Clare Dowling was born in Kilkenny in 1968. She trained as an actress and has worked in theatre, film and radio. Clare has had drama and children's fiction published and she writes scripts for Ireland's top soap, *Fair City*. She lives in Dublin and is married with one son and one daughter.

Don't miss Clare Dowling's previous novel, *My Fabulous Divorce*.

NO STRINGS ATTACHED

Judy is getting married on Saturday and it's going to be the happiest day of her life if it kills her. It's a military operation, but it'll all be worth it because marriage is for ever, right? But the night before the nuptials, fiancé Barry goes missing. Then his credit card shows up two days later in a nightclub in the south of France. A case of cold feet? Or worse, is it because he's being frog-marched up the aisle? Fanning her fury and grief is Lenny, Barry's best man. Lenny argues that relationships aren't permanent and that commitment ruins romance. With her fiancé romping around France, Judy just might be in the mood for a little romance — with no strings attached, of course . . .

Books by Clare Dowling
Published by The House of Ulverscroft:

MY FABULOUS DIVORCE

CLARE DOWLING

◆

NO STRINGS ATTACHED

Complete and Unabridged

CHARNWOOD
Leicester

First published in Great Britain in 2007 by
Headline Review
an imprint of Headline Publishing Group
London

First Charnwood Edition
published 2008
by arrangement with
Headline Publishing Group
a division of
Hachette Livre UK Limited
London

British Library CIP Data

Dowling, Clare
   No strings attached.—Large print ed.—
   Charnwood library series
   1. Love stories
   2. Large type books
   I. Title
   823.9′14 [F]

   ISBN 978–1–84782–078–5

Published by
F. A. Thorpe (Publishing)
Anstey, Leicestershire

Set by Words & Graphics Ltd.
Anstey, Leicestershire
Printed and bound in Great Britain by
T. J. International Ltd., Padstow, Cornwall

This book is printed on acid-free paper

For Siân

ACKNOWLEDGEMENTS

I'd like to thank my agent, Darley Anderson, and all at the agency. Special thanks to Clare Foss, my editor, and to all at Headline for their hard work and ingenious author events. Thanks to Breda Purdue and all at Hodder Headline Ireland. Thanks to Siân Quill for many enlightening discussions. As always, thanks go to Stewart, Sean and Ella for their patience, fortitude and encouraging cries of 'God, are you not finished with that thing yet?'

You are cordially invited to celebrate the wedding of

Judy Brady & Barry Fox

At the Church of the Holy Saints, Cove,
at 3pm on Saturday the 1st of July,
and afterwards at a reception in
Glenmallock House Hotel, Wicklow

RSVP

1

Angie was trying her best to talk Judy out of getting married. 'You don't really want to,' she said persuasively.

'I do,' Judy insisted

'You wouldn't if you really thought about it.'

'I *have* thought about it. We're getting married on Saturday — it's hard to think about anything else.' Indeed, she had spent many hours that morning worrying over the place settings for the meal. There was one particular uncle with whom absolutely everybody had fallen out and it looked like they would have to organise a table for him on his own.

'Ah, yes,' Angie went on knowledgeably, 'but you're only thinking of the nice bits like walking up the aisle, and Barry unpeeling your dress inch by inch on your wedding night, and two weeks in Barbados rubbing sunscreen into each other.'

Judy made a mental note: put sunscreen down on the blessed list. Then: where was the blessed list?

'That sounds lovely,' Ber chipped in dreamily. 'And having breakfast in bed and skinny-dipping in the Jacuzzi before having lots of squelchy, wet sex!'

Angie gave her a stern look. 'Contain yourself.'

'Sorry,' Ber said humbly. She tended to get very involved in other people's weddings. She maintained it was good practice for her own. She

3

had already earmarked a wedding dress, even though it would be a register office marriage, obviously, and decided on a menu for the meal — prawn cocktail followed by duck à l'orange. The only trouble was, it was all taking rather longer than anyone expected and the dress had begun to look not so much last season as last century. And nobody really ate duck à l'orange any more, although prawn cocktail had made a comeback. Still, it wasn't as though she had put down a deposit on the dress, as she had told the girls, and she could always change the menu. Really, she was quite lucky, if you wanted to look at it that way.

Angie fired up a fresh cigarette and looked at Judy kindly through the clouds of smoke. 'You see, right now you're blinded by romance.'

'Am I?' Judy thought, oh great, something else to impede her progress up the aisle. The four-inch satin wedding shoes were already proving quite a challenge. She had worn them around the house yesterday to get used to them, at one point pitching dangerously towards the television screen.

Angie nodded. 'Well, of course — look at you!' Judy did, warily, or at least at her knees. 'Giddy with love hormones. Senses awash with passion and longing. Half crazed at the prospect of getting that ring on your finger and galloping off into the sunset!' She wagged a finger at Judy. 'In fact, you haven't said a sensible word since you arrived here today.'

Judy had that pain in her forehead again. Yesterday, when she had gone to investigate it in the mirror, sure it was a big boil coming on — please, God, not four days before the wedding — she had discovered her whole forehead pleated in big wrinkles, right up to her hairline, like that woman out of *Star Trek*. She had taken a few deep breaths, along with several sniffs from a bottle of tea tree oil given to her by a friend who had herself survived a wedding, and her forehead had relaxed back down again.

People told her it was perfectly normal. Weddings were right up there with birth and death in the greater scheme of things (thank God they had bought the house five years ago or she would have been moving, too). Like childbirth, nobody told you how bad it was going to be because there was no sense in frightening the life out of you, and you'd find out for yourself soon enough in any case. Besides, the happiest day of your life doesn't come cheap, she had been vigorously warned; naturally, there were gallons of blood, sweat and tears to be shed first. Judy didn't know if there was a direct correlation between the degree of stress endured in the run-up and the happiness of the day itself, but if there was, hers should be off this planet.

'The point is that you're unbalanced,' Angie finished up gently. 'Incapable of making a rational decision.'

Judy *had* felt a bit unbalanced for several weeks now. She had put it down to the list-making and the endless entertaining of little-known relatives who dropped by with big lumps of Waterford glass. But if what Angie was saying was true, it wasn't wedding stress at all

5

that was waking her up in the dead of night in a cold sweat, but pure, unbridled happiness and lust.

'Barry and I have been living together for the last five years. We've known each other since we were children,' she pointed out cautiously. 'Do you not think we're over all that kind of thing?'

'Not at all,' Angie said. 'If anything, long relationships increase your longing for each other.'

'She's right,' said Ber vigorously, and she should know.

'Face it, Judy, love has turned your head completely. And I wouldn't be your friend if I didn't strongly urge you to look beyond the glamour of the wedding to the grim reality ahead.' Angie's voice dropped to a new, gloomy low. 'The back-breaking mortgage, the horrible mother-in-law, having to pop out babies one after the other while desperately trying to hold on to your career. You putting on weight and him losing his hair, or the other way around. Next thing you know, you won't be able to find a single thing to say to each other.'

There was a depressed silence. Outside, the sun retreated behind a big black cloud.

'Bloody hell.' Even Ber's relentless optimism had deserted her for once and she looked a bit fed up.

For two pins now, Judy was thinking darkly, she nearly *would* change her mind. Let them all swing! The whole shooting lot of them! She included in this the hairstylist who had imprinted her ear with a pair of tongs last week

6

during a test run, and Granny Nolan whose de luxe wheelchair was too wide for the church ramp and whom Barry said might have to be airlifted in.

Then, at the very last minute, she giddily realised that this whole conversation wasn't about her and Barry at all, but the Big Ignorant Fucker From Orlando, or Biffo for short. Of course! She went limp with relief that everything was fine after all, and that she was still getting married on Saturday.

To lovely, lovely Barry. Last night he had spent a whole hour coaxing her shoulders down from her ears, massaging them with his big warm hands, and murmuring soothing things like, 'Don't worry, I'm just going to give you a little jab,' and, 'You'll be fine, we've got your finger on ice.' (He had just come off a ten-hour shift at the surgery and it always took him a while to come down.) But she had felt a lot better afterwards, even without a jab.

Barry had that effect on people. He had been born with a bedside manner, his mother maintained, and had cheerily gone through childhood trying to push people down stairs and in front of cars so that he could see what the damage looked like. While other children were busy punching the stuffing out of each other, Barry could be found putting a plaster on Action Man, or inserting a thermometer up various cuddly toys. For a while they had been worried that he would turn out odd, like those silent, bearded men you see in documentaries about the unravelling of DNA, but thankfully they

7

caught him under a bush with the girl next door at fifteen, and it wasn't her tonsils he was having a look at.

He never grew a beard either, except for a charity event once. In fact, he had turned out quite handsome and was easily the most popular doctor at the surgery, although the competition, Dr 'Hairy' Stevens and Dr Yvonne Jacobs, who was permanently sick herself, wasn't that intense. He was particularly liked by older people — he had a genuine fascination with digestive systems — and could hardly venture into the local supermarket without being set upon immediately by gangs of elderly patients delighted to see him and asking if he could read the price on packets of fig rolls. When Judy would collect him half an hour later, having done the entire weekly shop, he would sheepishly extricate himself, and apologise to Judy. But his cheeks would be all pink — whether from pleasure, or from being squeezed by old folk, she was never quite sure.

Nobody ever accosted Judy in the supermarket. In fact, she tended to have the opposite effect. They all knew her from the library and they would flush guiltily upon seeing her and back away quickly whilst making stuttered excuses about books being eaten by dogs or gerbils or vacuum cleaners.

Barry joked gently that when she made her grand entrance to the church on Saturday afternoon, half the congregation would suddenly remember overdue library books and gallop out.

'I've been talking to the wall, haven't I?' Angie

8

said sadly now, taking one look at Judy's rosy, love-stricken face.

'Yes,' Judy admitted sheepishly. 'I'm sorry, Angie, but I love Barry and I'm getting married to him on Saturday!'

Ber clapped enthusiastically. 'Hurrah!' She confided to Judy, 'I was never really worried there.'

But there was still the problem of Biffo. He had left the country over a year ago now, although a bottle of his aftershave was still in Angie's bathroom cabinet. An oversight, Angie had explained when confronted, but Judy had her suspicions. Also, Angie had kept one of his Liverpool T-shirts, ostensibly as a duster, but Ber told Judy that she had once caught Angie sniffing it.

'Look, Angie,' Judy said, 'I know things might be slightly awkward on Saturday.'

Angie managed to look incredibly vague. 'Sorry?'

'You know who I'm talking about. Biffo.' His name landed on the lunch table like a stink bomb. Ber's nose wrinkled up and she began hunting around for a tissue.

For a moment Angie did a very good impression of not being able to place the name. 'Ah!' she said eventually. 'Biffo.'

And her mouth did a little wobble. Judy and Ber exchanged fearful looks — surely she wasn't going to break down in those terrible, keening sobs that were so heartbreaking that the whole café would be in floods along with her. She had drenched hundreds of ham sandwiches last summer, and a computer at work, which hadn't functioned since. You never saw such tragedy in your life, not even in *Terms Of Endearment*.

Of course, things hadn't been going so well for a while. Angie had spoken darkly of silences, and inexplicable black moods, and wild nights out with the lads. Sex had dwindled off. Then dried up altogether. Even the most civil inquiry as to what the hell was going on was met with a defensive shrug and a 'nothing'. In a last-ditch attempt to salvage the relationship, she'd splashed out on a hideously expensive trip to Rome, hoping that they could thrash things out. 'Oh, typical!' Biffo had said, cryptically, when she'd presented the tickets.

That very night he had announced that things weren't working out and that he was off. She had thought it was just from her apartment. But apparently she had driven him further than that: all the way to America, to be precise. By the end of the week he had handed in his notice at work, and his company white van, and had left the country without a backward glance.

It was impressive how Angie managed to smile wryly now and say, 'Judy, I appreciate your concern, but I think I can just about cope with meeting my ex at your wedding.'

'Of course you can,' Ber told her encouragingly.

'I'm sure we've both moved on,' she went on efficiently. 'I mean, I'm with Nick now.'

Ber gave a nervous little start. Nick was a stockbroker, like Angie. Every time they met him

he tried to talk them into investing in plastics as a pension. 'You're not going to stay young forever,' he would say sternly. Recently, he had amended this to 'youngish'.

He and Angie had been seeing each other for four months. She didn't laugh like she used to with Biffo, and he hated football, but things seemed to be going well enough.

But Judy had further news to break. 'Biffo is bringing someone to the wedding, Angie.'

Something crossed Angie's face briefly. But then she said calmly, 'He's perfectly entitled to bring anyone he wants to the wedding. *I'm* bringing Nick. I'm not saying it won't be awkward, but I think we can manage to be civil to each other.'

'I'll put you at opposite ends of the dining room,' Judy promised her. 'With your backs to each other.'

Angie waved this away as though it were entirely unnecessary. 'So who is she, anyway?' she asked brightly. 'His date?'

'Her name is Cheryl.' She didn't want to reveal anything else, such as the fact that she was a 26-year-old with legs like Barbie.

Ber didn't know about the legs, and said to Angie consolingly, 'She's probably dog ugly.'

'Oh, I'm sure she's not,' Angie said. She was very nice like that. Even despite everything.

'Well, he's not exactly an oil painting himself, is he?' Ber went on belligerently. 'Unless you were thinking along the lines of Rubens.'

You had be very careful how far down that

road you went, for a number of reasons, and so Judy said neutrally, 'She's American.'

'Well, I suppose I'll meet her on Saturday,' Angie said, putting an end to the conversation.

'Me too,' Ber said stoutly. 'And I'll have Vinnie warned not to let me drink too much.'

'Will Vinnie definitely make it along then, do you think?' Judy inquired.

Ber gave a little sigh. 'Well, we hope so.'

'How is Vinnie Junior's jaw anyway?' Judy hoped that she sounded concerned. Vinnie Junior was Vinnie's teenaged son.

'All right. They've wired it together but he can only drink out of a straw. And he can't talk at all, Vinnie says, but you'd hardly notice because he never really said anything anyway. All the same, Vinnie is keen to stick close to home.'

'Well, of course,' Judy murmured, thinking of the bout of gastroenteritis that had invaded Vinnie's house last month and curtailed his freedom, and his wife's unexpected summons to jury duty last year, or any of the serious rugby injuries that seemed to plague his two sons on a weekly basis.

But nobody ever said these things, of course. In fact, the whole thing had been going on for so long now that nobody even thought them any more. It was just the way things were, and they weren't likely to change at any time in the near future, no matter how optimistic Ber remained.

She was obviously thinking along the same lines because she said to Judy, rather enviously,

'What does it feel like? To be getting married?'

The list popped into Judy's head again and her stomach rose in revolt. But then there was Barry at the end of it all, and so she smiled and told Ber, 'Great. It feels great.'

2

Judy and Barry had known each other since they were three and a half. They would run into each other in the local shop, both of them stuffed into buggies, while their mothers engaged in endless pleasantries over their heads. They would look balefully at each other, Judy all buttoned up properly in her little red coat, and Barry sticky-faced and sulky that he wasn't allowed a lollipop. After about five minutes he would start squirming in the buggy and screeching that he wanted to go, NOW, and his mother would sigh and say that she wished to God she'd had a nice quiet girl like Judy instead of a thug like Barry who was up three times every night and wouldn't eat any vegetable only blessed turnips and that if she had to cook another one she'd puke (that was before she became chronically ill in later years and completely dependent upon Barry for a variety of pink and red pills).

When they were older, maybe nine or ten, she and Ber would sometimes run into him down on the beach after their mothers had bustled them all out of the door, saying, 'Go out and play — here ye are, living in a seaside town, and you never bloody well get out and enjoy it,' even though it would be blowing a gale-force wind down on the beach, and lashing rain, and the seagulls wouldn't even chance it. The adults, of course, would settle down to an afternoon of telly by the fire. 'And don't come home till dinner time,' they would order.

Shivering amongst the sand dunes, Barry would perform urgent imaginary surgery on Judy and she, bookish even then, would read aloud passages from works such as *She Loved Too Much* and *His Wicked Way*, pilfered from her mother's bedside cabinet.

These books had pictures on the covers of big dark men towering over wisps of women, many of whom were inexplicably in their nighties, even though it was plainly freezing outside. Neither would ever look particularly happy; generally the men scowled and the women looked like long streaks of misery.

' 'He looked at her out of dark, brooding eyes, and she felt a tremor run through her,' ' she would read out earnestly over the howling wind.

Barry would laugh nervously, before telling her gently, 'I'm afraid we're going to have to amputate your leg.'

While he was doing this, using a stray shell as a kidney bowl, Judy would continue with her reading. The carry-on of the lovers was something else: him pretending to be in love with another woman, her letting on she hated his guts. Judy couldn't imagine how they were ever going to get it together. She would fret and worry as each new twist would drive them further apart, until it seemed that he would zoom off in his power boat to Tunisia just as it was beginning to dawn on her that she mightn't loathe him as much as she did ten minutes ago. But then, miraculously, the whole thing would come together and they would fall into a passionate kiss, usually promptly followed by the requisite marriage proposal. It would all have been worth it in the end, and Judy would be greatly relieved and think, well, that was another pair sorted.

When the summer finally came, and the sun ventured out from behind the clouds, the big amusement rides would roll into town and set up all along the pier. They had names like Twister and Wild Thing and Boogie Blaster. At night the whole place was lit up with fantastic flashing lights, accompanied by the thunderous beat of 'I'm Too Sexy For My Shirt'. 'It'll corrupt them all,' the town elders warned.

By the time they were seventeen, Judy and Ber were certainly open to corruption, or at least tried to look as if they were, by wearing short denim skirts and lots of glittery eye shadow that kept getting into Judy's eyes and semi-blinding her. They would brazenly hang around the steps of the busier amusements, even though they had no money to actually get on them.

Barry did, though. He was an only child and because his father was the local auctioneer, everybody knew he was swimming in money.

That night, his chin was rather raw and red looking, with a lump of tissue paper stemming blood from a nasty little nick. Somehow it touched Judy's heart, and she felt all funny and tender inside.

'He fancies you,' Ber said, always alert to these things.

'Shut up, Ber.' She was scandalised yet thrilled

16

at the same time. Even though they had known each other forever, she and Barry had found simple communication difficult of late, what with Barry looking at his shoes and Judy trying to fight down boiling blushes.

Finally Ber left Judy at the steps of one of the amusements to go and buy a bag of chips between them.

Barry made his move. 'Do you fancy a ride?' he asked Judy. Then the colour drained from his face. 'I didn't mean . . . I meant on the helter-skelter.'

That was where they had their first kiss, that very night. It was lovely and intimate until the ride started to pick up pace, propelling Judy inexorably upwards in her seat until she ended up latched onto his eyebrow.

Their blushes were saved by Barry's departure a week later to Dublin, and medical school. Judy went to Dublin too, to get her degree as a librarian, but she never ran into Barry in all her years there. The two of them dated fellow students, goths, political activists, a couple of nurses in Barry's case, and they didn't really meet again until they were both back in Cove in their mid-twenties.

One Christmas in the local pub he got drunk and blurted to her, 'I still think about that night in the helter-skelter.'

When Judy didn't immediately reply, he moaned, 'Oh my God. You obviously don't. Shoot me, somebody.'

'No, I do. Not *all* the time, obviously.'

'I'm so embarrassed,' he said miserably. 'And I

diagnosed somebody with a heart attack today when it was only indigestion. I think he's going to sue.'

'He won't,' she found herself reassuring him.

'Really?' He locked his lovely, friendly brown eyes onto hers hopefully. 'I suppose you're going out with somebody.'

She was, but she wasn't that interested in him — he sniffed all the time, which was off-putting.

'Not really,' she said.

They went on a date the following week. It was easy and fun, with none of that getting-to-know-you awkwardness. They had already known each other all their lives.

'Do you think maybe we know each other *too* well?' she asked cautiously when, after a good few dates, sex loomed. 'Maybe there won't be any spark.'

'I'll make sparks all right,' Barry cried lustfully, and bore her off to bed.

They became such a familiar sight around town that people began referring to them as childhood sweethearts, even though Judy would point out that they hadn't dated properly until their twenties.

'Yes, but it's obvious you were meant for each other,' people would say, and after a while Judy didn't bother with the technicalities. She just began to believe it.

⋆　⋆　⋆

At the library they had hung a big sign up over the door: *Good Luck To Judy!*

18

'It's not very clear. People keep asking whether you're having an operation or something,' Annette fretted. She was head librarian and took these worries upon herself.

'I love it,' said Judy. She was embarrassed and pleased they had gone to the trouble.

'We have a bit of a party organised for you at coffee break,' Annette told her. Judy must have looked hopeful because she clarified quickly, 'There's no drink or anything, just some sandwiches and a Tea Time Express cake.'

'You shouldn't have,' said Judy, meaning it; she had her final dress fitting this evening.

'Yes, well, it's not every week you get married,' Annette said. 'And I've done a whip-round of the staff, they all chipped in.' She handed over an envelope. 'It's just a bit of cash for your honeymoon.'

'Thanks, Annette.' Judy was really touched now.

'Where are you going, Judy?' Marcia, the trainee, inquired chirpily.

'Barbados.'

'You should have gone to Ibiza,' Marcia advised earnestly. 'The clubs are great.'

Judy had seen the documentaries, and could just imagine herself and Barry lapping around a club to music that wasn't music at all, and then being covered with foam to cap it all off. Barry would probably go into doctor mode and try to save people from drowning, while she would flap about searching for her handbag. But then they weren't twenty-two any more. They were heading for their mid-thirties. They could still do the whole club thing any time they wanted, of course, but now it might also be a question of being let in, as Barry had pointed out.

'Maybe next year,' she murmured to Marcia. Secretly, she hoped that next year they might be heading to Butlins, or some equally family-friendly place. That was jumping the gun a bit, she knew, but they had talked about babies already, usually after a bottle of wine. Judy optimistically wanted four, while Barry declared himself happy with two. Then they would finish off the discussion by having a 'practise session'.

The afternoon passed quickly in the library. There was kids' club in the corner, with lots of little heads bent industriously over homework, although occasionally a lump of wet paper would land on the librarians' desk and Judy would go over with her arms folded sternly and root out whoever had the catapult.

It was holiday season too, and people were stocking up on books to lie on the beach with: fiction and romances mostly, but some people would insist on taking away big tomes on rebellions, and long-dead world leaders, as if to punish themselves for lolling on the beach.

'Is this any good?' a woman demanded, holding up a Barbara Cartland from 1962.

Judy explained, politely, as she did a couple of times a week, that neither she nor the rest of the staff had time to read all the books.

'Really?' The woman looked at Judy and Annette and Marcia, amazed, as though they were somehow reneging on their job descriptions.

But mostly people were nice, and a lot of the regulars came up to the desk to wish her well. 'Big day on Saturday!' they would joke. Or, 'It's not too late to change your mind!' That was from Mr Foley, who always gave Judy a little wink.

'Thanks, but I think on reflection I'll probably go through with it,' she had joked back.

Mr Foley got very serious then. 'You've got a good man there, Judy. The best. You could tell him anything, and you'd know it wouldn't go any further.'

It was as high a compliment as he could give, it seemed.

'That's true,' Judy assured him. 'I can't get a single thing out of him about what goes on in that surgery.'

Mr Foley nodded in approval. Mind you, some of Barry's other patients didn't seem so sure. They obviously suspected that Barry rang Judy the minute they were out the surgery door to whisper down the line to her about their various aches and pains and dysfunctions, because they always hung back in the hopes that Annette or Marcia would step up. When they were landed with Judy, they would stare in mortification at some point above her head, and give monosyllabic answers to her innocent questions about whether they wanted to put their name down for the new John Grisham that had just come in.

'I just heard the long-term forecast. It's going to be a beautiful day for you on Saturday, Judy!' Bill, the security guy, said as he passed by on his way back to the lobby.

21

The wedding photographer would be delighted. He didn't often get seaside weddings, he said. They would go straight to the beach from the church, just her and Barry, and do a shoot there. The photographer had arranged for a small boat and everything, it was going to be very romantic. 'Just cross your fingers that we'll get the weather,' he had warned, 'or else it could look like bloody *Jaws*'.

If she could, she would get him to take a photograph of her and Barry on the helter-skelter, just for old times' sake.

Barry loved the summer best, with the crowds and the buzz around the town, the whole place taken over by people in shorts. He always got a bit depressed around September time. After the excitement of the summer, he would complain that everything felt very flat and there was nothing to look forward to at all. Then there would be an outbreak of measles or something, and he would be in great demand, and he would be back to his old self again in no time at all.

3

Barry's old school friend Lenny was flying in especially from Australia for the wedding, although he had declined to let anybody know the precise time of his arrival. Then there was confusion over the flight number. It was equally possible that he would arrive via Amsterdam or Paris. Again, no forward communication had been received.

'Do we even know what he looks like?' Judy inquired rather grumpily. All her earlier good humour had been lost in the terrible race from the library to the dress shop, where she had finally taken possession of the wedding gown, along with some helpful hints on how to enhance her assets on the day using dark powder, although Judy had thought that providing cleavage was the designer's job. God knows the dress had cost enough.

'Oh, he's absolutely gorgeous,' Barry declared. It was unlike him to be so ebullient, especially about other men's looks. He added, carelessly, 'If you like that sort of thing.' Then, rather darkly. 'I haven't seen him in fifteen years. He's probably put on three stone and lost most of his hair.'

She noted that his own hair was combed carefully over the crown of his head.

'Barry,' she said, 'why have you still got your white coat on?'

'What? Oh, I was, ah, cold.'

Usually he wouldn't be caught dead in it outside the surgery, because he believed it made him look as if he was delivering bread. To dispel any such confusion today, he wore his stethoscope over the coat rather ostentatiously, and kept eyeing the crowd importantly in case anybody looked in need of resuscitation. Nobody did, except Judy.

'Do you really not remember Lenny at all?' he asked.

Judy could honestly say she didn't. But then she hadn't gone to Barry's secondary school, nor hung around on the usual street corners. She was always off to tuba practice or hockey practice or choir, for all the good any of it had done her. There she would be, lugging that great lump of a tuba past the gang of girls and lads outside Daly's shop, closing her eyes to the muffled giggles. 'Can I give it up, please?' she would implore her father, but he would never let her, not when she had begged for the blasted tuba in the first place, and for which he'd had to get out a Credit Union loan.

'I can't put a face to him at all,' she told Barry now. Lenny was obviously an unmemorable character who had probably grown into one of the grey, bland-looking businessmen who were filing out from international flights now, blinking owlishly and clutching briefcases and looking around hopefully in case somebody would step forward and claim them. Usually nobody did, and they would sigh and drift out towards the car parks.

In his crisp white coat Barry looked rather

dashing in comparison (she sometimes imagined him in medical dramas like *Casualty* or *Holby City*) and she was overcome with a fit of amour and she took his arm cosily and squeezed it.

'What?' he said, alarmed.

'Nothing. Just that we'll be back here on Sunday, that's all.'

In her new, red, going-away outfit.

'I suppose,' he said, rather muted. Possibly he had had Mrs Mooney back in with her ingrown toenails.

So she planted a little kiss on his cheek, and added, 'Going on our honeymoon. To the Bella Vista Hotel.'

' 'Where every room is full of love.' ' He said it with a silly French accent, even though the hotel was in Barbados.

Cross, she dropped his arm. 'I don't know why you're being like this.'

'What?'

'Laddish.'

'Don't be ridiculous. I wouldn't know how to be laddish. I'm a lovely, sensitive fellow, everybody says so. Mrs McBride admitted yesterday that sometimes she pretends to be sick just so that she can come into the surgery and talk to me. And I'll bet that goes for some of the others too.'

Judy was watching him suspiciously. 'What's that thing that you're doing with your hips?'

'What thing?'

'You're thrusting them out.'

'You're imagining it.'

'I am not! You're doing something all macho

25

and weird with them!'

He reined them back in quickly. Then a second later, when he thought she wasn't looking, he reached down and butchly adjusted himself the way you see rappers doing on MTV videos.

'Barry, has all this got something to do with Lenny?'

'Lenny!' He laughed, unconvincingly. 'Don't be ridiculous. No, I just needed to . . . let in a bit of fresh air down there, that's all.'

Judy wondered whether the wedding arrangements were unhinging him, too. It was possible. 'Barry, you don't seem yourself.'

'Me? What about you?' he yelped. 'The language out of you last night when we were going over the list! Fecking this and fecking that. And then drinking all that wine.'

'It was just to help me sleep.'

'A whole bottle?'

Anyway, it hadn't even worked. She had jerked upright in bed at 3 a.m. having had a terrible premonitory dream about fake tan — and that had only involved Barry. She herself had been falling from a very high place in the dream, a cliff or something, and as soon as that was over, she had fallen from a crane, and then from a hot-air balloon. In fact, there wasn't much she *hadn't* fallen from in her sleep last night.

'When was the last time we had sex?' she asked suddenly.

She didn't know who was more startled, herself or Barry.

He looked around. 'Jesus Christ, Judy, we're in a public place.'

'Sorry. I was just wondering.'

'About sex? Have you not enough else to be worrying about, what with the wedding on Saturday?'

'It's just that Angie has set me thinking.'

Barry shook his head. 'I don't know what kind of conversations you lot have at all.'

She persisted, 'Surely four days before we get married we're supposed to be a bit more, you know, passionate and excited and not able to think clearly because we're off our heads on hormones?'

'What?' Barry was looking at her very oddly, the way he did when he was sizing up patients for a course of Valium.

'Maybe the arrangements are doing our heads in,' Judy said bluntly. 'Maybe we're too bogged down by it all.'

'I know, the whole thing would sicken you,' Barry agreed heartily, 'but it has to be done, Judy. And anyway, isn't the honeymoon supposed to be for sex?'

'So we have to wait until then?'

He laughed. 'Come on, it hasn't been that long.'

'Which takes me back to my original question. When exactly was the last time we had sex?'

He could see she wasn't going to let it go, and eventually he hazarded a guess. 'Tuesday week ago?'

'Try last month.'

He looked shocked. 'No!'

27

'It's true.'

His brow furrowed. 'Did we not do it that night we got the Indian takeaway?'

'You fell asleep on the couch.'

'If you cast your mind back, I think you'll find we did it just before I nodded off,' he persisted.

'I'm positive.' In fairness, he had been in the surgery all day. 'Look, it doesn't matter.'

'Oh, Judy.' And he threw his arms around her in a comforting hug, and said, teasingly, 'We certainly can't have you going without sex now, can we? So let's rectify the situation at once. Immediately!'

And he looked around as if searching for a suitable place to have sex, but it was all very open plan, unless they were going to go into the toilets, which was a definite turn-off.

'Tonight,' he decided, masterfully. 'There'll be no talk at all about weddings — well, all right, fifteen minutes, max — and I won't take a single call from a patient convinced that they're having a heart attack. We'll open a bottle of wine, have something nice to eat, and then I think it's an early night for *you*, Judy Brady. Doctor's orders.'

He always said this rather smuttily and with a lewd wink, and Judy giggled. There was nothing wrong between them at all. They had just been too busy, both of them. They would have a lovely, cosy night tonight as a timely reminder of what all this wedding torture was really about.

Then Barry's face froze. 'I've just remembered. I told Lenny he could stay with us.'

'What?'

'You're going to kill me, aren't you?'

'Yes, Barry.'

'I'm really sorry, it's just for one night, I promise.'

Judy thought of her tights drying on the radiators all over the house, and the spare room that would have to be made up, and the list on the table. She thought of her romantic night in with Barry, gone now. Oh, he might be lovely, but sometimes he was as thick as a plank.

'Can he not stay in a hotel?' she said. 'Or with friends or something?'

'What, Hammer Moran and that lot?' Barry said incredulously.

At that, Judy placed Lenny. Hammer Moran, so named because of his habit of getting hammered on cider, had been the head of a group of local wide boys who used to drive up and down on the promenade on a rickety old motorbike, until one of them eventually drove it into a wall. There was one summer when Barry had briefly become infatuated with them and had tried to join up, and had even bought a pair of black leather pants, but he couldn't even smoke properly, and had been promptly kicked out. Judy remembered Lenny as a thin, dark boy who hung on the fringes of the group watching out of cynical eyes as everybody else fell about oafishly.

'They were such a bunch of losers,' she said to Barry. They used to whistle rudely at her and Ber and their crowd on the beach, and ask the colour of their knickers. Ber, the big eejit, used to tell them.

Barry immediately cheered up. 'They were a bit, weren't they?'

'I don't know what you ever saw in Lenny at all.'

'He was all right in school, when you got him on his own,' Barry said loyally. But he was looking more and more cheerful, right back to his old self, and he stopped adjusting his privates, and swinging his stethoscope around.

'What does Lenny do with himself now?'

'He didn't say,' Barry confided. 'But I gather he dropped out of college and was on the dole for a while. He's been in Australia for years now. For all we know, he could be a beach bum.'

Judy thought that might be going a bit far. She didn't even know why Barry had invited him to the wedding. It was obvious they hadn't had much meaningful contact since their school days. But Barry was diligent like that, keeping up old acquaintances. She herself ended up guiltily writing hasty notes on the inside of Christmas cards, such as, 'I can't believe another year has passed without seeing you!' Or speaking on the phone or anything else, despite promises in the previous year's Christmas card.

'I suppose it gives him an excuse anyway to come back,' Barry said with largesse. 'The wedding.'

'I'm sure he has family and friends here still that he'd like to see too,' Judy said, not knowing why she was defending a boy she had hardly known and certainly hadn't liked.

'Well, yes, of course,' Barry said.

There was a shout across the terminal. 'Barry!'

30

They craned their necks towards Arrivals. But there were only two women coming out, and some flight attendants.

The shout came again. Judy ascertained it was coming from somewhere above them and she turned.

An escalator was smoothly bearing down upon them from the upper floors, carrying aloft a tanned, black-clad man who seemed quite used to being high above the masses. He had a holdall slung casually over one shoulder. Judy wouldn't have recognised him except that he sardonically raised two fingers to his forehead in a mock salute at Barry.

She disliked him on sight.

Barry didn't appear to recognise him immediately either. Far from having put on three stone and gone bald, Lenny had remained trim and was the proud possessor of a full head of thick, dark hair. Also, for someone supposedly with no job, he was wearing a great deal of expensive clobber, most of it fine black leather. Designer sunglasses, a laptop and a mobile phone into which he murmured a few words before hanging up completed the effect.

Barry remained rooted to the spot for a moment, his stethoscope hanging rather limply, before he galvanised and galloped to the bottom of the elevator to greet their guest.

Judy walked much more slowly. She checked her watch discreetly — so much to do still — and stood at a polite distance as Barry and Lenny engaged in hugs and some rigorous backslapping. 'Great to see you, man,' Barry said. Man? Judy rolled her eyes.

'Barry,' Lenny said warmly, and without the kind of fawning that Barry was doing. 'I hope I didn't drag you from surgery.'

'They can do without me for one afternoon,' Barry said, very magnanimous. 'And you, what are you up to?'

'Oh, this and that. I'll fill you in later.'

And he looked past Barry at Judy. 'Hello,' he said, with the kind of blank look that said he didn't remember her at all.

'Hi,' she said briskly, and reached out to shake his hand. But he was already smoothly coming forward to kiss her, and she somehow ended up planting her hand on the crotch of his trousers.

She was mortified. 'Sorry.'

He wasn't put out at all. Very possibly he was used to women trying to get into his trousers because he just gave her a charming smile and said, 'I hope I didn't keep you waiting.'

She thought of her lovely wedding dress in a heap in the boot and said, 'Well, actually — '

Barry waved it away. 'Don't worry about it.'

'I nipped up to the bar for a pint of Guinness,' Lenny confessed. 'I've been dreaming of one for about ten years now.'

Barry chuckled appreciatively. Judy tried to see the funny side too, even as she wondered whether she had taken out that big oily wrench from the boot before she'd put the dress in.

'I'll take you out tonight,' Barry said, red-faced with pleasure. 'We'll have a few pints.'

'Well, we'll see how it goes,' Lenny said. Then, presumably tossing a bone to Judy, he said, 'I'm sure you're up to your eyes in wedding stuff.'

Stuff? thought Judy. This had been her *life* for the past eight months.

But Barry waved a hand and said, 'Oh, it'll keep.'

And he and Lenny exchanged a the-things-us-men-have-to-do look, and Judy was at this point quite sick of the pair of them, and she said loudly, 'Actually, we're very busy, yes. We have a hundred and fifty place names to handwrite, about two dozen phone calls to make and Barry has yet to write his wedding speech. If he's going to do one at all, that is.'

There was a little silence. And Judy thought, oh God, was there really that much to do yet? She felt the spasms start up again, and a warning tingle in her forehead.

She found Lenny giving her one of those looks that men reserve for women who they believe are half cracked, or pre-menstrual, or otherwise scary. She didn't care. She was a woman who was getting married on Saturday and it was going to be the happiest day of her life if it bloody killed her.

'We'll give the pub a miss,' Lenny told Barry.

But Judy didn't want to be too ungracious — Lenny was one of Barry's oldest friends, after all — and so she reluctantly offered, 'I can go on home by myself if you two want to go back up to the bar and catch up.'

But Lenny said, 'Thanks anyway, but we're both a bit tired.'

She was wondering how Lenny knew Barry was tired; surely he didn't look that haggard. But then Lenny turned to look back up the escalator with the kind of nakedly lustful look that made Judy feel embarrassed.

A woman was coming down it. Or rather, a vision, with long, black glossy hair, and exotic eyes. She was about six feet tall, most of it legs, and Judy felt squat and midget-like beside her. The woman was wearing what Judy could only describe as a negligee, but then again she herself was obviously hopelessly overdressed for the occasion in jeans and T-shirt. Under the negligee, the woman wore shiny vampish boots and had the kind of nails designed to leave big long scratches down men's backs. The false nails Judy had decided on for the wedding, and had thought rather risqué, were only stubs in comparison.

Beside her, Barry gawked, his eyes like saucers. He had described seeing such women to Judy before, but only in certain magazines.

The elevator disgorged the vision at their feet, and Judy was forced to take a step backwards or else be speared by the heel of one of the vampish boots.

'This is Charmaine,' Lenny announced, putting an arm round her, and letting his hand drop to rest on her bottom. Well, of course. She certainly wasn't going to be a Helga or an Assumpta.

Charmaine flicked lustrous, dark, disinterested eyes over them. 'Hi,' she said, in Americanised English.

Barry shot a fearful look at Judy, and then said to Lenny, 'You didn't tell me you were bringing somebody with you.'

'Oh, we just hooked up in Bangkok yesterday,' Lenny said easily.

'I'm dying for a cup of tea,' Charmaine confided to Judy.

There was little silence, then Barry said, 'Um, right! Well, let's go then!'

And he and Lenny set off across the terminal, leaving Judy and Charmaine to trail behind.

★   ★   ★

'She's looking for lemon in her tea,' Barry told Judy in the kitchen.

'What?' Judy's face was red and her hair wild from a quick dash around the house putting away embarrassing items while Barry stalled Lenny and Charmaine in the car with a lengthy description of what they intended to do to the garden once they had finished paying for the wedding. Which should be around 2014.

'She's lactose intolerant,' Barry explained.

'So, what, a drop of milk brings her out in lumps?'

'I have no idea, but I'd rather not find out,' Barry said. Of course he wouldn't, especially as his tongue was nearly hitting the floor every time she recrossed her giraffe-like legs on the couch in there. They mightn't look so nice covered in big red boils, Judy thought with uncharacteristic ire.

She hurled open the fridge. Lemons were not high on her shopping list at the best of times. Anyway, the fridge was full of make-up, after the girl who was going to do it for her on Saturday

35

morning had advised her that the fridge was the best place for it. Ber said that that was rubbish, that it was only nail polish you put in the fridge, and so Judy had put all that in too. There was scarcely room for a carton of milk. Which Charmaine couldn't have anyway.

'I'm sorry about this,' Barry said, for about the fifth time. The more he apologised, the crosser Judy got, which was irrational, but so was looking for a lemon four days before her wedding.

She eventually found half of one at the back that looked to have been there since pancake day. Barry cut off the mouldy end, sliced it, and then found two beers for himself and Lenny.

'They'll just have to take us as they find us,' he declared. Then, in the next breath, 'Have we not got any crisps?' He looked around as if expecting a packet to jump up at him from the worktop, along with a selection of delicious dips.

Judy could see their guests through the kitchen door: Lenny was sitting in the big armchair, one ankle propped on the other knee, as if he owned the place. Charmaine was perched on the very edge of the sagging couch and looking around as if she couldn't believe she had found herself in such pedestrian surroundings.

They were a difficult pair to entertain. Judy had tried to strike up a conversation with Charmaine in the back of the car — the two men had sat in the front and talked about sport — at one point mentioning her job in the library. Charmaine had cut that one short by saying, 'Oh, I don't read.' What she herself did was as yet unclear, but judging from the amount of expensive luggage Barry had had to stuff in the boot — on top of the wedding dress — it involved a fair bit of travel.

Lenny was no better. In the sitting room just now, Judy had asked about the flight and the weather in Australia, normal sort of questions, and he had answered them pleasantly enough, but with a little sardonic smile, as if he was more used to conversations about music or the stock exchange or the meaning of life, and that she, while pleasant enough, was a rather boring sort of person. He hadn't asked a single question of his own, not even about the wedding, which was an obvious conversation filler. The effort of it all had driven Judy's forehead up even further, making her look permanently startled.

She found two packets of Chipsticks in a press and hurriedly tipped them into a bowl. It wasn't great but it would keep them going till dinnertime. She hadn't yet figured out what she was going to feed everybody. Possibly Charmaine had other intolerances that had yet to come to light.

She handed the Chipsticks to Barry. 'Tell them they'll have to find somewhere else to stay tomorrow.'

He looked a bit wounded by this. 'You might be a bit more welcoming, Judy. He's my oldest friend.'

'You've hardly spoken to him in fifteen years.' Well, it was true.

'That's not the point. He's come all the way back for our wedding. The least we can do is

37

show our appreciation.'

That did it. She turned to face him. 'Barry, right now I don't have time to show Lenny and Charmaine my appreciation that they landed on me the week of my wedding. In case you haven't noticed, we have a big long list on that table over there, full of things waiting to be ticked off in red!'

'Oh?' he challenged. 'Earlier, you said you wanted to have sex!'

'I did not!'

'You complained that we were far too bogged down in detail and that we should put it all to one side and indulge in some hormonal madness!'

'You're twisting my words.' She elbowed past him and into the fridge again, where she dug out a jar of salsa left over from the Mexican evening they'd had ages ago. There was a thin layer of mould on the top of it. Maybe she could scrape it off.

'You were up for it, though, when I suggested that we get naked,' Barry said, in that annoying way he had of always wanting the last word.

'Well, I'm certainly not now!' Judy hissed. 'In fact, sex is the very last thing I feel like at this moment. And it might just be the very last thing I feel like on my wedding night!'

There was a noise by the door. Lenny stood there, hands dug casually into his pockets.

Barry was the first to recover. 'Beers are just coming up!'

'And the Chipsticks,' Judy interjected. Her face was very hot. She wondered how much he had heard. He was the kind of person who wore an all-knowing expression whether they actually were or not.

'If you don't mind, Charmaine and I are going to hit the hay,' he said. 'Jet lag and all that.'

'Sure,' said Barry, in that eager way that was beginning to grate on Judy's nerves.

'I hope you haven't gone to any trouble,' Lenny said.

'Not at all!' Barry assured him. He realised he was holding the two opened beers. 'I'll drink these myself.'

'And I'll have the lemon,' Judy said. She was trying to be funny, but Lenny just looked at her as though she was already sour enough.

'Good night,' he said. 'And thanks for putting us up. It's tough getting a hotel in a resort town at this time of the year. But we'll try in the morning.'

Judy felt this was directed at her, which she thought was very unfair given the effort she had gone to.

'No rush,' Barry said magnanimously.

Lenny did that two-finger salute thing to Barry again, who attempted to do it back, but he wasn't any better at it than he had been at smoking, and he gave up.

Charmaine didn't bother saying goodnight. A moment later they heard the hall door closing, and then the bedroom door.

Judy and Barry looked at each other, surrounded by lemon, beer, Chipsticks and mouldy salsa. After a moment, Judy laughed. Barry did too.

'God, sorry, Judy.'

'Me too.'

'I just didn't think.'

'No, it's me, I'm in a heap about the wedding. Give me one of those beers.'

They kissed and drank some beer and then Judy got down to the list. But she kept looking at the hall door through which Lenny and Charmaine had disappeared, which annoyed her, and in the end she got up and moved seats, so that her back was to the door. Opposite her, Barry was writing his speech, blinking at the blank page like someone who had wandered out of a cinema into the middle of a cold, drab afternoon.

4

'I refuse to be intimidated at your wedding,' Biffo declared.

'Good,' said Judy. 'Because I need you to bring up the gifts in the church, and make a speech after dinner.'

Biffo swiftly backtracked. 'Although perhaps it might be better if I stayed in the background. Given the circumstances that are in it. I mean, it'll be all Angie can do to make it through the day, without me standing up and making speeches at her. She might break a bottle over my head or something.'

'If you weren't my brother I'd break a bottle over your head myself right now.'

'I can see where your loyalties lie.'

'There are no sides in this one, Biffo.'

'There are always sides,' Biffo said darkly. 'And we all know which I'm on — the wrong one. Which Angie will no doubt go out of her way on Saturday to make perfectly clear to everybody.'

It was doubtful whether Angie would even recognise him. After a whole year selling luxury waterfront apartments in Orlando, Biffo was tanned a deep, mahogany brown. His mousy brown hair had, in contrast, got lighter in the sun. Startlingly, the hair on his chest had disappeared altogether, even though Angie used to complain bitterly about his big rug. Every

41

time he smiled, his cosmetically whitened teeth nearly blinded Judy. And he was so clean and smooth that you could nearly eat your dinner off him, as their father Mick had commented.

Several women had given him looks at the airport when he'd arrived. Toned, tanned men of any description were rare in Ireland, never mind reasonably good-looking ones. Privately, Judy thought he looked like a young George Hamilton.

She wondered what Angie would make of him. He didn't look much like the slightly slobbish, beer-guzzling, football-watching Biffo of a year ago, that was for sure. America had changed him, in more ways than one.

'I wouldn't worry too much about Angie on Saturday. She'll be too busy with Nick to bother denigrating you.'

Biffo scarcely flinched. 'And I'll be busy with Cheryl. Did I tell you she used to be a cheerleader?'

But for a man who was dating an ex-cheerleader, he looked very gloomy indeed.

'No offence,' he admitted to Judy, 'but I'm dreading your wedding.'

'I know,' Judy commiserated. 'In fact, I don't know a single person who's actually looking forward to it.'

Biffo said, more animated, 'Well, of course not. Weddings are a total pain in the arse. There's the expense for starters: the present and the rigout, and the overnight stay in the hotel, the volumes of drink that have to be bought. And you always get stuck at a table beside some woman who only talks about her children the whole meal. Then the food is usually brutal, and the wine runs out after the starters, and you have the whole night to go through yet. The DJ, the little sausages on sticks, dancing to 'Eye Of The Tiger' at three o'clock in the morning — it would turn your stomach. Then you stagger to bed after making a total fool of yourself in front of the staff, only to have to face them three hours later at breakfast. No, I can honestly say that most people can't stand weddings.' He saw her face. 'You were only joking, weren't you?'

'Yes, Biffo.'

He winced. 'Sorry. Put it down to jet lag. Anyway, Mum's looking forward to it. She'll have enough enthusiasm for everybody.'

It was true that Rose was delighted about the whole thing. She had gathered Barry and Judy into her big warm generous bosom, and cried. Then she had dried her tears and declared happily, 'I suppose I'd better go on a diet.' She had been on twenty-four diets in the past ten years, and had managed to gain two pounds on average with each one. You could tell which diet she was on by opening the fridge; it might be stuffed with cottage cheese, or nothing but eggs or, once, box upon box of strawberries, after she read that each strawberry contained ten calories but took thirteen to digest — it was a win-win situation, she had declared (she had gained three pounds on that one).

But she was never too downhearted, and everybody agreed that her little failures only made her more substantial and homely.

Judy's wedding gave her fresh impetus, though. She wanted to be able to stand proudly by her beautiful daughter and not have to suck her stomach in as usual for the photos. For three whole weeks she stuck rigidly to a grapefruit and ice cream diet she found on the Internet. Apparently the citrus in the grapefruit negated the calories in the ice cream so it was the same as if you were eating nothing at all. Unfortunately she managed to gain another two pounds. She gave up, saying to Judy cheefully, 'Ah, I'm fine the way I am,' and everybody relaxed again.

Judy's father Mick was much more muted about the wedding. And Judy his only daughter, the apple of his eye! And himself and Barry got on reasonably well too, although it was a poor man who didn't know how to change a washer or unblock a U-bend in his own toilet, Mick had declared. Still, it was handy that help was only around the corner in the shape of himself, and he would make Barry stand over him and watch, so that he would know for the next time. He similarly advised Barry on cars, and investments, and what he should do with his garden if he ever got around to it. Barry always managed to look grateful, and everybody thought Mick would be delighted at the engagement, and the prospect of many more years of imparting his vast knowledge.

But his reaction had been unexpected. 'Getting married? Don't be ridiculous. You're far too young.'

'Dad, I'm thirty-three.'

'What? You are not.'

'I am. I was thirty-three in January.'

You could see him doing the sums in his head, and not liking it.

He changed tack. 'That doesn't mean you should rush into anything. You should be out there enjoying yourself!' Then he'd suddenly looked worried. 'You won't be producing children straightaway or anything, will you?'

'Oh, yes,' Judy told him. 'Loads of them. I'm hoping you'll look after them while I'm at work.'

But Mick's sense of humour had deserted him. 'If you do have any, I don't want any of this 'Grandad' nonsense. They can call me Michael.'

Rose said not to mind him, that he had been a bit off since some form had arrived in the post for him advising him that he would shortly be eligible to apply for a travel pass.

And then Biffo flying home from the States first class and looking like he'd stepped straight from *Men's Health*, making everybody else feel even more ancient and boring. Not to mention his new girlfriend, who didn't look much out of her teens. Mick's back, already bad, had begun to ache much more, apparently, and everybody was sick listening to him.

'And there's Barry's family,' Biffo went on now, obviously anxious to make amends. 'They're only dying for Barry to get married. Mrs Fox dropped by the house yesterday to tell Mum what a lovely girl you were.'

'Really?' Judy was surprised. Mrs Fox had never given much indication that she was overly fond of her. But then Mrs Fox's health was so precarious that she didn't have much time to spare on anybody but herself.

'So what's she been saying about me behind my back then?' Biffo burst out. It had obviously been bugging him since he'd arrived two days ago but he had managed to refrain from asking so far.

'I take it you mean Angie.'

'Oh, I know exactly what goes on when women get together and drink wine, and call their exes terrible names and make fun of their sexual skills,' he said accusingly.

'If you must know, the very odd time your name *does* come up, I actually try to defend you,' Judy told him. 'As your sister, I'm in a bit of a difficult position, Biffo.'

'Stop calling me Biffo,' he complained.

'When you and Angie were together, I wasn't allowed to say a bad word against you, and now that you've broken up, I can't say a *good* word. So I've decided I'm better off saying nothing at all.'

That wouldn't do either, obviously, judging by the way Biffo shuffled around discontentedly in his seat. 'What's this Nick fellow like? Just so I know for Saturday. He doesn't have any defining features like only one eye or a pronounced limp or anything?' He looked hopeful.

'He's nice,' Judy said kindly. 'He's a stockbroker too.'

Biffo nodded as if all this was only mildly interesting to him. 'Good, good. So she's still selling those share things?'

It was hard to know whether he was feigning it or whether his vagueness was genuine. After all, he hadn't even known Angie had a job until about a month after they'd hit it off at a party in Judy's. He'd thought she was on the dole, because she certainly didn't act like someone who had somewhere to go in the mornings. Then one day he picked her up early for a date and nearly had a heart attack when he'd found her dressed up in all that scary stockbroking gear. 'It's only for show,' she had reassured him gently, and changed smartly into her jeans.

Afterwards, he was a bit embarrassed at how he'd tried to impress her in the pub by going on about his trainee job in the real estate business, and how they'd just given him his own white van. But Angie was always very interested in his work, far more than she ever appeared to be in her own, and Biffo soon relaxed back into his nightly monologues. He got a bit of a kick in the beginning telling his mates in the pub that he was dating a stockbroker, and he and Angie had had a few memorable nights out on the strength of her bonuses. Which were vast. And frequent. They had started saving them with a view to buying one of those big posh houses on the hill with a view of the sea. And a big driveway, with plenty of room for her big black shiny SUV, and his little white van.

'I own a few shares myself now,' he announced suddenly, and loudly. 'In the company that I work for in Orlando. If it floats on the stock exchange, I'll be worth a fortune. Not that I'm not already. We flew home first class, did I tell you?'

About four times.

'It's a good life over there, Judy,' he lectured, even though she hadn't asked. 'People look after themselves. Everybody works out, eats properly, they're at their desks at half past seven. There's focus, and drive and success if you want it. And the sun! No, moving out there was the best thing I ever did.' But he looked a bit gloomy again. 'I suppose she hates my guts. Angie.'

'I think she was more confused than anything.'

'I didn't mean to hurt her, you know,' he said defensively. 'It was just best for everybody.'

'In what way?'

'It wasn't going to work out, Judy, OK?' He looked stubborn.

There was no time to pursue it because the bathroom door opened down the hall and Charmaine stepped out, carrying a massive toilet bag, and wafting perfume in all directions. She was buck naked except for a tiny hand towel ingeniously draped to barely skim her vitals, even though Judy had hung a great big fluffy robe with a bunny tail on it on the hook inside the bedroom door yesterday evening.

'Hi,' she purred to Biffo. It was as if Judy didn't exist.

Biffo's eyes nearly fell out of his head. Charmaine tripped daintily down the hall and into the spare bedroom. Judy caught a glimpse of a bare brown leg sprawled across the bed. Lenny appeared to be fast asleep still, judging by the contented snores that drifted out before Charmaine firmly shut the door. He probably needed his rest after last night; Judy had lain awake into the small hours as the headboard in the room next door crashed merrily off the dividing wall. Barry had heard it too; he hadn't said anything but his jaw was making that little clicking noise that meant he was clenching it.

'Is that her?' Biffo hissed, having found his voice again. 'The model Lenny came home with from Bangkok?'

How he knew Lenny was even staying with them, never mind that Charmaine was a model, was beyond Judy. But she shouldn't have been surprised. The gossip network in the town was such that her mother had heard about her engagement to Barry before he'd got up off his knee.

'Who said she was a model?' Judy demanded.

'Well, it's obvious,' Biffo said. 'Is she coming to the wedding?'

'She hasn't been invited,' Judy said rather shortly. 'Look, I'll see you tomorrow night anyway,' she said, in an attempt to get rid of him. She had to get on with her list.

But Biffo was staying put. 'I might wait till Lenny gets up.'

'You don't even know Lenny.'

'I do! We went to school together too.'

'You were years behind him.'

'Only three,' Biffo said. 'He gave me a cigarette once,' he added nostalgically, as if regretting that he hadn't kept it and put it behind framed glass.

Judy could hardly believe how it was that Lenny, whose charm had been fairly limited and his prospects dim, had suddenly acquired mythical status amongst his former peers. And all because of Charmaine. Nobody would think twice about him if he'd come back with a homely secretary from Melbourne.

Biffo hung around a bit, but when it was obvious that neither Charmaine nor Lenny was going to appear any time soon (possibly Charmaine needed help drying off), he eventually rose to go. 'By the way. As a wedding present I'm giving you and Barry a timeshare in an apartment in Orlando.'

Judy was stunned. She and Biffo had always been close; she would hitch a ride to school on the crossbar of his chopper bike, and he in turn would try and get off with all her friends. But still, an apartment? She didn't know what to say.

'We can't possibly accept . . . '

'Of course you can,' he said, benevolently. 'I know the last present I gave you was a book token but that was back when I was nobody. You're looking at the new, improved Biffo, and nothing is too good for my big sister!' He added, 'Obviously, there are some conditions.'

It eventually emerged under intense questioning that they could have it for a couple of weeks off-peak. January to April to be precise.

'You'd have to pay for your own flights and the rest.' He added, 'And transfers. It's a fair bit from the airport. I'll organise the paperwork when I get back to Orlando.'

When he was gone, Judy got down to the list. There was so much to do yet. And Barry was no help because he was working. She was just having a few quick sniffs of tea tree oil when she felt someone standing over her.

'Morning.' It was Lenny, wearing the bunny bathrobe, and precious little else.

She quickly put away the tea tree oil, embarrassed.

'What's for breakfast?' he asked, with a leisurely scratch.

She blinked. 'Sorry?'

'Joke,' he said.

'Oh,' she said.

Now he thought she was a scary woman with no sense of humour. But Judy knew men like him; they didn't know how to deal with women who didn't giggle, or smile incessantly, or generally act nice. And if they didn't smile or giggle, they had jolly well better be sex bombs like Charmaine. Or else over fifty, and non-existent anyway. Oh, yes, she had his number all right.

'There's coffee made,' she told him, in her most humourless voice. She sounded a bit like Darth Vader.

'Thanks.' And he walked past her in the bunny robe. The pink fluffy bunny tail bounced on his bottom with every step, and Judy found herself watching with a morbid fascination as he walked to the cupboard, got a cup, and went to the coffee machine, with the little tail going *boing, boing, boing.*

'Where's Barry?' he inquired, turning round. Judy's head whipped away, but not before he'd seen her ogling his bottom. Which she hadn't been! And now he thought she fancied him. Oh, cringe. She could tell by the little knowing look in his eye, the certainty that he was so hot that no woman, not even poker-faced Judy, could resist.

'Work,' she said, clipped. 'He's a very good doctor, you know. Very dedicated. He's probably saving a life right now.' Well, that was highly unlikely, but for some reason she was anxious to talk Barry up; to impress upon Lenny that she *had* a man, thank you very much, a man who was engaged in vital duties right now, and that she had no reason at all to be ogling other men.

'Oh,' he said. She was sure he would take his coffee and go back to bed. But he was obviously in need of some respite from Charmaine because he sat down at the kitchen table opposite her. She was writing place names for the meal with a silver pen. He sipped his coffee and watched. It was difficult to concentrate under such scrutiny, and her fingers grew slippery on the pen.

'That looks like an awful lot of work,' he said, in that ironic, lazy tone that probably went down a treat in Australia but didn't cut much ice with a woman about to get married on Saturday and whose sleep he had disturbed last night.

'Yes, well, I suppose I should have just run them all off on the printer, batches of fifty at a time, but hey, I thought I'd go the extra mile, you know?'

He wasn't sure how to take that. 'Maybe. I've never done it myself.'

'Operated a printer?'

'Got married.'

'You never know,' she said. 'Charmaine might be the one.'

Judy didn't normally subject house guests to

52

such uncivil exchanges over breakfast, especially when she hadn't even given them any breakfast, but stress was making her reckless. Also he was using the list as a coaster for his coffee mug, and there were now big brown marks over the most important details (yet to be organised) of her entire life.

'I doubt it,' he said, obviously having given Charmaine's suitability as a bride some serious consideration.

'I hope she won't be disappointed,' Judy said, hardly able to believe her cheek. Barry would go mad at her if he heard her speaking to the great Lenny in such a fashion. She had heard him this morning furtively cleaning the bathroom before he went out to work, and when she had come downstairs there was a selection of Booker-nominated novels that they had dutifully bought but never quite got around to reading carefully laid out on the coffee table.

'I think she'll be pretty OK about it,' Lenny said, looking at her very steadily. 'Not all women want to get married, you know.'

Judy felt herself flushing, and she was trying to think up some appropriate retort, something that would wipe that revolting little smile off his face, but he wrong-footed her again by standing and adjusting his bunny robe, and asking briskly, 'Is there anything that you need gift-wise?'

'Sorry?'

'For a wedding present. Charmaine and me, we're going to take a walk around the town, I want to show her around. I was wondering if

53

there was anything special that you wanted as a wedding present.'

Perhaps it was the practicality of such a question coming from a sex god like Lenny — you didn't expect him to start inquiring about ironing boards or towel sets — or maybe it was because she didn't like him and didn't want anything from him, but Judy, queen of the lists and library cataloguer extraordinaire, just looked at him mutely like a rabbit caught in headlights. The names of everyday household objects fled completely from her mind, even that thing that you put two slices of bread into and they popped up brown. She was looking at it right now.

Lenny eventually prompted, 'Although I suppose you probably have everything.'

'Yes,' she admitted. 'We've been gathering it over the years.'

He looked slowly around the kitchen as if affirming that this was true. 'You pretty much have it all set up, don't you?'

There was a judgement there, on her and her wifely preoccupations before she was even married, and she felt herself go red again, and she said, neutrally, 'A gift voucher would be nice.'

'OK,' he said, and with another amused look he walked out.

As if anybody could live without a toaster, she thought blackly, whether they were married or single or just having mad sex with women like Charmaine every night of the week. The fact that she herself had one in her kitchen was no indication of anything at all.

5

Ber and Vinnie called around after lunch with their wedding present, an abstract painting of an egg in violent shades of orange.

'You already have everything,' Ber said apologetically.

'It's lovely,' Judy assured them. 'Thank you.'

'You're welcome, you're welcome,' Vinnie said. He said most things twice.

This was to cover up his permanent embarrassment. For starters, he was about twenty-five years older than any of Ber's friends, although she would dispute that. But he gamely wore clothes that were too young for him, and always inquired about their jobs and lives in a way that showed he had been listening to Ber. And on nights out he always offered to drive everybody in his sports car, although it wasn't really a sports car, just an uppity model of a regular car, and he drove it at the kind of sedate speed that said he would be far more comfortable in something with five doors.

But no matter what he did, how nice he was to them all, nothing could change the fact that he was Stringing Ber Along. As each year passed, and nothing changed, his expression in their presence grew more evasive and apologetic. Conversation had become increasingly difficult, and eye contact all but impossible. When Angie had got drunk at a Christmas party last year, and said all those things, Vinnie had actually crawled out of the room on all fours, although Ber had insisted afterwards that it was just those fourteen Jack Daniels.

Judy herself had tried to hate him many times, but found that she just couldn't. He so clearly hated himself that there seemed little point in adding to the man's misery.

And then there was Ber, of course, who wouldn't hear a word against him. Nobody, she declared, understood the situation unless they were in it themselves. Perhaps not, but they knew a love rat when they saw one, although with his combed-over hair and hangdog expression he looked more like an ageing accountant in need of a good night's sleep.

'Vinnie chose it,' Ber told Judy. She always gave Vinnie credit for any little thing at all, as if to boost his poor ratings. He shot her a grateful look.

'I hope you and Barry will be very happy,' he told Judy sincerely.

'Thanks, Vinnie,' she said, although the sentiment contained the possibility that they wouldn't be. Or maybe she was just reading too much into it. It was the sex thing, she thought. It had been playing on her mind since yesterday. She would pin Barry down tonight, maybe even literally, and they would just do it, and she would feel a lot better.

Ber interrupted this little fantasy by saying, eyes round, 'Is it true you have Lenny Jackson staying with you?'

'Yes.' Judy didn't even wonder how she had heard.

'And that he brought an actress with him?'

'I thought she was a model,' Judy said.

'She could be an actress-cum-model,' Vinnie offered, looking pleased at knowing the term at all.

'Oh, well done, Vinnie!' Ber said.

Judy didn't care what she was so long as she was gone from the house. She had left half an hour ago on Lenny's arm, wearing denim shorts that scarcely covered her bum and another pair of extraordinary boots. In summer! Everybody else was wearing flip-flops. Judy had been secretly hoping she would trip down the front steps, which were not designed for such footwear, but she glided down them as if she was on a catwalk. Judy gloomily conceded now that in all likelihood she *was* a model, and possibly did some acting in her spare time.

Ber was explaining to Vinnie, 'Lenny is this guy we used to know. A corner boy. Thought he was the bees' knees. Did you know him?'

'No, but I think I went to school with his mother,' Vinnie said sadly.

Judy was glad that Ber seemed to share the same memories of Vinnie as she did herself.

'And now look at him,' Ber said. 'Home with a babe on his arm and a career as a movie maker.'

'What?' Judy said sharply. Honestly, she had to go outside her own house to hear anything at all. 'He makes movies?'

'A friend of mine said they saw one of his films last year,' Ber confirmed.

57

'What was it called?' Judy went to the cinema quite a lot; surely Barry would have told her if they had been watching one of Lenny's.

'I can't remember,' Ber confessed. 'But apparently it wasn't mainstream. No real story to it at all.'

'Oh?'

'And at one point, this friend said that people started to take their clothes off.'

'All of them?'

'Sounds like top-shelf stuff to me,' Vinnie said with authority. He added hurriedly, 'Not that I watch any of that myself. Pure filth.'

Ber and Judy were bug-eyed. Well, they were fairly innocent in that regard. In Ber's case, extremely innocent, even though she was a mistress and everything, and you would think she'd feel a duty to keep up with these things. But she got all embarrassed and began giggling uncontrollably when people even kissed on screen, so hardcore porn was not something she would have a natural appetite for. Judy was scarcely more worldly wise, and if it wasn't for channel 46 on that cable package they'd bought last year, she would know nothing at all. 'You think Lenny makes . . . adult movies?'

Vinnie looked grave. 'There's very good money to be made in it, I hear. Fastest growing sector in the entertainment industry. In fact, it's become so accepted nowadays that some of these people even call what they do art.'

'Art!' Judy wondered if Barry knew. He had sounded rather hassled on the phone at lunchtime. But that was probably more to do with the screaming baby in the background — it was jab day at the surgery — than any discovery of Lenny's career in the arts industry.

Another thought struck Ber. 'She could be starring in one of his movies — Charmaine!'

Judy felt they were going too far now. 'Just because she's drop-dead gorgeous doesn't mean she's a porn star.'

'Does it not?' Ber said, disappointed. 'Still, at least we know about Lenny now.'

Judy tried to picture Lenny behind a camera in a grubby, dark room with a big bed in the middle of it all, or a couch or whatever else they used in these kinds of films (there was no point asking Barry, he wouldn't have a clue). And he didn't seem so glamorous now.

Ber was obviously thinking along the same lines, because she said, 'We used to think he was gorgeous. But in a cheap kind of way — do you remember, Judy? He used to always have two girlfriends on the go at the same time.' She shook her head in disapproval, and then said casually to Vinnie, 'Maybe you two should have a drink sometime, you have a lot in common.'

The words were out and gone so quickly that nobody was quite sure they had actually been said. Indeed Ber herself blinked as if she had momentarily lost the thread of the conversation. She gave herself a little shake, smiled brightly at Judy and said, 'We should go. I'm getting my hair done. Vinnie's going to be really sweet and drive me.'

Vinnie was too wrong-footed by her previous remark — if indeed she had made it at all, his hearing wasn't what it used to be — to bask in the glory, and just looked more miserable.

Plus, he was always driving Ber to get her hair done. Or her nails or her feet or some other part of her. She worked in marketing, and was always terrifically turned out, and a week never went by without some upgrade being required. And she hardly ever wore the same thing twice, except maybe shoes. When the shops saw her coming, they rolled out the red carpet in anticipation.

She had the time for all this, of course. She never had to rush home from work to hastily cobble together a runny shepherd's pie for a herd of children or a husband who would stroll in just as the cooker timer went off. So mostly she was hardly home at all. She shopped and went to the gym. She played golf and badminton and she swam. She read nine books a week and she met a different girlfriend every day for lunch. Dinner was always out, with another girlfriend, or her sisters, or some of the people from work. In the winter she went to the theatre and in the summer she went to barbecues, and she strolled in home every night at whatever time she damn well pleased. Naturally, she would rather see more of Vinnie, but until such time as that happened, there was very little stopping Ber from living her life exactly the way she chose.

'We're thinking of taking a holiday together after your wedding,' she told Judy now. 'Me and Vinnie.'

'That's great, Ber.' They had never been on a holiday together, for obvious reasons.

Ber looked full of excitement. She squeezed

Vinnie's hand. 'I know. It'll be lovely to spend all that time together. It'll be just like if Vinnie ever left his wife, or if pigs took off like 747s.'

This time there was no mistake about it: there was a deathly silence as the words settled over the room like poison. Ber looked the most appalled; she stood there with her mouth still open as if trying to snatch the words back. Vinnie was appalled too, but he was well used to public condemnation (if not from Ber), and he stared at the ceiling impassively, a jumping left eyebrow the only indication that he'd heard her at all.

Judy looked desperately at the orange egg propped up against a chair, her head tilted as if admiring it from another angle.

She didn't know how long they all stood like that; at least a minute anyway, and she was wondering how to break the deadlock when Vinnie's mobile phone rang, as it nearly always did at these gatherings. Everybody always assumed it was his wife, even though it hardly ever was, but he didn't help his case by always jumping guiltily and making furtive exits.

He made one now, rummaging around in his trousers pocket for the phone, whilst simultaneously bowing in agonised apology. 'Excuse me, excuse me,' he whispered miserably and repeatedly to Ber and Judy, before scurrying out of the room.

'Oh, everything's gone wrong!' Ber burst out.

Her usual cheerfulness had completely deserted her.

'What's happened? What has he done?'

She gave a screechy laugh. 'Vinnie? *Do*

something? That'll be the day!' Her hand immediately flew to her mouth in horror. 'There I go again. Stop me, someone.'

'Ber, calm down. Tell me what's wrong.' Judy cleared a space for Ber at the kitchen table and sat her down.

In a shaky voice, Ber said, 'Last night, my Pilates class was cancelled.'

'I'd give it up altogether if it's having this effect on you.'

'No, no. The thing is, I decided to go through one of the drawers at home instead — the Passport Office says they won't give me another new passport after the five I've lost already, and to go home and look for it. And I found all my old diaries, Judy, going right back to when I first met Vinnie. And I sat there, and I counted up all the dates we've had over the years even though I knew it was silly, but I still did it anyway. And you know something? It didn't take all that long.'

Judy was thinking that she never kept any diaries of her dates with Barry, and she felt a bit deficient, but it wasn't as if they only met up once a week for big romantic dinners, like Ber and Vinnie. There were other, more pedestrian outings like double appointments at the dentist, and lunch with his mother. She would hardly look back upon accounts of those with great nostalgia in forty years' time.

'Then I got a calculator and I worked out the weekly average.'

'Oh, Ber.'

'Zero point seven,' Ber said thinly. 'That's how many times, on average, we see each other a week. And not one of those is ever on Christmas Day, because he spends it with his family, or my birthday, because it's on New Year's Eve and he's on his annual skiing trip with his family. Usually one of his blasted kids gets horribly injured on some slope or other, and then I don't see him for a month.'

There was a note in her voice that Judy hadn't heard before. Ber knew it too, and she said, 'Listen to me. I've gone bitter, Judy.'

'Well, anybody would.'

But Ber shook her head. 'Counting up those dates, it did something to me. Everything has changed.' She gave a little laugh. 'I know you and Angie always thought I was a desperate fool, waiting around for him.'

'Well, yes,' Judy admitted.

'But I always enjoyed it, Judy. I always had a good time. And from the start I promised myself that I'd put a stop to things if I ever started getting bitter. And I have.' She clutched Judy's arm desperately. 'I'm going to turn into Glenn Close, I know it.'

'I really think you're being too hard on yourself, Ber. You're entitled to get fed up with the situation now and again.' Indeed, Angie always said that Ber was far too placid and accepting of the whole thing. A little blow-out was probably exactly what she needed.

'No, you should have heard me in the car over,' Ber said darkly. 'Making veiled cracks about his age, and his bald patch, and the way gaps have started to appear between his teeth. He didn't even know about the gaps, he pulled

63

over to the hard shoulder to have a look. And then,' she gulped, 'I moved on to his wife.'

'What did you say about her?' Judy asked fearfully.

'I couldn't even repeat them,' Ber said, looking scandalised. 'And there was Vinnie, looking over at me like I'm some kind of monster!'

Judy couldn't feel too sorry for Vinnie, although she could imagine his shock: sweet, lovely, optimistic Ber finally getting the boot in. It mightn't do him a bit of harm.

But it seemed that Ber was the one who couldn't bear it. 'I've made a decision, Judy. I'm going to give him an ultimatum tonight.'

'Are you sure?' Judy said, only because over the years her role in all this had evolved into one of practicality, caution, reason, to counteract Angie's stance, which would have Ber rushing out into the hall right now to grab Vinnie by the throat and shake him until he made up his mind.

'It's time,' Ber said, measured. 'I want to have someone, Judy. Like you have Barry.'

Judy didn't want to feel responsible for anybody else's relationship. 'Well, yes, but I suppose no couple is the same.'

But Ber was adamant. 'Maybe your wedding is making me rethink things, Judy. I'm not putting up with second best any more. And I'm going to say it to him tonight. Either he wants to be with me properly, or it's over.'

They could hear Vinnie wrapping up his phone call out in the hall, saying, 'Goodbye,' at least five times.

Ber grew tense again. 'Wish me luck.'

'You know I do.'

'Even though I know you think he'll probably stay.'

'His kids are nearly grown,' Judy said loyally. 'He doesn't have any other excuse.'

'That's exactly what I'm thinking,' said Ber, but there was something a little brittle about her as she rose to go.

6

'I never had sex with your father before I married him,' Judy's mother Rose told her cosily that afternoon.

'Stop, I don't want to know about your sex life,' Judy told her, horrified. She had only come over to help get her old bedroom ready, where she would spend the night before her wedding.

'I'm your mother and it's my duty to tell you about these things before you get married,' Rose insisted. Judy should have expected this; Rose was very liberal with her motherly advice to her children, and approached each new milestone with great zest. Judy still remembered the appallingly embarrassing 'chat' the day she'd got her first period, when Rose had described in great detail the inner workings of women, at one point drawing a diagram on the fogged-up bathroom mirror. When she had finished, it looked like a map of Africa with a leak at the bottom. Other chats had followed, such as the night before her Leaving Cert exams, and her first date, with a lad from across the town. Mostly these chats contained fairly good advice, the only really dud one being the one about the first date. 'Respect yourself, and he will,' Rose had told her with great confidence. But of course the boy in question had laughed derisively at Judy when she had refused to let him stick his hand up her jumper, and then had gone and told all his friends that she was frigid.

'Anyway,' said Judy, 'I already know about sex. I've been living with Barry for the last five years, we have sex all the time.' Well, some of the time. Up until the wedding had taken over, at any rate. But all that would be sorted out on the honeymoon, as Barry said. They'd be at it morning, noon and night. It was very likely that she wouldn't be able to stand up straight and make it down for breakfast in the mornings. 'So you don't need to draw any diagrams or graphs or anything,' she emphasised to her mother.

'Well, I think cohabitation is very healthy,' Rose declared.

'You must be the only mother in Ireland who's delighted her children are having rampant sex outside marriage.'

Biffo and his American girlfriend Cheryl had taken over Biffo's old bedroom for the week. Apparently, it wasn't so much the noise of rampant sex that was disturbing everybody as the constant whine of the en-suite power shower. Cheryl took at least two showers a day, morning and night, and sometimes one after lunch, although Rose was sure she never served up anything all that messy to eat. Biffo was just as bad, in and out like a rabbit, and he never used a towel more than once. Rose was killed washing and drying and ironing and Mick was killed complaining that he'd never be able to afford the electricity bill.

'It's certainly an improvement on our day,' Rose said with satisfaction. 'We didn't even know the facts of life, some of us. People were going into their wedding night not sure which end of them was supposed to be up.'

Mick had been sitting at the kitchen table throughout this. Now that there was a lull in the conversation he said, 'Has that poor girl not got enough on her plate, what with getting married on Saturday, without hearing all about our sex life? You're embarrassing her.'

It was a charge he frequently levied at Rose. She was too intimate with people, he maintained, too cosy, forcing upon them all kinds of private family business that didn't need to be aired at all. Quite often this business concerned himself, and half the neighbourhood knew how much he had paid into his pension fund, and what foods disagreed with him, and what the repercussions of these foods were. And you couldn't stop her talking about sex. Any excuse at all and she was off. The highlight of her week for years had been those candid camera-type programmes where people's trousers fell down, or men's willies inadvertently popped out. In fact, the very word willy used to be enough to set her off, or bonk or boob or anything like that. Then she would dry her eyes in satisfaction and wander off to the fridge.

'I refuse to get involved in this conversation,' Mick announced now. 'It's nothing but smut.'

But Rose winked at Judy and said, 'We're talking about sexual liberation here, Mick. How great it is that women in this day and age can make their needs and desires known. Just like Judy here.'

Mick and Judy looked at each other fearfully;

neither had any wish at all to get into her needs and desires, and certainly not her sex life.

Especially as she had been into Lenny and Charmaine's room earlier: she'd had to get the big honeymoon suitcase from the wardrobe, it was all perfectly legitimate. The aroma of expensive body lotions and aftershave had hit her at the door, and she'd had to acclimatise before advancing further. She had tried not to look at the bed, which was a tangled mess of well-used sheets, and the kind of implausible underwear — basques, and suspender bits, and bras so padded they could walk off by themselves — that made Judy feel undersexed and prudish. She half expected to see bumper packs of condoms spilling out over every available surface, and battery-operated sex toys, although she wasn't sure if she would recognise those as easily. Rose would have had a field day. There were no hang-ups in *that* bedroom, and it was fairly certain that all kinds of needs and desires were being adequately catered for. But then Lenny was in that business, apparently, and Judy couldn't help having a quick glance around to see if there was any video camera in evidence, and stacks of new tapes. She was relieved to find that there wasn't.

She felt better when she was back in her own bedroom amongst the cool pine furniture and with Barry's spare medical bag that he kept by the bed for night calls. As she packed her modest trousseau into the suitcase, she decided that there was something artificial about Lenny and Charmaine. Something contrived and not quite real, like a holiday romance that was nothing but euphoria, with no basis in reality at all. Imagine Barry's face if she produced some of that gear on their honeymoon! He wouldn't know how to get most of it off. That was, of course, if she had managed to get it on in the first place. She might have to get instructions from one of Lenny's movies.

Mick said, 'If you want my opinion, the world would be a better place if people kept their wants and needs to themselves and didn't go foisting them upon innocent people.' And he gave Rose a look as though she were the main culprit.

Rose's eyebrows jumped up. 'Isn't he turning into an awful grumpy old man?' she said to Judy. Then she remembered something and clutched Judy's arm. 'For God's sake, don't go without seeing the shoes I got for Saturday. I think they might be a bit too pink.'

It was difficult to know how they could be any pinker than the dress Rose would be wearing on the day. But then Barry's mother, Mrs Fox, would be wearing an olive-green affair that looked vaguely military, and Judy figured the two would cancel each other out. You won't miss her in the photographs anyway, Mick had said. He had been making the same joke for thirty-five years now and hadn't noticed yet that nobody found it funny any more.

'Have you managed to zip the dress up at the back yet?' Judy inquired.

'No,' Rose admitted. 'But I've three days to go yet. I haven't eaten a thing since breakfast.'

'Did Barry find out where that leak in the bath

was coming from?' Mick asked quickly, heading any talk about diets off at the pass.

'He's been up to his eyes, Dad, what with everything.'

'I can go around there if you want,' Mick offered, brightening.

'You're not fixing any baths with that back of yours,' Rose said briskly. She said to Judy over his head, 'Apart from anything else, I couldn't listen to him.'

Mick glowered. 'How many times do I have to tell you? My back is better.'

'If that's the case, why were you hobbling around last night?' She said to Judy, 'It was all he could do to make it over to the fridge for a beer and then back for the remote control, the poor pet.'

'That's right, make a joke,' Mick retorted. 'There's nothing funnier than people having injured themselves.'

Rose shot another look over his head at Judy as if to say, look what I have to put up with.

Suddenly there was an unearthly whiff of shower gel, deodorant and powder, and they were all united in trepidation. A second later Biffo walked in, looking faintly damp. He was followed by Cheryl, also dampish, and in a baby-blue tracksuit. At the sight of them both, so scrubbed and shiny, Mick gave a surreptitious sniff to his armpit.

'Hi,' said Cheryl, smiling around sweetly at everybody. Like Biffo, she had shockingly white teeth, but hers came from big glasses of milk, Judy just knew, not expensive orthodontics. Her

71

hair was glossy and brown and tied up in a girlish ponytail which swung jauntily as she looked from one member of the Brady family to the other out of incredibly clear blue eyes that surely had never been clouded by a hang-over or a bad thought.

At least around Charmaine Judy only felt short and fat; around Cheryl she felt short, fat, unhealthy and of poor character.

She had been surprised when Biffo had presented her at the airport. Lovely and all as she was, she seemed too anaemic for him. Especially after Angie.

But it was plain that Cheryl adored Biffo, judging by the besotted look she was giving him now. Biffo didn't notice. Probably he wasn't used to besotted looks — Angie hadn't been that hot on them, or indeed on any great public displays of affection. She had been more liable to tell him to get up to the bar, that it was his round.

'Was the water hot enough for you?' Mick inquired, with some sarcasm.

But Cheryl just nodded eagerly and said, 'Yes, thanks. You've been so good to us. I really hope we're not imposing.'

Well, of course, that made everybody feel just awful, and they all shouted at once, 'Of course not!' and, 'It's lovely to have you!'

With some fanfare now, Rose announced, 'I've got a lovely bit of prime steak for tea.'

There was a dead silence. Biffo and Cheryl exchanged looks of consternation. Rose grew uneasy and looked at Judy as if wondering what she had said that was so awful. Judy didn't know either. Steak was Biffo's very favourite meal, and the last thing that had passed his lips before he had boarded the plane for America.

He broke it to her gently. 'I don't eat red meat any more, Mammy.'

Rose was nonplussed. And she after going specially to the butchers and all, and making him take off every ounce of fat in honour of the health-conscious visitors, until there was nothing left only a bit in the middle. Four portions had cost a fortune. She wouldn't even tell Mick. He would go through the roof.

Mick said incredulously, 'What colour meat *do* you eat then? Blue? Green?'

Biffo was superior. 'White, Dad. Chicken, turkey — organic, of course. And fish sometimes, but only if it's wild.'

Mick was looking at him as though he were speaking in strange tongues.

'I'll make lentil bake later,' Cheryl told Rose apologetically. 'We should have said. Oh, I feel just terrible.'

You couldn't be angry with her, although Rose looked as if she was trying her best, but then she gave up and smiled warmly, and said, 'Ah, you're all right. Mick will eat it although too much red meat bungs him up these days.'

Mick looked mortified. In front of Cheryl! But Rose didn't seem to notice the glare he gave her.

'There is nothing wrong with my digestive system,' he blustered.

'He has quite a bad back though,' Rose confided to Cheryl.

Mick was very ruddy in the face now.

Cheryl looked him up and down with great interest, and said, 'You look in pretty good shape to me.'

Mick blinked furiously, unsure whether she was taking the mickey.

'You can always tell by looking at a person,' Cheryl elaborated, her blue eyes devoid of anything except pure niceness. 'Their skin, their hair, the way they stand. The minute I saw you at the airport, I said to Biffo, your dad is a good-looking guy!'

Mick looked totally unsure how to respond. He hadn't had a compliment in a number of years, and remained cautious. 'I suppose I *should* exercise more. I'm spreading a bit around the middle.'

'Oh, you're not!' Cheryl cried.

'Do you think?' said Mick, delighted.

Judy looked at Biffo, swallowing a smile. But Biffo was oblivious, and staring intently at some point over her left shoulder. She turned to have a look; it was a six-pack of crisps, smoky bacon flavour. But when he sensed her looking, he averted his gaze piously to the vegetable rack, and a big leek.

'You've just made his day,' Rose told Cheryl. 'Maybe now he won't be moaning for the rest of it.'

Mick ignored that and, buoyed up from the attention, said, 'Will we all go to the pub?'

Cheryl looked mildly shocked. It probably wasn't the norm to hit the local drinking den at two in the afternoon in Orlando.

'We've hardly had a chance to talk at all since

Biffo came home,' Mick said expansively. 'We could have a few drinks and catch up properly on all the news. You come too, Judy.'

Judy shook her head firmly. 'I'm going home. I'm getting married on Saturday, in case you've forgotten.'

'You then, Biffo. And Cheryl, of course.'

But Biffo, who had squandered most of his youth in pubs, shook his head and said, 'We can't go either, Dad.'

'You can have a mineral water, can't you?' Mick said, imploringly. 'No one's going to force you to drink pints.'

'We're going for a jog,' Biffo said firmly. 'Just down to Butler's Cross and back.'

That was about ten miles each way.

'Sit down and read the paper,' Rose told Mick consolingly. 'Have a bit of a rest.'

'I've been resting all day. I don't want a bloody rest,' he said somewhat irritably.

Biffo was fussing with the timer on his sports watch, which had nearly as many dials and monitors as the controls of a plane. Judy half expected him to say, 'Ready for take-off,' but he just hooked a thumb at Cheryl, and they jogged out into the sedate suburban street like two escaped tanned extras from *Baywatch*.

7

Barry rang from the surgery that evening just as Judy was arriving home. 'I'm overrun by people looking for repeat prescriptions to get them through my honeymoon. I can't get away.'

'Tell them there are two other doctors there if they need anything.'

'You know what they can be like,' he fretted.

'Just throw open the drugs cabinet and let them at it.'

He was never very amused at jokes like that. He took drugs very seriously indeed, and you couldn't get even half a Valium out of him for love nor money (although she knew very well he slipped some to his mother). Sometimes he would bring a bag of free samples home but only so that he could pore over the enclosed information leaflets. 'Look at these, Judy. Not only do they lower cholesterol but they clear your sinuses as well.' Or, 'These side effects are terrible! Drowsiness, dizziness, nausea, vomiting.' Try organising a wedding, Judy wanted to say, but she didn't, because he would be so happy there on the couch with his plastic bag of pills, his hair sticking out in that mad professor way that she loved.

'Are you coming home soon?' she asked him.

'I don't know.' He told her that Dr Stevens and Dr Jacobs were insisting on taking him out for a drink when surgery finally closed. He didn't

76

sound that enthusiastic; the Christmas drinks hadn't exactly been a blast. He assured Judy that he would be home by seven, to write the speech. And ring the priest. And confirm numbers with the restaurant for tomorrow night.

He sounded a bit put out.

'It's not my fault, Barry,' Judy said.

'Sorry. I just didn't think there would be so much to do, that's all.'

How he could have thought that was beyond Judy, especially since she had been warning him since January exactly how much there would be to do. Hadn't she drawn up reams of lists as a prelude to the Master List, and put them on the fridge where he couldn't fail to miss them every morning? Right about nose level? Nobody in their right minds could fail to grasp that getting married was a very complicated, detailed, messy, thorny, low-down dirty business, and it was a bit late for him to be complaining about it now.

And he was the one who had wanted a proper wedding in the first place! Well, so had she, in fairness. They had only briefly considered the possibility of getting married in Rome, just the two of them, and then there was Vegas where you could do it in five minutes flat. And you didn't even need witnesses, as Barry pointed out, but he had only been joking. He wouldn't be caught dead in Vegas, he'd be terrified of all those showgirls and slot machines, and Judy probably wouldn't be much better. 'We're too conventional,' he had declared happily.

It had never been in any doubt, really: they

would have a small traditional wedding in their home town with just family and close friends. And probably they should invite a few of his chronic patients, Barry tentatively suggested, whom he had got to know very well over the years. And Judy supposed she had better ask them from the library. And then there were those couples they had become very friendly with down at tennis. Suddenly, in the space of two weeks, the whole thing had ballooned and they'd found themselves with a guest list of one hundred and fifty. 'What have we done?' Barry had asked, scared.

'There's no need to take your vest off as well, Mrs Mooney,' she heard him say in a muffled voice on the end of the phone. Then he was back. 'I'm sorry, Judy, but I have to go.'

And that, of course, was the problem with ending up with the Great Irish Wedding: Barry was never available to organise any of it, because there was always some person sitting in his surgery with their clothes half on or half off. Also, he argued that some people, such as the baker who was making the wedding cake, got very sniffy at having to deal with the groom, and had kept urging him to check back with Judy, the implication being that he knew nothing at all about icing or tiers or anything like that. It was quite intimidating, Barry told Judy, if not downright sexist.

Very quickly the List became, and remained, Judy's domain. Was it any wonder that she was looking for Valium? Which he wouldn't even give her. She sent very dark thoughts down the phone at him now, and said, '*I'll* phone the restaurant.'

'No, no. I'll do it, I'll find a minute later on.' Often he did that, just to give the impression that he was pulling his weight. 'By the way, did you invite Lenny? And Charmaine, of course.'

They were having a meal the following night for the two families as a kind of a getting-to-know-you, even though they had known each other all their lives, as Mick had pointed out rather plaintively. Judy had explained that it was tradition. But Mick remained very unenthusiastic about it until he discovered that, for once, he wasn't required to foot the bill.

'I haven't seen Lenny since lunchtime,' Judy told Barry. Various reports had filtered through of sightings of the exotic pair strolling hand in hand down the high street, or taking a boat around Cove Head. Maybe Charmaine would fall in.

'Don't be too late. I'm cooking risotto for everybody,' she told Barry.

It was a belated attempt to make up for her lack of hospitality towards Lenny and Charmaine. She had checked with Charmaine earlier and she had no further allergies or intolerances, except perhaps to Judy's general sense of décor, judging by the way her nose kept turning up. She had also checked with Lenny and apparently there wasn't a hotel room available in the whole of Cove. She didn't even ask about B & Bs because somehow she knew they just wouldn't be his style.

She decided she would give them both a big

plate of carbohydrates tonight, and tomorrow morning she would firmly point them in the direction of the local park bench.

* * *

Angie knocked on the door five minutes later. She must have come straight from work because she wore a sleek grey suit and a pair of dangerously high heels.

The illusion was immediately shattered when she kicked them off, took a packet of Benson and Hedges from her briefcase, and lit up with a happy sigh. 'That's better.'

Angie managed to successfully combine smoking with stockbroking, high heels with football, and heavy drinking with going to Mass on Sundays. It stemmed from a good, solid rearing on a farm in the southwest, where there were no airs and graces, and nobody thought it was anything to get too excited about when she began to read aloud the barcode numbers off packets of cornflakes when she was two. Except that, with seven football-mad brothers, it came in handy to work out the league tables.

'How many points will Chelsea need to win the cup if Liverpool lose the next match at home but only draw away, given that they're already ahead by two points?' they would demand anxiously.

Angie would suck her thumb for a moment and lisp, 'Seven.'

'Good girl!'

They were vaguely proud when she began to

do so well in Dublin, even though they hadn't a clue what she actually did, and her brothers were more interested to see what kind of a car she would drive down in next.

'Is that a three-litre with satellite navigation and climate control?' they would ask enviously.

'It is.'

They had never ventured into her office: 'Sure what would we be going all the way to Dublin for?' Although Judy had. It was a futuristic building in the financial sector, all cold glass and chrome, and three secretaries vetted her before they finally allowed her up in the elevator to Angie on the top floor.

The other people in the lift were talking in some kind of strange, coded language.

'% 1.5 X 1000?'

'+ 812374 @ > 5 = trillions.'

'Ah! \$\$\$\$\$\$!'

And they had all smiled and rubbed their hands together in glee.

Angie had reassured her by saying, 'It's paper money. It doesn't really exist.'

She was always doing that, downplaying her own success. But she had lowered her voice and told Judy that sometimes it was necessary; that not everybody was delighted to know you were doing well. Judy had looked past her to the lifts, and the other stockbrokers, and imagined some kind of bloody turf war.

Angie took a worryingly long drag of her cigarette now and said tersely, 'I want to meet him. Biffo.'

'What?'

'Before the wedding. Just me and him, one to one.'

'Angie, is that wise?' Judy couldn't help feeling nervous. They had parted on such bad terms that any kind of meeting didn't seem like a very good idea.

'I know, but we need to clear the air, do you not see? We can't just turn up at your wedding with our new partners. It wouldn't be fair on anybody.'

'I suppose.' She didn't think for a moment that Biffo would agree to it.

Angie must have read her mind, because she lifted her chin and said, 'Tell him I won't hurt him.' She muttered, 'Although I should.'

'Look, I'll see what I can do, Angie, OK?'

There was a glum little silence. It was all such a bad ending to something that had started off so well.

Everybody had said they were made for each other. You never saw two people share so many interests: football, pints, laidback nights in the pub. 'I didn't know women like her existed,' Biffo had breathed in awe, shortly after meeting her. 'He's just like one of my brothers,' Angie had said happily. There was never a cross word spoken in their entire relationship, and everybody agreed that it would warm your heart just to look at the two of them on the beach on a Sunday morning walking off their hangovers or trying to rugby-tackle each other to the ground.

'Did he say anything about me to you, Judy?' Angie blurted suddenly.

'What?'

'Did I do something to upset him? Or say something? Was I too boring for him, or too crude, did I drink too much, or did he just not fancy me any more?

'Oh, Angie.'

'I must have done *something* wrong. He couldn't stand to be around me in the end.'

'I don't think that's true.'

'Come on, Judy. All those nights out with the lads. Those weekends spent at work. I just want to know what I did wrong, that's all.'

Judy looked at her lovely, intelligent, incredibly successful friend and said, 'And you don't think it might be anything to do with your job?'

Angie gave a screech of incredulous laughter. 'Judy Brady. We're living in the twenty-first century here.'

'You are. Biffo may not be.'

'Look, whatever else we say about Biffo, he has never pulled a testosterone tantrum over my job. It's a desk job, for God's sake. Boring as hell.'

'You make a lot of money, Angie.'

She waved this away. 'So what? I've never made an issue out of it. I've never done the whole I-earn-more-than-you thing. In fact, we hardly ever even mentioned my job, that's how much of a non-issue it was.' She took another deep drag of her cigarette and glared owlishly at Judy over her stockinged feet, which she had now propped up on the table. There was a hole at the toe of her tights. 'I mean, look at me. Do I look like some kind of a threat to you?'

'Not right now, no.'

After a minute she admitted, 'All right, so

maybe I wasn't *unaware* of it. But it wasn't a big deal, Judy. Look, I know what guys can be like over the whole job thing, OK? With Biffo I made absolutely sure that my job wasn't an issue from the word go. And he's never given any kind of vibe that he had a problem with it.'

Judy shrugged. 'It was just something he said yesterday about shares.'

Angie glowered afresh. 'Then let him say it to my face.'

'I'll talk to him, set up a meeting.'

'Good.' She ground out her cigarette. 'So what's she like? This Cheryl? Just so I know for Saturday. She's not a size twenty-two or anything?'

'She's a fitness instructor,' Judy said regretfully.

Angie looked surprised. Then the corners of her mouth reluctantly lifted. 'Here, do you remember that time Biffo took a cholesterol test from one of those mobile clinics outside the shopping centre, and they made him sit down before they'd give him the results?' Then she got a grip on herself and she said to Judy fiercely, 'Now look what you made me do! I don't want to speak badly about Biffo, OK? Or at least any more than I already have. Fair play to him if he's found a fitness instructor. I'm glad for him. Delighted, in fact! Well, not delighted, obviously. But I've met Nick, after all. So all that's left is for me and Biffo to draw a line under the whole thing and go our separate ways.'

★   ★   ★

Barry wasn't back at seven. Or eight. The risotto had dried out, and so Judy added a splash of white wine, and watched as it dried out again. She rang him on his mobile but either it was switched off or he was in a dungeon somewhere. By nine, the risotto had disintegrated to the texture of baby food and Judy had drunk half the bottle of white wine. The priest rang, irritated that Barry hadn't been in contact with him to approve the music that would be played at the wedding. 'We had 'Saturday Night Fever' last year on CD and don't want a repeat.'

Judy apologised for Barry's oversight, and read out the hymn list, hoping she wasn't slurring her words. When the phone rang again ten minutes later, she was sure it would be Barry, saying he had been called out to a patient, or some other plausible explanation, and she hurried to pick it up.

But it was Mrs Fox, his mother. As usual, she didn't waste any time on pleasantries.

'I need to speak to Barry,' she said in a low, urgent voice that Judy was used to, and that usually meant that something was wrong.

'He's not here.'

'Oh,' said Mrs Fox. You could hear her indecision on the phone. Then she evidently decided that Judy was better than nothing. 'Could you tell him that thing has happened again?'

'The same thing as before?' Judy inquired.

'Yes,' Mrs Fox whispered. 'He said it was nothing to worry about. That it would pass and maybe to take a spoon of Milk of Magnesia, and that if I wanted I could look it up in that medical encyclopaedia he gave me for Christmas. I wish I hadn't now.'

In Judy's opinion a medical encyclopaedia was the very last thing he should have given her, and that a big bottle of brandy or a couple of DVDs would have been far better, but he had insisted that if she could read about things herself, then she wouldn't be ringing him up all the time. The upshot was that she was now perpetually alarmed, which meant that she rang them up twice as much, a fact Judy could have predicted. But as Barry kept saying, she didn't have anybody else except him. He had a duty to look after her.

'Maybe you should go into the hospital if you're worried,' Judy suggested. 'Get yourself checked out.'

That usually did the trick. 'Oh, I'm sure it's nothing *that* serious,' Mrs Fox said, already sounding more robust.

'Why not have a couple more spoons of Milk of Magnesia?' Judy suggested. 'It's fairly harmless stuff, and it might help.'

Mrs Fox was always delighted with any bit of advice, not to mention more medication. 'I'll do that. Thanks, Judy.'

When the phone rang for the third time, at half past nine, she was so hopping mad at Barry — and getting slightly worried — that she snatched it up and said, tersely, 'Hello?'

There was a slightly startled pause on the other end. Then a female voice, rather throaty and low, asked to speak to Lenny.

'What?' Judy snapped. She'd forgotten all about him.

'I heard he was back and staying with you,' the woman said.

'And you are?' Judy asked.

'Oh, just someone he used to know.' Intimately, judging by her throaty little laugh.

Judy was cross. Not content with availing himself of free bed and board the week of her wedding, Lenny was now clogging up her phone line with calls from old flames. Or old colleagues.

'He's not here,' she said, starting to sound like a broken record.

'Can I leave a message — '

'Sorry.'

Now Judy began to worry about Lenny and Charmaine too. Supposing it was true and they *had* gone out in a boat around Cove Head? Supposing Charmaine *had* fallen overboard? She wouldn't have been caught dead in a life jacket and would have sunk like a stone. Lenny would have jumped in after her like some kind of macho hero, muscles flexing. Or maybe he wouldn't, that kind usually didn't put themselves at any risk. He might have just sat there and watched her go under. Or maybe he *had* gone in after her, but the sheer weight of her jewellery and sodden hair and thigh-high boots had dragged them both under . . .

Judy stood there in the gathering dark wondering whether she should raise the alarm. What did one do in these circumstances? Ring the coastguard? Oh, she wished Barry were here. He was good in a crisis. She would try his mobile again, immediately.

It went to voicemail again. She was just leaving a stream of curses on it when she heard the front door open. The hall was full of loud laughter and chatter and general good cheer. She heard Barry shout, 'Judy? We're home.' Then Lenny's voice. Whatever he said elicited an eruption of giggles: Charmaine, who up to now had shown no sense of humour whatsoever.

The expression on Judy's face soon put a stop to all that. Or, rather, it would have if anybody had troubled to look at her. Instead they crowded into the kitchen and trampled past her, taking off coats and smelling of sea air and, worse, chips, which they waved around in big greasy brown bags.

'I ran into Lenny and Charmaine in the pub,' Barry said by way of explanation. He tried to plant a kiss on her cheek, but missed. His own cheeks were rather florid and he wore a big toothy smile. He was, Judy realised, pissed.

'Blame us, Judy,' Lenny said. 'He tried to leave but we wouldn't let him.' He gave her a slightly wary look, as though expecting her to burst into flames at any moment. Which she would have, of course, if she hadn't had an audience in him and Charmaine, and so she was forced to say to Barry, civilly, 'You could have rung.'

'I tried twice from Lenny's phone but you were engaged,' Barry protested. 'My battery was dead.'

'He did,' Lenny said, backing him up like they were a pair of schoolboys.

'Have you any vinegar?' Charmaine inquired.

'I'm starving,' Barry declared.

What could she do? If she starting bleating about ruined risotto and wedding lists she would look churlish in the extreme. And anyway, she felt Lenny watching her again. He wasn't nearly as drunk as Barry, and he was standing near him protectively, as if to save him from this dragon of a fiancée who was out to ruin his few remaining nights of freedom.

Judy wouldn't give it to him. So she smiled merrily around at them all, and said to Charmaine, 'Vinegar is second press over. I'll get the plates.'

They sat around the kitchen table eating chips and drinking cans of beer, and Barry kept sighing blissfully and saying, 'This is just great!' as if he'd never had a better evening. The very same man who would only eat chips once a month because they clogged up your heart, as he liked to warn Judy. And who started whingeing if he was kept out any later than nine and missed his collection of medical dramas (he didn't care about any of the characters; he just enjoyed spluttering incredulously at all the technical bits and shouting, 'That would *never* happen in a real-life situation!').

'We were in some kind of member's section in the pub,' he regaled Judy happily now. 'Lenny kept buying cocktails — and the price of them! — and those posh beers and he wouldn't let me put my hand in my pocket the whole night long.'

'Well, you're getting married on Saturday,' Lenny said, as though this was a perfectly reasonable explanation for pouring drink down Barry's throat and getting him rat-arsed.

89

'And the music, Judy. Cuban. Fantastic!'

'He's a good dancer,' Charmaine told Judy, as though she was surprised.

So was Judy. Barry hadn't set foot on a dance floor since that holiday in Spain six years ago when he'd nearly broken his ankle doing an implausible twirl, and had to go straight home and prop his leg up on a pillow. Or rather Judy had got the pillow, and the ice, and the painkillers, while Barry had lain there moaning and complaining that the pillow wasn't high enough. He might be a good doctor but he was a terrible patient.

'You're not so bad yourself,' Barry told Charmaine with a rakish wink, and made a kind of a lunge at her. His hand landed on her thigh; with an expert twist in her seat, Charmaine shrugged him off like an irritating fly. He almost lost his balance and went crashing to the floor.

Judy looked into her chips, mortified and furious.

Barry just righted himself and barrelled on with, 'And then we got a taxi to the slot machines. We should go there some night, Judy, we haven't been in years. Lenny got three stars on a fruit machine and it started spitting out coins in all directions. Hundreds of them, you never saw anything like it. How much did you win, Lenny?'

'Just ten euro,' Lenny said.

'Yeah, but in five cent pieces!' Barry was like an overgrown child now. But maybe it just was her, thought Judy. The other two didn't seem to notice.

'Your mother rang,' she told him.

There was a damp silence. Judy was further embarrassed. But Barry always liked to know when his mother rang. 'But it's not important,' she added quickly.

The atmosphere never quite reached the same high after that. Barry opened more beers, despite protestations — 'Come on, one more for the road' — and Charmaine began to yawn, and Lenny tapped his fork against the tabletop as if he had suppressed energy.

Judy, feeling responsible for the slump, attempted to kick-start the conversation. 'So!' she said to Lenny. 'I hear you're in the movie business.'

She hadn't meant to say that. Or maybe she had. She was curious to see how he would explain it.

Lenny looked up. Cagey, she thought. 'I wouldn't exactly call it that.'

'Oh?' said Judy, an eyebrow jumping up. 'And what *would* you call it? Art?'

From Barry's face she guessed that he already knew about Lenny's profession; they had probably been discussing the cultural signifi- cance of *Deep Throat* down in the pub.

Lenny shrugged. 'Maybe. I prefer the term documentary.'

'Documentary!' Judy spluttered. 'I suppose that's one way of putting it.'

Lenny was slightly wary now. 'Do you know of another term?'

'I could think of several,' Judy declared loudly. 'I don't think I need to list them off here.'

Lenny remained guarded. 'Have you seen any of my stuff?'

'I most certainly have not. And nor has Barry. But I know of someone who watched one last year.'

'Did they like it?' he asked eagerly.

'I have no idea. I can only imagine that it fulfilled requirements. It had lots of naked people, after all.'

Lenny looked briefly puzzled and then his forehead cleared. 'Ah!' he said. 'The one on the Melbourne surfers. That went down very well, actually.'

Judy felt colour creep up her face. 'It was about surfers?'

'Yes. A documentary.' He was watching her closely now, the beginnings of a smile on his face as he guessed that she had somehow got it wrong.

Barry wagged a finger and said loudly, 'Don't be so modest, Lenny. It was a huge cult thing, Judy, the spirit of the sea and all that. Nominated for an Academy Award and everything.'

'What?' said Judy feebly.

'We didn't win,' Lenny assured her. 'Just in case your friend was wondering.' He raised an eyebrow pointedly. She blushed wildly.

'The nomination didn't hurt, though,' Barry said, very loud now. 'That always ups the takings at the box office, doesn't it?'

'For movies. Documentaries hardly ever make it to the big screen,' Lenny said patiently.

'Go on, I bet you make a packet. How much

would you make in a year on average?'

It was clumsy and gauche. Judy gave him a warning glance, which he didn't see. He was too drunk.

'Not as much as I'd like,' Lenny joked, expertly rescuing the moment. Judy found herself giving him a grateful look, the first sympathetic feeling she'd had towards him since she'd met him.

There was an odd, whistling noise; Charmaine had fallen asleep on the table, her mouth gaping open.

Lenny gave her a bit of a shake. 'Hey, baby.'

But there was no response at all from 'baby', and he pulled her coat up over her, but otherwise seemed dispassionate.

'Maybe it's time to say goodnight,' he said.

But Barry was all wound up. 'It's great how it turned out for you all the same, isn't it, Lenny? You drop out of college, arrive in Australia penniless and look at you now. Flying all over the world, winning awards, making millions even though you won't admit it.'

Lenny shrugged. 'It's just the way it turned out. And I don't make millions, or anything like it.'

'The point is that you took a risk,' Barry insisted. 'You didn't just sit here like the rest of us.'

There was a belligerence about him, a fractiousness that was out of character. It was probably all the beer and cocktails. He had never really been able to hold his drink.

'You make it sound like we've done nothing

with our lives,' Judy said lightly, trying to jolly him out of it.

'And what *have* we done?' Barry demanded. The belligerence seemed to be directed at her now.

It was Lenny who said, 'Not too badly, I'd say. A doctor with your own practice. A nice house. A good woman.'

He shot Judy a wicked little look.

'I think I'm going to be sick,' Barry suddenly announced. He lurched up from the table and stumbled from the room.

There was an uneasy silence around the table, punctuated only by the sounds of violent heaving in the bathroom. Judy should go to him, although it was possibly the last thing she wanted to do right now.

She stood. 'Sorry,' she said awkwardly to Lenny.

He looked steadily back at her. 'You don't have anything to apologise for.'

There was another burst of heaving from the bathroom. Judy nodded rather jerkily at Lenny, and left the room.

8

Barry's mother had been poorly ever since her husband Gerry had died. There hadn't been a thing wrong with her up until then; in fact, she used to compete every year in the Ladies' Tournament at the local Lawn Tennis Club with great success. She used to be a great woman for a round of golf, too, and would regularly take a brisk walk around Cove Head at the weekends.

But it had all been downhill in recent times. She was plagued with a series of inexplicable symptoms, such as periodic bloating and a dull thudding behind her left ear, though not at the same time. With each new development she would be over like a flash to sit on a stool under the main light in the kitchen, her mouth already open to say 'aagh'.

This morning she arrived looking particularly under the weather, and accompanied by two of Barry's aunts who were over from England for the wedding, and who wanted to deliver a lovely piece of Wedgwood. With much tutting, they settled her on her usual stool in the kitchen. She winced on impact.

'What's wrong? What's the matter?' Barry croaked. He was only out of bed five minutes and looked a fright. His eyes were painful-looking slits in a big, puffy face the colour of lard. When he bent down to his mother he gave a beery burp.

'She drank a bottle of Milk of Magnesia,' one of the aunts told him, reverentially.

'What?' he said now. 'A whole bottle?'

'She said Judy told her to.' They all swivelled to look at Judy, bar Mrs Fox who was clutching her stomach and giving a low moan.

Judy said, 'I did not, I said a couple of spoons.'

'It's not Judy's fault. I should have read the label,' Mrs Fox said bravely. 'But when she said it was harmless, I figured I could drink as much as I liked.'

Normally Barry would have roundly reproached Judy for giving out such advice, but this morning he hadn't a leg to stand on, and so he mumbled, 'I'm sure she was only doing her best, Mum.'

'It's been a terrible night,' said the first aunt. 'For us all.'

'This morning we said we'd better bring her straight over to Barry,' the other said respectfully.

They thought the sun shone out of Barry. Not only was he the only living male left in the whole family, but he was a doctor too, which automatically made him better than the nephews of all their friends. And he always sent them a Christmas card, and took them out to dinner in the hotel when they came over to visit, and listened with interest to their problems with their boiler. He was, quite simply, lovely.

'Let's have a look at you then, Mum,' he said.

The aunts began to relax. Barry was in charge now and they could hand over responsibility. They shot a sideways look at Judy, not trusting that she appreciated him quite as much as she should. Or, indeed, that she deserved him at all.

Mrs Fox lay down on the couch in the living room. It was debatable who was sicker, as Barry tottered over to her unsteadily. He poked and prodded; Mrs Fox moaned and groaned. He asked a few murmured questions such as, 'How many times?' and squeezed her hand sympathetically. Through all this he refused to look at Judy, either through embarrassment or because any sudden movement of his head would visit a lot of unpleasantness on everyone.

She was left to stand on the sidelines with the aunts, who remarked, 'We had lovely weather in Surrey when we left.'

Finally, Barry pronounced, 'I think a dose of Arret should do the trick. We have some in the press. Could you look after it, Judy? I feel a little light-headed, I might go and lie down.'

And he staggered out of the room.

The aunts and Mrs Fox looked at each other in alarm. 'Poor Barry! Is he all right?'

It was on the tip of Judy's tongue to tell them all that poor Barry had got completely bladdered the night before and only had himself to blame.

But she reluctantly covered by saying, 'He's just nervous over the wedding.'

'Really?' The aunts were most surprised. Barry had never been known to suffer overly from nerves before. 'Still,' said one bravely, 'he has so much on his plate.'

'Like what?' Judy inquired politely.

'Well, all his patients, Judy. That surgery is a huge responsibility for anybody. And there's all his charity work too, and now a wedding on top of it all.' They looked at Judy as though she was being most inconsiderate for foisting such a thing upon him. She was going to ask them what charity work they were talking about, and then remembered that meals on wheels run he had done two Christmases ago. Just the one run. But the two aunts and Mrs Fox had that mad glint of adoration in their eyes and she knew she would only bring terrible trouble upon herself if she said a bad word against Barry and so she managed, diplomatically, 'It's a busy time for us both.'

But of course they thought she did nothing, only sit around reading books all day in the library, and they gave her no hope whatsoever.

'I just hope he'll be able to get through Saturday,' one of the aunts said with a sigh. She patted Mrs Fox's arm. 'And you, of course. You know, what with Gerry being dead and everything.'

Mrs Fox started nervously at the mention of death, but she said, bravely, 'Yes, well, there's nothing we can do about that now.'

Gerry Fox had passed away two years ago. It was completely out of the blue and a terrible shock to everybody. A fit 62-year-old man, who didn't drink or smoke, with no family history of anything at all except bunions, to drop dead just like that in the middle of a department store! Mrs Fox was in the dressing rooms trying on skirts, and had sent him off in search of a size 12, which he never came back with. He had always hated shopping, and she blamed herself for months afterwards, because it was the only explanation there was; even the postmortem was worryingly inconclusive. If they had found a great big lump somewhere, or a heart screaming out for a bypass, it would have been some consolation. If it could happen to Gerry, Mrs Fox had kept saying, then it could happen to any of them.

At least she still had her son, everybody consoled her. Look how great he was over the whole funeral! Tearing strips off the undertakers over the colour of Gerry (they'd gone too heavy on the rouge) and giving Mrs Fox a sleeping pill when she declared that she hadn't slept in three days.

A month later, she asked for a full medical check-up, just to be on the safe side. Naturally, Barry had obliged. Then she got the house tested for radon. When she wanted to move because there was an electricity pylon a hundred yards away, he spent a whole evening showing her websites on the Internet that proved such things were completely harmless.

Judy had urged him to take her out for a game of tennis. Or to see a film or something. Take her mind off things, rather than humouring her. Barry had got a bit offended at that. Mrs Fox was his mother, suffering from bereavement, and he would comfort her any way she wanted.

Judy dispensed the Arret now, having first carefully read the instructions, and made tea for everyone, and admired the Wedgwood.

'It's dishwasher proof and everything,' one of the aunts assured her.

'But I wouldn't risk it all the same,' the other one cautioned.

They eventually took their leave when it became apparent that Mrs Fox was feeling better. Also, Judy was afraid that Charmaine or Lenny would wander in at any moment in a state of extreme undress, and undo the effects of the Arret. There was still no sign at all of Barry as she ushered them out and into the rental car that the aunts had hired.

'See you at the meal tonight,' Mrs Fox said, placing a dry kiss on Judy's cheek.

'Oh, yes, we're all looking forward to it,' the aunts said eagerly.

Amid much clashing of gears, they finally left.

Judy went back to her list. She was very behind. Worryingly, she wasn't worried, or at least not as worried as she had been up to now. Maybe she was suppressing it, and it was all building up inside her like a time bomb, and she would eventually explode tonight, or tomorrow morning, and it wouldn't be pretty.

Barry appeared just as she was trying to summon the energy to ring the hotel. She didn't turn to look at him.

'Sorry, Judy,' he eventually said. He looked marginally less close to death than he had an hour ago.

'For what?' she said. 'Leaving me to entertain your aunts, or making an ass of yourself in front of Lenny and Charmaine last night?'

'I did not!' He looked queasy again.

'At least admit it.'

'I was merely having a good time.'

'Do you even remember half of it?'

'Yes,' he said bravely, casting a furtive eye

around the kitchen for clues. He caught sight of a brown bag. 'Chips,' he said. 'We had lovely chips.'

'Yes, before you practically made a pass at Charmaine.'

That jogged his memory. His Adam's apple bobbed in fright. 'Don't be ridiculous! I was simply trying to give her a friendly . . . hug.' Without giving her a chance to retaliate, he went on, 'You've just never given her a chance!'

'Charmaine?'

'Or Lenny. Dead set against them from the word go!'

'Don't be stupid, Barry,' she said, even though it was probably true. And anyway, weren't they supposed to be discussing *his* bad behaviour rather than her perceived prejudices?

'Once you get to know them they're very nice people,' Barry told her. 'You should have come out with us last night, Judy.' It obviously didn't occur to him that (a) she hadn't been invited, and (b) they were getting married in two days' time and there was quite a lot to do. 'We had some fantastic chats last night about travel, and film-making and Naomi and Claudia and, um, Kate.' In case she needed clarification, he added, 'Models. Charmaine knows them all.'

Judy was scarcely able to believe she was listening to this. 'I had no idea you had such an interest in the fashion world.'

'Well, I don't,' Barry admitted. But then he rallied again, and looked rather loftily at her out of bloodshot eyes. 'I'm just saying, Judy. Maybe we need to open our minds more.'

101

Judy did a double take. 'Sorry?'

'Broaden our horizons. Embrace new experiences. That sort of thing.'

'I see,' she said carefully. 'And would you have any suggestions on how we might do that?'

For a moment he looked stumped. Then, stoutly, 'Maybe we should travel more.'

'We're going to Barbados on Sunday, Barry.'

'I know, but I mean exotic places, Judy,' he said, more animated. 'Forget the touristy stuff. Let's go off the beaten track.'

'Literally?' Judy inquired. It was difficult to imagine him in khaki shorts trying to fend off a rhino in the African bush with a stick. She would probably be more use; at least she had managed to stay awake during *Out Of Africa* whereas Barry had fallen asleep.

'Well, no,' said Barry, obviously thinking the same himself. 'I mean places like Singapore. Johannesburg. Mexico City, even!' He was really pushing the boat out now.

Judy said, 'Well, yes. I'd love to. It sounds great, but would you be able to get away from the surgery?'

It was a completely practical question — the honeymoon alone had caused conniptions in the roster — but Barry went off the deep end again. 'If you want to do it enough, you can find a way, Judy.'

You'd think that she personally was holding him back from his hitherto undiscovered dream of becoming a seasoned traveller.

'Maybe we'll plan something for next summer then,' she said.

The conversation had a bizarre feel about it. The list sat on the table, screaming out with urgent things to be done for the wedding, which was in exactly forty-eight hours' time, while they discussed next summer's holidays.

She had the sense of things slipping out of control, and she wasn't sure how to claw them back. And Barry standing there, so belligerent, so caught up in himself at a time when they were meant to be preparing to be together for life.

Judy got up, and picked up her handbag, and her mobile phone.

'Where are you going?' he said, surprised.

'Out,' she said. The way she felt right now, she might just hop on a plane and do some travelling herself.

'But what about the list?' he said. He was worried now; he didn't want her to go.

'It'll sober you up,' she promised him, and left.

★   ★   ★

She found Ber at home cleaning out her fridge.

This was unprecedented. Ber didn't clean, no more than she cooked, did laundry, or hoovered. She used to have someone come in and do it, but they resigned under the weight of the task, and Ber had been living more or less in filth and disarray ever since.

Nobody outside her immediate circle of friends realised this, although the Passport Office had a good idea. She always looked so good for starters (all the new clothes she bought were

103

partly to hide the fact that she never got around to washing the dirty things at home). She never invited any kind of scrutiny by throwing dinner or cocktail parties, and even Judy and Angie were discouraged from calling round. She just got up in the morning out of her bombsite of a bed, picked her way across the mounds of things on the floor, grabbed a banana from the kitchen (there was no other fresh food of any description) and closed the door on the whole lot of it. The night routine was the same, except that she usually didn't turn on any lights so that she wouldn't have to look at the mess.

Vinnie had no idea at all of Ber's slovenly side. He had only been to the house five times in their entire relationship (Ber had had to hire in industrial cleaning staff on each occasion). They always met in hotels, or parks, or cosy restaurants, and Ber would turn up looking gorgeous as usual, giving no hint at all of the carnage she had left behind.

Her dirty little secret had remained just that.

'Fuck this,' she said now, and emerged from the fridge, red-faced. 'Why don't they make self-cleaning fridges, like they do cookers?'

'Is your cooker self-cleaning?' Judy asked.

'Don't be asking me questions you know I can't answer,' Ber said crossly.

Ber's 'at home' image was also somewhat at odds with her public persona. Today she wore giant grey tracksuit bottoms and appeared to be still wearing last night's make-up. She looked at Judy, pushed back a handful of greasy hair, and immediately demanded, 'What's eating you?'

'Me? Nothing.'

'Wedding arrangements getting on top of you?'

'Something like that.'

She wanted Lenny to leave her house. It was a sudden and powerful feeling. His very presence was somehow insidious.

'I came over to find out how you got on last night.' She needed to immerse herself in someone else's man trouble. 'Have you news?'

'I have,' said Ber steadily.

'And . . . ?'

'He's moving in.'

'What?

'Why do you think I'm cleaning out the bloody fridge? I found cheese in there from nineteen ninety-nine. Isn't that sick?'

But she was grinning all over her face.

'Oh, Ber. That's marvellous.' If anybody deserved something to work out right for them, it was Ber. All her years of loyalty and patience and optimism had finally paid off. Love *would* overcome, as Ber herself would say. It must be nice to be right, Judy thought.

'I nearly talked myself out of it,' Ber admitted. 'Gave myself the whole if-it-ain't-broke-don't-fix-it speech. Convinced myself that backing him into a corner wasn't a good idea. But you know something, Judy? He got there before me.'

'What?'

'He said he'd been thinking and thinking about the things I'd said yesterday. That he deserved them. That the whole arrangement had been terribly unfair on me and that it was a

105

miracle I had waited around for as long as I had!'

'He said all that?'

'Twice. You know how he gets when he's nervous.'

'Oh, Ber.'

'So it's all sorted,' Ber said triumphantly. 'He's moving in Friday.'

'Bloody hell, Ber. That doesn't leave you much time.'

The bathroom alone would take a week. So many years' worth of newspapers were stacked in the living room that they practically blocked out all natural light. And the downstairs toilet wasn't somewhere that Judy even wanted to go.

Ber just waved a hand casually. 'Oh, it'll be fine. I've got a big shed at the back that I'm just going to pile everything into.'

Judy thought she was joking. But she wasn't.

'Come on and let's have a glass of wine,' she said, dismissing the filthy fridge with another casual flick of her hand.

There were no glasses to be found, or at least ones without any mould in the bottom of them, and so they ended up sipping out of a couple of eggcups.

'He's already told his wife.'

'What did she say?'

'She was pretty OK about it. She'd suspected for ages he was having an affair. She threw some plates and stuff at him, but I think it was more because it was expected than anything else. We're going to meet on Friday.'

'What?'

'When I go over to pick up Vinnie and his stuff. She suggested it. And his kids were pretty cool about it. They just wanted to know how big my TV was, for when they come and visit.' She gave a little chortle of glee. 'It's mad, isn't it? All these years, waiting and wondering, and in the end it's all working out brilliantly!'

It certainly seemed to be. Judy looked at Ber's blissful face and felt a pang of envy. Which was crazy. She was getting married on Saturday, for heaven's sake. She was just cross with Barry at the moment, that was all. It was bound to be a little more difficult to summon a swoon or a sigh.

Ber was busy painting a romantic picture of her new life. 'I can just see it all now, Judy. Vinnie and me curled up in front of a roaring log fire — once I clean it out, of course — watching *When Harry Met Sally* and drinking a nineteen eighty Bordeaux. And all the sex we could possibly want at the drop of a hat! Vinnie's very passionate, you know.'

Judy wondered whether he routinely did it twice. 'I hope it works out for you, Ber.'

Ber gave another gloriously dismissive wave of her hand. 'This is everything I've dreamed of, Judy. I'll never be a mistress again. I'll be a bona-fide live-in lover!' She looked at Judy. 'I used to look at you and Barry and think you were so lucky. You never had to come home to an empty house — a dirty, empty house — and a Marks and Spencer's dinner for one.' She said, simply, 'I can't wait.'

★ .★ ★

Judy arrived home rosy-cheeked from wine, and talk about affairs and husbands leaving wives. When she thought about it, her friends were really quite cosmopolitan and exciting, and Barry needn't go shouting about how brilliant Lenny and Charmaine were. They only seemed exotic because they were new in town; if you saw the pair of them in their own surroundings Judy bet they were probably just like anybody else.

She heard the television on in the living room. Football, it sounded like, and she could see a big pair of stockinged feet plonked on the coffee table. Unbelievable!

'I hope you haven't been sitting there the whole afternoon,' she called rather threateningly, as she hung up her coat.

But it was Lenny watching the television. 'Just for the last half hour,' he told her.

Her face was stinging. 'Obviously I meant Barry.'

'Obviously.' He gave her that look again, as though she were some kind of ogre who was perpetually out to harass Barry. 'He's gone out,' he told her.

'Yes. I can see that now.'

'He said to tell you that he has the list.' He made the list sound like some horrible, niggly thing that she had drawn up in pursuit of the perfect wedding; a rigid and pretentious blueprint for a dream day that she was ruthlessly determined to have.

To counteract this, she gave a careless smile,

and said, 'Oh! That old thing.'

There was a little silence now. When it became apparent that he wasn't going to hold up his side of the conversation, she asked, 'Where's Charmaine?' Not that Charmaine was generally any great addition to a conversation, but she might come in and start snogging Lenny or something, which would remove the need for her own presence at all.

'Gone,' Lenny told her.

'With Barry?' She couldn't imagine that Charmaine would have much interest in the finer organisational points of a wedding. But maybe she was harbouring hopes that Lenny might pop the question and wanted to get in a little prep. In that case, someone should tell her about Lenny's determination to remain a bachelor.

'No. I mean she's left.'

Judy almost looked around, as if he was joking, and Charmaine would really be under the coffee table. 'You mean, for good?' The suddenness of it, the lack of announcement was unsettling.

'Yes.' She saw that he wasn't a bit unsettled. In fact, he glanced at the score on the television.

'Did you two have a . . . row or something?'

Lenny laughed at her consternation. 'She's got a modelling job in Berlin, Judy. She flew out this morning.'

Judy felt slightly foolish for assuming there were dramatics behind her departure. 'A job! I see. Good for her. Are you going to join her after the wedding?'

'In Berlin?' He looked amused at the very notion.

Judy cursed herself for ever having starting this conversation. 'Sorry,' she said. 'I didn't mean to pry into your arrangements.'

Lenny shrugged. 'We don't have any arrangements. She's gone her way and I've gone mine, that's all.'

Judy blinked. 'It's . . . over?'

'What, you don't think two people can meet up, have a perfectly good time for as long as it suits them both, and then move on with their lives without any screaming or gnashing of teeth?'

'Well, I — '

But he cut her off by lightly slapping his forehead and saying, 'I forgot. Of course you don't — you're getting married.'

She was getting a bit tired of his pot shots about her marriage. 'What has that got to do with it?' she said stiffly.

'Well, it's all about the big commitment, isn't it? In it for the long haul and all that. Thick and thin.'

'I'm surprised you can sound so disparaging about something you've never actually tried.'

'You haven't either.'

'No, but I happen to believe in commitment to people,' she said loudly, feeling under attack. 'I actually *like* long-term relationships, and . . . and stability and being able to recognise the person in the bed beside me!'

'What, and you think that makes you a better person?'

'I didn't say that.'

'You're acting like it. And that I'm somehow inferior for having a relationship that lasts less than eight years and three months and two days.'

Which was pretty much exactly how long she had been going out with Barry, give or take a few days. She didn't know how he had found that out. Probably prised it out of Barry in the pub last night, whilst giving him a diatribe on how confining marriage was. Oh, yes, Judy could see how it had all happened now.

'Since you ask,' she said, 'yes, I do think you're shallow. And selfish. And full of yourself. And that you like only the nice bits in life and you'll leave the rest. And that's fine. Great! But it's not the way I operate and I'm quite happy with that.' She was all puffed up now, and she waited for his furious rebuttal, but he just leaned forward suddenly and asked, in a low voice, 'Have you ever slept with other people?'

Judy couldn't believe it. He was making a pass at her! In her own home. Two days before her *wedding*. And the bed not even cold from Charmaine. Oh, he was an unbelievable piece of work.

She clutched her handbag like a shield to her chest and told him icily, 'I have no interest or intention of sleeping with you, so you can . . . sling your hook somewhere else!'

Lenny looked briefly startled. Then he waved a hand impatiently. 'I don't want to sleep with you, Judy.'

'Oh.' Her face was aflame. She lowered her handbag.

'I mean, here you are, locked into this big relationship with Barry for the last however many years. Before you met him, did you see other people, Judy? Did you sleep with other people?'

Judy should have walked out of the room. But she was so mortified over her misconceived notion that he was propositioning her that she couldn't; her very attractiveness was at stake here, and she had to defend herself. So she flung the handbag aside and planted her hands on her hips and bellowed at him, 'I'll have you know that I have slept with a great many people!' At least four, including Barry. She should have left it at that, of course, but she barrelled on with, 'And those were just the ones I *agreed* to sleep with!'

There was a horrible little silence. She had a feeling he was going to burst out laughing, which would jettison altogether any small, lingering traces of her sex appeal.

But he didn't. He just nodded in approval. Honestly, what kind of a twisted mind did he have at all?

'That's something anyway,' he said.

What exactly, Judy didn't have the slightest idea. She should of course have retaliated by asking him how many people *he* had slept with but she had a feeling that the sheer numbers would leave her so shocked that she wouldn't be able to say her vows on Saturday. To dear, sweet, earnest Barry (unbeknownst to him, his star was rising meteorically in her affections. She could have ended up with someone like Lenny).

'Is there anything else you'd like to know?' she asked him with great sarcasm. 'Maybe whether I've travelled at all, or whether I have a second language?'

She was quite pleased with her riposte, but he just said, 'No. That's about it.'

He turned back to the television. Judy hopped from one foot to the other a couple of times, uselessly, before eventually leaving.

9

Biffo was suspicious of Angie's request to meet him.

'Why?' he said, swigging furiously from a bottle of mineral water and wiping his lathered brow. His physical agitation wasn't entirely brought on by Angie; he and Cheryl had just done an hour of step aerobics in the living room, with the inventive set-up of a selection of footstools and pouffes. Cheryl was upstairs finishing her shower now. Apparently there had been a brief panic when the water had dried up and the whole thing had stalled, but Mick had got up on a chair with his toolbox, and had fixed it in no time at all, despite Rose's protestations about his back. Cheryl had been very grateful; in America, you would have had to call a plumber, an electrician, and most likely a tile guy before you even touched your power shower, and wasn't Mick a regular Mr Fixit.

Afterwards Mick had gone around the house whistling some tune that nobody initially recognised, but which Rose in the end guessed was 'Wild Thing'.

'I think she just wants to make the peace.'

Biffo shook his head grimly. 'I know that woman. She'll have spent a whole year thinking up terrible insults and character assaults that she'll unleash upon me just as soon as she gets a can of cheap beer inside her.'

Biffo didn't drink any more. That was probably the most surprising facet of his transformation in America. Cheryl was teetotal (she had taken the pledge along with fifty-seven other teenagers in a big hall in her home town, applauded by all their parents. There was a photo of the moment hanging on their apartment wall, Biffo told Judy. Judy thought it was creepy.) It wasn't that Cheryl didn't *let* him drink — he wouldn't put up with that, he told Judy, shoulders flexing — but it was difficult to enjoy being rat-arsed and talking shite when Cheryl had her earplugs in and was doing lengths up and down the communal swimming pool.

He didn't watch football, either. They didn't show it much on the channels in America, and American soccer wasn't the same at all. He had got into baseball in the last while though, and Cheryl said that he had finally taken down his posters of Beckham and Best, and that he hardly ever cried any more in his sleep.

'I don't think it's a good idea,' he said at last. 'What are we going to do, shake hands and hug each other like everything is OK?'

'It wouldn't be necessary if you'd finished things a little more civilly this time last year.'

'So that's it,' he said. 'She just wants to rake over the whole thing again!'

'You didn't exactly rake over it the first time. You just upped and left.'

'I did what was best for both of us,' he said stubbornly. 'Look, I know it seemed sudden at the time, Judy, but if I'd stayed it would only have got worse.'

'What would, exactly?'

Biffo looked as if he wasn't going to enlighten her, but in the end he couldn't help himself and he burst out, 'Oh, you have no idea what I had to put up with, Judy! The snide little remarks in the pub. The jokes about men and aprons. The lads in work used to ask me why I bothered turning up at all, when I could just stay home and put my feet up instead. It gets to you in the end, Judy. And as for trying to talk it over with Angie, her answer to everything is an all-expenses paid weekend in flipping Madrid!'

'It doesn't sound too bad to me.'

'That's exactly the kind of thing I'm talking about!' Biffo yelped. 'That kind of scurrilous, low remark! You have no idea, Judy, how demeaning it is to go out for a night on the town and have somebody else pay for every single thing!'

'Did you try staying at home?'

That earned her another black look. 'People see us as a joke — men who are in relationships with women who earn loads more. We're the butt of every smart remark. People don't realise that we have feelings too!'

'Sorry, Biffo,' Judy said, trying to sound sincere.

'Oh, look, it doesn't matter now anyhow,' he said moodily. 'It's all over and done with. I'm not going to gain a single thing by meeting up with her.'

'She hasn't a clue about any of this, you know.'

Biffo looked cynical. 'She couldn't be that slow.'

'But Biffo, you didn't tell her that was why you left. How do you expect her to know?'

Biffo thought about this.

'All right,' he announced unexpectedly, 'I've changed my mind. I'll meet her.'

'What?'

'Maybe we do have some things to talk about after all.'

Judy was suspicious. There was a peculiar look on his face.

'I don't want any fights, Biffo.'

'No, no, of course not. Look, it's all in the past now, Judy. We might as well meet up to put it to bed.' He blushed furiously. 'That was a Freudian slip, obviously.'

'Obviously. I'll set something up.'

'And you'll be there, won't you, Judy? Just to break the ice.'

Judy didn't want to be there in the morning, listening to Biffo and Angie discussing the finer points of their break-up. Plus, it was the day before her wedding, and she was pretty sure that if she consulted her list she would find that she had a hair appointment, or something to do with nails or make-up or some damn thing. But at the end of the day, Biffo was her brother, and Angie was her friend. And if it hadn't been for her, they never would have met in the first place.

'OK,' she said reluctantly.

'Thanks. And I think it might be best if we don't tell Cheryl about this.'

'It's not illicit, Biffo. You didn't even suggest it.'

'Yes, but if she knows there's a meeting with

117

my ex she'll go off the deep end and start asking me where our relationship is going and all that, and right now I just don't know, OK?'

It was fairly obvious what Cheryl thought; you never saw anybody pour a bowl of no-fat, high-fibre, low-carbs, wholewheat cereal as lovingly as Cheryl had for Biffo that morning at the breakfast table, Rose said. Meanwhile, Rose and Mick were left to mow their way through the mounds of Sugarpuffs and Frosties that she had bought in for Biffo; they had been his favourite cereals before his conversion. And Rose was not supposed to be eating anything at all. But that resolution had already been blown out of the water the night before, with her consumption of two steaks and all those chips with Béarnaise sauce, and other assorted non-organic odds and ends that she had got in specially for Biffo and Cheryl and which neither of them would touch.

'I thought you were getting on well,' Judy said.

'We are,' Biffo insisted. 'Cheryl and I, we're equals.' But being equal didn't seem to light too many fires, judging by the look on his face. 'Maybe it's just funny, being home again. Things will be fine when we get back to Florida.'

The air was filled with the by-now familiar smell of bath products. Cheryl. But no, it was Mick who walked into the room. He was freshly bathed and had shaved, and stank of Old Spice. Biffo and Judy looked at each other in alarm.

'Whose funeral are you going to?' Biffo immediately inquired.

'What? Nobody's,' Mick replied.

Judy said, 'Dad, I think you've got the day

wrong. I'm not getting married until Saturday.'

Mick puffed up defensively. 'Can a man not have a wash around here without being interrogated? I just fancied a bit of a clean-up, that's all.'

Biffo and Judy exchanged another astonished look.

Rose arrived in from the kitchen, round and homely in a frilly apron, and holding a packet of tofu. She said to Biffo, 'Can I make sandwiches out of this?' Then she got the smell off Mick, and her hand flew to her mouth. 'Who's died?'

'Nobody!' Mick shouted. For some reason Rose's inquiry seemed to get under his skin the most. 'Biffo here can take as many showers a day as he wants and you don't say a word about it!'

'I do,' Rose insisted. 'We all do. We're blue in the face commenting on it.'

Mick ignored that. 'But the minute I do, everybody thinks there must be something wrong! Nobody would dream of saying anything nice.'

Rose said, hastily, 'You look lovely.'

'Oh, too late,' said Mick.

'Could you two have this discussion in the privacy of your own bedroom?' Biffo said with a sigh.

'Are you joking me?' Mick said. 'You can't get in the door of the place. Not with the piles of clothes and shoes and handbags, and a dead bird on the bed.'

'That,' Rose said condescendingly, 'is a feather boa.' She said to Judy, 'I found it in Top Shop. It'll set off my dress on Saturday just beautifully.'

There was still no hope at all of her actually getting into the dress, but Rose was confident that by tomorrow things would have improved, seeing as she hadn't eaten a single thing that day so far. Plan B was a packet of safety pins that she had bought in the chemist.

She said to Mick, 'Do you want a tofu sandwich? I'm not having any, so there's plenty.'

'I'm tempted,' he said, 'but no.'

'You then, Judy. You'll stay for lunch, won't you?'

'I can't, Mum. I've got a million things to do, and then the wedding rehearsal at seven.'

'We never had a rehearsal, did we, Mick?' Rose said mistily.

Mick looked past her as the door opened and Cheryl walked in. She had nothing but a towel wrapped around herself. She looked straight at Mick.

'The shower's gone again,' she said apologetically.

Mick puffed up a bit. 'Leave it to me.'

He set off after Cheryl, his tool kit in hand.

'Mind your back,' Rose called after him.

'My back is fine!'

★ ★ ★

'Are you going to promise to love, honour and obey Barry?' Lenny inquired of Judy.

'Of course,' she said. 'And cook for him, and clean up after him, and provide sexual services on demand.'

'Wow,' said Lenny. 'Maybe this marriage lark

120

is better than I thought.'

They were standing on the steps of the church where the wedding rehearsal was scheduled for seven. Barry was parking the car, having decided that his blood alcohol level had sufficiently lowered for him to drive. Thankfully his form had improved through the afternoon. Probably because he had been away from Lenny, Judy believed. There was no more loose talk about exotic holidays or models, at any rate.

One thing was now firm in Judy's mind: Lenny was a bad influence, a poisonous presence out to blight her wedding day. She was able to see him for what he was, but Barry was a more impressionable sort. You couldn't let him open the door to a salesperson for fear that he would be talked into buying a goat for Africa or getting a whole new set of gutters for the house. He hadn't an ounce of cynicism in him. She loved him for it, even though they'd had to cancel a weekend away to pay for the guttering.

'I hope I didn't offend you earlier,' Lenny said. 'About the sex thing.'

Judy stiffened. How could any woman not be offended when a man declared that he didn't want to sleep with her? Oh, she might pretend she didn't care — as if she would want to sleep with Lenny anyway! — but it still would have been nice to be *asked*. Even if it was obvious she wasn't his type, which was a tall, leggy, model-like creature with masses of hair. Tonight, Judy felt at her most squat. She didn't think she had ever felt more gnomish in her life before. And her hair was too short. She was practically bald, for God's sake. And fat. And her nose was too big, even though she had never worried about her nose before.

Another thing was becoming clear in Judy's mind: Lenny was very bad for her self-confidence. In his presence she felt inadequate, boring, unattractive.

'Not at all,' she said, icily. 'Over the years I've come to accept that not every man on this earth wants to sleep with me.'

He looked briefly confused. 'I meant my asking about your past sexual partners,' he clarified.

'Oh!' She had exposed herself again; now he would think that she had obsessed the entire afternoon about sleeping with him. That she was heartbroken because he didn't fancy her!

She told him loudly, 'You didn't embarrass me. I have nothing to hide. Nothing to be ashamed of.'

His eyebrow lifted. 'Meaning I have?'

'Your sex life is your own business,' she assured him sweetly.

'Like you, Judy, I'm an open book,' he said back.

'I have no doubt at all about that.'

He laughed. 'You know, I can't remember the last time I was so disapproved of. Probably back at school.'

'And has it ever occurred to you that you behave like a schoolboy?'

'Do I?' He seemed genuinely surprised by this.

'Bucking the system. Blowing raspberries at convention. Rebel without a clue.'

'And what are you, Judy? Head girl maybe,

with your little badge and your sense of responsibility and your earnestness.'

He made it all sound very insulting.

'I don't care what you think about me,' she said, with a brave laugh, even though she did.

'I think you're kind of cute, actually,' he said.

Cute! That was even more insulting than being branded uptight and earnest. It carried with it a hint of ridicule, of not being taken seriously. Teddy bears were cute. Small children dressed up in their Sunday clothes were cute. Cute was not good.

And you're a right plonker, she opened her mouth to say back, a big tart who can't keep it to yourself, but she only managed to get out, 'Now, listen here!' in her best head girl voice before Barry blundered up the steps towards them, tripping on the third step and almost falling on his face. This was nothing to do with alcohol or its after effects. No, it was his new black wedding shoes, which he had belatedly decided that he had better break in before Saturday. And from the way he kept tripping over them, they were at least two sizes too big. But he would insist on buying them after a busy Saturday at the surgery, where he spent the whole day standing and running up and down stairs, and his feet had been two big smelly swollen lumps when he had presented them to the sales girl for fitting.

Plus, they squeaked. Loudly. Judy felt a mixture of pity and annoyance as he hopped on one foot now, the better to examine the shoe on the other.

'Maybe I can oil them or something,' he

muttered. 'Anyway! It's great to see that you two finally seem to be hitting it off. I could hear you laughing down the street.'

'Only with derision,' Judy said stonily. She had meant this for Lenny, of course, but Barry thought it was aimed at him and, defensively, he looked at his shoes again and said, 'They'll be fine, OK? I'll stuff some tissues in the top or something.'

'And they'll need a polish before Saturday too,' she said. The toe of the left one was already scuffed. 'We haven't even got any black shoe polish.'

She could sense Lenny observing this little exchange with some amusement; thinking probably that they were already behaving like a long married couple, hapless Barry and bossy Judy.

Well, he knew nothing about relationships. Not real relationships, anyway, where people stuck around long enough to find out each other's little faults, instead of just bonking their brains out and then moving on. Barry and Judy had a whole past together, a history of shared experiences and moments and feelings. They'd had the ups and downs (she thought about the guttering again) and the bits in between. And she liked that. She *loved* that. She loved their Sunday mornings together, and the way he called her honey pie when nobody else was listening.

They were good together. Sometimes they were great together. She wouldn't change it for anything, and certainly not a couple of nights of exotic sex with a beautiful stranger. Not that anybody was offering, of course.

And so she swept past Lenny haughtily and put her arm firmly under Barry's elbow, her fiancé, and they walked together through the church doors.

Inside, it was cool and empty. They stood still for a moment at the back of the church, breathing in the slightly musty smell.

'Imagine,' she said to him softly. 'This will be us on Saturday.'

The sense of occasion seemed to touch him too, and he looked around with a mixture of trepidation and excitement before smiling down at her tenderly.

Then, a sly voice in her ear: Lenny. 'Look at that. Someone's got here before you.'

There was a coffin at the top of the church. Judy felt a bit queasy. It seemed like a very bad omen or something, and she clutched Barry's arm. He squeezed her hand reassuringly.

Then Lenny, Mr Comedian, followed up with, 'I hope that wasn't a patient of yours, Barry.' And Barry broke into a volley of sniggers, despite his best attempts to look sombre.

Judy was furious: imagine making fun of the dead! Well, actually, she was crosser about yet another intimate moment ruined. She rued the day Barry had asked Lenny to be best man. Anybody would have been better. Even Biffo.

Eventually Barry got a grip on himself, and went off to study the Stations of the Cross with the intensity of one who hadn't been in a church properly for many years. His shoes creaked loudly with every step.

When Lenny found no conversation with Judy, he wandered off to study a rack of pamphlets on addiction and alcoholism. Good, she thought. It might improve him.

'Hi!' There was a clatter of high heels at the back of the church and in came Ber, gorgeous in a very tight dress and with her hair freshly done. 'Sorry I'm late,' she said, squeezing in beside Judy in the pew. 'I was clearing out my lingerie drawers so that Vinnie can have some room for his jocks tomorrow.'

Her words reverberated around the empty church, and came back to them, amplified.

'Sorry,' she whispered, chastened. Then, briskly, 'So, where's this creep Lenny?'

Judy had instructed Ber on the phone earlier: her prime function as bridesmaid on Saturday would not be to hold up the bride's veil but to Keep An Eye On Lenny. Now that he had dispatched poor Charmaine (Judy had started to feel sorry for her; she had probably been dumped), it was pretty much certain that he would hit on one of the wedding guests on Saturday. Judy had already re-jigged the seating plan so that he would now be sandwiched between the aunts from Surrey, although there was no guarantee he wouldn't make a pass at one of them. But with Ber watching his every move, and with Vinnie as muscle should things get nasty, she felt she was doing what she could to protect the other wedding guests from his rampaging sexual advances.

'Over there. I should warn you now, he'll try

126

and win you over with charm. But it's very superficial. Once you scratch the surface there's not much there.'

But Ber was looking over with glee. 'You didn't say he had grown up to be such a ride, Judy!'

'Ber!' Honestly, you could take her nowhere. 'I've told you. He's a creep. King of the one-night stand.'

'So is he free right now?' Ber asked keenly.

Judy rolled her eyes. 'I thought Vinnie was moving in tomorrow?'

Ber sobered. 'Oh. Yes.' Then she brightened again. 'Still, there's no law that says I can't look, is there?'

Lenny knew very well that he was being discussed, of course; he studiously finished a leaflet on family planning and carefully put it back. Then Judy watched as he pretended to have some interest in a picture of the Virgin Mary holding a fat baby Jesus, a very holy expression on his face. Finally, only when he considered that they had sufficiently admired his profile did he lazily turn in their direction. A quick flash of a sexy smile; a slow strut over. What a performance, Judy thought. Beside her, Ber smacked her lips.

Judy didn't bother with flowery introductions. 'Lenny, Ber. Ber, Lenny.'

Lenny reached past Judy to shake Ber's hand. 'I remember you,' he said to her warmly.

Ber, who was supposed to be giving him the evil eye, was delighted. 'Do you?'

'Of course I do. You used to give us a terrible time.'

Ber laughed flirtatiously. 'You probably deserved it.'

Judy felt it was time to head any trouble off at the pass and so she told Lenny meaningfully, 'Ber's boyfriend is moving in with her tomorrow. His name is Vinnie. They've been seeing each other for donkey's years.'

Ber gave her a little cross look, as though she was spoiling the party. Lenny, Judy noticed, didn't seem all that put out at Ber's unavailability.

'I come all the way back from Australia and all the best girls are gone,' he teased instead. Ber played up by laughing in that way that men seemed to find very pleasing. Judy wasn't any good at all at flirtatious laughing; the one time she had tried it she had sounded like a drowning horse.

But Lenny wasn't looking at Ber. He was looking at her. Teasing her, of course. Sending her up. She resisted the uncharacteristic urge to stick her tongue out at him, and changed the subject.

'Where's Barry?' There was no sign of him.

'He's probably made an escape,' Lenny told her.

She looked at him. 'You're very predictable, do you know that?'

'I thought you liked predictable.'

'You haven't a clue what I like or don't like.'

Ber was looking from one to the other, her smile gone; obviously Judy hadn't made it clear how badly relations had deteriorated.

'Oh, look!' Ber said, relieved. 'The priest!'

But the priest wasn't going to lighten the

atmosphere too much. He began by consulting his watch with a sigh, and said, 'I suppose we'd better get going.' He looked at them out of humourless, rheumy eyes. 'The bride?'

It took Judy a moment to realise that everyone was looking at her. She pitched forward clumsily. 'I guess that would be me.'

'Come up, please. And the groom?'

Barry was eventually tracked down by the squeak of his shoes to one of the balconies, and brought down. The priest's irritation grew. Any hopes Judy might have had that the rehearsal would be a cheerful, romantic warm-up to Saturday were swiftly dashed. The funeral of the person in the coffin was due to take place in half an hour, Fr Maguire told them tersely, and he was up against time. He raced them through their wedding vows — Barry got so flustered that he agreed to take Judy as his awful wedded wife — before ushering them out the door just as the mourners started to arrive, weeping and wailing. To make matters worse, one of them recognised Barry, even though he tried to duck behind a statue of St Bernadette.

'Dr Fox! I wonder could you take a look at this? I don't like the colour of it.'

Ber had stayed behind to ask the priest whether he could bend the rules a little, and marry her and a divorcé.

Lenny and Judy found themselves outside on the steps again, staring at the hearse.

'Cheer up, Judy. We'll all be dead some day.'

'How profound.'

'In fact, if looks could kill, I'd be dead right now.'

'I'd imagine you're fairly immune to dirty looks.'

'I know, but for some reason yours hurt.' Judy drew herself up haughtily (it only added a quarter of an inch to her stature, but anyhow). 'Do you know what your problem is?'

'Tell me.' And he folded his arms over his chest, as if he were enjoying himself. At her expense, naturally.

'You're jealous,' she announced.

'Of what?'

'Me and Barry.' That sounded rather conceited, not to mention a bit unlikely, and so she hurriedly clarified, 'People like us, I mean. People who get married.'

He laughed merrily. 'I'm jealous of people who get married?'

'Well, you seem to spend an awful lot of time putting it down. You know what they say.'

'What *do* they say?'

'That often it's a cover-up. To hide the fact that you want it for yourself.'

'Great,' scoffed Lenny. 'I'm being dissected by a pop psychologist.'

Judy was rather wishing she hadn't started this. 'I think you make fun of me all the time because you're afraid of commitment. It's much easier to pick up women at stopovers in airports and spend the weekend having mad sex and . . . and licking foodstuffs off each other!' Lenny's eyebrows shot up at that. Judy hurried on, 'I think you're terrified of commitment

130

because it means you have to invest a bit of yourself, you have to work at things, instead of just falling back on your one-liners and your good looks!'

There was a bit of a silence following this.

'Whew,' said Lenny. 'At least you think I'm good-looking.'

Judy clarified quickly, 'In an objective way.'

'Naturally,' he said. 'Well, I'm sorry that you seem to have such a low opinion of me. But you're wrong, Judy. I don't go in for the happily-ever-after stuff because I don't believe that two people can spend their whole lives together. Oh, they can grit their teeth stoically and get on with it, sure, out of a sense of duty and responsibility and all that, and because they've got this great big wedding ring on their finger.' She felt this was aimed at her. 'They'll have the kids and the mortgage and the holiday home in France, and one morning they'll wake up and there won't be a thing holding them together except routine.'

'And you know this for a fact, do you?' Judy scoffed.

'I know that people don't stop growing and changing the day they walk up the aisle. They're not going to be the same people in twenty years' time. And the person who's right for them then is not the person they're hitched to.'

'That's very cynical,' Judy said.

Lenny shrugged. 'Maybe. But at least I'm not fooling myself, Judy.'

10

The evening didn't improve with the family
meal. Somehow Barry and the restaurant had
got crossed wires over the booking, and they
ended up two places short, which meant that
everybody would be sitting on top of everybody
else around the big long table.

'Still, it'll be cosy,' Judy said. She was
determined to make the best of it. In fact, it
seemed very important that they had a nice night
tonight. She already had a pain in her face from
smiling at all the restaurant staff in the hopes
of convincing them that she was a blissful
bride-to-be.

But Barry just glowered back. 'I suppose that's
aimed at me. Oh, there goes Barry, making a
balls of things again!'

'I didn't say that,' she said. His mood was
grim again. To compound matters, he had
stepped in dog poo on the way to the restaurant
in his new wedding shoes.

'Come on, Barry. Let's enjoy ourselves
tonight.' And she tried to kiss him, to bring a
smile to his face, but he was too busy loosening
his tie as though he were being suffocated, and
she nearly got an elbow in the face.

'What, with my hypochondriac mother and
your perma-tanned brother, and Mick going on
about the leak in our bloody bath? And let's not
forget the two eccentric aunts. Oh yeah, I'd say

132

we're going to have a ball.'

Judy was worried now. Barry normally never said anything really mean about anybody. And especially not his mother or his aunts. Mick, maybe: all his advice was starting to wear a bit thin. But Barry always humoured him; he was good at that, it was part of what made him a great doctor.

'They're our families, Barry,' she said. 'They just want to wish us well. That's all.'

'You mean they want to see us married off just like them.'

'What?'

'It's the herd mentality. Safety in numbers and all that. They've all knuckled down to it, and they just want to make sure we do as well.'

Judy had no idea where all this was coming from. Nobody had ever put pressure on them to get married. It was as if the words weren't his, as though he had borrowed them from somebody else.

'Where's Lenny?' she said, instantly suspicious.

'Gone to the pub.'

'What?' The last time she had looked, he had been right behind her — looking at her bottom, actually. Probably reaffirming to himself how unattractive she was, and pitying poor Barry who would end up with nothing at all to say to her in twenty years' time.

'He said the dinner was a family thing, he didn't want to intrude.' Very convenient, Judy thought. 'He's probably having a nice quiet pint in O'Grady's right now.'

133

And Barry looked so bad-tempered and resentful that Judy found herself blurting, 'Don't let me hold you back if you want to join him.'

'Don't be stupid, Judy.'

'I'm not the one being stupid.' She had to blink hard. She was hurt, and confused, and upset. Not only had Lenny said horrible things about married people — she hardly ever had to grit her teeth stoically when it came to Barry! — but her fiancé was also moping about like a surly teenager and having mood swings that would alarm a menopausal woman.

But there was no time to pursue it because the restaurant door opened and in tottered Mrs Fox. 'I hope I don't pass on anything,' she announced immediately. 'My tonsils feel a bit swollen.'

She began to press the sides of her throat delicately as though fingering a couple of beach balls.

'If your tonsils were that swollen you wouldn't be standing,' Barry informed her tersely.

Mrs Fox looked at Judy. Judy just shrugged. She wasn't going to take responsibility for Barry's lousy mood, although undoubtedly somebody would blame her.

And, actually, Mrs Fox was going to. 'He's had a lot on his mind recently,' she told Judy, as if urging her to be more understanding. 'What with his father dying and everything.'

And you phoning him up three times a day about your glands and your hypertension and the coating on the back of your tongue, Judy thought. But then she felt bad and she managed a smile and said, 'I suppose.'

Next up was Judy's lot. Mick was wearing a rather flashy suit that he hadn't worn since the last big family occasion about nine years ago. It looked a bit small for him. He seemed afraid to let his breath out in one go in any case, and spoke in short, terse sentences that didn't require too much puff: 'All right, Judy?' 'Pint of Guinness, please,' and, 'Did you fix the leak in the bath, Barry?'

Biffo was in a brilliant white shirt, which made his tan even darker. He seemed preoccupied and immediately ordered a double mineral water on the rocks from the waitress. Cheryl was like a prom queen in baby pink, and lit up one whole corner of the room with her healthy glow. She looked a bit nervous at the way everybody got down to the serious business of ordering drink before wasting any time on hellos.

The other side of the room was lit up by Rose's deep purple dress. The dress size was probably a little optimistic, and it stretched too snugly across her belly and hips, giving her the look of being wrapped in cling film, but she was glorious all the same. She had teamed it with lots of jangly jewellery and strappy sandals and had gone all out on her make-up.

She came over with Mick in tow, and immediately enveloped Judy and Barry in a big hug. 'I can't believe you're getting married on Saturday!' She was already filling up.

Nobody knew how she was going to get through the day on Saturday. The handbag she had bought would only fit three packets of travel tissues.

'I know,' said Barry politely. 'It kind of snuck up on us all, after all these years.'

Judy gave him a look. Was he being sarcastic?

But Rose was nodding vigorously. 'You'll make a lovely couple,' she informed them with great authority. 'I always said you were made for each other, didn't I, Mick?'

'You did,' he said dutifully.

'Excuse me,' Barry said abruptly, and walked off to a waitress. From the motions he was making with his hands, he appeared to be ordering a very large drink.

Judy felt she had to excuse him to her parents. 'He's a bit tense tonight.'

Rose put her arm around Judy's waist warmly. 'The groom is often more nervous than the bride, you know. But everybody expects them to be all macho and masterful and they feel it would be letting the side down if they were to show any hint of nerves at all.'

Judy felt better. 'Do you think?'

'Of course. Mick had to get blind drunk before he'd marry me, didn't you, love?' She laughed raucously. 'Really, it should have been the other way around.'

'Thanks, Rose,' he said.

'Ah, I'm only joking you.' She looked at him, a bit concerned. 'Are you all right in that suit? You look a bit hot.'

The loud query only made him look hotter.

'I'm fine.'

The restaurant door swung open again, announcing the arrival of the two aunts from Surrey, who immediately set upon Barry with

136

the kind of delight that elderly people always seemed to feel in his presence.

'There's Barry!'

'Oh, isn't he lovely?'

'Come sit between us, Barry.'

Judy could see his sudden flash of impatience, his determination to resist, but they wore him down with pats and strokes and lavish compliments, until after about two minutes his face grew all ruddy with pleasure and his whole mood lifted.

He allowed himself to be borne along between them to the table, where they perched either side of him, never taking their eyes off his face.

That was the cue for everybody to move to the table. Rose hurried off to the bathroom to take off her tights, which had gone into a very painful roll around her stomach.

Cheryl commandeered Mick to ask his opinion about the menu.

'What's gruel?' she said.

Mick had to choose his words carefully for fear of alarming her. 'Well, it's an old-fashioned Irish dish that uses the, um, less popular cuts of meat.'

'He means the guts,' Biffo shouted up.

Cheryl looked horrified. She turned back to Mick immediately for assistance.

'Can you find me something vegetarian, non-wheat, and non-dairy on the menu?'

Mick looked across at Judy, stumped. 'I'll try,' he said, dubiously.

But Cheryl seemed to have every confidence in him. 'Geoffrey never told me what a great guy you were.'

'Geoffrey?' Mick looked confused.

'Biffo,' Judy supplied.

'Oh! Yes, of course.' Mick looked down at Biffo rather balefully. 'Did he not now?'

'He just said you were retired and had a bad back.'

Biffo got another look thrown at him.

'What?' he said to Mick.

He was saved by the arrival of Mrs Fox at the table, who plonked herself down at the other side of Mick, and leaned across him heavily to say to Cheryl, intensely, 'Someone told me you're a doctor too.'

'No. I'm a fitness instructor.'

Mrs Fox digested this and obviously decided that it was in the general field. 'You're very healthy looking,' she said enviously. 'Very muscular.'

Petrified, Cheryl looked to Mick once again to save her.

'This is Barry's mother,' he explained.

'I haven't been well at all recently,' Mrs Fox told Cheryl, even though she hadn't asked. 'Barry won't say it, but I know he thinks it's all in my head. But if it's in my head, how come my tonsils hurt?'

Ber couldn't come to the meal because she still had mountains of things to shift before Vinnie officially moved in tomorrow, and she didn't want a single thing to spoil his arrival, not when she had been mentally planning it for the best part of a decade. Everybody else at the dinner was family, a fact that Biffo leaned over to carefully check with Judy, out of the side of his mouth.

138

'You haven't invited Angie along or anything, have you?'

'She's actually at the cinema tonight with Nick.'

Biffo looked disappointed and unthinkingly reached for a big hunk of white bread. Two places down, Cheryl noticed and frowned. Both of them had given up wheat. But then Mrs Fox leaned over again to show her something on her elbow, drawing her attention away.

'Is it serious?' Biffo asked Judy.

'I don't know. They're only going out four months.' She didn't want to be disloyal to Angie, so she added, 'They seem to be getting on well.'

Biffo looked even gloomier. 'I don't know what she was doing with me at all. Slumming it, I suppose.'

'Biffo, Angie's not like that.'

In fact, part of the attraction of Biffo was that he was the total opposite of the people Angie normally associated with. 'Natural' was how she euphemistically put it. But then she was natural too, when she took off her suit.

'I guess I'll see her tomorrow anyway,' he said, rather cryptically. 'I don't suppose you thought to ring ahead and ask them if they have anything macrobiotic on the menu, did you?'

Down the table, Barry seemed back to himself. At any rate, he shot Judy a look that could be termed conciliatory, or possibly ashamed, but that might be going too far.

Rose plonked herself down beside Judy, stuffing the discarded tights into her handbag. 'There's a great feeling of freedom down there now,' she confided.

139

Judy wasn't sure whether this was a good idea or not, but she went ahead anyway and asked, 'Have you any advice to give me?'

'What?'

'On marriage, Mum. Any nuggets of wisdom that I can take to the altar with me on Saturday.'

Rose was delighted to have her advice sought, rather than always having to give it out like a dose of medicine. 'Never go to bed on an argument, or a sink full of dirty dishes.'

'That's it? That's all the advice you have to give me?'

Rose was surprised at her tone. 'Well, what do you want me to say, Judy?'

That it was all going to work out brilliantly, of course. That she and Barry would not only become husband and wife on Saturday, but that the rest of their lives would be full of tinkling laughter, and romantic dinners, and no bills at all, and lovely children, and hardly any mortgage, and that they would still be together at ninety. Still with eyes only for each other, even if they were ugly old crones on Zimmer frames and with hair growing out of their noses.

That was just idealistic. But she wanted something to counteract Barry's odd behaviour. Some reassurance.

'You'll start out marriage together, just you and Barry,' Rose said, 'and you'll end up together. Just the two of you. Remember that.' And she looked down the table for a moment at Mick, who was diligently showing Cheryl something on the menu. Then she let out a laugh, and squeezed Judy's hand. 'Your little face is terribly worried looking, Judy.'

'Oh, someone just said something earlier.'

'Who?' Rose demanded.

'It doesn't matter.' She hoped the person in question was having a very bad pint in O'Grady's right now. It would serve him right. Or maybe being picked upon by a couple of local thugs whose seats he had inadvertently taken.

'Don't listen to anybody, Judy,' Rose said spiritedly. 'Not even me. At the end of the day, you and Barry will have to make your own mistakes.'

Oh cheers, thought Judy. The night just kept on getting better and better.

On cue, Biffo started banging his spoon off the side of his glass. 'Speech! Speech!'

And nobody had even ordered their food yet. In the dim lighting, and with a couple of mineral waters in him already, his teeth shone manically in his tanned face.

Barry was trying to fend off Biffo's exhortations. 'Won't there be enough speeches on Saturday?'

'Hear, hear,' said Mick, fervently.

But Biffo kept banging his spoon off the side of his glass, until eventually Barry hauled himself reluctantly to his feet.

'This is ridiculous,' he grumbled, embarrassed.

Oh, why couldn't he just stand up with some degree of pleasure and say a few words? Why did he have to have a big drink of his pint as if to fortify himself? They were surrounded by their closest family, after all. He was supposed to be

141

enjoying himself, not looking as though he were on his way to the dentist.

'I'll start by thanking everybody for making the effort to come along tonight,' he began rather heavily, as though there were ten inches of snow outside and a threatened rail strike. Judy sat up straighter and smiled valiantly at everybody, determined to look as though she, at least, was having a marvellous time, whatever about the groom.

Barry nodded around to them all. 'Mum, Mick, Rose, Biffo. Sorry, I mean Geoffrey. And the lovely . . . ' He looked at Cheryl blankly. 'His lovely girlfriend. My two aunts. You're all very welcome.' He looked at Judy. 'And Judy, of course, who had no choice.'

They tittered around the table. It was an improvement, even if she wasn't fond of the tenor of the whole speech. And Barry began to relax into himself, used to having lots of mainly older people looking at him expectantly, hanging on his every word.

'I'll have to go through all this again on Saturday,' he said quite jokily.

You couldn't keep up with his mood swings these days, Judy thought darkly. But then she remembered how he had been a few days before his final exams, or the time they had bought the house. He wasn't a person who dealt with stress well at all. He was a worrier; he didn't sleep well even the night before a medical conference, because he wasn't that keen on big crowds or having to put on a public show.

'Nothing he liked better than a good night

142

out,' he was saying now, at the top of the table. Judy wondered for a moment whether he was talking about the absent Lenny. But no, it was his father. 'Not too late, mind,' Barry cautioned. 'And he was a great man for a jar, not that he ever drank more than the one. But he still knew how to have a great time.' He amended this to, 'A goodish time.'

Mrs Fox was misting up. Barry rambled on to address his aunts, and to thank them for making the trip all the way over from Surrey, as though it were Outer Mongolia. He thanked Mick twice for letting him have his daughter, oblivious to Biffo's tittering. Rose got a mention too, something along the lines that if Judy turned out to be half the woman her mother was, then he would have his hands full. Nobody was sure whether this was a compliment or not, and puzzled looks darted across the table and back, and Rose sucked her stomach in just in case.

Ten minutes later Barry was still going strong, and thanking all his friends from medical school even though none of them were actually present. Judy was coming to two conclusions: firstly, if they didn't order soon, the restaurant would be closed for the night; secondly, Barry wasn't going to mention love, or her, or his feelings for her at any point in his speech. Not that she was in favour of public outpourings of emotion generally, but he could at least say he was looking forward to making her his wife on Saturday.

'There's just one last thing to say.' He looked around. Here it came now, thought Judy. 'We have a spare seat in the car home, two at a squeeze, so let us know if you want a lift.'

Everybody clapped, and Judy kept smiling around at everybody the whole night long.

★ ★ ★

'Barry, are you all right?'

'What? Of course I am. I've never been better.'

Under the light of the street lamp outside the restaurant, he looked haggard and baggy-eyed and ancient, and Judy could see exactly what he would look like at seventy. John Cleese, she realised with a start.

'You seem a bit down.' Plus, he hadn't praised her beauty and intelligence and handiness with a garden strimmer to their families tonight.

'I'm fine,' he insisted, looking up and down the deserted street a bit impatiently. A stray chipper bag blew up and wrapped itself around his leg and he pulled it off, swearing under his breath. 'This godforsaken town.'

'What's wrong with this town?'

'Nothing, Judy,' he said coldly, as if she wasn't as enlightened as him, and was mistakenly under the impression that they were actually living in Paris.

'Goodnight, Barry! Goodnight, Judy!' It was the aunts, the last to wander from the restaurant. 'We'll see you on Saturday! The big day!'

This only served to drag the general mood even lower.

'You'd think they'd never been to a wedding in their lives before,' Barry said.

144

Judy tried to stay smiling. 'Maybe they haven't.'

He looked at her. 'You're taking it all in your stride, aren't you? The whole thing.'

'Actually, Barry, I'm not. But it's something we decided to do presumably because we *wanted* to do it, because we love each other, and I'm going to try to get through the stress of it as best I can, and enjoy the day on Saturday if that's at all possible.'

Some of what she said seemed to get past Barry's boorishness because he rubbed his eyes and gave a little tired sigh.

'I'm sorry, Judy.'

'You don't have to be sorry. Just talk to me, Barry.'

He took her face in his hands and gave her a look of such ferocious intensity that she was briefly scared. 'You're so great, do you know that?'

There was something about the way he said it that made her heart speed into a nervous gallop in her chest. 'I'm not, I'm horrible half the time. I have very mean thoughts quite often that I never tell you about because I'm so ashamed of them, and lewd ones occasionally that just . . . revolt me! Plus, I'm impatient, and bossy, and I care too much what people think of me, and I really can't stand Marcia in work but I still let on to like her.'

Barry smiled. For the first time in days he looked like himself. *Her* Barry, with his good-natured, open face, his eyes crinkling up at the edges.

'Maybe there's something about weddings,' he said.

'I feel I'm not myself at all,' Judy agreed. 'I feel I've turned into some monster who only goes around organising things.'

They smiled at each other.

'I'm sorry about tonight,' he said. 'I know you think I should be sweeping you off your feet instead of having an attack of last-minute nerves.'

Judy felt relief flood through her.

'It's normal,' she said. 'I'll probably go to pieces in my mother's house tomorrow night.'

But Barry wasn't to be consoled. 'I'm supposed to be the strong one in all this. The one taking charge. I'm a physician, for God's sake!'

'That doesn't make any difference,' Judy soothed. 'Us librarians have great inner reserves of strength. It's all that quiet time by ourselves.'

And she put her head on his chest. She could feel his heart beating, strong and familiar under her ear, and she felt reassured. Rose had been right. In fact, Judy decided that she thought *more* of Barry, now that he'd had a slight case of the jitters. It just showed you that he had been thinking hard about the whole thing.

'I'm glad we talked about this,' she said warmly.

'Me too.'

She ran a hand over his chest. 'Will we go home?'

'Now?'

'It's nearly midnight, Barry. I thought we

might do a bit of catching up on some things we've let slide recently.'

And she wasn't talking about the list.

You would think he'd have jumped at the chance. To make up for his gaffe tonight, if nothing else. But he shifted from one foot to the other and said, 'I told Lenny we might meet him for a drink.'

Alarm bells went off in Judy's head, as they always did where Lenny was concerned.

'Now?'

'He's in a club down the town.' He added hastily, 'It won't be a big session or anything, just a drink or two.'

They had the rest of their lives together, she told herself, so she shouldn't make a big deal about one night. But it still hurt that he didn't want to come home with her.

'You know, I'm tired. I think I'll just go on home.'

He could have tried to persuade her, to say that the night wouldn't be the same without her.

'Are you sure?' he said, already reaching into his pocket for the car keys.

'Perfectly.'

'And you won't be mad at me or anything? It's just, it's my second last night as a single man and all that!' And he gave her a crooked smile.

'I won't be mad.'

He planted a kiss on her cheek. 'You're the best, Judy.'

11

The day before Judy and Barry's wedding dawned blue and clear. Judy held her breath and listened to the weather forecast for the weekend on her car radio, sure that gale-force winds and thunderous rains would lash through the entire country tomorrow, taking her veil with it. But Bill at the library had been right: the weather would be even better tomorrow. The sun would split the stones, and they would put the Mediterranean to shame. For once. Instead of Iceland, or India during the monsoon season.

Judy cautiously let her breath out. Or some of it, anyway. She didn't think she would be able to let it all out properly until tomorrow.

She parked and ran quickly across the road.

The minute she walked into the library, Marcia looked her up and down and inquired, 'What happened to you? You look great.'

It was the result of an entire morning spent at the beautician's, where she had been plucked, waxed, buffed, bleached, sprayed, and painted. 'He won't recognise you when we're finished,' they had told her reassuringly. She had hardly recognised herself. The rather sleek creature that had looked back at her from the full-length mirror in the salon bore little resemblance to the Judy who had walked in. She looked, she thought, like a woman who was getting married in the morning.

Annette came over. 'What are you doing here, Judy?'

It had been decided that the best place for Biffo and Angie to meet was the library. It seemed to fulfil everybody's requirements: a neutral place (Angie), where they didn't serve alcohol (Biffo) and where they would be obliged to keep their voices down (Judy).

Biffo was already there. It took Judy a moment to recognise him. He was wearing a suit, which was probably a designer label even though Judy hadn't a clue about these things. But it looked extremely expensive. His hair gleamed with gel and setting lotion, and his tan was so robust that it looked sprayed on. He had on another ostentatious watch, and what appeared to be a diamond stud in one ear. You could smell him from the desk, and under his arm he casually clutched the property supplement of the newspaper.

The whole package had been carefully constructed to reek of money and success, and had probably taken him hours to put together.

'He's your *brother*?' Annette asked, agog, when Judy explained her mission.

'Yes,' Judy admitted.

'We thought he was one of those American entertainment solicitors, or a media mogul or something.'

'Well, I think he's gorgeous,' Marcia announced. 'Will you introduce me?'

Judy was tempted; she would love to see how Angie would deal with Marcia muscling in on the action.

'I could but I won't, for your own sake,' she said regretfully.

She went over to Biffo.

'Oh, hi, Judy,' he said, trying to pretend that he wasn't all dressed up like a dog's dinner.

'Is that the suit you're wearing to my wedding tomorrow?' she inquired.

'It might be. I thought I might give it a little airing.' But he was nowhere near as casual as he was letting on. His upper lip was covered in sweat and his eyes kept flying to the door.

'She's late,' he complained.

'Where's Cheryl?' Judy asked, just to remind him that he had a girlfriend.

'Giving Dad a massage.'

'*What?*'

'Well, she has some training in sports injuries, Judy. Dad was doing so much moaning about his back this morning that she offered to treat him.'

'And he let her?' Judy was astonished.

'She insisted. He was mortified at first, but she assured him she wouldn't hurt him and in the end she persuaded him to take off his shirt and lie down on the floor.'

Judy imagined the scenario. Then Rose's face.

'She gives a great massage,' Biffo confided in Judy. 'He'll be a new man when she's finished with him.'

Judy asked, 'Do you think they still have sex? Mum and Dad?'

Biffo looked appalled. 'That is very possibly the most . . . scurrilous suggestion you've ever made, Judy!'

'What? I'm just wondering, that's all — at

what age people decide they're not going to make the effort any more.' She hoped it wasn't as early as thirty-three. 'Or whether people still want each other even after years and years together. They might want each other even more.' Passionate pensioners; now there was a thought.

Biffo was wilting. 'Stop. I feel sick.'

'They didn't just do it twice in their lives, Biffo, to produce you and me.'

Biffo still looked like a disgusted five-year-old. 'There are some things you just don't talk about, Judy. And your parents having sex is one of them, OK?'

'Yes, but you must be curious as to what holds people together, Biffo. Apart from their children, that is. If the sex thing is gone, the physical attraction, then there must be something else.'

'Yes,' he snapped. 'I believe it's called marriage.'

Then his head whipped round to the library door even before it opened. Judy heard him swallow as the doors slid back and Angie walked in.

If Biffo had dressed to impress, then Angie had played it down. She wore a pair of jeans and a hoodie top with runners and had her hair tied back in a ponytail. She looked like the girl next door, and nothing at all like a hotshot stockbroker who could sell you shares in your own granny.

Talk about game-playing. Angie strode forward defensively, and Biffo stepped up importantly. There were so many vibes flying back and forth that Judy wanted to duck.

'Well, well,' said Angie, as her eyes did a slow sweep from the tips of his sun-kissed hair down to his shiny American shoes. You could see that she was gobsmacked. He endured it defiantly, his chin lifting so much that he was practically looking at the ceiling. 'You've changed,' she said, eventually.

'Yes, well, I've gone up in the world since you last saw me,' he pointed out, unnecessarily. He gave her the up-and-down treatment now, finishing up on her nicotine-stained fingers. He crooked an eyebrow disapprovingly. 'Still smoking, I see.'

'Yes,' she said evenly. 'I haven't felt the need to change at all, Biffo.'

'Maybe I should go,' Judy murmured.

But nobody was listening to her.

'You wanted to talk?' said Biffo, haughtily.

'I'm sure it won't take long,' Angie said grimly.

Biffo made a great show of consulting his massive, gold watch. 'I can spare an hour.' The implication was that he had to rush off somewhere to close a multimillion pound property deal. 'How about we go somewhere quieter?'

'Fine. Let's step outside,' Angie snapped.

'It'd be nicer over coffee,' Biffo said.

'Coffee?'

'I've booked us in for afternoon tea in the Four Seasons,' Biffo said efficiently. 'My BMW is outside.'

'Are you winding me up?' Angie said suspiciously.

'Absolutely not,' Biffo said. He shot a look at her jeans. 'That's if they'll let you in.'

With a rather astonished look at Judy, Angie let herself be borne out of the library by Biffo.

* * *

She said her final goodbye to Barry at the house.

'Have you got your toothbrush?' he said.

'Yes.'

'And your pyjamas and everything?'

It was unlike him to be so practical. But he probably didn't want to get all mushy and romantic given that Lenny was sprawled on the sofa eating Pringles and watching Sky Sports. You would think he would have the sensitivity to make himself scarce at a tender moment like this. But he probably didn't want to pass up on the amusement value he would undoubtedly extract from the situation. He had been watching closely the whole day long as Judy and Barry had dashed in and out like lunatics, shouting into mobile phones and clutching the list, which still wasn't finished. When Barry had appeared from the barbers, with his hair cut up around his red, shiny ears, Lenny had laughed out loud. Barry had actually got cross with him. It looked like the love affair, at least on Barry's part, was beginning to wane. He hadn't even wanted Lenny to accompany him to the dress hire shop to collect the suits. Lenny had insisted anyway.

Judy had thought Lenny would run a mile from all this last-minute wedding stuff. But perhaps her words yesterday had hit home.

Perhaps he was rethinking his shallow, superficial life and had developed a sudden yen to get hitched.

Yeah, right, she thought cynically.

'I think I have everything,' she told Barry now, deliberately angling her back towards Lenny. But he wasn't a man who took a hint, obviously. There was a crunching noise as he popped another Pringle into his mouth.

'And you'll go to bed early tonight?' she said to Barry in a low voice. She didn't want to get all schoolmarmish and bossy, but she didn't think he could handle any more late nights. Himself and Lenny had come home at about 2 a.m. last night. At least Barry hadn't been drunk. He had got into bed beside her very quietly and fallen straight asleep. Or, at least, he hadn't responded when she had whispered his name.

'Don't worry, Judy. I'll look after him for you.' That was Lenny, on the sofa, no doubt being sardonic.

'Now, why doesn't that reassure me?' Judy quipped cheerfully. Well, at this stage of the game she felt she could afford to. She was getting married in the morning and, despite his best efforts, Lenny hadn't managed to sabotage the whole thing.

But nobody laughed at her little joke.

'I don't need anybody to look after me, OK?' Barry said, bristling a bit. This seemed aimed more at Lenny than her, and she was surprised.

But Lenny just gave Barry a look before turning back to the TV. 'Fine'.

'I'll walk you to the car,' Barry told her,

picking up her overnight bag and going out. Great, thought Judy. They could have a last romantic goodbye and a kiss.

It only remained to say goodbye to Lenny. 'I guess I'll see you tomorrow,' she said.

'You will,' Lenny said.

She had been prepared to leave it at that. After all, nobody could accuse them of having hit it off over the past week. There was no need for any misplaced joviality or anything like that.

But Lenny was getting up from the sofa and coming over to her. He obviously felt obliged to make a thing of it. She was going to extend her hand, but remembering what had happened at the airport, she quickly let it drop.

'Goodbye, Judy.'

'Um, goodbye.'

For a minute she thought he was going to give her his two-finger salute. But then he took her by surprise by bending down and kissing her on the cheek.

His lips were warm and dry and she gave a little jerk as though she'd received an electric shock.

He smelled of Pringles and other nice things.

'I do wish you well, you know,' he said.

He didn't step away and Judy found herself looking up at him. His eyes had little flecks of gold in them, she noted. He hadn't shaved. He was gorgeous. She wanted him to kiss her again. What?

Thankfully, normal brain function suddenly resumed as if after a brief but alarming malfunction. 'Lovely!' she said, baring her teeth

155

in what she hoped was a smile. 'See you tomorrow! Don't forget the rings!'

She began to back away from him. It seemed very important to put as much distance between them as possible.

He was looking at her peculiarly. 'Is something wrong, Judy?'

'With me? God, no! No, I'm great. I mean, I'm fine.' Before he could guess what thoughts had been going through her head — how he would laugh — she turned round and ran for the door.

Out at the car, Barry had already put her suitcase in the boot, and opened the driver's door for her. Obviously he didn't have any protracted goodbyes in mind. Judy found that she didn't care. She felt odd; all hot and nervous and for some reason she found it difficult to look Barry in the eye. She felt guilty, she realised.

Barry was looking at her closely. 'I hope you're not coming down with a temperature.'

'It's just excitement,' Judy assured him. Well, she could hardly confess that it had been a brief but blinding flash of low-down dirty lust for his best man. 'Look, I'll see you in the morning.' She wanted to get away. She would feel better in her parents' house, all safely wrapped up in her wedding preparations again. There would be so much to do that she wouldn't have a moment to think.

But Barry wanted to talk, blast him. And he had that funny look back on his face now, like trapped wind. She hoped he wasn't going to go on about his last-minute nerves again.

156

'What, Barry?' she said.

She waited. At the kitchen window, Lenny appeared. Arms folded, he looked at the two of them, inscrutable.

Judy met his eyes briefly, before looking away quickly.

So did Barry. When he turned back to Judy, he shrugged, and said, 'Nothing. I'll see you in the church tomorrow.'

12

There were lots of tears in the Brady household the night before Judy was due to get married. And those were just Mick's.

'More hot water!' he said mournfully, as Rose brushed past him with two big fluffy bath towels and a bottle of bubble bath. 'Has anyone considered how I'm going to pay for this?'

Rose said briskly, 'Judy here is getting married in the morning. You hardly expect her to turn up dirty, do you?' She handed over the towels to Judy. 'I have fish pie on for dinner, your favourite. And you're in charge of the remote control for the whole evening. So if Benny Hill here' — and she jerked her head towards Mick — 'wants to watch football or anything just tell him to get stuffed, OK?'

Mick said to Judy, 'She thinks that's hilarious. She's said it about ten times already.'

Rose chipped in, 'You might want to watch your step around the place, Judy. You're liable to find people lying around the floor half-naked. You don't want to twist your ankle for tomorrow.'

'I told you,' he said robustly. 'Cheryl was doing a detailed examination of my back. She is the one who discovered, where everybody else has failed, that I have a weak disc.'

'With the amount of moaning and groaning

158

coming from you, I'm surprised she only found the one.'

'I assure you, I wasn't enjoying myself down there.'

'Well, of course not,' Rose commiserated. 'How could any man enjoy himself with a twenty-six-year-old astride him on the floor?'

'Your problem is that you know absolutely nothing about physiotherapy. Cheryl has a diploma in sports injuries. She treats people like me all the time. And I take umbrage at you making fun of her professional skills.'

'It's not her I'm making fun of,' Rose said back.

Mick ignored her and said to Judy, 'She thinks it was all those years of bending over, for work. Apparently a lot of plumbers and people in the trade end up with back problems.'

Rose threw her eyes to heaven over by the sink.

'Maybe you should set up a support group or something,' she said.

Mick rounded on her. 'Surely the important thing is that I'm now able to walk from here to the living room without experiencing pain? Or is that a joke to you too?'

'Oh, it's a laugh a minute around here all right these days,' Rose snapped back.

Judy stood between them, clutching the fluffy towels and the bubble bath to her chest, looking from one to other. The mood had gone rather sour.

There was a creak from upstairs, and then footsteps running lightly down the stairs. Cheryl.

159

Judy braced herself for a ray of sunshine.

But Cheryl's lovely face was clouded over today. Probably by thoughts of environmental pollution or world debt.

But no. She inquired, tersely, 'I thought I heard the front door.'

'That was just Judy,' Rose told her, very kindly indeed for someone whose husband had recently been discovered semi-naked under Cheryl.

'Oh.' Cheryl's face grew even darker. So preoccupied was she that she didn't even say hello to Judy, or ask her how she was bearing up for tomorrow, the standard questions.

'What's wrong?' Judy inquired.

'Well, er, Biffo hasn't come home when he should have,' Mick explained.

Judy tried not to look guilty. 'What do you mean?'

'He went out this afternoon for a George Foreman fat-free grill while I was giving your father a massage,' Cheryl told Judy. 'He said he'd only be an hour. We haven't seen him since.'

Judy discreetly checked her watch. Biffo and Angie must have had many, many cups of afternoon tea by now.

But she said nothing. It would only upset Cheryl more to find out that he'd had a covert meeting with his ex-girlfriend.

'I'm sure he'll be home any minute,' she said rather weakly.

'It'll be all right, love,' Mick assured Cheryl. 'He'll walk in that door any minute, you'll see.'

They all looked at the door for a few minutes but nothing happened.

'Are you sure it's OK for me to stay over tonight?' Judy asked Rose a bit awkwardly. It sounded as if there was already enough going on the house without her inconveniencing everybody by taking pre-nuptial baths and no doubt wanting everybody to dress up in the morning and come watch her get married. 'It's only a silly tradition anyway, it's not like I'm trying to convince anybody I'm a virgin.'

But Rose immediately put a stop to that kind of talk. 'Judy, darling! Of course you're going to stay, I wouldn't have it any other way.'

Secretly, Judy was glad. Not that she was *afraid* to go back to her own house or anything. In fact, she felt rather foolish now at her hasty flight — and all over a harmless kiss from Lenny! Just as she suspected, the minute she set foot in the chaos of her parents' home, rationale had come quickly to bear. All right, so Lenny *was* good-looking, in a smooth kind of way. There was the remotest possibility that she *might* fancy him. So what? Just because people got married didn't mean they stopped having sexual feelings (no matter what Biffo thought). It wasn't as though she was desperate to act upon them; she wasn't fantasising about ripping his trousers off or anything, and dragging him into bed.

She just had, she realised. Horrified, she switched her mind to Barry. She would spend a few quality moments imagining *his* trousers coming off.

But somehow the fantasy took on the feel of a comic strip and she stopped, uneasy.

Rose was saying, 'I suppose we're all a bit

emotional about tomorrow. But nothing's going to spoil your last night here as a single woman, Judy.'

She gave Mick a look, and he rowed in with, 'Absolutely not. Go and have your bath. Use as much hot water as you like.' Generously, he offered, 'I'll even boil an extra kettle if you want. And we'll all have a nice drink for ourselves tonight, eh? Settle the nerves for tomorrow.'

'And I'll make some special herbal tea that'll help you relax,' Cheryl offered, obviously eager to make up for stealing Judy's thunder, today of all days.

And Judy gave in and let herself be cosseted and fussed over by everybody, listening to their words of encouragement about tomorrow, trying to block out the fact that she had, within the past several hours, developed an attraction for her fiancé's best man. Who wasn't even worthy of it. A guy whose behaviour and values were so opposite to her own that they might as well be different species.

As if to counteract all the bad karma surrounding her, Judy filled up a huge bath after dinner and tipped half the bottle of bubble bath into it. She would give herself a good scrubbing, she decided, to rid herself of any unchaste thoughts about other men, and she would turn up at the altar tomorrow in her white frock, a vision of purity and holiness, and marry her lovely Barry.

By the time night fell, she had talked herself into believing that the whole Lenny thing was just a temporary aberration brought on by stress.

162

She was, after all, a bride-to-be, and there was no accounting for what irrational thoughts she might have before tomorrow. Lenny wasn't even her type! She didn't go for men who were all dark and chiselled with smouldering eyes and laconic grins, and a body that was shortish but perfectly formed.

She was salivating, she realised. She must stop this, now. It was madness.

Thankfully, Ber arrived just as Judy was hunting about frantically for her tea tree oil.

'Great!' Judy cried. If anybody was romantic and gooey-eyed, it was Ber. She would deliver a blow-by-blow account of Vinnie's big move, complete with passionate sighs and overblown statements. It would be enough to coax even the most addled bride into the mood.

But Ber confounded expectations somewhat by announcing, 'What a bloody awful day.'

She went on to apologise for her appearance so late in the evening; she would have been by earlier except that Vinnie had a lot more possessions than he'd let on, and it had taken several more trips from his house to hers than originally planned. And he was quite particular about the packing of it. Everything had to be wrapped in two layers of newspaper, which quite dampened the euphoria of the whole thing.

'Most of his things aren't even very nice,' she confessed to Judy. 'And I don't know where I'm going to put it all.' She paused. 'I thought we'd spend the afternoon drinking champagne and making love, and instead we ended up trying to find a drawer for his socks.'

163

They were sitting on Judy's single bed, like they used to do years ago as teenagers, talking about boys and sex and about Ber's worry that the single cigarette she had smoked behind the toilets on the beach would give her lung cancer.

'And I'm a bit suspicious at how cheerful his wife was to see the back of him,' Ber went on. 'She was altogether too friendly to me. Gave me a big hug and everything.'

'She was probably just covering her heart-ache.'

'Maybe,' Ber said. You could see she wanted to believe it.

But not as much as Judy. 'She's more than likely drinking herself into oblivion as we speak,' she insisted.

'You're right,' said Ber. 'Or having a senseless one-night stand with a complete stranger in a motel.'

She looked almost wistful for a moment, but then she said, briskly, 'Now! I brought you this.'

And she rooted in her handbag and extracted a half bottle of brandy. 'For your nerves.'

'I'm not too bad actually.' She'd already had Cheryl's herbal tea, and a vodka and Diet Coke supplied by Mick, and had a feeling that any more mixing of drinks wouldn't produce good results.

'I'll have it so,' Ber said. She took the top off and had a big slug, and it seemed to settle her.

She gave Judy a rather coquettish look. 'So? How's the bride-to-be?'

'Do you ever have thoughts about other men?' Judy blurted out.

Ber reared away in alarm, spilling the brandy. 'Jesus Christ, Judy.'

Judy was sorry now she'd ever said anything at all. 'I was just wondering.'

'It's the night before your wedding,' Ber said sternly. 'We shouldn't be having a conversation like this. We should be discussing love and romance and Barry's dimples.'

'He doesn't have any.' Lenny did, though. Right in the middle of his chin.

There she went again!

Ber was looking at her very closely. 'Are we talking about someone we know here?' As if it made a difference.

'No,' Judy lied. 'Look, it was kind of a lust thing.'

'Ah!' said Ber, immediately relieved. 'I lust after other men all the time.'

'Do you?' Judy felt a big cloud lift.

'Well, of course. In work I'm surrounded by gorgeous men. You can't get away from them. And we have a unisex loo and everything.' She confided, 'Some days it's all I can do to keep my hands off some of the younger ones.'

This was possibly too much information, but Judy lapped it up anyway. And there she had been thinking that there was something wrong with her! That she had done something terrible the day before her wedding.

'It's natural to notice other men, Judy. But I've chosen Vinnie over any of them, for all kinds of reasons. Just like you've chosen Barry.' She wagged a finger at Judy. 'You know what they say. Just because you're getting married doesn't

165

mean you can't look at the menu.'

That didn't sound quite right, but Judy was prepared to go with it anyway. She was relieved and delighted that the Lenny thing truly meant nothing, only that she was completely normal. Mind you, that was by Ber's definition.

'Barry's mad about you,' Ber finished up, even though it hadn't been in question.

'I know,' Judy said, smugly.

Ber was right: she and Barry had chosen each other over anybody else, they had made a commitment to each other that couldn't or shouldn't be undermined by a very fleeting attraction to someone else.

And to Lenny, of all people! He couldn't commit to next week. Barry was so superior in practically every way that Judy couldn't think *why* she had found him even remotely attractive.

Sex, she thought. It came back to that again. She and Barry were simply missing a bit of passion in that area of their lives. She had only looked at Lenny with a twinkle in her eye because she was frustrated, pure and simple.

Maybe this was her cue to spice up her and Barry's sex life. After all, they had been together for years, things were bound to have become a little stale. She might even suggest they experiment in the whole area of foodstuffs, seeing as she had brought up the subject recently. Barry had never expressed any urge to lick things off her bare skin before, but possibly she was underestimating him. After all, he had never actually been propositioned by anybody holding edibles (not that Judy knew of, anyway).

166

He might love it! He might want to take all their meals in the bedroom.

'Are you all right now?' Ber said, concerned.

'I've never been better,' Judy answered happily.

'I'd better get home to Vinnie in that case. We're having our very first night together tonight!'

'Oh, Ber.'

'I know, it'll be marvellous.' Her lustful look dimmed a little. 'Mind you, we have to shift one hundred and thirty beer mats off the bed first. I didn't even know he collected the things.' She rallied with a brilliant smile. 'Imagine! *So* many things to discover about him!'

When she had gone, Judy lay on her bed for ages, fantasising about tomorrow in a way that she hadn't really done up to now. And why shouldn't she? All the arrangements had been made, the list had been got through (or most of it anyway). The whole thing was in motion, and Judy could let herself be swept along on it, the happy bride, and her feet wouldn't touch ground again until the honeymoon was over and she and Barry had landed back in Dublin airport, blinking and disorientated and probably wondering where in the name of blazes their luggage was.

She couldn't wait.

There was a sudden crash downstairs, which sounded suspiciously like someone falling in the front door. This was followed by a high-pitched scream from Cheryl.

Then, Rose's voice, 'For God's sake, keep the

167

noise down! Judy's getting married tomorrow and she's trying to go to sleep.'

Getting married or not, this was too good to miss. Judy jumped out of bed and went down the stairs.

Biffo was standing in the hallway. Or, rather, lurching about in it, hands grasping for something to hold on to. His suit was very rumpled looking, and something that looked suspiciously like Guinness had been spilled down the front of his white shirt. Finally he stumbled back against the coat stand and kind of balanced there, but could fall again at any moment. His eyes were sunken drunkenly in his head, and he slurred something that sounded like, 'Sonny is great,' but which Judy deduced was, 'Sorry I'm late.'

Rose, Mick and Cheryl stood around him in a silent semicircle as if at a freak show. One of Cheryl's hands was clasped to her mouth in horror. The other slowly rose to point at Biffo. Judy was sure it was to decry his drunkenness, to point to the nasty stain down his front.

But she just moaned, 'Look!'

They all did, even Biffo. And there it was: a tray of curry chips protruding from his jacket pocket, the yellowish contents dripping down the side of his lovely trousers, and the accompanying cheap white plastic fork about to fall out. He had obviously tried to hide them before coming into the house.

'Whose are those?' he said now, in a pathetic attempt to shift the blame. To Cheryl, he swore, 'I never saw them before in my life.'

To cap it all, a packet of Benson and Hedges fell out of his trousers pocket and landed incriminatingly at his feet.

In what was obviously a desperate stab at damage limitation, he stumbled forward towards Cheryl, his arms outstretched to hug her. 'Sorry,' he said, and hiccupped.

'Get away from me!' Cheryl screamed in terror, and took refuge behind Mick.

As Mick argued afterwards to Rose, what else could he do except shield her? Biffo was in a terrible state; you couldn't let him near anybody, and certainly not somebody as clean as Cheryl. Mick tried to redirect him towards Rose. Rose was furious, but managed to side-step just in time. Biffo ended up landing with a thump at Judy's feet on the stairs.

He blinked up at her earnestly. 'I'm really happy for you and Barry, Judy. I mean it.'

Then, like some hideous movie baddie who couldn't be killed, he rose unsteadily to his feet again.

'Where have you been?' Cheryl demanded.

Biffo blinked as his brain slowly processed the question and generated a reply. 'In pubs,' he mumbled. He wiped some saliva from his mouth. 'Give me a hug.'

And he lurched towards her again, arms outstretched like Freddie Kruger.

'I'm a teetotaller!' Cheryl cried in disgust, and pushed past him and up the stairs.

★   ★   ★

In her dreams, Judy heard bells ringing. Ah, she thought — wedding bells. Of course. They had a lovely cheerful happy sound, and she smiled to herself and turned over in the bed.

They were going on a bit, the bells. She was getting slightly fed up of them. Honestly, it was difficult for a bride to get any sleep with the racket.

Then she heard voices. They were coming from downstairs. Was Biffo still wandering around drunk? It had taken half an hour to persuade him to lie down on the couch, as everybody agreed that Cheryl would probably not welcome him upstairs.

Judy woke up properly and looked at the little pink alarm clock on her locker. It said ten to seven. In the morning? She looked at the curtains and could see sunlight creeping through.

There were footsteps on the stairs now, and Mick poked his head around the door. He was bleary-eyed and in his dressing gown.

'It's that Lenny fellow,' he said, scratching his head.

'What?'

'I told him you were still asleep. But he insisted on seeing you. At this hour of the morning!' Mick looked a bit worried. 'I'll give him the boot if you want.'

Not many people called around at that hour of the morning, and when they did it generally wasn't to impart good news.

'No, no.' Judy swung her legs out of bed and

170

reached for her robe. 'I'll come down. You go back to bed, Dad.'

'Are you sure?'

'Yes.'

All kinds of things crowded into Judy's head. Accidents, mostly, or emergencies of some kind. Had he and Barry gone out on the batter last night again, and were dropping by on their way home? Worse, had he lost the wedding rings?

More implausible still: had the same fire shot through his veins yesterday when he had kissed her, and had he lain awake the whole night long chewing on his knuckles in anguish, before deciding to come and prostrate himself at her feet this morning and beg her to call off her wedding?

Ridiculous, she told herself. Ludicrous. But she ran down the stairs quickly anyway, smoothing down her hair and hoping to God that the puffiness under her eyes didn't resemble two recently released air bags.

Lenny stood just inside the front door. His hands were dug deep into his pockets, and his face was ruddy from the morning air. He seemed anxious, awkward. It was the first time she had ever seen him like that. It made her feel even more nervous, and she self-consciously tightened the belt around her robe.

'Hi,' she said. Her voice came out all husky from sleep. She quickly cleared her throat.

'Hi.' He looked past her, up the stairs, then into the living room. 'Look, this might sound stupid.'

'What?' she said.

He was watching her very intensely.

She didn't for the life of her know what he was going to say. She held her breath.

'Did Barry by any chance stay here with you last night?'

'Barry? No, of course not, I left him at the house with you.'

'He's not there now.'

'What?'

Judy couldn't immediately understand what he was saying. Barry, not at the house? What was he talking about?

'Did you check the bathroom?' she said automatically.

'Judy, I mean he's gone. The bed wasn't slept in last night. His car isn't in the drive.'

There was a noise in Judy's ears. A buzzing. Some self-defence mechanism, no doubt, to block out the words.

'Judy, are you all right?'

13

Judy had never fainted in her life before. Not that she hadn't tried. All around her, others of a less sturdy disposition would cunningly wriggle out of hockey practice or training day at work by simply hitting the decks, all white and delicate looking, and have to be brought around gently with wet facecloths and sweet tea. But despite her best efforts, and blotting paper in her shoes once, Judy remained determinedly upright through exams and never-ending school assemblies, not to mention the occasional personal drama where fainting would have been a rather nice touch.

And now, finally, it had happened to her. *Was* happening. But where was the facecloth, the sweet tea? Instead she felt herself being hoisted rather unceremoniously into the air.

This was accompanied by an expletive: 'God, she weighs a ton.'

Please, let that not be Lenny, she prayed. Someone, somewhere, was taking pity on her because the next thing she heard was, 'I hope my back doesn't give out again.'

It was her father carrying her.

Then she felt herself being laid down rather roughly on the sitting room couch. A big hard book dug into her neck. And there was a very unpleasant smell off the cushions. Curry chips, she realised. And stale beer. Biffo must have been roused to make way for her.

Then, her mother's voice. 'I think she's coming round.'

Judy opened her eyes to find Rose, Mick, Cheryl and Biffo huddled over her like a rugby scrum, and she nearly screamed.

'Give her some air,' Rose instructed. They all shuffled back a bit. 'Are you all right, love?'

For a moment she didn't know what had happened. Had she been hit by something? The big truck that her mother had been warning her about since she was a little girl?

Barry was gone.

It landed back in her brain with a nasty thunk, and she wished she could faint again. Block it out. But she couldn't, and she just lay there as if all the stuffing had been knocked out of her. She felt hollow, unreal. She thought she might be going to be sick.

'Don't try and sit up, love,' Rose cautioned. 'You've had a terrible shock.' So had she by the looks of it. Her face had that startled look of one roused brutally from their sleep. Mick had deep furrows down both sides of his mouth. Cheryl, in fluffy pink pyjamas, stood close to him as if for protection. Biffo looked like the dead, but drink was to blame for that, not Barry's disappearance.

Barry, gone. Judy just couldn't get her head around it. Gone where, for heaven's sake? The day of his wedding?

Then, it came to her. Sweet relief flooded through her.

'He's probably at the shops,' she announced to Rose.

Rose looked startled. 'What?'

'Barry. That's where he's gone. To get black shoe polish.' Her stomach stopped churning.

'Did she hit her head when she fainted?' Mick worried to Rose.

Judy almost smiled at their lack of comprehension. All this worry for nothing! 'For his wedding shoes, Dad. We have none left at home and he probably remembered it last night.'

Rose looked at Mick. Mick looked at Cheryl. Cheryl refused to look at Biffo, who was still in his crumpled suit from yesterday, and stinking of beer.

'Where would he get shoe polish at this hour?' Biffo ventured, obviously in the hopes of impressing Cheryl with his detective work. It didn't cut any ice, judging by the way her nose rose in disdain.

He had a point, Judy reluctantly conceded. But then she remembered something.

'They have all-night shopping in Tesco's now,' she announced proudly.

They were all looking at her as though she had completely lost her marbles.

'I don't think that's very likely, love,' said Rose, sorrowfully. 'Lenny says he's been gone the whole night long.'

That was a problem, all right. Thankfully another, very logical, thought struck her. 'He could have gone to visit a friend. He has lots of friends. Maybe he just lost track of time and slept there for the night.'

There was a perfectly reasonable explanation for this. There must be. It was just a question of finding it. Determined, she pulled herself up on the couch a bit. They all tried to help, patting her and adjusting her dressing gown, and Rose moved the book.

'I'm fine,' she insisted. 'I just want to find Barry, that's all.'

'We all do,' said Rose.

But none of them was coming up with any likely suggestions. Probably the shock was only sinking in with them too. Plus, they obviously didn't know Barry's routine the way she did. The places he might go. She must think, quickly.

'He could have gone for a walk,' she said. Maybe somebody should write these down. 'He often drives down to the beach and goes for a walk. Has anybody checked down there?'

'Not yet,' Mick said.

'Will you have a cup of sweet tea?' Rose said.

'Yes, please,' Biffo said with relief. 'And a bit of a fry-up — I mean muesli — to settle my stomach.'

'I meant Judy.'

But there was no time now for sweet tea, even though Judy was parched. It was beginning to dawn on her that there was a great possibility that Barry was hurt. Seriously injured. Or even worse. Why else was he not ringing them? Why else had he not come home? He would never worry her, or his family, like this.

'We need to check the beach,' she said, panic rising now. 'He might have got disorientated in the dark. It's easy to happen. He could have been forced to take shelter for the night. Someone needs to go down there.'

Why were they all standing there looking at her like she was barmy?

'The whole of Cove is lit up like a Christmas cake,' Biffo said. 'You couldn't get disorientated on that bit of a beach if you tried.'

Rose gave him a thunderous look.

'That's not true!' Judy said hotly. 'There are plenty of places you could get lost!'

She couldn't believe Biffo's insensitivity. Barry could be shivering by a rock right now, with nothing but a thin jacket on him and a packet of Polo mints to keep him from starving. Wouldn't you think Mick or Biffo would at least go and check the car park down there? 'And has anybody rung the hospitals?'

'I'm going to do it now,' Mick said. But not with any great urgency, that much was obvious.

'Lenny has gone back to the house,' Rose said, in the same kind of sorrowful voice as if she were speaking about the dead. 'He'll let us know straightaway if he shows up there.'

'How is he going to show up if he's drowning right at this moment on the beach?' Judy screeched. He wasn't even a strong swimmer, his mother had left him in armbands for too long. 'Or at the bottom of a ditch somewhere in his car? He probably needs a critical blood transfusion as we speak and none of you care!'

'We do, Judy,' Rose said. 'Don't get upset.'

How could she not get upset? Her fiancé was missing. And her whole family was behaving as though he had just selfishly decided to wander off on his wedding day without telling anybody! Judy was furious on his behalf. Did Rose, all of

177

them, really think so little of Barry that he would do something like that? To her? To his family?

Something terrible had happened to him, Judy knew. Because what other explanation was there?

Her family were still looking down at her with the same odd expression.

'What?' she demanded. 'Surely you don't all think that Barry would just . . . run out? On his own wedding? On me?'

Nobody answered. Biffo shifted his gaze.

Judy pushed herself roughly off the couch, and past them.

'Judy,' Rose called after her.

'Leave me alone.'

★ ★ ★

Word travelled fast. All morning long Judy could hear the phone ringing downstairs. Often it wouldn't be answered because everybody was already on their mobile phones. At around half past nine people began to arrive. Cars drew up outside. The front door opened and closed repeatedly.

But for a house full of people and ringing phones, there was an eerie calm. You couldn't hear a single voice, only the occasional sob, which could have been anybody's. The only thing Judy was sure of was that it wasn't hers. She hadn't shed a tear yet. In fact, she was strangely dry-eyed for someone whose fiancé had disappeared into thin air, as she had heard Mick murmur out in the hall.

Nobody came near her in her bedroom.

178

Nobody dared. She rocked back and forth on her bed, still in her pyjamas, and ignoring the cups of sweet tea which Rose left outside her door every fifteen minutes with a little call: 'Here's another one if you feel like it.'

Ten o'clock came and went, when Judy by rights should have been turning up at the hairdressers. Then, eleven o'clock, which was her make-up appointment. At some point between the two, Judy stopped worrying that Barry was seriously injured, and started to desperately hope that he was. She got down on her knees by the bed like she hadn't done since she was a child, and she prayed sincerely to St Anthony that Barry would be found semi-conscious in an alley somewhere, or in a ditch in his car (preferably near a supermarket that sold shoe polish) trapped behind his steering wheel. Nothing too life-threatening, obviously, and preferably nothing that left hideous scars. But she caved in on the scars too. Just let him turn up in any old state, and she would be glad.

And, in time, after they had put him back together, they would have a nice bedside wedding ceremony at the hospital, just close family, and she would tenderly feed Barry a bit of cake, and they would all laugh jovially about the night he had fallen down a lift shaft, or whatever.

Just let him be hurt, she begged St Anthony. Sorry, Barry, she added. But there could be no other explanation for his absence on the morning of his wedding. Because he would not do this to her. She knew him too well, they had been together too long. There was no way he would just leave her high and dry like this unless something serious was wrong.

At about eleven o'clock, there was a knock on the door and Rose came in tentatively with a tray full of cups of sweet tea.

'Would you ever drink one of these,' she said apologetically. 'It's just that I'm running out of cups.'

Judy took one, even though she didn't think she would feel hungry or thirsty ever again.

Rose sat down on the side of the bed and put her big warm hand over Judy's cold one.

'Judy, the very last thing I want to do right now is upset you any more.'

'No,' Judy agreed.

'But at some point in the next hour we're going to have to make a decision about the wedding arrangements.'

'We're not cancelling it,' Judy said. 'Not yet.'

'It's gone eleven, Judy. We have to give people notice.'

'I don't care about giving people notice! Can we not at least give him a chance to turn up?'

Rose said nothing. You could tell by her face what she was thinking.

But Judy went on stubbornly, 'Did Dad get through to the hospitals?'

'He did. Barry isn't there, Judy.'

'They mightn't have his name. He might be unconscious. And he has no distinguishing birthmarks or anything, except that mole on his bottom. They might have him filed under the name of John Doe.'

She knew how desperate she sounded even to herself. But she didn't care. She had a rising sense of apprehension, of dread, that she was trying hard to fight down but it was a losing battle.

'They said they definitely don't have him, Judy.'

'Well, what about the guards?'

'Biffo went down to them — he felt a lot better after he had thrown up. Anyway, they said they couldn't do a thing until someone is missing twenty-four hours. But they were very good about it, they checked through the night reports, said they would tell us if his car turned up.'

Judy felt as though she were being hit by a series of little missiles. But she kept going.

'And the train tracks?'

There had been two suicides on the train tracks in the last year. Young men, around Barry's age. She didn't think there was the remotest possibility, but then again she had never dreamed that something like this would be happening to her either.

'No,' Rose said decisively.

Judy let her breath out slowly; with it went the last hopes that this whole thing was somehow out of Barry's control.

Rose squeezed Judy's hand. 'Ber's downstairs, ringing around all your friends. Leaving messages for him to ring if he turns up. And I got on to the surgery, and even a few patients. Discreetly, of course. They'll let us know straightaway if there's any news.'

Judy said, 'He went because he wanted to, didn't he?'

'Judy . . . '

'Didn't he?'

Rose looked a bit fierce. 'Now you listen to me. This might seem like the worst day of your life, Judy. But we're going to get through it, OK? So we'll just take it one hour at a time and we'll see what happens.' she consulted her watch. 'And right now, we need to decide whether to let the guests know if the ceremony has been postponed.'

Judy said, dully, 'Tell them it's postponed.'

'All right,' said Rose. 'You just stay here. I'll sort out everything.'

And she would. You could tell by the look of her. She was a woman with a purpose, a woman whose daughter needed her.

And so the decision was made. Judy's wedding would be cancelled. It was over before it had even begun.

She burst into tears then, for the first time. Great big gulping sobs that shook her whole body and left her short of breath. Like a baby, she wailed, 'Don't go, Mum. Don't leave me here by myself.'

Rose immediately sat back down on the bed and gathered Judy up into her arms.

'You poor pet,' she kept saying. 'You poor pet.'

The sympathy set Judy crying even harder; the tears streamed down her face, and her nose ran like a tap all down Rose's front.

'How could he have done this to me?'

'I don't know. I just don't know.'

For a couple of hours Judy went into a kind of deep freeze. Shock, probably, or at least that's what Rose said. Judy herself had little memory of it except for the crying and the sweet tea. Rose poured the stuff into her in between violent crying bouts. The tears came in waves, and drenched them both, and then they would abate, but only for a few minutes, as if to conserve energy for the next session. Then, gradually, she exhausted herself and grew quiet except for a few lingering, hiccupping sobs.

'That's the worst of it over now,' Rose told her, patting her consolingly.

There was a knock on the bedroom door. 'Get away!' she shouted protectively.

'It's only me,' called Mick.

Rose went scuttling over to the door to let him in.

'We've a crowd of about fifty down there,' he said. 'We're running out of tea bags fast.'

'Let them drink coffee,' Rose ordered.

But Mick came in anyway and hobbled over to Judy. His back had apparently popped out again under the strain of lifting her. 'Are you all right, love?' he said.

That set her off again, and she cried on his shoulder for a minute or two while he patted her back like he used to when she was a child. 'None of this is your fault. You know that, don't you?'

'Go on down to the guests,' Rose told him impatiently. 'I think I have things under control here.'

'So I'm no use whatsoever, is that what you're saying?'

'What?' she snapped.

'Oh, nothing,' he said, and turned his back on her and made for the door.

Judy sniffed. 'You go on down too, Mum.'

'I won't leave you.'

'I'm fine. Anyway, I need to get dressed and stuff.'

'Are you sure?'

'I'd like a bit of time to myself.'

'We'll pop back up in half an hour or so,' she assured her.

They went, quietly closing the door behind them.

After a few minutes Judy made herself get off the bed and go out into the bathroom and clean herself up. Everything the beauticians had worked so hard to achieve yesterday was sadly undone. Her cheeks glowed with freshly burst veins and her new eyelash tint had been completely washed away in the sea of tears. The only small consolation was that her eyebrows hadn't grown back, although given the swollen, puffy state of her eyes, it would nearly have been a mercy if they had.

She had a pain in her chest. It felt like her heart being crushed. She looked at her tattered reflection in the mirror, wondering whether this could really be happening to her. On her wedding morning. It seemed incomprehensible. It felt like some kind of sick joke. Maybe Barry would ring at any moment, falling over himself with apologies, explaining that he had spent the night at the sickbed of a dying person and had completely lost track of time.

Because that was the sort of thing he would do. *Had* done, a few times. He was full of compassion like that, Barry, Judy thought fiercely. He was not the sort of person who would wilfully disappear without explanation and leave everybody sick with worry.

A horn hooted outside. She drew back the curtain and looked out of the bathroom window. Mick hadn't been joking: she saw that cars were parked all the way up the street now, some of them with Kerry and Mayo registrations — people who had already been on the road hours before they'd received the call.

Oh, she could just imagine the scenario.

'Turn back. The wedding's cancelled.'

'What? I can't hear you, we're on this godforsaken country lane in the middle of nowhere, not a mobile phone mast in sight.'

'I said turn back. Barry's after running off.'

'Barry's running late? That's great news, so are we, but we'll be there by half past three, all right?'

And when they had all found the church empty, or were too far into the journey to turn back, where else would they congregate but the Brady family home?

The noise level had risen considerably from downstairs. You could even hear the odd laugh or two, the way you do at funerals once the initial gloom has worn off. Judy could hear Uncle Benny's voice now, booming through the ceiling. He played the mouth organ, usually without any

185

invitation, and it was probably only a matter of time before he started up.

She saw a van pulling up on the road outside now. Someone got out and opened the back and began to unload trays of what seemed to be samosas and pakoras and carry them to the house. The whole day was taking on an Indian theme, which only served to increase her sense of confusion and disbelief that this was really happening.

The tears threatened again. Just as her eyes were finally starting to go down a bit too. She took several big breaths and fought them down.

She opened the bathroom door, only to come face to face on the landing with one of the neighbours who was waiting to use the loo.

'Oh, hello, Mrs O'Reilly!' Her voice came out oddly cheery.

Mrs O'Reilly looked like she wished the ground would swallow her up. Judy escaped before any condolences could be extended, and barricaded herself in her room again. Rose had left more sweet tea in her absence, she saw, and a little plate holding some pakoras.

What was she going to do? Sit in her room all day while the noise level continued to rise downstairs, until eventually a party would break out? It was only a matter of time. She had already heard a few notes that sounded suspiciously like a mouth organ being warmed up.

She put on her clothes from yesterday and brushed her hair. Then she went and lifted her wedding dress, which had been pressed and patted and arranged to perfection on a big padded hanger hanging from a hook on the back of the door, and she jammed it into the wardrobe. It was a squeeze, given that the wardrobe contained every coat she'd owned since she'd been about five, and which Rose had saved. But she managed to shove it in, using her foot at one point, and roundly closed the door on it.

There.

Then she left the bedroom and slowly descended the stairs.

Biffo was the first person she saw. Greenish and weak looking, he was pressed up against the wall at the bottom of the stairs, being talked at by Aunty Mary and Uncle Tom.

'We'll break his two fucking legs for him if we ever catch him,' Uncle Tom was saying.

Aunty Mary was nodding in a bloodthirsty fashion beside him and saying, 'It'll be the last time he'll run anywhere for a while.'

Biffo looked up and caught sight of Judy. He straightened quickly. Aunty Mary and Uncle Tom's expressions melted into a sickening sympathy and they shuffled back a bit as if to give her and her grief plenty of room.

Biffo met her at the last step.

'You don't want to go in there,' he warned, looking in towards the living room. 'They've started drinking and everything. Some of them want to go out looking for him, but so far Dad has managed to hold them back. Uncle Finbarr has a pitchfork in the back of his car and everything.'

187

Judy looked beyond him and into the living room. It was full, with people packed five and six to a couch, and others sitting on stools and chairs borrowed from the kitchen. Two more perched on the arms of Granny Nolan's wheelchair. The air was thick with cigarette smoke and the buzz of chat. Rose was efficiently handing around big plates of ham sandwiches. She had a word for everybody, without actually saying anything at all. At the other side of the room Cheryl was trying to tempt people with a healthy selection of crudités.

'Do you not have any samosas left?' someone asked her, peeved.

Mick walked in from the kitchen. 'More whiskey, anybody?' he asked, and was immediately set upon by a small crowd.

Rose hurried over to restore order. 'There's plenty for everybody,' she said firmly.

The thought of walking in there was nearly more of an ordeal than what she had already been through.

'You don't have to prove a point here, Judy,' Biffo told her.

'I'm not trying to.'

'If it was me, I'd turn around and run for the hills.'

'I'd consider it, only there's no other way of getting out of the house, Biffo.'

Unless she was going to scale the ten-foot wall in the back garden.

'Oh.' He thought quickly. 'I'll lower you down onto the street with a rope from your bedroom window.' He swallowed rather nauseously again.

188

'That's if I don't pass out.'

Even in the midst of her own trauma, Judy felt sorry for him. He looked terrible, and very in need of a kind word, judging by the looks Cheryl was throwing his way. His alcohol binge the previous night had obviously wreaked terrible havoc on their relationship, not to mention his appearance. His neck seemed swollen and his tan was a bit blotchy; a reaction to the curry chips, Judy had heard Rose say earlier.

'Were you with Angie last night?' she asked.

Biffo gave a nervous look around to make sure Cheryl wasn't in earshot. 'For God's sake, Judy,' he hissed. 'All right, I was. But not in the biblical sense, OK? We just went drinking, that's all.' Another wave of nausea obviously passed over him. 'My God, that woman can drink. I'm seriously out of practice.' But there was something rather triumphant about him all the same. 'Between you and me, I showed her a really good time last night. I'm sure she'll tell you all about it.'

Cheryl shot him another look. He went back to chewing on a crudité disconsolately, as if hoping it would get him back in her good books.

'I'd have thought you had more on your mind now than me and Angie,' he said.

Well, yes. She had been looking for a little light relief.

He patted her arm awkwardly. 'Judy, I'm sure Barry didn't mean to . . . he's not the type to . . . ' His brow worked furiously as he strove for something comforting to say. Then, 'Amnesia. He could have got a wallop on the head. It happens to people all the time. Well, not *all* the time obviously. But you never know. He might be found wandering up Grafton Street in his pyjamas and they'll all think he's a concert pianist or something.'

'Maybe,' said Judy, trying to find some cheer in the thought. 'Thanks, Biffo.'

She descended the final step and stood at the living room door. She took a deep breath, and walked in.

Rose was the first to see her. She gestured frantically towards the kitchen and hissed, 'Go out the back! Mick will give you a leg up over the wall.'

Today might indeed be the worst day of Judy's life; she might have been betrayed, humiliated and scorned by her husband-to-be; her blotchy face might have the colour and surface appearance of Mars, but there was no way she was going to exit this house by getting a leg-up over the back wall.

She was not the one who had done something wrong, she reminded herself fiercely. And she wouldn't behave as if she had.

Aunty Jane saw her now. And her cousin Deirdre. A hush gradually fell over the room, helped along by whispered comments such as, 'There's Judy!' and 'God love her,' and 'Would you stop gawking at her, Bert.'

Gawk they did. Most of them, anyway. Some didn't meet her eyes at all as she passed through. Mortified, no doubt. She probably would have been too, had she been in their position.

Others were kind. Her cousin Deirdre reached

out to touch her hand. Mick gave her a heartening wink from the other side of the room. And there was Ber, with Vinnie. Vinnie went bright red and looked at the floor. Ber marched over and gave her a quick, hard hug, and whispered, 'I'm so sorry, Judy.'

Then she stepped back, to let Judy on her way.

Finally Judy made her way through them all. Before she left she wondered should she say something. Maybe apologise. Shrug helplessly, and say, 'Sorry about this.'

But it wasn't her fault. Maybe some of them thought it was — a lovely fellow like Barry wouldn't have gone for nothing. Judy herself was sure that he hadn't. But the way he had gone, without notice to her or to any of them, without courtesy or courage, well, let him apologise for that.

She opened the front door and left.

14

After escaping the house, Judy's first stop was the shop. She bought seven Mars bars, three packets of Rancheros, a large Toblerone and a two-litre bottle of full-fat Coke. When the shop girl gave her a look, Judy explained to her, 'My fiancé has just left me at the altar.'

The shop girl laughed. 'Good one. I must remember that.'

Judy started into her cache as soon as she left the shop, stuffing wrappers into her pocket as she went. By the time she had walked to her house — her and Barry's house — she was chock full of cocoa products, caffeine from the Coke, and a mounting rage.

The big bollox, she swore to herself, as she found her key and dug it into the lock. The big, dirty, lying, spineless bollox.

Please God, let him be found alive, she prayed, so that she could finish him off herself. She would do it slowly, using his own surgical instruments, and she wouldn't bother with an anaesthetic.

Grimly, she looked around. The place was exactly the same as she had left it yesterday. Irrationally, she had expected it to be empty, as though he would have taken all the furniture or something. Anyway, it seemed that he had vanished in the dead of night — not the best time in the world to be loading up the boot.

She pictured him now, sneaking out of the house like a thief, and her anger grew.

The next stop was the bedroom. The bed was dressed exactly as she had left it yesterday morning; he had not slept in it at all. Probably too busy planning his getaway. She began pulling out the drawers.

It didn't look like anything was gone at first. But she knew his clothes better than she would have liked — she generally got stuck with the ironing — and she saw now that several things were missing. A nondescript white T-shirt. His new-ish jeans. Some socks and underwear. His toothbrush was still in the bathroom but the new, spare one was gone.

She stood frozen for a moment in front of the open bathroom cabinet. She didn't know whether to be glad that he hadn't calculatedly filled a huge suitcase with everything but the kitchen sink, or furious that he had made a half-thought-out effort to cover his tracks. Did he think she wouldn't notice the missing toothbrush, the white T-shirt that she had ironed millions of times? Had it not occurred to him for a second that it was more worrying when someone disappeared without taking anything at all? That the people left behind — Judy — might think that that person was injured or ill in some way, or even dead?

She was spitting with fury now as she marched into the living room and continued her detective work there. A small amount of cash was gone, and the car keys, obviously. His passport and driver's licence were always kept in the glove compartment of his car anyway. She didn't know what else to look for apart from that. What did people take with them when they ran away? As little as possible from their old lives, probably. And certainly not their fiancée, the person they had intended to spend the rest of their days with. Definitely leave that old wagon at home.

She could still feel him in the house, smell him even, and she stood very still, trying to find her way into his mind. What had he been thinking last night? What had made him go? Why hadn't he told her?

But no answers came back at her. He felt as remote from her now as he had been in the last few days. She saw now that he had been preparing himself to go, even if he hadn't realised it at the time. He just hadn't had the bottle to prepare her.

The phone erupted in the kitchen.

'Oh, shag off,' she told it.

Then she thought: it might be Barry. She knew it was pathetic. But she dashed for the phone anyway, her heart hurting.

'Hello?'

'Judy? It's Christine. Your cousin Christine from America? We've just heard the terrible news — '

Judy butted in. 'Have you seen him? Barry?'

There was a startled pause. 'Here, in Kentucky? Well, no, but I'll keep an eye out — '

'Thanks.' Judy hung up. She wanted to cry again. Shit. Every emotion seemed turned upside down. She still didn't really believe it. Even after what he had done, she would still give anything if he walked through the door right now. She choked down the last Mars bar in the hopes that it would make her feel better. Thanks, Barry, she thought. You have just condemned me to a lonely life of comfort eating and stretch pants.

She was angry again. It felt good. Or at least better than weeping and wailing, and rocking back and forth like a candidate for an asylum.

'Drink!' she cried, relieved. She would get completely scuttered. Why not? Blot the whole thing out and all that. And she wouldn't have Barry standing over her shoulder tut-tutting about her unit intake. And when she was finished with the drink, she would go looking for his medical bag and she would take one — no, two! — Valium out of it without producing a prescription in the world. *That* would be one in the eye for him.

In great form now, she dug out a full bottle of white wine from the fridge in the kitchen. Then she retrieved her secret stash of cigarettes from behind the bread bin.

Thus armed, she sat up on the high stool by the breakfast bar and puffed away, a glass in her hand. Give her an hour and she would probably break into a rendition of 'I Will Survive'. Heck, give her ten minutes — the wine was going straight to her head. Maybe she should have lined her stomach with a couple of samosas first.

She drank and smoked and tried to ignore the silence in the house. This was what it was going to be like, living alone. Nobody to say, 'Honey, I'm home!' Nobody to share dinner with, or fight with over the duvet. Nobody who cared if you lived or died, until the neighbours eventually got the smell, she thought, very maudlin indeed now.

Music, she decided. That was all the place needed. A jolly tune to cheer everything up. To hell with Barry. She would be quite happy without him, just her and the Bee Gees.

She went to the CD player and put on 'Stayin' Alive' (which was almost as good as 'I Will Survive') and she sang along loudly and did a little shimmy around the kitchen, dropping cigarette ash on the floor. So what? It was her kitchen now, and she could do anything she liked in it. If this was freedom, she thought, then she loved it! She wished he could see her now. She wished he knew that, far from wailing in the corner curled up into the foetal position, she was having a ball.

Then it hit her like a thunderbolt: she would tell him. She would ring him up on his mobile and tell him.

Why had nobody thought to ring him? She couldn't believe how blind they had all been. Barry, the doctor, who wouldn't be caught dead without his mobile phone! He wouldn't even go to the bathroom without it in case there was an emergency. All right, so it was possible that he wouldn't answer, but she would leave a message on his voicemail. Wherever he was, he wouldn't be able to resist checking in to see if Mr Keane had been on about his arthritis.

She fired up another cigarette and skipped over to the phone. She would enjoy this. She wouldn't even ask him where he was. She would let on she didn't care. 'Listen, you creep,' she would say. 'You toerag. I hope you're having a great time in a lay-by, or a dingy B and B, or wherever you're holed up. I hope it's everything you wished for! I'm sitting in the kitchen by myself drinking and having an absolutely marvellous time.' Actually that sounded a bit sad. She would say nothing about being alone, and she would turn up the Bee Gees very loud so that he would think she was having a party. Then she would finish up by saying, 'Don't hurry back. I'm doing fine without you. I will survive!' Without hiccupping in the middle, preferably.

He would be gutted. Distraught. She was nearly cackling now as she dialled and held the phone to her ear. It began to ring at the other end. Good. She took a breath in readiness.

In tandem, another phone began ringing somewhere in the house too. Her own, probably, in her bag in the hallway; Rose trying to find out where she was and finding the landline engaged.

Judy followed the sound, still on the house phone to Barry.

It wasn't her mobile. The sound was coming from the hall table. And there, in the small drawer tucked in the underside of the table, she found Barry's mobile phone nestling under a selection of pizza delivery leaflets and taxi numbers.

He had left it there deliberately, she knew. He had obviously decided that his phone, his lifeline, was not something he wanted or needed to take with him. It had seventeen new messages.

'Barry, it's Lenny. Where are you?'

197

'Barry, Mick here, about half seven. Listen, we've just had Lenny over . . . '

'Barry? This is your mother.'

Judy stopped at message five. She turned the phone off and dropped it back into the drawer.

An hour later, she had drunk the whole bottle of white wine, and run out of cigarettes. The CD player had flipped on to the Smiths and she was so depressed that she could hardly lift her head from the countertop.

'What's wrong with me?' she asked the bowl of fruit which happened to be in her line of vision. 'That my bridegroom couldn't face me this morning?'

She didn't get any satisfying answer.

Still, there would be plenty of time in the coming days for blame; hours and hours to examine her faults, to go over her character flaws with a fine toothcomb, pinpointing exactly what it was about her that had driven Barry away. The idea was enough to make her puke.

If her stomach weren't so empty, that was. Curry chips, she thought. She wondered if Biffo would get her some. He obviously had sources. But she didn't want to ring her mother's house. They would all know she was drinking in the middle of the day and they would say, 'Poor Judy!' and she just couldn't bear it.

The kitchen door opened and Lenny quietly walked in.

'Hello,' he said.

Judy jerked upright in shock. For some reason she had thought he would be gone. Back to Australia, or to a hotel, or something. She had not expected that he would stay in her house once Barry was gone.

But there he stood in the flesh. The man whose trousers she had fantasised about ripping off. The man who had broken the embarrassing news to her that morning that her groom had up and gone.

Her tongue, thickened by white wine, got stuck several times before eventually coming out with, 'I didn't hear you come in.'

'I've been in my bedroom all the time.'

Sweet Jesus. The Bee Gees. 'I Will Survive'. Going around shouting 'bollox'. Judy felt the last remaining drops of blood drain from her face.

'You needn't have bothered,' she told him ungratefully. 'He's not going to turn up.'

Lenny wasn't put out by her tone. 'I didn't stay for Barry. I wanted to be sure you were OK.'

In a rather high-pitched voice, Judy said, 'Thanks anyway, but I don't actually want your pity, believe it or not.'

'I wasn't offering it.'

'What, then, do you want to gloat? To say 'I told you so'?'

'Don't be silly. Look, why don't I make you something to eat?'

His concerned reason just inflamed Judy further. 'You're just delighted by all this, aren't you?' she spat. 'Good for Barry, you're probably thinking. Another poor man freed from the clutches of a hormonal, broody, marriage-obsessed woman! Every one of your little theories about relationships proved in one go. You must be thrilled with yourself. And then you come around to break the news to me this morning, all mournful and wringing your hands. When really you wanted to let off a bunch of party streamers.'

Lenny stood impassively through all this. 'Are you finished?'

'No,' said Judy, regally. She paused. Then, 'I was going to say something else, something quite important, but I've actually forgotten it. But if you'll give me a minute, it'll come back to me.'

'Look, Judy, it's been a rough day for you. You look pretty tired and upset.' He didn't say drunk, which was quite nice of him. 'You'll probably see things a bit clearer tomorrow.'

She didn't want to see things a bit clearer tomorrow. She had a feeling it would only get more unpleasant. And she would have a hangover now, too.

'Why don't I take you back to your mother's?'

'No,' Judy said stubbornly. 'This is my house. I'm staying here. Anyway, there'll be a big party going on by now, and I couldn't face it.'

'All right, but I'm going to ring Rose. Let her know you're here.'

'OK,' Judy conceded. She found that she liked Lenny taking charge. It made her feel tragic and vulnerable and strangely attractive.

'And maybe you want to wipe your face,' he said kindly. 'There's a big ring of chocolate around your mouth.'

Judy's face flamed. 'Actually, I'm going to bed,' she said quickly.

It was only five o'clock in the afternoon. Had the day gone according to plan, they would have been having a champagne reception in the hotel now.

She wondered vaguely had somebody alerted them to the fact that nobody would be showing up. Oh well. They were bound to have guessed by now.

She stood unsteadily and made for the kitchen door. Lenny accompanied her, as though afraid that she would keel over or something.

At the door he turned to look at her. He said quietly, 'I know we haven't seen eye to eye in the past week. But I'm really sorry this has happened, Judy.'

She looked at him levelly. 'You know, I don't think I believe you.' And she walked out past him and shut the door.

She had brought her mobile phone with her and she put it on the pillow next to her. Some part of her was certain that Barry would ring. That, wherever he was, the enormity of his act was beginning to sink in. Wouldn't panic be rising? His Adam's apple, always a good indicator of his mental state, would be bobbing up and down furiously at the sheer preposterousness of what he had done: running out on her like that! The love of his life. On his own wedding day, without a word to anyone. And all over a case of wedding nerves, or whatever it was.

It's all right, Barry, she thought drunkenly. I forgive you. Or at least I might once I bash you over the head.

She could clearly imagine him outside a public phone booth right now on the side of a lonely, dusty road, trying to summon up the courage to ring her, to cry down the line at his foolishness and regret at hurting her.

Just come home, she would say to him. Just come home and we'll work it out.

The phone remained silent all night long.

15

The Garda who took her statement was very understanding about the whole thing. In fact, it turned out that he had been treated by Barry at the surgery only the previous week for a suspected hernia, and knew him well.

He gently asked for a description of Barry's car, and what he was wearing when he was last seen.

'Pyjamas,' Judy admitted. 'We think. It was night time, and there's a pair of them missing.'

'I see.' He made a careful note of this. 'Did he take anything else with him that you know of?'

She handed over a neat list. Along with the clothes and new toothbrush, she had discovered other items gone too: his sunglasses, and a wad of cash they had put by to tip people on the day of the wedding, such as the hotel staff, and the money to pay the priest. He had taken one of the Booker-nominated books from the coffee table too.

'This is very helpful, to have such a comprehensive list,' the Garda commented, taking the sheet of paper.

'Yes, well, that's what I do.'

'Pardon?'

'Make lists.'

He wasn't quite sure what to make of that. 'He's taken quite a few things really, hasn't he?' he observed.

You could tell what he was thinking: packing sunglasses and a book was hardly the action of a man who had raced from the house in a state of wild panic and disorientation.

'He doesn't get much of a chance to read normally,' Judy told him. Well, it was true. There was no need to go assuming all kinds of things just because Barry had taken a single book.

'And then there's the timing of his departure.' He was looking at her sympathetically but meaningfully.

'Yes,' said Judy. There was no sense denying it. 'But that doesn't change the fact that he's missing. Or that he might be in trouble somewhere.'

He made a kind of a non-committal noise. He asked some more questions: who might Barry know, what places did she think it likely that he might go to.

'West Cork,' Judy said immediately.

'Sorry?'

'We went there on holidays once. He really liked it. He could very well be in the same hotel right now.' Wandering around the lobby, confused and regretful and trying to find a way to come home.

'Or the midlands,' she said. For some reason she kept imagining him driving aimlessly around small towns, existing on fish and chips and bottles of fizzy orange. He would have grown a nasty bit of stubble by now and would probably be smelly, and people would call security when they saw him hunched sadly over his steering wheel in some dark corner of a supermarket car park.

The Garda dutifully wrote it all down.

'But I'll ring the hotel in West Cork myself,' she assured him. 'You'll obviously be too busy following other leads.'

He looked up, and cleared his throat. 'In these cases, there's not actually a lot that we can do.'

Judy didn't understand. 'You said yesterday that we had to wait for twenty-four hours to report him missing. We have, and now I'm reporting him missing. Are you not going to send out an APB?'

She was hoping he knew what that was, because she didn't. Possibly it was an American term.

'Or contact Interpol.' She felt on safer ground with that.

'We'll conduct our investigations,' he assured her. 'I'll file this report straightaway.'

'File it where?' Judy asked rather querulously. 'In that big filing cabinet over there?'

He didn't mind that at all. He laid the report aside and said, 'Look, I know this is all very upsetting. Understandably you're worried. But the facts are that once a person is over eighteen, they're free to come and go as they please without an explanation to anybody, hard and all as that is to accept.' He said all this very apologetically. 'It would be different if, for example, we suspected foul play, or we felt that there was a chance at all that this person might have come to some harm. Or if there was an issue of mental health. Is there?'

As though anybody who walked out of their own life could be completely sane! Was stress and pressure and worry not enough? Did a box on a list of mental disorders have to be ticked too?

Apparently so.

'If you mean is he bonkers, then no,' she said coldly. 'Not clinically anyway.'

The Garda took that one on the chin. 'Pressure can do very strange things to people. Some people cope better than others. Some people can't cope at all.'

Judy felt terribly culpable again, as though this whole thing were all her fault.

'He proposed to me,' she told him loudly. 'I didn't propose to him. Everybody seems to think I got him up against a wall and held a double-barrelled shotgun to his head, and said, marry me or else!'

There was a sudden nervous scuttle out at the desk at the mention of the shotgun. But when they saw that Judy was armed with nothing more than a list, they all relaxed again.

'Would you like a cup of tea?' the Garda asked.

She knew she must look desperate and pathetic; down at the police station wailing and demanding that they get her man back. A man who quite obviously didn't want her any more. But she kept her head high and stood. 'No, thank you. Thanks for your time.'

He insisted on accompanying her out to the exit. Judy felt sure they were all looking at her, the other Gardai and the various young offenders scattered about the waiting area. The news would be all around town by now: there she is, look! That one that the doc ran away on.

The Garda turned to her reassuringly on the steps. 'The vast majority of people who go missing like this come back. Usually within a very short period of time too.'

'Yes.' She just wanted to go now.

'You might want to contact one of the missing persons helplines. They're a great support.'

'Lovely!' said Judy, cutting him off and running down the steps.

★ ★ ★

Afternoon tea had been quite an experience with Biffo. He'd ordered champagne and cocktails along with the Earl Grey, complained about the sandwiches being stale even though they weren't, and then proceeded to lavishly tip everybody in sight.

'It was awful,' said Angie.

But the afternoon hadn't ended there. Not by a long shot. He'd then squired her in his hired BMW into town, belatedly informing her that he had booked them dinner at Restaurant Patrick Guilbaud, even though she was stuffed to the gills after all those stale sandwiches. There followed more champagne. And a wine bar afterwards, where Biffo had loudly ordered 'the best bottle of plonk you have', scarcely flinching when he was presented with a one thousand euro bottle of Château Lafite. Angie had wanted to crawl under the table.

The agony didn't end there. He hired a horse and carriage to trot them around St Stephen's Green, and Angie had spent the journey huddled down into her coat hoping to God that nobody would recognise her. Biffo was so drunk that he was waving out regally at people as though he were royalty.

'Then he tried to tip the horse,' Angie recounted.

After ten laps of the green, a fit of hunger had overtaken him, hence the tray of curry chips on Dame Street. The smell of the curry sauce obviously evoked some deep nostalgia in him because he had then made a pass at Angie. She had given him a robust tongue-lashing; so robust that he had begun to shake and tremble. But it transpired that, after a whole year of clean living, his system had gone into toxic shock, and in the end she'd got them a taxi and pushed him out at the Brady family home.

'I'm only telling you all this to take your mind off Barry,' she told Judy.

'No, no, I'm glad of the distraction.' Judy was, even if it felt like she was listening to it all from some place outside herself.

'All he talked about the whole night long was his salary and his car and his flipping condo by the beach. Which he was careful to point out was much bigger than my apartment, and had a pool as well as the beach, and which he would own in full by two thousand and nine. At one point I thought he was going to get out the mortgage deeds and show them to me.' She shook her head incredulously. 'He wouldn't let me pay for a single thing all evening. Not even a round of drinks. Every time I turned around he was flashing his credit card and saying, patronisingly, 'This one is on me.' Like I was the poor relation or something! Can you believe it?'

Judy could and did. It had been obvious from the moment she'd seen Biffo in the library that he had an agenda. Possibly he had been planning it for a whole year now.

Angie lit up a fresh cigarette and said, grimly, 'You were right, Judy. It *was* my job.'

'Did he admit it?'

'Did he heck! He was too busy flashing his cash, scoring points off me. The cheek of him! I never once treated him like that, Judy — all that patronising bullshit — in all the time we were going out together, even though I was earning five times what he was.'

'Ten, surely.'

'Well, yes, but he thinks it was only five.' She yelped. 'See? I even lied about how much I earned to protect his feelings! Pussy-footing around him so that he wouldn't feel emasculated! Always making sure that he never felt uncomfortable or awkward, or that he was somehow less important in the relationship just because I earned more. Jesus, Judy, I couldn't have done more!'

'I know, I know,' Judy soothed. 'Bloody men,' she said, because she felt it was warranted, given the circumstances.

'I mean, what am I supposed to do? *Not* be successful in case he couldn't handle it?'

'Definitely not,' Judy said firmly.

'I know, but I can't win. Men can climb up that ladder as far as they want and it only makes them more attractive. When we do it, we have to bend over backwards to be sure that everybody else is OK with it! Your brother needs to grow up, Judy.'

'Yes, but did you feel anything?'

'What?' Angie snapped.

'I'm just wondering. Apart from all the job stuff, what it was like, seeing him after a year?'

'Oh, fine,' said Angie, burying her face in her handbag.

'There's nothing left between you?'

'Not a thing.' She rooted some more in her bag.

'They're on the table, Angie. Your cigarettes.'

'Oh! Right. Thanks.' When she reluctantly lifted her face, there was quite a bit of colour in it.

Judy lifted an eyebrow.

'Look, it's just nostalgia, OK? Nothing more.' She hid behind a cloud of smoke. 'Did I tell you Nick is taking me on safari the week after next? For my birthday.'

'You didn't,' Judy said drily.

'Oh, look, I don't want to talk about me any more.'

'I don't want to talk about me, either.' She was afraid that if she started, she would only start crying again, and she'd just finished the last bout half an hour ago. 'Right now, I just want to keep busy.' And she handed Angie some scissors and a stack of brightly coloured cardboard.

'Um, what are we making?' Angie asked

reluctantly. Arts and crafts had never been her thing.

'Posters of Barry,' Judy clarified. 'To put up telephone poles and bus shelters and things.'

'What?'

'Well, it's the next logical step, isn't it? After reporting him missing to the guards.'

Judy could see that Angie was as stumped as anyone. And why not? Lovely, kind, dependable, cheerful Barry, running off like that! A man who had been happily dating Judy since the turn of the century. What depths of inner angst could possibly have sent him running from his own house in the dead of night in his pyjamas and taking nothing only an overnight bag and some snacks from the fridge? (Judy had discovered a packet of sausage rolls missing.)

Angie said, bluntly, 'Look, I know you don't want to talk about it, but there may be some things, some explanations, that you haven't thought of yet.' She paused delicately. 'For instance, he doesn't have any debts, does he? Barry?'

'No,' Judy said regretfully. It would have been so easy.

'You mightn't have known,' Angie argued. 'I see it all the time in work. People buying up thousands of euro worth of shares, and you just know they're living out of their car.'

'He doesn't owe a penny,' Judy said. 'And he doesn't have a drinking problem, or a sex addiction problem, or a medical malpractice suit that I don't know about.'

'He wasn't prone to bouts of depression, or

chronic doubts about career or self-worth?' Angie said hopefully.

'No, no, no.'

Angie cleared her throat. 'And there's no possibility at all that he had . . . someone else?'

'No possibility at all,' Judy said apologetically. It would have been lovely if there had been. Well, horrible, obviously, but yet so nice and easy and tidy! But however much Angie and even she herself might wish the explanation were this clear-cut, it just wasn't.

'So I guess,' Judy said, 'that just leaves me.'

Angie stubbed out of her cigarette rather fiercely. 'That's nonsense, Judy.'

'Why? There's no other explanation.'

'Just because we can't immediately understand why he left doesn't automatically mean you're to blame.'

'Who else is there to blame.'

'His mother,' Angie said immediately. 'She has him ruined, everybody says so. And his aunts from Surrey. And his father for dying on everybody like that. And his patients. Some of them treat him like he's God.'

Lenny didn't feature anywhere in this list. But he lurked around the back of Judy's mind: the catalyst amongst the pigeons.

Judy said, quietly, 'Look, one thing is certain in all this — Barry did not want to marry me yesterday morning.'

Angie couldn't argue with this, although she looked as though she would like to. She let it drop.

'I don't know what you're making posters for,' she said.

Mick had said that too. Ber hadn't, but had been thinking it, Judy knew. It was disconcerting how everybody seemed to think that she should have abruptly stopped loving him after what he had done to her. It made it difficult to confess worry or concern for him. But if you turned it around, if she had been the one to disappear unexpectedly the day before her wedding, would Barry have stopped loving and caring about her?

Angie said hesitantly, 'Nobody made him leave, Judy. He went because he wanted to go. There's a chance that he doesn't want to be found, you know?'

'Then let him tell me that himself.' She gave a tired sigh. 'Look, Barry is out there somewhere on his own. Upset, probably. I would rather he came back, and then at least I would know he was safe. That's all.'

Angie said gruffly, 'You're too loyal, Judy.'

'It's for me too.' Judy didn't want to look too virtuous in all this. 'Yesterday he waltzed out of my life without an explanation in the world. At some point in the next week he's going to run out of underwear and what's going to happen then? Is he going to waltz back into my life the same way he left it? Am I supposed to sit here wondering when or if I'll hear his key in the front door? Or whether he'll ring today or tomorrow or not at all?'

The phone began to ring.

'Jesus,' said Angie. 'That's spooky.'

Judy nearly broke her leg running for it.

213

'Hello?'

It was the credit card company. They wanted to alert her to some unusual patterns of spending. Was she or the other account holder on holiday at the moment?

'Where?' said Judy foolishly, immediately thinking of some dingy town in the midlands.

She was told France.

16

Biffo wanted to go after Barry with a baseball bat.

'Uncle Tom and Aunty Mary will come with me, and our cousins from Mayo, they all have chainsaws. We'll get the ferry over tonight and hire a big van and throw everything in the back. Don't you worry, Judy, by the time we're through with him, he'll be sorry he was ever born.'

His tan was looking slightly faded today. It just went to show you what a week out of the sun could do. And his teeth were less white or something.

But maybe it was just her. The shock of discovering that Barry wasn't writhing in turmoil in the midlands but romping around France had possibly affected her vision. Certainly, nothing looked the same now. Or at least the same as it had two hours ago.

France. She tried to think why. He had never expressed the slightest interest in France. In fact, he'd grumbled that he didn't know the language and that they ate disgusting things like snails.

'Oh, you're a great help, you are,' Mick told Biffo. He was back to being a grumpy old man again. 'You'd be better off going after Cheryl. Imagine letting her jog off up the road like that by herself!'

215

Biffo shifted guiltily. 'I told you. I've pulled a tendon.'

'Yeah, from lifting pints.'

'You just can't stop on about that, can you?'

'I've never been so embarrassed in all my life,' Mick declared. 'Poor Cheryl must think we're nothing but a crowd of drunken paddies! I don't blame her, you know. For kicking you out of the bedroom and refusing to talk to you.'

Biffo looked at him suspiciously. 'I don't know what you're taking such an interest in the whole thing for.'

Mick said back, 'It's hard to keep out of it when the whole house is in uproar. Everybody going around banging doors and sleeping on couches!'

'Yes, well, we'll be going back to Orlando in a couple of days,' Biffo replied shortly. 'You'll have the whole house back to yourself then.'

At that, Mick looked glummer.

Judy heard all this sniping as if through a fog. Her brain was still having considerable difficulty transplanting Barry from a rundown B & B in rural Ireland to the sunny south of France. She couldn't have been more surprised had the credit card number showed up on Pluto.

'Are you all right, love?' Mick inquired. 'More sweet tea?'

'No. I couldn't bear it.'

He gave a fatherly sigh. 'I just don't understand why you didn't cancel the card.'

'I didn't think of it, Dad, OK? Cancelling the card wasn't the first thing on my mind.' Anyway, by the time she'd picked the phone back up off the floor, the credit card person had gone.

'You can still do it,' he said. 'It's not too late.'

'It's a joint card, Dad.'

'Exactly!' He was getting himself worked up now. 'So just cancel the thing and I can guarantee you that he'll be home here in forty-eight hours. Money is power, Judy.'

It was hardly the most attractive way of getting one's groom back, cutting off his line of credit.

'No,' she said flatly. He would probably think she did it out of petty revenge.

'At least let Biffo here go and kick him in the nuts then,' Mick begged, even though a minute ago he had thought it was a terrible idea. 'We can't just sit here and do nothing!' When it became obvious that Judy intended to do just that, he ranted, 'When I think of everything we've done over the years for that fellow! All the washers and screws and burst pipes that I've fixed for him! And then he turns around and thinks he can treat us like this.'

Mick was going to take umbrage on behalf of the entire Brady clan, that much was obvious. His cheeks were ruddy with hurt. 'I just hope you're never going to take him back, Judy. Not after all this.'

Oh, great. Now she was charged with preserving the dignity of the whole family.

'I have no idea if I'll ever lay eyes on him again, Dad. He might decide he likes France so much that he wants to stay there. He could be growing olives as we speak, or tending a modest vineyard in the sun!'

Actually, she was intrigued to know exactly

217

what he *was* doing in France. Practising medicine? Were French people as a whole sicker than anybody else?

The answer was about to become clearer. Rose came in from the hall, the phone in one hand and a piece of paper in the other. Her curly hair was sticking out in all directions and she had a big knot of worry in her forehead.

'Well?' Mick demanded. 'What did they say?'

Rose had been appointed to take up with the credit card company where Judy had left off, to find out exactly where the card had been used.

But she just commanded, 'Make more sweet tea, quick.'

This was serious. Mick stumbled to the kettle. Biffo looked resigned to the possibility of more trouble.

Judy just waited passively. She'd had so much bad news in the last few days that another bit wouldn't hurt.

Rose sat beside her and said, gently, 'I've said nothing bad about Barry so far, Judy. You know that. I've tried to find explanations, excuses. I put it down to pressure and stress, or that mad mother of his, or his father dying under a rail of skirts. I told myself that he wasn't as strong as you, that he was that little bit immature in some departments. It was hard, but I managed to hold on to my calm these past few days when all around me other people were losing theirs.' She shot a look across at Mick. 'But I'm sorry to say that I was wrong, Judy. He really is a desperate, rotten, filthy, lowlife scut and if I got my hands on him right now I'd throttle the life out of him

218

and burn what was left in the back garden.'

They all reared away a bit. Rose had never before spoken of throttling anybody, not even the person who had invented the GI diet.

'Brace yourself,' she said grimly. Then she lifted the piece of paper and began to read.

Barry had bought a one-way ticket from Rosslare to Roscoff, costing one hundred and eighty-nine euro. He'd also hired a cabin whilst on board.

Then, one night's accommodation in a hotel in Paris. Two hundred euro. But it was peak season and possibly he hadn't been able to find anything cheaper.

Breakfast in the Grand Hotel had cost him forty-five euro.

At this point, Mick broke in. 'Forty-five euro for *breakfast?*'

'That's what it says,' Rose confirmed tensely.

'It was probably a full Irish, with sausages and black pudding and toast and everything,' Biffo said. There was a terrible note of envy in his voice. Then he seemed to get a firm grip on himself. 'Go on, Mum.'

Barry had charged petrol to the card a hundred miles south of Paris.

Then, some clothes. Well, he'd taken very little with him.

'Dolce and Gabbana,' Rose said, her lips growing tighter.

Biffo let out a little low whistle at that.

Judy said nothing. She sat at the table, motionless and sick. Rose read on. Further south, he had checked into another hotel. A further two hundred euro. Then, at eleven o'clock that night, thirty euro was charged to an establishment called 'La Piste Rouge'.

'What could that be?' Mick asked, mystified.

'My French isn't great, but if you were to translate that it's something like the Red Alley,' Rose offered.

The Red Alley? Wild glances flew back and forth across the table and everybody tried, and failed, to picture Barry in such a place.

'I'd say it's a nightclub,' Biffo said eventually. From the look on his face, it wasn't the kind of nightclub that anybody at the table would be familiar with.

Judy was flummoxed. Barry, in dubious nightclubs in France? He hated them. You couldn't drag him to one kicking and screaming.

'We're nearly finished,' Rose assured her.

There were two final entries. A hotel in the Riviera, and some pleasure boat hire company.

'He can't swim,' Judy said. It was a foolish thing to have said, but it was the only thing that came to mind.

There was a very long silence after Rose finished. She folded up the piece of paper and laid it carefully in the middle of the table, as if it would self-destruct in five seconds.

Nobody looked at Judy. They were all too kind.

'Well, I can't believe it,' Mick said at last. 'Here we all are, tearing our hair out over the whole thing, and it looks like he's off holidaying in the south of France.'

It certainly cast a whole new light on Judy's

modest plans for a poster campaign in the midlands. It left her feeling foolish and duped and completely ridiculous. All this time she had been fretting about him lost or injured or unbalanced in some lonely small town, never suspecting for a moment that he would be whooping it up on the Riviera without her.

She felt as if she had been slapped in the face. She wanted to crawl under the kitchen table and never come out again. It was one thing to have your husband-to-be suffer an unexpected panic attack. People could understand that. People could have sympathy. But it was quite another for him to be discovered cavorting about in one of the most exclusive holiday destinations in the world. He might as well have put two fingers up at her and their whole life together.

Oh, she would never live this down. Never, never, never. She might as well just emigrate or something. She'd go to Peru or South-East Asia and settle in a modest fishing village where nobody knew her.

'At least we know now where he is,' Rose said at last.

'Is that supposed to make me feel better?'

Rose thought about that, then eventually conceded, 'No. But I bet a sandwich would. Or a big bowl of chips with gravy.'

'No. Thanks anyway, Mum.'

'I don't blame you,' she commiserated 'I can't eat a thing myself since this whole thing started. I'm after losing five pounds. And I can't even enjoy it.'

A wretched gloom settled over the room. They

all stared dejectedly at the floor or the crack in the wall over the cooker. Occasionally somebody would sigh or shake their heads in despair. The sweet tea that Mick had made grew stone cold and nobody made an attempt to make a fresh pot.

Judy supposed she should be touched by everybody's misery. At least they were on her side. None of her family would think that her life was so petty and boring that Barry had to run away to France in search of excitement. Or maybe they would, but they'd have the decency not to say it.

She had no idea how long they all sat like that. She lost track of time. Eventually she was startled into awareness by the kitchen door bursting open.

'Hi!' Cheryl chirped, back from her run. Then: 'What are you all doing sitting in the dark?'

'Barry's having a great time in France,' Rose said, by way of explanation. 'Turn on the light, there's a good girl.'

She did, and they blinked owlishly at each other. Judging by Mick's puffy eyes, he had been asleep. But he brightened considerably as Cheryl fanned herself with a piece of paper and said, 'This map you drew me was great, Mr Brady. I went jogging right up the top of the hill, like you showed me. It was much better than following the usual old routes.'

'Well, it's a poor man who doesn't know his own locality,' Mick said modestly.

She adjusted her tiny white shorts and said, 'Phew! I need a cool drink.'

222

Biffo shot out of his chair like a bullet from a gun. He extracted a bottle of mineral water from the fridge and handed it to Cheryl.

'It's sparkling,' he offered.

For a minute, it looked as though she was going to hurl it at his head. But no, she accepted it with a curt little nod to acknowledge his good deed. This was obviously a great improvement in relations, because Biffo looked surprised.

'Did you go far?' he inquired tentatively.

'About seven miles,' she said, civilly. Then her face clouded over a little. 'Trucks and vans and guys in BMWs kept hooting at me on the road. Do you think they were trying to warn me of something?'

It was Rose who answered. 'Not at all,' she said kindly. 'It's probably just men in their late middle to old age experiencing some kind of a crisis. It's very sad, really, but quite common, I hear.' She stood briskly. 'I'd better get that lentil pie on for dinner.'

She walked out, slamming the door.

Mick bolted out of his chair too, his face puce. 'It's very hard to put up with your mother these days. Oh, I've tried to be understanding. I've tried to put it down to Barry's disappearance. God knows it's taking its toll on us all. But it doesn't excuse the kind of vicious comments she's been coming out with — usually aimed at me, I have to say — and then nearly taking doors off their hinges. Well, if she can do it, so can I!'

And he stomped out the other way, giving the door a good slam.

'If I ever get that way, shoot me,' Biffo said.

Cheryl looked from him to Judy, unsure. 'Am I off beam here, or are your parents having some issues?'

Judy wasn't about to discuss her parents' relationship with Cheryl. 'Like Dad says, it's a stressful time for everybody.'

'And I'm sure it's not helping, having us staying here too,' Cheryl commiserated.

'I'm sure it's not,' Judy concurred, as Cheryl's shorts rode up another inch. Cheryl, bless her, had no idea at all how lovely she was; her whole attention was now fixed on Judy.

'I haven't really had a chance to say it before, Judy, but I'm so sorry about you and Barry.'

'Thank you, Cheryl.'

'You must be very angry right now.'

'I'm fairly spitting mad, all right,' Judy agreed.

'But, you know, I believe in giving people second chances. We all make mistakes. Sometimes horrible mistakes.' Across the table, Biffo stiffened. 'Nasty, dirty, offensive mistakes that make you wonder if you really knew that person at all.' He was bright red in the face now. 'But it doesn't mean that you stop loving people, Judy. Maybe it even makes you love them a little bit more, because they're human.'

Biffo sat very still.

'I'd better go freshen up,' Cheryl said. Then, in a soft voice, she said to Biffo, 'Maybe you'd like to move back into the bedroom tonight?'

Biffo looked over his shoulder as if she might be talking to someone else. 'Me?' he said.

'Yes. You, Geoffrey.' And she gave him a look

of such tender love and devotion that Judy had to look away.

'Ah, er, um, OK,' said Biffo, always one to rise to the romance of the moment.

'See you later,' Cheryl promised him, and jogged out.

'It looks like you're forgiven,' Judy said.

Biffo just sat there. He was probably still stunned at his good fortune.

'I think I'm still in love with Angie,' he blurted out.

'What?'

'I know. I can't believe it. After a whole year away from her. It's not fucking fair.' He buried his head in his hands. Along with his fading tan, she saw that there was dirt under his fingernails. He was fraying at the edges. He was turning back into the old Biffo before her very eyes.

'This is serious.'

'Tell me something I don't know.' He gave a low groan. 'And I behaved like such an idiot the other night!' He lifted his head to look at her out of one eye. 'I'm sure she's told you.'

'Just the highlights,' Judy assured him.

'Look, I know it was stupid, OK? I know it was just getting back at her. But for once we were out for the night and I wasn't broke, Judy. I didn't have to worry that the cash dispenser would tell me to fuck off. I was on her level, or near it. I could treat her instead of it always being the other way around. And do you know something, Judy? It felt really, really good, and I'm not a bit sorry!' His

225

defiance quickly dwindled away. 'Although from the look on her face at the end of the night I'm not sure she enjoyed it as much as I did.'

'Probably not. Why didn't you tell her any of this a year ago?'

'Tell her what? That I deeply resented her job when she went out of her way to make sure that there was nothing to resent? Some women might have dropped the odd comment, but not Angie. She never once rubbed my nose in, Judy. If you had to go out with a woman who could buy and sell you, then Angie's the one. She was so cool about the whole thing, so fair, that I couldn't turn around and say, hey, I feel like a piece of shit in this relationship. Because it wasn't her fault, it was mine.'

'So what are you going to do?'

'Do?'

'If you're still in love with her . . . '

'So what? She can't stand the sight of me.'

'You don't know that.'

'Come on, Judy. Anyway, she's with Nick now. I'm with Cheryl.'

On cue the power shower jumped into action upstairs and the whole house shook. The sugar bowl began to vibrate on the table and Judy moved it away from the edge.

They both looked up at the ceiling.

'Do you love her?'

Biffo looked caught at this question. 'I don't want to be on my own,' he blustered.

Something must have crossed Judy's face

because he said quickly, 'Not that there's anything *wrong* with being on your own. Absolutely not! No, I'm sure you can live a perfectly satisfactory life here without Barry. I mean, you have a good steady job, friends, a nice house with even more space in it now that it's, um, less crowded. And Dad's always there to fix your bath for you. And you can still go down to the Cove Arms on a Friday night, and Spain once a year, and with Mum around you'll never be stuck for company on Christmas Day.'

When he laid it all out like that, Judy felt like running off to France herself. She wondered now whether Barry had drawn the same, damning little picture of their lives together. Had he suddenly decided that routine and tradition had become boring and staid? Perhaps the prospect of one more Friday night in the Cove Arms had been too much for him and he had just snapped.

Funny how he had given no indication of his discontent up to now.

To look at him you'd think he was as happy as Larry. But maybe it had all been festering away just under the surface, like a great big boil. Maybe he had been waiting for one last thing to push him over the edge; or, rather, into a swanky hotel on the Riviera.

'Biffo!' It was Cheryl, calling down from the bathroom upstairs. 'I've forgotten my shampoo. Could you bring it in to me?'

Cheryl forgetting her shampoo would be like a drunk forgetting where they had stashed their bottle of vodka. It was obvious that she had something else in mind.

Biffo looked at Judy. He looked trapped.

'It's a dirty job but someone's got to do it,' she said.

'Shut up,' he said, and stomped up the stairs.

17

Judy refused to get out of bed for three days. The sheets got smelly and there were bits of jam and crisps down the front of her pyjamas from her night-time forays into the kitchen, but she didn't care. She didn't brush her hair and what looked like a giant fur ball formed on the back of her head. She took to watching afternoon confessional programmes on the bedroom telly, finding great comfort in other people's stories of misery: My Ex Left Me For Her Rottweiler, or My Husband Is A Bigamist. At least he wasn't the type to run away from marriage in order to 'find' himself, Judy thought venomously.

She found that the shock was wearing off. At least there wasn't that same sharp sensation of having been punched in the stomach. It was sinking in that he was gone, and that he had no intention whatsoever of phoning home.

She didn't think she had ever felt so worthless in her entire life. Well, it was hard not to. Anybody would have in the circumstances. Rejection oozed from every pore like poison, as she lay there obsessing about long-legged French showgirls strutting their stuff in places called 'La Piste Rouge'.

And her legs *were* short. She might as well face it. Her hair was straight and brown and unexciting. Her personality was stubbornly uncharismatic. Her aspirations were stunted and hideously limited to things like job satisfaction, maintaining friendships, and to be happy. Happy! What a pathetic person she really was. Mediocrity might as well be her middle name. And bossy, of course. And the list-making would have to go in there somewhere too.

In her deepest moments of self-hate, she would crawl right under the duvet and huddle there in a little ball, only surfacing now and then for a packet of crisps. Of course, her skin broke out in spots with all this maltreatment, and she added that to her list of repulsive traits as well.

No wonder Barry had run off! How could any man possibly be happy with the likes of her? Obviously she, and the life they would have had together, had repulsed him so much that he couldn't even hang around long enough to tell her to get lost to her face.

She went back to wishing him dead. She renewed her prayers to St Anthony that a showgirl would lose her balance and spear him through the heart with one of her stilettos.

At some point during the day Rose rang. Judy wasn't quite sure what time exactly, but the sun hadn't gone down yet so it must be early evening.

'I'm worried about you,' she announced. 'I'm coming over.'

'No,' Judy said, rather tragically. 'I want to be alone.'

'Lenny says you won't get out of the bed.'

Judy was surprised to learn that Lenny was in contact with Rose. She hadn't seen him since that night in the kitchen. She heard him coming and going all right, pottering around the house and in and out of the shower. Once he had called through the door to ask if she wanted anything to eat. 'No!' she had shouted defiantly, expecting him to offer again, to try and persuade her, but he hadn't. Not even the next day, when she was ravenous and would have eaten the leg off the bed. She'd had to sit there while the delicious smell of garlic and onions had wafted under her door from the kitchen.

'I don't know what he's doing, still hanging around here for.'

'He told me he has a month to kill,' Rose offered.

Judy was again taken aback at how much Rose knew about Lenny.

'Still, with all his money you'd think he'd move into a hotel or something,' she said churlishly, even though she had never liked sleeping in the house on her own those nights that Barry had been out on calls, or away at a medical conference.

'He's been very good over all this, you know,' Rose said. There was an odd note of fondness in her voice. 'He was over here yesterday, keeping everybody's spirits up. And he spent the evening with Mrs Fox, she's in a terrible state altogether.'

'Oh.' Judy had presumed that he had been out drinking in the local pubs and trying to pick up women. So far he had shown no signs at all of a caring side to his personality.

'Would you not come over for a while?' Rose pleaded. 'I'm making shepherd's pie.'

'No.'

'This isn't like you, Judy. To go off the deep end like this.'

'You hardly expect me to be jumping around the garden.'

'Judy, this is not your fault,' Rose lectured. She said this a couple of times a day. Judy half expected her to pop over and drag up a diagram of all her pros and cons, making sure the pros won out. 'This is entirely Barry's decision and no reflection whatsoever on you.'

'Do you think he'd have run out if I had been Charmaine?'

'Who?'

'Oh, it doesn't matter. Some model.'

Rose scoffed, 'Look, whatever notions Barry has in his head, he'd never end up with a model.'

Judy was sure that if she thought about this long enough, she would find that it wasn't too flattering to her either.

'Even if he did meet one, he'd be too frightened.' Rose was emphatic.

'He obviously doesn't want a staid life with me,' Judy said, her lip curling up in a bit of a sulk.

'Judy Brady, I am not listening to this kind of talk from a woman who is intelligent and mature and who knows there is more to life than running off to France in search of God knows what!' Judy could picture her face at the other end, round cheeks flushed.

'Now,' she said, finishing up. 'What are you going to do for the rest of your life?'

'I don't know yet, Mum.' Surely she didn't expect her to have made all kinds of life decisions. It hadn't even been a week yet. In theory she should have been on honeymoon, revelling in her newly married status, and perhaps even sneaking a peek at a pregnancy magazine in one of the local shops when she went up for ice creams.

Without warning she began to blub again.

'What is it?' said Rose, alarmed.

'Babies,' Judy cried. 'I'm not going to have any babies now.'

'You will,' Rose said encouragingly.

'I'm thirty-three. Do you know what it's going to be like trying to find a man who hasn't heard that I drove Barry away? Then to persuade him to marry me, and all before I'm thirty-eight?'

'Well, you'd better get out of bed in that case,' Rose said briskly.

'Mum!'

'You haven't got much time to spare.'

'Stop it. I was only joking. Kind of.'

But Rose had obviously decided that her softly-softly approach wasn't working and she was implementing the tougher-tougher approach. 'I'm going to ring back in an hour and if you're not out of bed I'm going to send Mick over. His back is bad again, and Cheryl's been out the whole day, so you can imagine his mood.'

The truth was, Judy was getting a bit fed up in bed. Apart from the hunger, she was sure that the red patch on her bum was the beginnings of a bed sore. And if she didn't shake off some of the food crumbs the mice would move in.

She was also sick of her own emotions. When she wasn't wishing that Barry's testicles were being ripped off, she was crying heartbroken tears and keening with a piercing sense of loss and betrayal. All it took was the sight of his razors in the bathroom and she would be off, her whole body convulsed in sobs. Five minutes later she would be fingering the same razors with murderous intent.

It was exhausting, this yo-yo of emotions. She felt as raw as a January wind. Even as the realisation of his departure sank in, even as the credit card debits from France kept rolling in (dinner for what was probably two the night before last in a restaurant called Chez Michel), she still could not believe he had done this to her. Her fiancé, her best friend. The man she had known since they were babies.

Or thought she had known. Maybe she hadn't known him at all.

But of one thing she was sure: lists were very dangerous things. Potentially lethal in the wrong hands. There was nothing guaranteed to make a man skip the marital home quicker than pinning a big list of TO DOs on the fridge door.

Men weren't the only victims. What about the poor list makers? Writing things down and ticking them off only gave a false sense of being in charge, in control.

Which Judy wasn't, of course. She had planned so hard for this wedding, had thought she had taken into account all eventualities, and yet she could never have foreseen how things would turn out; that Barry would wake up one morning and decide that there was something better out there for him.

She could feel the tears rising again. 'Got to go!' she squeaked to Rose.

'Are you out of bed?'

'Yes,' Judy lied.

'One hour,' Rose said threateningly.

Thankfully there was another spate of confessional type programmes on and she had dried her tears and was just settling down to enjoy the topic How Come I'm Always The Other Woman when there was a rap on the door.

'What?' she called, ungratefully. Surely that wasn't Rose over already. She'd just hung up on her.

But it was Lenny's voice outside. 'I'm cooking dinner.'

'No thanks,' she shouted back, her stock response.

There was a silence, and she assumed that he had gone off again. He really was a selfish, uncaring brute, she thought.

Then: 'If you're not out here in ten minutes, I'm going to come in.'

Everybody was at her today! Threatening and coercing her! Well, she wouldn't give in. She would barricade the door or something.

But she didn't have anything to barricade it with, no handy chair or a plank and selection of nails. She didn't think Lenny really would come in, but on the other hand if he *did*, she would just die if he saw her sprawled akimbo on the bed, unwashed and eating crisps.

She got out of bed. She climbed hurriedly into the en suite shower, albeit muttering and cursing under her breath. She washed her hair and combed out the big lump at the back. She couldn't do much about the fake tan they'd sprayed on in the beautician's, which was coming off very unevenly and leaving big dirty brown streaks behind. Oh well. It wasn't as though anybody would be looking at her naked body in the next few days. Or very possibly in the next decade. Nobody would ever touch her again after this. Instead they would stand in small groups at street corners and point at her as she went past, whispering, 'There's that awful woman who drove away lovely Dr Fox. He diagnosed my mother's emphysema, did I tell you that?'

When she was washed and dressed and had her hair dried, she was surprised at how much better she felt. In the mirror, she looked more or less the same as she had five days ago, before all this happened. She had half expected gaunt cheeks and sunken eyes, testament to her anguish, but if anything her cheeks looked a little rounder due to all the crisps she had eaten.

It was good to be up and about again. She was taking back a little bit of her life.

★   ★   ★

Lenny was cooking in the kitchen when Judy entered. He was in a T-shirt and one of Judy's pastel aprons. On any other man it would have looked effeminate. But he, of course, managed to look stunningly virile, a fact that Judy couldn't help noticing even though her heart was in about nineteen different pieces.

236

'Hungry?' he asked.

Judy jumped guiltily. 'No! Um, I mean not especially.'

Lenny looked at her sternly. 'I counted twelve packets of crisps when I emptied the bin this morning.'

Her face burst into colour.

'You've got to start eating properly, Judy. And it wouldn't hurt to cut back on the wine too. I counted a good few bottles of Riesling.'

She decided to go for the haughty approach. 'Your concern for my health is touching. In fact, your concern all around is touching. I suppose Barry put you up to it.'

'What?'

'Maybe he asked you to look after me once he was gone. To salve his conscience!'

'No,' Lenny admitted, kindly. 'He didn't. It was actually your mother.'

'My mother?'

Her face was now so hot that he could nearly cook the dinner on it.

'She was worried about you being here on your own. Especially with the whole staying-in-bed routine. She was afraid you might do something stupid.'

He gave her a look that made her feel defensive and small in about equal measures.

'Yes, well, I'm fine now as you can see,' she blustered. 'So there's no need whatsoever for you to protect me from myself, or cook dinner for me.'

'Look,' he said, with a sigh. 'I'm cooking for myself anyway. Have some if you want. Don't if

237

you don't want. It doesn't make any difference to me.'

That took the wind out of her sails. He wasn't into this persuasion thing at all. But probably all supremely selfish people were like that, she thought darkly. Thinking only of themselves, never bothering to cajole anybody else into something that was really for their own good.

She thought now of all the cajoling Barry had required over the years. A man so gifted in the surgery, yet helpless when it came to choosing the correct sized shoes. And Judy always there to smooth things along.

No wonder that sometimes they didn't feel like sex.

Defiantly, she reached for the bottle of red wine open on the counter. Lenny's eyebrows shot up. Ignoring him, she poured herself a glass.

'I suppose she told you about Barry,' she said stiffly. 'My mother.' It was inevitable, seeing as the two of them seemed so cosy. She should have warned Rose not to say anything until they had decided on a cover story: maybe that Barry was on some kind of journey of contemplation in the peaceful countryside in France. A time of reflection, of renewal, that kind of thing. The credit card stuff could be minimised; she would talk vaguely of petrol expenses, and light lunches in modest roadside cafés.

But Lenny said, 'The whole thing. She even showed me the credit card statement.'

Cheers, Mum, Judy thought. Her cheeks did their Christmas tree thing again.

'So!' she said, trying desperately to put a

positive spin on it. 'At least we know where he is.'

'Yes.' He was watching her keenly as if for signs of disintegration.

'I mean, we know he's not dead or anything.' More was the pity.

'We do.'

She took a careless gulp of wine as if they were having some mildly interesting dinner party conversation. 'Yum! This is a delicious wine.'

'Judy, it's a three ninety-nine bottle of plonk that I got to cook with. I wasn't thinking of actually drinking it.'

It was sickening, this habit he had of seeing right through her. She placed the wine glass balefully down on the counter.

'Yes, but my tastes would be simpler than yours. Unsophisticated, I suppose, you'd call it. But some of us are happy in our ignorance. Or were, anyway.'

Lenny put down his wooden spoon and looked at her. 'Go on,' he said. 'Say it. You know you've been dying to.'

'What?'

'You blame me for Barry going.'

'I do not!'

'Yes, you do. It's written all over your face.'

'Barry leaving was obviously his own decision. I'm not blaming anybody else for that.'

'Are you sure about that, Judy?' And he bent down to get an onion. She was presented with his bottom. It was lovely, all round and firm. Barry's was sort of long, if you could have such a thing as a long bottom. At least, it started at his

239

waist and ended quite a bit down his thighs, without ever really plumping out satisfyingly in between.

'Sorry, I didn't quite catch that,' Lenny said, straightening again to look at her.

She hid behind a cough.

'Come on, Judy. Nobody's under any illusions here. I know you can't stand me, so why don't you just give it to me straight?'

The cheap wine made her bold. 'All right then, seeing as you ask, maybe you *did* have something to do with it.'

Lenny began to peel the onion, glancing up at her with great interest. 'Go on, then.'

'Well, there was all the drink, for starters. Nights out, and cocktails, and beer! He was sozzled the whole week — and out of his routine! Plus, he had very little sleep, what with you and Charmaine bonking morning, noon and night. I wouldn't be a bit surprised if the whole thing was enough to unbalance him and he ran off somewhere to get a bit of peace and quiet!'

'In a lap-dancing club in France? Biffo told me about the Red Alley.'

Oh! She glared owlishly at him. And to think that she had once thought she fancied this man! He was nothing but a home-wrecker. A saboteur of perfectly good marriages.

'Surely you can do better than that, Judy.' He was chopping the onion expertly with a sharp knife. She prayed that he would lop off a couple of fingers.

'I have nothing else to say.'

'Do you want to know what I think?'

'Not really.'

'I think that you can't stand the idea that Barry is obviously having a good time when really he should be lying half dead in a ditch waiting for you to rescue him.'

'That's . . . rubbish!'

'Listen to yourself. 'Out of his routine.' He's not a baby, Judy.'

She was furious now. 'I can't believe I'm sitting here being lectured by a man who calls his own girlfriends 'baby'!'

Lenny shrugged. 'Some women like that. I don't think you're one of them.'

'I most certainly am not!' she thundered. 'Say whatever you like about me and Barry, but we have never called each other by anything only our proper, grown-up names!'

'Yes, and maybe that was part of the problem.'

He had gone too far now. 'You think you know everything, don't you?' she said slowly. 'You waltz back in here after ten years away, with your Oscar-nominated job and your model girlfriend and your brilliant life, and you don't care about the people who have to live here all year round. You're like one of those tourists who come here in the summer, throwing your money around, and making everybody else feel that their life is totally crap in comparison!'

Lenny looked at her impassively. Judy knew she should stop now, but she couldn't.

'Most of us have the wit to know you're just a flash in the pan. But there's poor Barry after believing the whole thing! Thinking that he can have that too! And now he's after jacking

241

everything in to go cruising up and down the Riviera thinking the streets are going to be paved with . . . international models!'

Lenny looked mildly startled at that. 'You have quite a low opinion of him, really, don't you?'

'I think he has the capacity to be led astray.'

'By me?'

'I think you influenced him, yes.'

'By my choice of girlfriend and my routine indictments of marriage?'

'If you like.'

'Possibly you think I drew him a map and slipped him some money, too.'

'I wouldn't put it past you. Let's face it, Barry would never have had the imagination to do something like this by himself.'

Lenny shook his head impatiently. 'Actually, Judy, if you must know . . . ' Then he stopped.

'Know what?' Although she didn't really want to know. She had a feeling it would be unpleasant.

'Seeing as we're both speaking so truthfully here,' Lenny said, 'I should tell you that I knew he was unhappy. That he was thinking of calling off the marriage.'

Judy felt sick.

'I tried to persuade him to tell you. To be honest about it if he was having second thoughts. I told him that it wasn't fair to let each day go by and not say anything.'

Judy's brain flashed up the image of Lenny standing at the kitchen window, like a school-master, looking out at them as they stood at the car that day. And Barry looking back at him. Irritably.

She thought of the way Barry hadn't wanted her to go for a drink with him and Lenny after the meal that night. And the way he had crept into bed so silently and soberly afterwards.

He had been out talking about her to Lenny. Telling Lenny that he was having second thoughts. Confiding in a virtual stranger about the most intimate details of his relationship with her, while she had remained oblivious.

'I didn't know he was going to run off,' Lenny told her. He looked awkward. 'Obviously if I had, I would have warned you or something.'

'That's very decent of you,' she told him with a wobbly smile. Otherwise she would cry.

'Judy — '

'No, I mean it, honestly. Oops — more honesty! But isn't it nice to have an honest chat every now and again? To clear the air, so to speak.' She was rabbiting now. But anything to hide her distress at this latest blow. Lenny — Lenny! — had known that her wedding wasn't going ahead before she herself did.

At that moment, she hated Barry with a viciousness that took her by surprise. It felt good.

'He just didn't want to hurt you, Judy.'

'But he did in the end anyway. Far more than if he'd just told me to my face.' She had lost her appetite for dinner. She finished off her wine and stood. 'Goodnight, Lenny.'

18

Mrs Fox called around the following morning.

'Come in,' Judy said.

Mrs Fox's shoulders were hunched cautiously, as though she expected Judy to lob something at her at any moment, and she would have to duck. 'Are you sure it's not a bad time?'

'Not at all. I'm just sorting through a few things.'

It was surprising how much there was to do when someone did a runner. What with the post that was piling up on the hall table and all those telephone calls to return, there was very little time to sit around licking wounds. The morning had passed licking envelopes instead — six bills had to be paid, and Barry's subscription to *Medics Today* had to be renewed, even though it was unclear whether he would be back in time for the next issue.

What was even more surprising was her ability to deal with it. In some ways she hadn't any choice; the phone had gone at nine thirty with a call from the surgery, wanting to know whether they should book a locum for the week after next, when Barry should have been back from honeymoon. It was all very embarrassing and awkward. Judy had told them, in quavering tones, to go ahead and book. But she had dealt with it. And she had set to the rest of it. It felt peculiar at first, to be opening his post and returning calls on his behalf. But there was nobody else to do it.

'I won't stay long,' Mrs Fox said, stepping in.

'Your sisters aren't with you?' Judy inquired.

'No. They didn't see much point in staying on, now that we know that Barry is . . . ' Mrs Fox trailed off painfully.

'Not in trouble at all but having a super time in France?' Judy supplied helpfully.

Mrs Fox just looked at her. 'We don't know that for a fact.'

'Oh? He spent three hundred euro in a jewellery shop yesterday. I check in with the credit card company every morning.'

The jewellery debit was a surprise. Perhaps he had splashed out on some diamond cufflinks for himself. Or a gold medallion for his chest, in keeping with his new Lenny-type image.

Or maybe what he had bought hadn't been for himself at all. Maybe it had been for somebody else.

It was an interesting thought, and not one that Judy felt up to pursuing too rigorously at the moment. But why not a new woman? To go with his brand new life?

Mrs Fox looked further pained at this revelation. Perhaps Judy should have spared her. But she wasn't going to subscribe to this 'poor tortured Barry' scenario any more. Especially as it was the furthest thing from the truth.

'I came around to apologise for him,' Mrs Fox said stiffly. 'If anybody can. I know I should have come by earlier but I didn't know what to say. Then I thought I'd write a letter and post it but nothing I wrote sounded right.'

This was unexpected. Mrs Fox looked very pale and there was a thin sheen of sweat on her upper lip. It obviously had cost her a lot to come here today.

Judy felt for her. 'It's not your fault.'

Mrs Fox seemed to gather strength. 'No, I can't believe he's done this,' she declared. 'And to such a nice woman as you, Judy! Did you know that the night Barry told me you were engaged was one of the happiest of my life?'

Judy felt awkward now. She had had no idea that Mrs Fox had been that fond of her. Certainly she had covered her delight very well at their engagement party, but then Gerry Fox had only been dead a year, and everybody said that it must have been very hard on her. Barry had been extra attentive that night, and had driven her home early and been persuaded to part with another sleeping pill.

She didn't seem all that well today either. Apart from looking rather hot, her eyes were darting about all over the place.

'Well, thanks,' Judy said awkwardly. 'But obviously I'm not expecting you to be on my side in all this.'

'Oh, I'm totally on your side,' Mrs Fox declared.

'What?'

'If I could get my hands on him, I'd wring his neck,' she said, rather enthusiastically. 'He's just like his father, you know. The minute you take your eye off them, they're gone!'

Judy was very taken aback at all this. Mrs Fox

had never spoken about Barry in anything but glowing terms.

Judy ventured, 'I don't know if you can compare the circumstances . . . '

Mrs Fox flicked a hand disparagingly. 'Maybe it's something in the genes. Unreliable.' She grew quite chummy now. 'You could have had a lucky escape, Judy. Imagine if you *had* married him. He might have run off on you regularly, you'd have had to put one of those tracker things on his ankle and monitor him by satellite, the way they do with prisoners on parole. Do you mind if I use your bathroom?' Without waiting for a response, she tottered off at speed. 'Maybe you'd put on the kettle for a nice cup of tea, and we can have a good old chinwag about the whole thing.'

She closed the hall door firmly after her.

Bemused, Judy filled the kettle at the sink. The last thing she had expected was Mrs Fox's sympathy in all this. But then why should she be the only one hurt and upset at Barry's actions? Mrs Fox must feel betrayed too, and duped and fooled. Why shouldn't she be just as angry?

Judy wondered whether this would herald a new closeness between her and Mrs Fox. They had got on well enough before Gerry Fox had died, playing tennis together every now and again. But then, with the onset of Mrs Fox's ill health, she seemed to become a barrier between Mrs Fox and Barry; someone who had to be got around on the phone or at the front door in Mrs Fox's quest for comforting advice and the occasional prescription drug.

She was in the bathroom a long time. The tea grew cold. Eventually Judy went down the hall and tapped on the bathroom door.

'Mrs Fox?'

There was no reply. Judy began to wonder whether she had fainted or something — she *had* looked rather hot — and she tried the door.

The bathroom was empty.

Could she have gone on home? Perhaps she had realised how disloyal to Barry she had sounded, and had nipped off before she got herself into worse trouble over tea.

A noise came from the bedroom.

Judy went in to find her straightening up guiltily.

'Oh, hello, Judy! I was just making the bed for you. I'm sure you're far too upset to bother with housework. Would you like me to give a quick once-over with the Hoover while I'm here?'

Judy didn't reply to her prattle. She was looking at Barry's medical bag which was open at Mrs Fox's feet.

'I, um, was just looking for an aspirin,' Mrs Fox said.

She had something in her pocket. If it was an aspirin, it was the biggest aspirin they'd ever made, and must weigh about a pound.

'Have you got Barry's prescription pad?' Judy asked.

Mrs Fox's eyes blazed. 'Are you accusing me of being a thief?'

'It's illegal to forge prescriptions.'

'I have no idea what you're talking about.'

'Mrs Fox, I can see the top of the pad poking out.'

Mrs Fox's hand flew down to cover the pad. 'And anyway, even if it is, he's my son! And you two never got married, which makes me his next of kin and I can help myself to anything I bloody well want!'

It was all an act, Judy saw: the sympathy, the siding with her. Mrs Fox just wanted to throw her off track so that she could sneak in here and get her hands on some drugs, via Barry's medical bag.

'Please give it to me.'

'No,' said Mrs Fox.

There was a brief impasse. Mrs Fox stood like a frightened but fierce rabbit, clutching her pocket as if expecting Judy to wrestle her to the ground at any moment. Judy was wondering whether she should just step out and lock the door and refuse to let Mrs Fox out until she handed over the pad.

But then she realised she didn't actually care enough.

'What are your symptoms?' she asked eventually, just for something to say.

Mrs Fox blinked. 'What?'

'You must want drugs for something.'

'If you must know,' Mrs Fox said haughtily, 'I have heart failure.'

'That sounds nasty. Who diagnosed it?'

'Well, nobody. But if Barry were here, I'm sure he would. I looked it up in my book instead. I have all the symptoms.'

'In that case you should probably get down to

the hospital fairly pronto.'

Mrs Fox glared. 'You make it all sound so easy.'

'But it is. If you're seriously ill, you should get yourself seen by a specialist.'

'I don't need a specialist. Barry is perfectly capable of diagnosing his own mother.'

'Actually, I don't know if he is.'

'What?'

'I think he just tries to help in the way he knows best.'

'Oh, so *you're* a medical expert now!' Mrs Fox was very upset now. 'You don't know what these last few years have been like for me, Judy. I can't sleep more than a few hours any night. I'm over in that big rambling house on my own, with nobody to keep me company, nobody to turn to in the middle of the night if there's a noise downstairs. These were supposed to be my twilight years, you know. We had it all planned. We were going to go on a cruise, and drive in a camper van around Europe, and sit out in the back garden in the evening reading books. Then all of it, all the plans, gone in a flash, without a warning in the world. I can't even go down to that graveyard to visit him because I get too upset.' When she was finished her lip was trembling. 'I just wanted a few sleeping pills, that's all.'

'I'm not sleeping either, Mrs Fox.'

'Will I get you some pills too?' Mrs Fox offered generously.

'I don't want pills.'

'But Judy, they're great. You close your eyes

and next thing it's morning.'

It sounded very tempting. Any kind of diversion from reality sounded tempting. But the downside was ending up like Mrs Fox, who had made a career out of her health in an attempt to avoid grief.

'Barry would let me have them,' Mrs Fox said now, as if sensing that things weren't going her way.

'Have you tried hot chocolate?' Judy said. 'It doesn't work miracles, but I find that sometimes it helps.'

'Hot chocolate!' Mrs Fox thought she was having a joke at her expense. 'I always knew you were a cold person. Even with Barry gone missing, here you are sorting through his things like you're perfectly fine about the whole thing! Like you're over it already!'

'Give me back the pad, Mrs Fox.'

'He's not dead, you know. So stop packing up his things as though he were.'

She flung the prescription pad down on the bed and stalked out.

★   ★   ★

That afternoon Judy collected up all their wedding presents.

'People have awful taste really,' Ber complained, holding up a clock that told the time with two miniature scalpels instead of hands. She had come over to help.

'That's from his best friend in medical school,' Judy told her.

251

Ber put it back into its box. 'Are you sure you want to do this?'

'Absolutely.'

'But these are your *wedding* presents, Judy.' She looked pained.

'Yes,' Judy agreed, 'and seeing as I'm not actually getting married, I have to give them all back.'

'All of them?'

'Yes.'

'Could you not, like, keep some things as a consolation prize?'

'Ber!'

'Those are damn nice towels, Judy. You deserve them.' She added generously, 'And Vinnie and I certainly won't accept the egg painting back. It's yours.'

It was the one thing Judy had been looking forward to getting rid of, along with the clock.

'Just so long as you're not acting too hastily,' Ber said.

Judy sat back. There had been quite a nice atmosphere up to now, as they had sorted through various presents and roundly admonished people's lack of taste.

'What, maybe you think I'm horribly callous too?'

'No.'

'That maybe I should preserve the whole house exactly as he left it, on the off chance that he might come back? Refuse to wash his dirty clothes and build a shrine around his used cereal bowl in the sink?'

Ber was undeterred by Judy's outburst. 'He's

252

barely been gone a week, Judy. Just take your time, that's all. You might feel differently tomorrow.'

Judy felt differently nearly every five minutes, never mind tomorrow. But of one thing she was sure. 'However this thing turns out, we are not getting married, Ber.'

'Well, not right now, obviously.'

'Not any time soon.'

'I'd feel the same way. But that doesn't mean you mightn't work things out.'

Judy looked at Ber incredulously. 'Please tell me what I have said or done to make you think that I would, for one moment, still want to get back together with him?'

'You wanted to make posters of him two days ago. And put them up all over the midlands.'

'Yes, well — '

'And put out an APB on him.'

'That was before I discovered he had ditched me for a life in the sun.' That came out very angry and bitter. But she was. There was no point in pretending otherwise.

'So that's it?' Ber asked. 'Are you saying it's over?'

'I don't know!' Judy didn't want to think about this. She was still trying to come to terms with his disappearance, never mind think about how she might feel when he came back.

If he came back at all.

And if he did, whether she could ever trust him again.

And if she would ever *want* to trust him again.

There were too many ifs. And even if

253

— another if — they were all resolved, nothing would ever be the same again. That much she knew. And right now she didn't know whether there would ever be a way back.

'Hello, hello.' Vinnie stood in the doorway, his hands dug deep into his flannel trousers, not quite daring to enter the room. He hadn't yet managed to entirely shake his air of mortification, even after he had done the right thing by Ber. Neither was he all that comfortable at being in the house of another love rat, aka Barry. But he stood his ground and managed to look Judy straight in the eye. 'I've finished the first run,' he said, with the kind of authority he had never possessed before.

'Oh, well done!' cried Ber.

Vinnie had been appointed to help drop the presents back, and had been despatched an hour ago with a garden ornament and a family-sized bread bin. The boot of his sports car wasn't designed to carry anything larger than a set of golf clubs, and Judy would probably have to take back the lawnmower and smoothie maker herself.

Vinnie blossomed under Ber's praise as always. He smiled at her with a devotion that Judy hadn't seen before. Moving in together had obviously been the best thing that had ever happened to him. And look how Ber had softened around the edges too! She was looking indulgently at him now, and she had swapped her glamorous outfits for a comfy pair of jeans.

'What's next?' he said, with a bit of a swagger.

'That microwave,' Ber said, gratefully. 'I've put

an address label on it and everything.'

Vinnie hoisted it up. He looked at the label under his chin. 'Waterford?' he said, after a moment.

That was about a hundred and twenty miles away.

'That's right,' said Ber brightly.

'I'll be gone hours.'

Judy protested: 'Ber, I'm not asking Vinnie to go all the way down to Waterford.'

'Oh, he loves travelling,' Ber said, pushing Vinnie towards the door. 'See you later!'

'But — '

'Drive carefully now.'

She gave him a lingering kiss and then shut the door on him. She turned to Judy. 'He's doing my head in.'

'But Ber . . . you've been so happy all week!'

'That was all for show,' she said grimly. 'By the end of day two I was ready to take a knife to him.'

Judy bitterly regretted drinking all the white wine in the house. Lord knows they could certainly do with some now. 'You've only just moved in together. You have to give things a chance.'

But Ber was looking at her balefully. 'You should have warned me!'

'What?'

'I thought it would be all romance and passion and having big bubble baths together. Not Vinnie clipping his toenails in front of *Inspector Morse*.'

Judy felt she had to defend herself. 'I never let on that living together was full of romance and

255

passion! On the contrary, in fact!'

Ber was looking at her oddly. 'But you and Barry, surely there was still some spark?'

Now Judy began to feel very inadequate. 'Well, yes, of course. I mean, passion just naturally . . . evens off, that's all.'

To about once a month, in their case. And sometimes you could hardly even call it passion; more like an obligatory fumble after a bottle of wine and a curry.

'Maybe I just had this big dramatic ending built up in my head,' Ber said gloomily. 'That he would finally leave his wife after all these years, and we'd set up this cosy love nest together, and fireworks would explode twenty-four hours a day. Instead, he's using my anti-wrinkle cream on the dry patch between his toes, and playing his Status Quo collection.'

'He has a Status Quo collection?'

'It's just all so ordinary, isn't it?' Ber looked completely deflated.

'I suppose it's called domesticity, Ber.' But it sounded very hollow. Judy didn't know how much stock she put in domesticity any more. Or familiarity, and routine and sameness; all the little comforts that she and Barry had woven their lives around, and still would be, if he hadn't decided it wasn't good enough any more.

So how come it was good enough for her?

Maybe it was all a con; the glue that kept you together long after you should have broken up.

'So ask him to leave,' she said.

Ber was shocked. 'What?'

'Tell him it's not working out.'

256

'I can't do that!'

'Why not?'

'He left his *wife* for me, Judy! He can't just turn up there a week later and say he's coming back!'

'She might take him.'

'He's not a dog, Judy.'

'I'm just saying. She might have missed him.'

'I doubt it. She's had new carpets put down, and her hair restyled,' Ber snapped.

'Could you not leave him somewhere? The shopping centre maybe?'

'Judy!'

'Sorry, sorry.' For some reason she was feeling very giddy. It was entirely inappropriate in the face of Ber's relationship crisis, and indeed her own, but she couldn't help it. She felt strangely light and free.

'I'll have to talk to him,' Ber said, with a sigh. 'Try and draw up some boundaries or something. And get a lock put on the bathroom door, for both our sakes.'

'Just don't settle, Ber,' Judy said rather fiercely. 'Whatever you do.'

Ber looked at Judy, worried. 'Are you going to go all wild on us, Judy? And start sleeping with people and letting your hair grow long?'

'I have no idea,' Judy admitted. 'But I'll keep you posted.'

Ber went home a few minutes later, saying she wanted to enjoy her own house without Vinnie cluttering it up. Judy went down to the car with her, to make sure that she took the painting of the egg back. When she got back to the house,

257

there was a message on the answering machine.

For a minute she thought it was one of those pre-recorded telesales messages telling her she'd won a luxury cruise, because there was lively music in the background.

Then: 'Judy, this is Barry. Look, I'm really sorry I left the way I did. I know I should have told you . . . but you were so excited about the wedding, I just couldn't bear to hurt you.' There was a brief pause. 'Anyway, I just wanted to let you know that I'm safe and well. That's all, really. Goodbye, Judy.'

Then he hung up.

19

'Do you want to go to the pub?' she blurted out to Lenny that evening.

'What?' He looked completely stunned, as though she had dealt him a very hard blow to the side of the head.

She tried to make it sound less scary. 'Just down to Maguire's for a drink or two.'

For a minute she thought he was going to say no. He certainly looked as though it was an unappealing prospect, to say the least. As the seconds stretched, she began to bitterly regret her impulsive invitation.

What was she doing, anyway? She didn't even like this man. What on earth were they going to talk about for a couple of hours in a pub?

But the alternative was sitting in at home alone, replaying Barry's message over and over until the tape ran out. She had already listened to it nine times. Like a bad Eurovision song, it didn't get better with more air time.

I just couldn't bear to hurt you ... So, really, he had been thinking of her all along and not himself at all. Judy, with her ridiculously high hopes and expectations of getting married on Saturday! She was practically setting herself up for a fall. And poor Barry had to shoulder the responsibility of letting her down. Which he couldn't bear to. Because he was too sensitive and nice. So he had been forced into running off instead.

It had become her fault. That much was plain.

He had only phoned to let her know that he was safe and well. In case she was too distraught with worry and grief. Or in case she hoped that his phone call was an attempt at reconciliation. Firmly, bravely, he had declared that 'that was all'.

There was no mention at all of her own safety and wellbeing in any of this. Neither was there any intention of ending this limbo; of letting her know whether he intended coming back next week, next month or never. There was no contact number or address.

But maybe he was afraid that if he gave out such information, she would leap on the next plane over, her wedding dress in her suitcase, and cry and plead with him to change his mind.

Which he didn't want. That much was also plain.

It was his tone that said the most. He had sounded relieved that he had got the answering machine. Now he was able to assure himself that, this time, he had tried to do the right thing — after all, a letter would have been much easier — and it wasn't his fault that she wasn't there.

In a bare week he had become detached, uninvolved, unemotional. And not just from her. There was no mention of his mother, or the surgery or anything to do with his real life in Ireland. He was only in France, but he might as well be on another planet.

'OK,' said Lenny.

Judy had almost forgotten all about him. 'What?'

'OK, I'll go for a drink. If you still want to.' He looked a bit wounded that she had blown so hot and cold on him. But he wouldn't be used to that sort of thing, of course. Women only ever orbited around him adoringly.

And why not? He was just back after a walk on the beach, and he was beautifully wind-swept and buffeted, his dark hair a sexy, damp mess and his cheeks all ruddy.

He was, quite simply, gorgeous. And available. At least for the next couple of hours anyway, unless he had managed to pick up someone on the beach, which wasn't outside the realms of possibility.

Something shifted in Judy's head.

'Great,' she said. 'I'll just go and change.'

* * *

In the bedroom she hurled off her jeans and T-shirt and, after two quick blasts of deodorant, crawled into a vaguely sluttish red top that Ber had passed on, and a short black skirt that revealed plenty of (slightly streaky) brown leg.

In the bathroom she brushed her teeth and gargled as quietly as she could. She applied foundation, eyeliner, and mascara, even though it made her eyes run like hell. Her hair was still determinedly a bob, but she brushed it till it shone and put half a canister of hairspray on it. She added high heels and some perfume down her cleavage, and then looked at herself in the bedroom mirror.

She wasn't sure about the results. She didn't look like herself, at any rate. But then she didn't want to be herself tonight. In fact earnest, capable, sensible Judy was the very *last* person she wanted to be.

She thought of Barry, and the music in the background of his message. She wondered whether he was in La Piste Rouge again tonight. Maybe he had taken time out between 'personal dances' to make the obligatory phone call home to her. She was furious all over again.

But she didn't have to sit by passively and just let all this be done to her. For the past week she had been powerless. A casualty in Barry's quest for fulfilment. What about her own fulfilment? Her whole life had been thrown up in the air and had landed in pieces. She could pick them up but she didn't have to put them back the same way.

For too long she had ignored the gaps in her and Barry's relationship. Explained them away. The lack of passion and spark and excitement. Perhaps sure that marriage would solve everything.

If, indeed, it could solve anything.

She could hear Lenny turning on Sky Sports. The very thought of him was making her heart beat faster than seemed healthy. How was it possible to not actually like someone, but still want to bonk their brains out?

She supposed it was called lust. Sex with such a person would be extremely enjoyable but ultimately meaningless. The kind that Lenny enjoyed. No strings attached.

Which was exactly what Judy wanted. Because right now she needed a bit of passion to light up her life.

At the bedroom door, her nerve wobbled briefly. For a moment she felt out of her depth. Did she really want to do this?

But just as quickly she rallied. She owed Barry nothing, and herself everything, including some great sex. And with Lenny's good looks and vast experience, he should surely be capable of providing a half memorable night.

And she fancied him. Like mad. All right, so he didn't fancy her, which was a slight impediment but that was before. He mightn't have fancied librarian Judy in her jeans and T-shirts, but wait till he saw the new, improved version. He wouldn't be able to believe his eyes! Tonight she would show him her dangerous side (she felt a bit silly even thinking that, but it was all part of psyching herself up).

She wondered where she had put the bumper pack of honeymoon condoms. Perhaps Barry had taken them with him to France. No matter. Lenny would be bound to have hundreds, if not thousands.

With that thought in her head, she opened the bedroom door and walked out into the cool air of the landing.

The football game was still on. She could see his feet propped up on the coffee table as she made her way down to the living room.

His face was interesting when she walked in,

her high heels clicking on the wooden floors. She hadn't realised the pesky things would be so noisy.

'I'm ready,' she said.

He didn't say anything for a moment. Well, he was probably stunned by her attractiveness, hidden this past week under buckets of tears and baggy T-shirts. Naturally it would take him a moment to put down the remote control and descend upon her.

'Judy?' he eventually said, sounding very unsure.

'Well, yes,' she said.

'I didn't realise we were dressing up.' He remained annoyingly static. Did she have to do all the work here?

'I thought we might, you know . . . ' She didn't want to come right out and say 'sleep together', not at this early stage anyway. It would be crass. She settled for, 'I thought we might get to know each other a bit better.'

He digested this for another moment. Then, carefully, 'I thought we were going to the pub?'

Did he not realise that she'd never make it to the pub in these shoes? For someone who could read female signals like the palm of a hand, he was being surprisingly slow on the uptake.

Or, more likely, it was her who was reading the signals wrong. Horribly wrong. The realisation crept over her like rising damp. She saw now that he was not being slow at all but rather desperately trying to find a way out of this. Lenny was, for once in his life, thoroughly discomfited and she was the unfortunate cause of it.

'Do you know something?' she said, with great dignity. 'I don't think I'm ready for this.'

There was a little silence.

'I'm glad you said that, Judy,' he said gravely.

She just bet he was.

'Anyway!' she said, smiling like a lunatic. 'I'll see you later.'

'Where are you going?'

'To the pub.'

'On your own?'

'Of course,' Judy said cheerily, as though she regularly sat up at bars wearing short skirts and too much make-up. 'See you later!'

She hurried out into the hall, her high heels clattering across the floor like machine-gun fire.

Lenny came out after her. 'Don't be silly, Judy, I'll come with you.'

'No, no. I wouldn't force myself upon you.'

'Stop, Judy. Listen, you look . . . really lovely. Very attractive. I mean, if you weren't so . . . not ready, as you say yourself . . . well, who knows!'

'Oh, fuck off.'

'OK, I deserved that.'

'You don't have to try and make me feel better.'

'I'm not.'

'Let's face it, in normal circumstances you don't have any criteria, do you?'

'What's that supposed to mean?'

'You're a big tart.'

'I suppose by your exacting standards, yes, I am.'

'So don't give me that you're-so-vulnerable-I-couldn't-possibly-take-advantage crap. You just don't find me attractive!'

He looked at her, a bit cross now. 'This is all about you, Judy, isn't it? What about my feelings?'

'I thought you didn't bring any feelings to sex?'

He wasn't very amused at that. 'Maybe I'm not that keen on being a revenge shag.'

'What?'

'I'm guessing all this has to do with Barry.' He looked her up and down disparagingly. 'I don't blame you for wanting to give him a good kick in the goolies. Just don't bring me into it.'

He turned his back on her and stalked back up the hall. Judy went tottering after him, impeded by her high heels. She stopped to kick them off. One of them flew up to the ceiling and broke the lamp-shade. Lenny ducked. He gave her a look as though she had done it on purpose. He shook his head in disapproval and turned into the kitchen.

She found him at the fridge getting a beer.

'This has nothing whatsoever to do with Barry,' she challenged. How dare he! Even though he might be right. A little bit. But, honestly, she was sick and tired of hearing about Barry. As though her whole life still revolved around him, even though he was gone. Could she not do something for herself for a change without everybody thinking it had something to do with Barry?

'Judy, just go away.' He looked completely fed up.

Judy was confused now, as well as embarrassed. She said stiffly, 'Fine. Sorry. Obviously I misread the, um, situation.'

'That's putting it mildly. I can't remember the last time I was so insulted.'

Judy was gobsmacked. '*You're* insulted?' She was the one who was rejected here!

'In case you haven't noticed, I don't have a huge amount of difficulty attracting women. Sorry if that sounds conceited. I certainly don't have to rely on grudging offers by women as superior as yourself.'

'I am not superior!'

'No? Admit it, Judy. You wouldn't touch me with a bargepole normally.'

'You wouldn't touch *me* with a bargepole!'

'I'd be afraid you'd try and get me up the aisle,' he agreed.

'I can't believe you just said that.'

'It's true, though.'

'It is not true! Having just lost one fiancé, you hardly think I'm after another?'

'So what are you after then?'

She could have walked off. She could have just gone back to her bedroom and taken off the short skirt and sluttish red top that was biting into her under the arms and got back into her comfy jeans and sexless T-shirt. And then sat on her bed feeling even more miserable than before; so miserable that she would end up drawing up lists of things to do in order to improve her life.

Or she could just improve it right now.

'Sex,' she told him bravely, even though her voice did a nervous little dip in the middle and it came out sounding a bit like 'socks'. She looked him straight in his lovely, if rather suspicious, brown-flecked eyes. 'I haven't had any in an age, or at least any that was worth it.' Sorry, Barry, she thought automatically. But why should she be the one apologising? He was the one who had fallen asleep during an Indian takeaway.

'There are places you can go to pay for these things, Judy,' Lenny advised her kindly. 'But I'm not one of them.'

He turned his back on her and walked off.

20

'How's Lenny?' Rose inquired the following afternoon.

'I have no idea,' Judy snapped. 'We're not joined at the hip.'

Rose's eyebrows rose. 'No, but you're sharing a house together. I thought you might pass each other in the hallway every now and again.'

Oh, if only she knew. Judy was still smarting. Every time she thought of her tight red top and short skirt she was overcome with a fresh bout of smarting, until her face felt like it had been slapped all over. Hard.

'We are not sharing a house. He is a reluctant lodger only because my mother put pressure on him.'

'Well, the company is doing you the world of good,' Rose said emphatically. 'You've a lovely bit of colour in your cheeks this morning.'

Judy suffered a further bout of silent mortification. Honestly, she needed therapy or something. Maybe she was suffering from a rare fiancé-disappearing syndrome, in which all her mental faculties, including her judgement, went out the window, and she would go around propositioning entirely unsuitable men that she didn't even like. And then be turned down. Baldly.

She had snuck out of the house as soon as dawn had broken. Her embarrassment wouldn't let her stay under the same roof as him. She had been sitting at her mother's kitchen table for about eight hours now, and Rose kept looking at the clock and asking her should she not be on her way, but Judy had kept saying, 'Oh, in a minute!' So far she'd had her breakfast and lunch there, and Rose had asked an hour ago if she wanted her dinner too, and she'd said yes.

With any luck Lenny would have gone to the pub when she got back and she wouldn't have to face him at all that day.

'He's a lovely fellow,' Rose declared now.

Judy stiffened. Why did her mother have to keep going on about him? 'You hardly know him.'

'I remember him from when you were children,' Rose said fondly. 'He was a bit cheeky-looking, but with a heart of gold. You always knew he would turn out right in the end.'

Judy felt like telling Rose that he had grown up into a serial womaniser who probably drank like a fish and more than likely had an STD.

Which hadn't bothered her too much last night. She had been too busy trying to get him into her bed. Or his, she wasn't fussy. Oh, lord.

'It's a shame he can't find a nice woman to settle down with,' Rose mused now.

'I don't think it's for the want of offers,' Judy said rather tersely.

'I suppose not. He's very good-looking. Very sexy.' She had a worryingly frank look on her face; Judy guessed that she would shortly begin to speculate on his sexual experience in graphic terms and she moved swiftly to head her off at the pass.

'I don't think he wants to settle down, Mum.' To put it mildly.

'Oh, I wouldn't mind that,' said Rose, as if she came across commitment-shy men every day of the week. 'It's a question of timing, isn't it? You just wait until he gets into his late thirties and he'll start hankering after children and nights in by the fire and a nice woman to snuggle up beside.'

'I hope that isn't directed at me.'

'You? Well, hardly.'

'Good,' said Judy, and was then unreasonably put out by the fact that Rose wasn't considering her as a contender for when age finally caught up with Lenny and he decided to hang up his condoms.

'Although if I were you, I wouldn't waste too much time hanging around waiting for ET to phone home again.' Rose was quite proud of the ET quip and had already used it twice. Judy had filled her in on the phone message from Barry. They had dissected it in detail over the course of the day, and come to the conclusion that they were no wiser after it. Trying to see inside men's heads was like looking into the abyss, Rose had declared.

Judy didn't enlighten her now that she certainly hadn't wasted any time, not in the sexual arena anyhow.

Lenny had thought last night was about revenge. And maybe some of it had been. But mostly Judy had been trying to be liberated. To

271

turn the Barry experience into something positive, the way that other women seemed to do in the face of disaster.

Instead she had felt like a kerb crawler. Even in Lenny's own little unprincipled world, she had offended some moral code. What a hopeless failure she was in the seduction department.

She had obviously been very wrong to assume that he would take whatever was offered. Or maybe what she had offered wasn't in the slightest bit attractive to him.

To compound her feelings of rejection, Mick arrived and threw at her, 'Don't tell me you're still here?'

'I'm going in a minute,' Judy lied. After she got her dinner. But judging by the smells coming from the cooker, she wasn't all that sure she wanted to stay for it.

Mick sat down and dived behind a newspaper. Rose's dinner preparations hit a new snag at the sink. 'Don't tell me there's no hot water? That pair, I'll murder them.'

Biffo and Cheryl had arrived back from a jog an hour ago. Obviously they'd used up the contents of the immersion. Which was strange given that they had their power shower.

'Um,' said Mick, from behind his newspaper.

Rose looked at him. He shifted the newspaper up higher. She went over and pulled it down.

There was a moment of silence. Then she asked, 'What's happened to your hair?'

He tried to pass it off. 'My hair? Nothing.'

'Mick, it's black.'

Judy looked too. Rose was right: it *was* black.

'It's always been black,' Mick said defensively.

'Not for at least twenty years,' Rose said. 'Is that what you were doing upstairs all this time? Dyeing your hair?'

Mick's cheeks were horribly red now, in contrast to his newly black hair. It sat on his head like a shiny, unnatural cap. The tops of his ears were black too. 'Don't be ridiculous.'

'You have. Oh, Mick!' And she clamped a hand over her mouth.

Across the table, it was all Judy could do to hide her own laughter.

It was too much for Mick. He jumped up from his chair. 'Women can do what they like to try and improve themselves, but if men so much as change their clothes they're the subject of complete ridicule and derision! When you women stop availing yourselves of plastic surgery, and make-up and diets' — he said this last bit very loudly — 'then you can poke fun at us!'

'Did you leave it on for too long?' Rose asked sympathetically. 'The dye? Still, you'll know for the next time, when your roots start showing in six weeks' time.'

'You're just loving this, aren't you?' he said, coldly. 'It's just made your day.' He walked stiffly to the door. 'I'm going to put the immersion back on again.'

When he was gone, Rose looked at Judy, wide-eyed. 'He goes and makes a total fool of himself and then gets all upset when people notice.'

'Maybe we shouldn't have laughed at him.'

273

Judy felt bad now. Mick had looked really upset.

'What else are we supposed to do? Entertain him?' She planted a hand on her hip — Rose, who had never known a moment of self-doubt in her life, who had failed every diet she'd ever gone on, yet had never once been bowed by any of it.

'Let's not say anything else about his hair,' Judy said.

Rose shrugged and said, 'All right, but it'll be very hard not to.'

Biffo and Cheryl came down, as clean as two new pins. All was right with Cheryl's world again, judging by the serene look on her face, and the way she hung possessively onto Biffo's arm. He looked very much more subdued. Obviously the tryst in the shower the other evening hadn't taken his mind off Angie. He failed to perk up when Rose announced, 'I've made that healthy couscous pie you wanted.'

'Thanks, Mrs Brady. You've been so good to us,' Cheryl said sincerely. 'I'm sure you'll be glad to see the back of us on Friday.'

'Nonsense!' Rose said. Every time she wanted to say something nasty to Cheryl, she had told Judy, the words just died on her lips. The girl was just too nice.

Mick walked back in, wearing his reading glasses, as if hoping they might somehow distract attention from his hair.

Biffo immediately said, 'What the hell happened to your hair?'

'Nothing!'

274

Cheryl was looking closely now too. 'It's very black.'

'Yes, it is,' Mick said, clipped. He didn't quite meet her eyes. 'I just fancied a change.'

Biffo was greatly cheered up by Mick's hair disaster. 'What did it say on the pack, Midnight Madness? Black Velvet?'

'Biffo,' Rose chided. 'Your father thought it was shampoo he was putting on, didn't you, Mick? It was all a horrible mistake.'

Mick thought she was poking further fun at him, because he gave her a look and said, 'It wasn't. I knew exactly what I was putting on. And I can talk for myself, thank you.'

'Well!' said Rose, her jaw tight.

The air was tense as everybody sat down to partake of Rose's couscous pie.

And, from the look of it, Judy was a bit sorry that she hadn't elected to go home after all. But that would have meant facing Lenny and she wasn't sure she was up to it yet. Would she have to apologise? Certainly he had acted so insulted that an apology might be warranted. Which was a bit rich, really. After putting himself out there as someone who enjoyed nothing more than an uncomplicated sexual dalliance, his outrage seemed a bit far-fetched to Judy.

Between Mick's hair, the horrible couscous pie, the tightness around Rose's mouth, Biffo's obvious yearning to be somewhere else and Judy's morbid dread of having to face Lenny, the dinner table was rather more silent than usual. Only Cheryl kept the conversation going with a chirpy account of her family. Her father was a conservative, God-fearing Republican who worked in Washington on various pieces of legislation for Congress, most of which seemed to be anti something — anti-immigration, anti-abortion, anti-welfare state.

'I don't think he's that keen on me either,' Biffo said.

'Oh, that's not true!' Cheryl cried. 'Especially now that you've stopped drinking.'

The conversation limped on until dessert, which was something Rose had valiantly tried to do with steamed organic fruits.

By that stage the signature music for *Who Wants To Be A Millionaire* was playing in the sitting room, and Judy wouldn't be able to put off going home any longer. With any luck, Lenny would be out. But luck hadn't exactly been on her side lately.

She was spared by the surprise arrival of Angie.

Mick let her in, and she walked into the kitchen in her full stock-broker clobber — the suit, the heels, the make-up, the dollar signs in her eyes — and nodded around slowly, her eyes finally settling on Biffo. Top marks for a dramatic entrance anyway.

'Sorry to interrupt your dinner,' she told Rose.

'Not at all,' Rose said gratefully. 'We were all looking for some excuse not to eat dessert.'

Cheryl was suddenly alert. 'Biffo, who's this?'

Biffo, of course, was nearly on the floor with embarrassment. 'My ex,' he said miserably. 'I was going to tell you about her, but there didn't seem any point after the wedding was called off.'

'Hello,' said Angie to her cheerfully. 'Nice trackie bottoms.'

Cheryl was left looking down at her tracksuit in confusion, not understanding that in this part of the world, tracksuits were only worn as fashion statements, and that nobody would dream of actually going jogging in them.

Angie crooked an eyebrow dangerously at Biffo. 'I'd like a word with you.'

⋆　⋆　⋆

In the intervening days since the Night Of The Curry Chips, it had apparently dawned on Angie that Biffo had lied to her over the breakup.

'You're a coward, Biffo Brady.'

'I most certainly am not!' He recovered well from his surprise and rose to challenge her. Cheryl went wordlessly upstairs to her room. Rose and Mick wanted to stay, but Chris Tarrant could clearly be heard though the glass door asking whether an oryx was (a) an animal, (b) a precious jewel, (c) a fictional mystical creature, or (d) a household detergent, and Rose hadn't been able to contain herself. 'An animal!' she cried triumphantly. Then: 'Although I could have sworn I cleaned the toilet with it the other day.' Then Mick said over her, 'No, no, you're wrong, it's a precious jewel, I remember reading it somewhere.' Rose countered with, 'You're always reading things but you can never remember where you read them.' Mick argued back, 'At least I read and try to impart my knowledge to you.' Rose said, 'Oh shut up, let's go see what

Chris says,' and they hurried off into the living room cosily. It was almost like old times, and you could nearly forget that there was any disharmony between them at all except for Mick's hair, which sat on his head like a large, malevolent bat.

Only Judy was left, trying to choke down Rose's dessert, which seemed to be some kind of fruit crumble, except that the crumble bit had the taste and texture of sand.

But if this was what she must endure to put off facing Lenny, then so be it. She chewed on a mouthful and listened to the argument over her head.

'You let me think all along that the break-up was something to do with me!' Angie said accusingly. 'That it was my fault! That you didn't love me any more, or that I was terrible in bed or that I smelled or something. But really there was nothing wrong with me at all, was there?'

'None of us is perfect, Angie — '

'It was you and your own pathetic lack of confidence that was at fault!'

In the living room, the volume on the telly was turned up. The stakes must be getting higher.

Biffo lifted his chin. 'It's very difficult to nurture self-confidence when your girlfriend is the one stumping up for your entertainment and your holidays and even the pint you're drinking in the pub!'

'Poor you,' Angie said, her voice dripping with sarcasm. 'I didn't hear you complaining at the time. If I remember correctly you quite enjoyed all the things I paid for!'

'See?' Biffo yelped. 'I knew you felt that way all along! Superior. Even though you were always very careful to hide it. But deep down you had a sense of entitlement just because you earned five times as much as I did!'

'Ten, actually.' This registered with Biffo, and he let out a little gasp. There was a strangely triumphant look on Angie's face. 'And I've been hiding my bonuses too.'

'What?' Biffo looked rather weak now. It was obviously all much worse than he had thought.

'I only told you about every third one. I stashed the rest in an account in the Cayman Islands.'

'And you come here accusing *me* of lying to *you*? When all along you were telling me a big fat pack of them yourself!'

'I wanted to spare your feelings. I didn't want to make you feel inadequate.'

'Oh, well, aren't you great! Thank you so much, Angie, for your consideration.'

'Shut up, Biffo. The way you acted every time I got out my credit card told me that you wouldn't be able to handle it. So if I lied, it was because you forced me into it!'

Biffo looked a bit peculiar. 'Do you have any idea how galling it was for me to have spent the whole day driving around in that fucking white van putting up FOR SALE signs, and getting savaged by dogs, and working most weekends, when you would spend a third of that time in a nice air-conditioned office earning more in one hour than I did in a day?' He must have done a swift recalculation based on her revelations

279

about bonuses, because he amended this to, 'In a week.' He briefly closed his eyes in pain. 'So, yeah, I resented you, Angie! And your lovely, cushy, air-conditioned job!'

Angie looked a bit dangerous. 'Is that what you think of it? An easy number? Something anybody can do?'

'Well, no, obviously not *anybody*.'

'You're damn right there. I make as much as I do because I'm bloody good, Biffo.'

'I know you are.'

'But you never said that to me.'

'What?'

'You never said, I'm really proud of you, or congratulations, or anything like that.'

He was silent.

'You didn't, because you were too busy with your wounded male pride to even think of my feelings! Well, I'm sick of dumbing down for men like you. My own family never said well done to me, not even once. I'd have hoped the guy I loved at least would.'

'God, I'm sorry, Angie.'

Judy ate the last spoon of her crumble. She would sense the argument had come to a head and was wondering what way it would end up.

'Why didn't we talk about any of this?' Angie asked.

Biffo looked deflated, all his belligerence gone. 'Because we were pretending the problem didn't exist.'

'And your way of dealing with it was to leave without giving a reason why.'

'I know. I'm sorry. I was an idiot.'

It was the admission she had obviously been waiting for. She took a little breath and said, 'You were. And you threw it all away for nothing.'

There was a little silence then, and it looked like Biffo was going to say something, to go forward to her, maybe even to tell her that he still loved her.

But Angie said briskly, 'I think I'm done here.' She nodded at Judy, then gave Biffo a last look. 'Nick is waiting for me outside.'

Then she turned and left.

⋆　⋆　⋆

Judy was finally forced to leave when the nine o'clock news came on, and Rose began asking whether she should make her up a bed for the night.

When she drove up outside her own house, all the lights were off. The curtains weren't drawn. When she went in, the house was silent and empty.

'Lenny?'

She had a little speech rehearsed. She would begin by apologising for any offence caused and state that it had not been her intention to foist upon him any unwanted sexual advances, or to make him feel that he was on a par with those who charged for their services. She would try to sound sincere. Then she would suggest that due to the embarrassment caused all around, it would be better if he got the hell out of her house and checked into a swanky hotel. Which

281

he should have done last week.

'Lenny?' she said again.

He wasn't there. He may have gone to the pub, or for a walk on the beach or something.

The door to his bedroom was open. Unable to resist, she had a peek in.

The bed was neatly made and his suitcase was gone.

21

Judy went back to work the following Monday morning. They all looked as if they'd seen a ghost.

'Judy?' Annette reached out to touch her, as though to make doubly sure she wasn't actually an apparition.

Marcia, being very young, just kept looking at her with a mixture of pity and admiration that she'd had the bottle to show her face in public at all.

'I'm due back today, aren't I?' Judy said briskly, consulting the roster. In another life, she would have been back from honeymoon two days ago.

'Well, yes,' Annette said. She was nearly in contortions with the agony of it all. 'But I didn't want to put any pressure on you. And you can take more time off if you want. There's some kind of provision for, um, compassionate leave.'

'To be honest, I've had a gut-full of compassion,' Judy said. 'I just want to get back to work.'

Now that she had driven not just one man away, but two, it seemed that her career was probably the best option left to her, if not the only one. Forget romance, marriage and sex, she would from now on dedicate her life to books. She would gently encourage the youngsters over in the children's corner to stop throwing crayons at each other and go on a mystical journey with C.S. Lewis instead. She would strive to further literacy amongst disadvantaged groups, she would fund a mobile library, she would take the classics to the masses. And, alone in her narrow little single bed at night, she would think about Barry and Lenny, and she would take solace in the fact that her books would never leave her.

Although if they could they probably would.

'Next!' she shouted viciously, which was hardly the best start to her new goal in life.

Annette and Marcia were also seriously impeding her efforts to nurture a love of books in the public by making her have numerous tea and coffee breaks. Then they set her doing cataloguing work at the very back of the library, behind a giant computer, where she wouldn't have to face the public at all. For good measure, Annette put a big sign on the desk saying, 'Do Not Disturb'.

When they tried to insist that she take a two-hour lunch break, she had to have words with them. 'I'm fine, OK? I'm not on top of the world — my fiancé ran off the day before my wedding, after all — but now I just want some normality back in my life.'

Marcia was round-eyed that Judy was mentioning the terrible topic at all, and Judy had an urge to say it all again. In fact, the best thing would be to get up on the desk and announce to the whole library that she was back, her fiancé had indeed relocated to France (she wouldn't mention Lenny, not least because she had no idea where he had relocated to — probably

284

Australia) and could they all return any overdue books at their earliest convenience. It would certainly clear the air.

But instead she was forced to endure a series of embarrassed looks as the regulars plodded up to the desk, after first hanging around in the hopes that Annette or Marcia would become free.

'Morning, Mrs O'Reilly.' Judy greeted each customer steadily.

'Morning, Judy.' At least Mrs O'Reilly met Judy's eyes. She had been a patient of Barry's too, so his disappearance was a double whammy. 'How are you?' she asked bravely.

'I'm OK. I'm not doing too badly at all.'

The inquiries stopped at Judy's health. Nobody at all mentioned Barry. She supposed she couldn't blame them. What could they possibly say? Sorry to hear that bollox left you at the altar? Or, chin up, there'll be another one around the corner? In their situation, Judy herself would not have known what to say.

In the end, she stopped expecting anything from them, and they lapsed gratefully into inquiries about when the next Joanna Trollope was due in. Tomorrow would be easier, she knew. And in a few weeks' time the whole thing would have settled down and be absorbed into local history, dredged up only in the pub every now and again, and at other weddings. She could just hear it now: do you remember how Barry Fox ran off on Judy Brady that time? Did he ever come back from France in the end? Of course, she's still in the library, bless her. But very

285

cheerful, despite everything. And a great lover of books. If not for her, half the children in Cove wouldn't be able to read their own names, but she has them devouring Shakespeare like it was *The Beano*.

Judy was rather short with the next customer. She didn't want to get the cheery soul tag, the isn't-she-great-to-have-coped-with-it-all badge of honour. The alternative was bitter and twisted, but on balance she thought she'd rather be that. And now there was Lenny on top of it all, complicating things, making her feel even worse than she already did.

She had no idea where he had gone. There had been no note left anywhere — she had got down on her hands and knees and looked. No goodbyes of any kind. He had just taken his stuff and gone.

He had obviously taken her advances even worse than she'd thought. He must have been really appalled to go like that, so suddenly without even the most cursory goodbye. Was she really that revolting? Was he really that sensitive? It was a mystery.

On the other hand, leaving was what he did. She wondered whether he left other women in so brutal a fashion. Did he wait until they were in the shower before throwing his things into a bag and fleeing out the fire escape? He was even more of a lowlife than she had previously thought.

Well, Australia could have him, she decided. They were welcome to him! He should come with a government health warning, or a little tag that said, 'Might leave unexpectedly at any moment.'

As indeed should Barry.

There was no getting away from the fact that men were leaving her life with depressing regularity. By the time five o'clock came she didn't know whether she was glad she was back, or whether she should plump for the compassionate leave after all.

'How was it?' Annette asked, sympathetically.

'The first day back at work as the spurned fiancée? Pretty par for the course, I'd say.'

'Nobody's said a bad word against you, Judy. I wouldn't let them anyway.'

'Thanks, Annette.'

'If they've been gossiping about anyone, it's been Barry.'

'Yes.' Judy didn't want to get into a discussion about Barry, and his motives, and what an idiot he was to have left such a lovely woman as herself behind.

Especially as she didn't feel very lovely right now. She felt angry and mean and resentful.

'See you tomorrow,' she said, heavily, and took home *Ulysses* with her, just for punishment.

★ ★ ★

It had finally started to dawn on Vinnie that Ber was a slob.

'Just because he went into the cupboard under the stairs and found all these dirty things,' she complained. 'After I told him not to go in there and everything.'

'What kind of dirty things?'

'Oh, you know — clothes, shoes, dinner plates.'

'You put dirty dinner plates in the cupboard under the stairs?'

'Just once,' she said crossly. 'And he makes such a big deal out of it! Like he found out I have a criminal record or something.' She thought of something. 'I must make sure he doesn't go in the attic. I could board it up or something, couldn't I?'

'I thought you two were going to sit down and sort some domestic stuff out,' Judy said.

'Yes, but I thought that meant telling Vinnie not to use my hair-brush and to stop eating out of the fridge. But before I got a chance to say anything, he produces this big piece of paper that he says is a cleaning rota.' She nearly shuddered. 'You know me, Judy. I don't clean.' She saw Judy's face and got crosser. 'What's so funny?'

'You thinking that you're the only one who has to adjust.'

'Well, it's true. You know how impossible Vinnie's been! I think I've done pretty well to put up with as much as I have. Did I tell you that he likes to watch reruns of *The Good Life*? At four o'clock in the morning?'

'Whereas you, of course, have been a dream.'

'Vinnie's had no problems whatsoever with me up to now,' Ber declared. 'And why would he? I'm exactly the same as I was when we were having an affair.' She was wearing grey, shapeless tracksuit bottoms, not a scrap of make-up, and had probably left the kitchen in tatters behind her.

She may have seen some irony in this because she added, 'And anyway, even if there were some very minor adjustments to be made on my part, we always said we'd never change for a man. Do you remember? Every Saturday night in the pub we'd have ten vodka and tonics and we'd all make a pledge that no matter how nice a man was, how wonderful and how much we were in love with him, we would still never change a single thing about ourselves just to make him happy.'

'The changes Vinnie are suggesting sound more to do with health and safety than happiness, Ber.'

'I don't care.'

'Plus, those pledges were made when we were all young and beautiful, or at least attractive, and weren't looking forty in the face.'

'Forty is years off yet,' Ber said bravely, even though it wasn't that far off. 'I am who I am, Judy. He can take it or leave it.'

'Would it help if you didn't call it change? If you called it compromise instead?'

'God,' Ber spat. 'I hate that word. It's such a fucking wishy-washy, half-arsed word. Everybody gives in a little bit, just enough to feel resentful but not enough to make the other person happy. What's the use of that?'

'Then maybe you should build a wall down the middle of the house, and one of you could live on one side and one on the other.'

'That's not a bad idea.' Ber looked fed up.

'Oh, I don't know, Judy. I always thought Vinnie was the ancient one. You know — likes his routine, a bit set in his ways, same cereal every morning except on Sunday when he has eggs.' She said darkly, 'But maybe it's not him at all. Maybe it's me. I've got too used to the freedom of single life and I'm too selfish to change.'

'It's a possibility.'

'That I like my life more than I like Vinnie?' Ber looked horrified.

'Why don't you try cleaning the bathroom?' Judy suggested.

'What?'

'Just to see how it feels.' Judy felt a bit of a fraud, dishing out advice when she herself had a rather catastrophic record in the domestic bliss department.

'That, Judy, is a slippery slope. If I give in on that, what else will I have to give in on?'

'Make him give in on something too.'

'Until we're both so busy giving in that we won't even recognise each other any more? We'll just be some drab, middle-aged couple like you see in the supermarket on a Saturday morning, arguing over which type of biscuits to get.' She looked completely depressed. 'If I'd wanted domesticity I'd have married someone years ago, Judy. With Vinnie it was all about the passion. Not cleaning the fucking bathroom.'

Ber's language also appeared to have suffered some deterioration since Vinnie had moved in.

'Where's Lenny?' she inquired, looking about. It was as if Lenny lived there, and not Barry at all.

'Gone.'

'Gone? Where?' Ber demanded.

'I have no idea. Probably Australia.'

'That was a bit sudden, wasn't it?'

'Oh, you know Lenny. He comes and goes,' Judy said breezily, as if it made not a whit of difference to her in the world. 'To tell you the truth, I'm glad to have the house back to myself.'

In fact, the house felt emptier than ever. When Judy came home in the evenings from the library, there were no lovely welcoming smells coming from the kitchen, no bottles of Miller beer in the recycling. There was nobody to have a feisty exchange with over breakfast.

She missed him. Everything seemed rather flat and colourless now that he was gone. The air in the house seemed unnaturally still, crying out for a bit of life. Obviously she missed Barry too, but in a completely different way. His absence made her feel that she had forgotten to bolt the back door. She woke in the night feeling that something was wrong, that some vital, secure part of her life was gone.

'I know the feeling,' Ber said rather gloomily. 'And you might as well enjoy it, Judy, while you can.'

'What's that supposed to be mean?'

'Well, I suppose Barry will be back at some point.'

'Ber, I have to hand it to you. Nobody has remained as optimistic as you for a reconciliation.'

'I'm not championing any reconciliation at all,' Ber insisted. 'I'm just pointing out facts. And the facts are that Barry simply won't last without you.'

'He's lasted pretty well so far.'

'Pah,' said Ber rudely. 'Who wouldn't last a week or two away on their own, with oodles of money and adrenaline to keep them going? But that will wear off, Judy. And then he'll realise that without you, he's nothing!'

'Oh, Ber.'

'I'm not just trying to flatter you,' Ber insisted generously.

Judy hadn't been flattered. The opposite in fact.

'He's always needed someone to ground him,' Ber announced. 'People like that always do.'

So what did that make her? A great big lump of concrete? A ball at the end of a chain? With a list, of course.

'In that case,' she said, 'let's hope he finds himself.'

Ber thought she was joking and laughed. But then she gave a big heavy sigh. 'I suppose I'd better get home and clean the bathroom. Honestly, I had far more fun as a mistress.'

Judy lasted the week at the library. She had a crick in her neck from holding her head so high, and she was fed up of scrambled eggs for tea every night. But finally Friday came, and she declined an invitation from Annette and Marcia to go to the pub and went wearily home instead.

The dead air hit her the minute she opened the front door. And she had forgotten to put the bin out — it had been Barry's job — and it had started to stink. It wasn't easy being single all

292

over again. It would take some practice, this business of refuse disposal, and coming home to no one, not even a cat. She would start tomorrow, she vowed. But right now she just felt like crawling under the bed covers and bawling her eyes out.

There was a postcard on the mat, under an electricity bill. The picture on the front was of bright sunflowers. The postmark said Marseille, and there was just one word written on it: 'Sorry'.

22

She half expected Barry to phone over the weekend. She didn't even want to stray too far from home in case he did. She did her housework, and ironed her clothes for next week, and went over numerous little scenarios and conversations in her mind. For instance, what she might say if he told her he had made a terrible mistake and wanted to come home. Or what she would say if he told her he'd bought a small vineyard in the Rhône Valley and was taking a crash course in winemaking, and could she please send on half the proceeds of the sale of the house. (The second response was considerably easier, and shorter.)

Anything was possible. She was jittery and nervous all day Saturday, barely able to stay in one room.

He didn't ring, of course. She was raging with him, and raging with herself for working herself up into thinking that he would.

'Sorry' meant just that, obviously. At least he'd said it. At least he'd acknowledged that he had done her a great wrong.

It was one hurt less.

On Saturday night, Biffo came over with a sixteen-inch pizza and ten cans of beer.

Judy's first thought was that they were for her, to cheer her up, but he swiftly disabused her of that notion by sinking his teeth into a slab of extra pepperoni, and washing it down with half a can of beer.

'I've left Cheryl,' he blurted, when he could talk again. He wiped his mouth. 'God, I needed that. If I see another piece of tofu I'll puke.'

Judy was confused. 'Hold on a minute here, Biffo. You've left Cheryl? Where?'

She hoped he wasn't going to say halfway up the Wicklow Mountains. Or on the outdoor athletics track at UCD.

'At home, of course,' Biffo said impatiently.

'You mean . . . you've broken up with her?'

'Yes.' He looked as if he almost couldn't believe it himself. He seemed invigorated, more alive or something, even though he was all stubbly and Judy could detect the faint whiff of BO off him. It would appear that he had skipped his morning shower. Things were in crisis indeed.

'What happened?' she asked.

'Well, it's Angie, isn't it?' he said.

'She didn't call around again, did she?' There had been no word from Angie since that night. But then Judy remembered that she was on safari, with Nick. She was probably sitting astride an elephant right now, having a leisurely smoke.

'The way she stood in Mam's kitchen the other night,' Biffo said dreamily, 'and ate the head off me, and called me a coward and all that.' He looked off into the middle distance. 'I was a complete fool to have broken things off with her.'

He drank back the rest of the beer and, thus

295

fortified, said, 'Cheryl's a lovely girl, don't get me wrong. But my life with her, it was nearly like a dream, Judy. All that exercise and eating right and washing the whole time . . . that's not me! That's not the real Biffo.' As if to illustrate his point, he gave his armpit a leisurely scratch. 'I think I was so burnt by the break-up with Angie that I went for someone the total opposite of her, and buried my true self,' he told her earnestly. 'Because let's face it, Judy, deep down I'm an easy-going slob.'

'Yes,' Judy agreed.

'And I'm happy with that. Delighted! The night out with Angie was fantastic, even though I made a total tit of myself. It was just like old times — we completely connected, you know? I was trying to explain it to Cheryl.'

'You . . . told Cheryl about that night?'

Biffo looked wounded. 'Well, yes.'

'I thought you didn't want to tell her.'

'That was before I knew I was going to break up with her. But Angie has made me see how hurtful it was when I didn't tell the truth to *her*, and I decided that I wouldn't ever do that to another woman. So I was completely upfront with Cheryl. No holds barred.'

'What exactly did you tell her?' Judy inquired carefully.

'Everything!' He looked very relieved. 'I told her that I would never normally go for a woman like her, but that I was probably on the rebound from Angie, who had always been the love of my life. And that it was nothing personal, that she was a really lovely girl, and that the whole thing was my fault for never being able to love her even half as much as I loved Angie. And that I thought all that health stuff was empty and superficial and a load of crap, but that I wished her well in the future.'

'Oh, Biffo.'

'Nicely, of course,' he said quickly.

'There's no nice way of saying all that!'

'What?' He looked put out now. 'She seemed to appreciate it.'

'She was probably too gutted to speak.'

'It wasn't like that at all,' he insisted. 'She was completely fine about it, Judy. She even wished me well for the future.'

It was possible that she was even more of a saint than Judy had given her credit for. Judy herself would probably have taken a sharp knife to Biffo.

'We can't win,' Biffo complained. 'If we're not honest, we're in the dog house, and if we *are* honest, that won't do either.'

'It's called diplomacy, Biffo.'

'Anyway, it's done now,' Biffo said. 'And Mum and Dad are being very nice to Cheryl. Dad especially. He tried to coax her out for a walk and everything. He didn't really leave her side all day. You'd never think he'd be so good in a relationship crisis, would you?'

'No,' Judy murmured. She wondered what Rose was doing. Probably packing Cheryl's suitcase as fast as she could. Or Mick's.

'Now I just have to work things out with Angie,' Biffo said efficiently.

'What?'

'It's obvious we're meant to be together, Judy. She feels it too, but she just won't admit it.'

'You might want to clarify that one with her. She's on safari with Nick at the moment.'

'That's not serious,' Biffo said dismissively. 'I saw the look in her eye the other day, Judy. If it hadn't been for all that job stuff, we'd be living in that big house overlooking the sea, happy out.'

Judy didn't want to point out that the big house overlooking the sea was rather dependent on the job stuff.

'No, I'm glad we had that row,' he expanded. 'It cleared the air, brought it all out in the open. We were never going to be happy while she was trouncing me in the earning stakes.' He vowed, 'And now that we know what was wrong, I'm going to try and win her back.'

Judy didn't quite follow. 'But how is it going to be any different this time? Even if she *does* take you back?'

Biffo was smiling all over his face. 'Because I'm making a whole heap of money now too, Judy. I might have been a lowly estate agent driving a white van this time last year, but now I'm a big hotshot flogging luxury waterfront villas with balconies and private swimming pools.' He sounded as though he was reciting from a brochure. 'I'm not the poor relation any more, Judy. I'll be a fully paid-up member of the relationship!'

'Except that you'll be in Orlando, Biffo.'

But Biffo had thought of that too. 'OK, sure, so we're looking at a long-distance relationship for a couple of years. But I'll expand into the

Irish market, Judy. I'm going to open a branch here. Do you know how many rich Americans would like a small holiday home in Ireland? I could do a roaring trade in traditional cottages with thatched roofs and maybe a cow or two out the back. I'll make a fortune!'

Judy felt she should sound a word of caution. 'You might want to see how Angie feels first.'

'Well, of course,' he said. 'But it makes sense, Judy. And she doesn't have to go around downplaying her success. It's a win-win situation.'

He cracked open another can of beer as though it were already in the bag, and looked around. 'Where's Lenny?'

The very mention of him sent Judy's synapses crackling furiously.

'He doesn't actually live here, Biffo. If you must know, he's gone back to Australia.'

Biffo looked gutted. 'Really? He never even said goodbye or anything.' His case of hero worship didn't seem to have diminished any.

'I think he had to leave in a bit of a hurry,' Judy fudged.

To her relief Biffo didn't pursue it. He just said, 'Can I have his bed tonight so?'

'What?'

'Well, I can hardly go home. Not with Cheryl there. It wouldn't be fair on her.'

'I suppose not.'

She must have looked unwelcoming because Biffo said, 'It'll just be until Friday. Then we'll both be gone back to Orlando.'

'Better make sure they don't seat you

together,' Judy advised.

'Of course,' said Biffo solemnly. 'Although, you know, I don't honestly think she'd mind. I couldn't have broken up with a nicer woman.'

★ ★ ★

Poor Cheryl was taking the whole thing rather badly. Her lovely face was marred by shadows, and her blue eyes stricken with grief. A cup of sweet tea sat on the table in front of her, cold and untouched.

'She's been sitting in that exact same position since yesterday afternoon, when Biffo broke up with her,' Mick said to Judy in a low voice. 'Hasn't even moved to take a shower.'

Neither had he, by the looks of it. He looked a bit scraggy and tired, being unused to all this female angst. His black hair was less shiny, too, and it was obvious he hadn't had time to run a comb through it.

The reason for this swiftly became clear. 'Mick?' said Cheryl from the table. 'Do you think I could have another cup of sweet tea?'

'Of course you can, love!' He said to Judy with a little sigh, 'I should never have started her on the sweet tea. She's looking for a refill every ten minutes, and then she doesn't drink the blooming thing.'

He set to making it. Cheryl's eyes flickered to him every now and again, as though he were the only stable force in her otherwise shattered world.

'Where's Mum?' Judy inquired.

Mick jerked his head towards the living room. 'Inside watching the television. Well, it's a bit of an awkward situation, isn't it? You know, what with Biffo over in your house and Cheryl here.'

'Is my tea nearly ready?' Cheryl asked at the table.

'Coming, coming!' Mick said, trying to sound cheerful. Out of the side of his mouth he asked Judy, 'How is Biffo anyway?'

At the mention of him, Cheryl stiffened at the table.

Judy lowered her voice to a whisper and said, 'All right.' For Cheryl's benefit, she added sombrely, 'In the circumstances.' She didn't want her to know that he was flat out in the spare bed sleeping off a massive hangover, having celebrated his freedom till two o'clock in the morning with beer and cigarettes.

'Who would have thought it would all end like this,' Mick said, with a heavy sigh.

At the table, Cheryl began to cry.

From the look on Mick's face, it wasn't the first time that day, and it wouldn't be the last.

'What's wrong now, love?' he said, kindly.

'Biffo,' she said.

'I know, it was kind of a rhetorical question . . . Judy, bring over those tissues there, would you?'

But Cheryl didn't want anything to do with Judy. It was Mick she hung on to as she sobbed her little heart out all over his shirtfront.

'You're all right now,' he told her, giving her back an awkward pat, and meeting Judy's eyes over her head. He looked as if he'd like nothing more than a nice quiet pint in the local and a read of the paper.

Judy noted that the volume on the telly in the living room had been turned down.

Eventually Cheryl's tears dried up, and Mick fixed her up with more tea, and a bit of toast if she fancied it. 'I know it's not wheat-free or anything like that, but I think you could probably let up on yourself at a time like this,' he advised her.

Cheryl managed a small smile. She told Judy, 'Your dad has been great in all this. I don't know what I'd have done without him.'

'I'm only doing what anybody would do,' he said. Well, anybody apart from Rose.

'I mean it,' she insisted. 'You've been just like my own dad.' She added, just so there was no confusion, 'He's a really great guy.'

'Thanks,' said Mick.

Cheryl filled up again. 'Actually, do you think I could phone him?'

Mick must have sensed an opportunity to hand over the responsibility to somebody else because he said, 'Well, of course you can! Go right ahead.'

But Cheryl looked lost again. 'I've never been out of America before. I don't even know the international code.'

Mick looked stoic. 'Do you want me to help?'

'Would you?' She gave him a brilliant smile.

He limped out after her and down the hall.

Rose was standing in the living room doorway, her arms folded across her chest. The television was on behind her.

'What does she want him to hold her hand for now?'

Judy felt this was a bit unfair. 'He seems to be managing the situation pretty well, Mum. She's very upset.'

Rose, of course, immediately felt bad. 'Ah, I know she is. I tried to bad-mouth Biffo last night, just to make her feel better, but she wouldn't hear a word of it. She hasn't got a mean bone in her body.'

She looked very gloomy at that.

'How is Biffo?' she asked.

'Hung-over.'

Rose tsked. 'I'll send back some aspirin with you. And I made a big pork pie just to cheer him up. I had to make it in the bathroom because Mick said it might upset Cheryl.' She looked a bit dangerous again. 'I don't think he's ever been as concerned for any of us the way he is about her.'

'I don't think there's anything in it, Mum. Nothing . . . like that.'

'It's pathetic,' Rose said flatly.

She looked as tired as Mick. But what with Barry fecking off to France, Biffo's bust-up with Cheryl, and Mick's peculiar behaviour, it had been a stressful summer for her.

She wasn't so tired though that she failed to pick up that there was something up with Judy.

'Did anything happen, Judy?'

'No, no.' Then she decided to come clean. She was dying to confide in someone. 'Barry sent a postcard from France to say he was sorry.'

'Did he now,' Rose said slowly.

'I don't really know what to make of it.'

'Do you think he wants to come back?'

'I don't know, Mum.'

'He might be laying the groundwork.'

'Or he might just be apologising to make himself feel better.'

Rose tsked again. 'I hate to hear you talking so cynically.'

'How can I not be cynical after what he did?'

Rose looked troubled. 'I know. It's a hard thing to get over all right. You'd have to ask yourself if you could, Judy. Or if it would always be there, between you.'

Judy didn't even want to think that far ahead. But with the postcard, she felt Barry was forcing her into it, which made her want to resist all the more. She wasn't going to let him pull her strings all the way from France.

'It mightn't be my decision anyway,' she said. 'He mightn't even come back.'

'Or he might be waiting for some sign from you.'

'It's up to him,' Judy said stubbornly.

Rose was the one who looked a bit cynical now. 'In a lot of relationships there's a stronger one and one that needs a bit of a push. You must see it yourself.'

Had she? She didn't know.

Mick came back in with a shopping bag and his wallet. 'She's on the phone to her dad. I managed to reverse the charges, and with any luck she'll be on for a good while.'

'Where are you going?' Rose demanded.

'Down to the shops,' he said. 'She asked me to

get her some granola bars.'

'Granola bars!'

'I know, Rose, God knows we could do without the special dietary requirements in the middle of all this,' he snapped. 'But she wants the damned things and I said I'd get them.'

'Of course you did,' Rose said, her voice dripping with sarcasm.

'*You* go get them then,' he said, thrusting out the shopping bag. 'Instead of standing there passing remarks, when you did nothing the whole morning to help out!'

'My help wasn't wanted. Only yours.'

Mick lifted his chin. 'And that just kills you, doesn't it? That somebody else might have some use for me.'

'Use!' said Rose. 'Is that what you call it?'

'And what would you call it?' Mick demanded.

'Sad,' said Rose. 'That's what. Age comes to us all, Mick. But it doesn't mean we turn on those near and dear to us just because they remind us of how long we've lived, and make a fool of ourselves over someone young enough to be our granddaughter!'

'You'd have to be crude about it, wouldn't you!' Mick shouted back. 'It's not about that at all!'

Rose looked at him, white-faced. Then she grabbed up her handbag and the car keys, and left.

23

Judy went for a walk on the beach that afternoon. She needed a break from all the drama. And some time to think about what Rose had said.

She had never thought of herself as the strong one in her and Barry's relationship; she was just the one who made the lists. The efficient, down-to-earth one, who kept the house ticking over while Barry was on a mission to inoculate every child in Cove against measles, mumps and rubella. His work was important; there was no doubt about that. She wondered now whether this was subtly reflected in the way they had managed the relationship. Certainly she seemed to have done more than her fair share in most areas. But she hadn't resented it; it was just the way things were. And anyway, in most couples wasn't there one person driving things, even if it wasn't that obvious to the casual eye?

Judy wondered whether she had done too much driving, and whether Barry had become too comfortable being the backseat passenger.

He would be doing his own driving in France, in every sense of the word. She wondered whether he was finding things out for himself, as Rose had hinted. It would be interesting for him if that were the case. Interesting for both of them, maybe, if he came back.

She walked for hours along the water's edge.

Teatime must be approaching because families began to pack up and go, and people walking their dogs whistled to them and began to make their way up to where their cars were parked.

Soon she was the only person left on that part of the beach. She would go home in a minute and check in with Mick to see whether everything was OK.

She had been trying to ring Rose on her mobile all afternoon. But Rose didn't have her mobile phone on, or else she wasn't answering it.

Judy was worried about her. She had never gone off like that by herself in the car. They'd had their rows over the years, her and Mick, quite colourful ones at times, but they'd never had a serious falling out like this.

And over Cheryl.

If indeed it was over Cheryl at all. If the bickering was anything to go by, the seeds of it had been laid before she'd ever come on the scene.

It seemed to Judy that all around her, everybody was falling apart. No couple was safe, it seemed, from angst and change. Oh, if she could get her hands on *She Loved Too Much* and all its relations, she would put them through the shredder at work, every last one of them.

There was a man approaching across the sand. Rather purposefully. Judy squinted into the lowering sun. It looked very like Lenny. It *was* Lenny.

She stood rooted to the spot until he reached her. He looked at her unsmilingly.

'What are you doing back from Australia?' she

blurted. 'Did you forget something?'

Lenny said impatiently, 'What are you talking about? I wasn't in Australia.' Then, rather querulously, 'What's Biffo doing in my bed?'

His bed? Judy felt confused, and warm.

'He seems very hung-over.'

'He is. He broke up with Cheryl yesterday. He's staying for a while.'

Lenny's eyebrows jumped up. She wasn't surprised. At that moment, it looked as though no member of the Brady family could manage to hold any relationship together.

Best to start with the basics. 'Lenny, where were you the whole week?'

'West Cork, visiting relatives.' He dug his hands into his pockets and looked at her hard. 'I was going to leave you a note, but actually I was too hopping mad.'

He still looked mad. Judy was rather amazed that he had obviously kept it up for the whole week.

'Look, I didn't mean to offend you, OK?' she said. 'I thought you'd be up for it, so long as it suited everybody and nobody got hurt.'

Certainly, he had led her to believe that that was the way he operated.

But he looked even more hurt now, if you could believe it. 'If it's sex you want, Judy, go to any club on a Saturday night. I'm sure you'll have no problem scoring, especially in that red top.'

Ooh. That one hurt.

'I can see I wasn't entirely clear,' she said stiffly. 'I didn't mean I wanted just sex. I meant I wanted sex with, um, *you*.'

He continued to look very suspicious. 'Me?'

'Yes. Not with some desperate, pissed old guy in a club,' she qualified.

'That makes me feel much better,' he said cautiously. 'I think.'

There was a slight thawing in the air.

'I didn't realise the whole idea would be so repugnant to you,' she finished up humbly.

'It's not that,' he said impatiently. 'Look, Judy, you can't go around doing that to people.'

'I know,' she said. 'It was very low of me. I just feel sick when I think of how much I hurt your feelings.'

'Are you making fun of me?' He looked mad again.

'No, no, no. I'm just trying to clear the air. And, just for the record, I didn't do it to get back at Barry either.' Although that would have been a bonus, but there was no need to mention that now.

'Right,' he said, at last.

'So . . . are we friends again?'

'We were never friends, Judy.'

'What are we then?'

He considered this. 'I have no idea. Something strange and abnormal. The word exasperating comes to mind.'

'You're probably right,' she agreed. That didn't quite explain what he was doing back here again, in her life, her home. She decided she wouldn't ask. It might only bring on another fit of bad temper from him.

'So, no sex then?' she said. Hastily, she added, 'That was a joke.'

He looked a bit wrong-footed again. And, if she were being honest, she wasn't really joking at all. The week in West Cork had done wonders for him, he looked healthy and fit and well fed and her fingers were itching to get at him, to push him down onto the wet sand and have her wicked way with him.

'Sex,' he declared, 'would be a very bad idea, Judy.'

'Would it?' she said.

'Think about it. You and me, we have completely different ideas on pretty much everything. But certainly relationships. You just wouldn't be able to play by the rules.'

Well now, she wasn't going to be spoken to like that, as though she were some kind of hillbilly when it came to sex. 'Whose rules exactly are we talking about here? Your rules?'

'Yes. And I wouldn't be able to play by yours. Because if we agreed to sleep together — which we haven't — we'd wake up tomorrow morning and you'd already be planning a rerun.'

'You really think you'd be that good?'

He didn't like that. Mr Sex himself. 'I'm just saying. Your mind doesn't work in the short term. Only the long term. It's not a fault. It's just the way you are.'

'I've recently been dumped at the altar. Maybe I'm not thinking long-term any more.'

'You're still the same inside,' he argued. 'You'll get over this and you'll meet some guy and you'll get married eventually.'

'That's so patronising!' She was mad now.

'Don't fight it, Judy. It's in your DNA. Your genes.'

'All right, if you're going to push me about it, then yes, I think that two people *can* make a long-term commitment to each other. Just because Barry ran off on me doesn't mean I've stopped believing in romance and commitment and . . . longevity!'

Lenny's eyebrows shot up. 'That should be a quote of the week.'

'Shut up.' She was a bit embarrassed. 'There's no need to make fun of me just because you like to spread it around.'

'I'm getting a little sick of these cheap shots about my promiscuity.'

'So you're admitting that you *are* promiscuous?'

'Judy, you seem to be slightly confused between being loose and being able to live in the moment. They're very different, let me assure you.'

'What exactly is 'living in the moment'? Inability to think and plan ahead?'

'No. Unwillingness to get bogged down in 'what ifs' and 'I wonder where this is going'.'

'That's a typical male view that betrays your own reluctance to commit.'

'I don't have commitment problems. You, on the other hand, have problems at the other extreme.'

'I'm overly committed?'

'Yes. You hang on to everything, even when it's obviously past its sell-by date.' She thought he was alluding to her T-shirt, a leftover from a

Simple Minds concert twenty years ago. But he said hurriedly, 'I am not talking about you and Barry here, by the way.'

Judy blustered, 'At least I don't have a problem sustaining relationships.'

'I don't have a problem sustaining them either.'

'Yeah, for like two hours.'

'Judy, stop it. If it doesn't last, it's because neither of us wants it to.'

'So what happens?' Judy was quite enjoying herself now.

'What do you mean?'

'Do you, like, get up in the morning and say, bye now, I'm off?'

'Oh, you'd like that, wouldn't you?' he said. 'That would fit in perfectly with your narrow view of men and women and how they operate within relationships. The poor, duped woman, and the big fecker who's had a ride and who can't get out of the place fast enough.' He shook his head in wonder, as though she was some kind of extinct species. 'Judy, you need to stop reading the Mills and Boons in that library of yours, and move into the twenty-first century.'

She would never, ever tell him about *His Wicked Way*, she vowed there and then. Never.

'I'm just intrigued as to how you operate, that's all,' she said.

'How I *operate*? Surely you mean to choose another word. A less offensive word.'

He really could be very prickly. Judy was amazed again at how thin his skin was. Imagine getting offended over something like that.

'All right, how you start and end relationships.'

'Often I don't end them. Often she does. Mostly it's a completely mutual thing, Judy. People with the same interests and outlook tend to come together, just like, say, people who want to get married.'

'And I suppose that's not aimed at me and Barry either.'

'Oh, Judy. I'm talking about freedom here. No preconceptions, that's all. No agendas. Sometimes it's about sex. But sometimes you don't have sex at all, you just do nice things together. Like we're doing now — I mean, *we're* not having sex.'

'Not at the moment, no.' Judy couldn't quite believe she was having this conversation.

'And quite right too.' He sounded relieved.

Judy was offended. 'You make me sound like the back of a bus.'

'I didn't mean that — '

'That you'd have to take medication before you could face it.'

'Judy, stop.'

She went on heatedly, 'And it's rubbish to say that women always go in with preconceptions. Like we're always after some massive commitment! Sometimes we just want big long hot sex too!' That came out sounding very odd, but she kept a poker face anyway. 'Anyway,' she said. 'Back to how you leave women. What do you do?'

He looked exasperated. 'What any normal person does, Judy. I tell the other person in the relationship that I don't want to be in it any more. What, do you think I just slip out while she's not looking?'

It was horrible, the silence. Judy felt sick.

'Shit. God, I'm so sorry, Judy. I didn't mean to say that. I just meant . . .'

'You meant you would never do what Barry did.'

He hesitated. Then he shrugged and said bluntly, 'No.'

It had to be some kind of sick irony, Judy thought. There was Lenny, who had probably had casual sexual relationships with half the super-model fraternity, yet would never behave in a cowardly fashion. And Barry, honest, dependable, straight Barry, would and had.

'Are you all right?' he asked.

'Fine.' The tears rose. She blinked rapidly but they wouldn't go away.

'Oh, shit,' he said.

'I'm OK. Really.'

'Come here.'

The next moment, she found herself all wrapped up in the nicest, strongest hug she'd had in ages. He was lovely and . . . meaty, she thought. It wasn't the most flattering term, but that didn't matter. She felt warm and safe, which was odd, given that Lenny and security didn't go hand in hand. The wind whipped around them but she didn't even feel it.

At some indefinable point, the comforting hug went on a bit too long and mutated into a let's-get-up-close hug.

And then the moment passed when she could

have withdrawn without too much loss of face.

The upshot was that she found herself locked into a semi-passionate embrace that she seemed completely powerless to break.

From the look on Lenny's face, he found himself in a similar predicament.

'What's going on here?' she asked.

'I'm not sure,' Lenny said carefully. 'But maybe we should just enjoy the moment.'

That was his answer to everything. Even after they'd had a great big serious discussion. Even after they had decided that under no circumstances were they going to do what they were now doing.

But then Judy suddenly decided, what the hell, why not? Barry was gone, she was free, and Lenny was here.

'OK,' she said.

She scarcely got the word out before they were kissing so passionately that a nearby flock of seagulls took fright and jumped into the air. Judy didn't notice. She was too busy observing that there were great advantages to kissing a shorter man. Preferably a shorter man who looked and felt like Lenny. Oh, it was lovely. She had thought he might be a bit smarmy, given his vast experience, but he wasn't a bit, you could nearly think he meant it. And, she thought, there really was something in this theory about enjoying the moment, especially when it went on and on in a most satisfying way.

In fact, the only thing that eventually wrenched them apart at all was her mobile phone, ringing insistently in her pocket.

They broke apart, rather breathless, and in Judy's case, slightly sheepish.

'Excuse me while I take this,' she said. There was no reason to dispense with common manners just because they were now, apparently, having sex. Or the beginnings of it. Even though they had said that they wouldn't go there under any circumstances.

It was Mick. He said rather urgently, 'You'd better come over here. There's been a bit of an incident.'

24

The story went like this. While Rose had been driving around fuming, and Mick had been at the supermarket trying to find granola bars, Cheryl broke into the drinks cabinet under the television, and consumed four cans of Heineken, a quarter bottle of vodka, some sherry that had been there at least ten years, and a bottle of Powers' whiskey. She didn't like that much, apparently, because she tried to mix it with a can of Rose's Slimfast Chocolate Shake and some ice cubes from the freezer.

'The kitchen was carnage,' Mick whispered. 'You never saw anything like it. Then she must have got hungry, because there were pizza boxes from the freezer and empty packets of Bacon Bites all over the floor.' There was more. 'And not one morsel of it organic.'

She then slept some of it off in the front garden. Several neighbours saw her in passing, but thought that she was only sunbathing. Upon waking, though, she stood in the middle of the garden berating Biffo at the top of her voice for the whole street to hear.

'And the language out of her — you wouldn't hear a truck driver coming out with some of the things she did.' There was a shocked look about him.

'Go on,' Judy urged.

Cheryl then proceeded to finish off the bottle

of whiskey before getting up on the roof of Biffo's rental BMW and repeatedly smashing the empty bottle down on the windscreen.

'Thousands and thousands of euro worth of damage. The rental company said on the phone that they're going after him for every cent.'

Tiring of that, Cheryl then went on a rampage through the house, fuelling herself with Rose's cooking wine as she went (the drinks cabinet was empty at this point). Biffo was clearly the target. She had gathered up every article and item belonging to him: clothes, CDs, shoes, all his hair and body products, even his suitcase, and two photos of him as a plump, smiling child that had had pride of place on the piano.

She then built a big bonfire out in the back garden.

'Quite a good one too,' Mick said, impressed despite his upset.

She had then got the lawnmower from the garage, and got up on it and drove around on it a few times until the garden resembled one of those cornfields with mysterious circles in the centre, only hers were more unsteady. Then, with the ingenious use of a pipe taken from the back of the washing machine, she siphoned out the petrol from it and poured it onto the bonfire. She took a box of matches from the mantelpiece and sent most of Biffo's earthly possessions towards heaven.

An examination afterwards by fire officers deduced that she had correctly built the bonfire far enough away from the house so as not to pose any danger to it. Rather, it was the combination of the petrol and Biffo's highly combustible hair products that caused the blast that blew out half the kitchen.

Luckily Cheryl was uninjured, as she was upstairs being sick in the bathroom at the time. In fact, it was unlikely that she'd even noticed that the house was on fire, because a taxi pulled up around the same time as the smoke alarm went off. Cheryl was next observed on CCTV in Dublin airport, checking in, and looking a lot calmer after the carnage, and completely unrepentant. It was presumed that she was now back in Orlando.

'There's an awful lot of smoke damage,' Mick said. 'Rose had left your wedding dress out in the hall to take back to you, Judy. I'm afraid it's ruined.'

Judy didn't know whether to look upon that as an omen or just simple misfortune. 'Don't worry about my wedding dress at a time like this, Dad. I was probably never going to wear it again anyway.'

'Do you want a cup of sweet tea?' he said, quivering, even though he looked more in need of one. Then, 'Oh, I forgot. We have no electricity.'

Power had been cut to the house until the full damage could be assessed. But right away the chief fire officer had helpfully been able to tell Mick that the back wall of the kitchen had been completely blown out and was lying in the garden. Mick and Judy were looking straight out through the huge hole and into the back garden. The rain came down, battering the plastic sheeting that covered the gap, and letting in a gust of cold wind, even in July.

'Rose is going to kill me altogether when she sees this,' Mick said, looking out forlornly.

'It wasn't your fault, Dad. You weren't even here.'

'I shouldn't have gone for the granola bars. I didn't even want to go for the bloody things, I was exhausted. But she kept asking me, Judy. I know now that she didn't want them at all. She just needed to get me out of the house so that she could set fire to it.'

He looked outraged.

'She mightn't have been as calculated as that. The urge might just have come upon her.'

But Mick wasn't having any of it. 'It was all an act. Letting me think how useful I was to her. How great I was in a crisis.'

'You *were* great in a crisis,' Judy assured him. 'You were brilliant, Dad.'

Mick rubbed his eyes roughly. 'I know you all think I was a desperate eejit. Imagine getting all puffed up just because some young one tells me how brilliant I am because I can change a light bulb. But sometimes it's very hard not to feel like the fall guy around here. The retired old codger in the living room with the bad back, no use to anybody. The funny thing is that I don't feel old at all inside. I only feel about twenty-four.'

A gust of wind brought more ash in and it settled over them like a blanket.

'Did you talk to your mother?' he asked. 'Because she's not answering her mobile phone to me.'

'She probably just needs to let off a bit of steam.'

Mick didn't look cheered. 'Can you stay for a while?'

'Of course I can,' said Judy. But she couldn't help thinking rather longingly of her own house, and Lenny, whom she had left in the kitchen. They hadn't had a chance to say much to each other, not with Biffo there, running around half naked and looking for something to put on so that he could hitch a lift over with Judy to assess the damage. They had simply exchanged a very long, rather warm glance, and Judy had said, 'See you later.'

She had a knot of anticipation in her stomach. And apprehension too. They couldn't just ignore what had happened on the beach. They would have to acknowledge that it was either a mistake or else something they wanted to pursue.

The kitchen door — or rather, what was left of it — creaked open and in walked Biffo. He had been upstairs to see what mark Cheryl had left up there.

'Why does everybody keep looking at me like that?' he complained. 'You'd think all this was my fault!'

But there was an air of excitement about him. A woman had actually burnt a house down for him! Well, inadvertently. And only a bit of the kitchen. Still, it was more than most men could claim. He'd never admit it of course, but Judy just knew that, in his head, he had suddenly acquired a glamour that he had never previously enjoyed. And probably never would again.

321

'You were the one who kept saying how well Cheryl was taking it all,' Judy pointed out.

'How was I to know that she'd turn into a lunatic?' Biffo yelped.

As if Cheryl were still there, a bit of wood from the roof broke off and landed with a mighty hiss on the floor at their feet.

'Jesus,' Biffo breathed, slightly awed at the scale of the destruction. 'Imagine, I've been living with Cheryl nearly a year, and she's never done anything like this before.' It was all to do with her passion for him, in other words. He was even standing a bit taller. 'Obviously the thought of us not being together was too much for her.' And he looked off into the middle distance like an International Man Of Mystery.

Mick said, 'We'll have to get a quote straightaway from a builder.'

'I suppose.' Biffo was only mildly interested.

'We'll have to get it rebuilt right away, we can't live like this.' He said to Biffo, 'I can pay the deposit if you've no ready cash here.'

Biffo paid attention now. 'Sorry?'

'You can pay me back when you get home to America.'

The situation was suddenly looking a lot less glamorous. 'Me? Pay for this?'

'Well, she was your girlfriend. You hardly expect us to.'

'But I already have to pay for the damage to the car!'

'The kitchen will be at least fifty on top of that,' Mick advised.

Biffo's brow worked furiously for a moment.

'I'll have to get a bank loan,' he said at last.

'That's a good idea, son.'

'I'm going to sue her for damages,' he vowed now. 'When I get back to America. I'll take her to court and make her pay for the car and the kitchen!'

'Don't forget your clothes and personal effects,' Mick chipped in, rather maliciously. 'And the back garden. The whole thing will have to be relaid.'

Biffo was nodding furiously. 'I'll get her for the whole lot! And I'll throw in mental anguish too!'

'Add my name to that petition,' Mick ordered.

Judy had a sudden and terrible desire to laugh. The whole thing had the air of a reality TV show — When Good Girlfriends Go Bad, or something like that. Half the audience would be stunned and horrified by the antics, while the other half would be screaming, 'You go, girl!' and clapping with glee.

Judy had no interest in property damage as a form of revenge. But her reaction to Barry's departure seemed very tame in comparison. Would she have felt better had she vented her anger in some way? Built a bonfire out the back and burnt all his things? Or cut all his clothes into squares and posted them to him . . . where?

That was the problem: how to damage someone when you can't actually find them, and they refuse to check in to see what havoc you might have wreaked? At least Cheryl hadn't been left in helpless fury.

There was a noise behind them. They turned to see Rose slowly picking her way across the charred ruins of her kitchen, the car keys dangling from her hand.

Her face was white.

Mick turned to go to her. 'Rose,' he began.

She held up her hand, as if to ward him off. She looked around slowly. Her lip quivered. 'My kitchen. It's destroyed. The whole thing.'

She burst into tears: her kitchen, the hub of family life, gone up in smoke. It was where she had reared her children, and gone on her many diets, and sat in to watch the portable television at nights to get away from Mick. Without her kitchen, she was adrift, lost.

'What happened?' she said.

Nobody answered immediately.

Eventually it was Mick who said, 'Cheryl.'

'Cheryl,' Rose repeated, as if she had expected nothing less, as if Cheryl had become the bane of her life.

'It'll be all right,' Mick said.

Rose flung a hand in his direction dismissively and cried harder. 'Look at it! It's ruined. How can it be all right?'

'Because I'll make it all right,' Mick told her. 'I have contacts, friends in the business. I'll get them around here in the morning and we'll rebuild it, OK?'

'This is not like fixing a U-bend in a toilet,' she told him dully.

Mick took some umbrage at that. 'Look, if you don't mind me saying so, I know what I'm talking about here, so why don't you leave this one to me, OK? I'll sort the whole thing out.'

And he pulled up a charred kitchen chair, and

put his coat down on it to protect her skirt from the ash.

'Do you want to sit down?' he asked.

She eventually sat.

★　★　★

Judy drove home to her own house an hour later. She left Rose and Mick silently eating chips and burgers from the local chipper, sitting on the burnt kitchen chairs. Biffo had elected to say behind. He had discovered that Cheryl had thrown his wallet on the bonfire too, and he was holding dollar bills over the sink trying to wash the charred bits off.

It would be just her and Lenny tonight in the house. Her heart was jumping violently around her chest as she drove fast down the road. She had no idea what would happen next. Would there be a follow-up? Did she *want* a follow-up? If she did, and if there was, how would she feel about it in the morning?

And what did it mean for her and Barry?

She took her foot off the accelerator.

She needed to think about this before she rushed in and did something stupid, like have wild sex with a man she desperately fancied. But that was all it would be. There wouldn't be any tomorrows with Lenny. Was she OK with that?

On the other hand, there had been a lifetime of tomorrows promised from Barry, and in the end he hadn't delivered on a single one.

Oh, just go for it, one part of her brain urged. It'll only end in disaster, another, more rational part, said back.

She decided she would read the signals. Lenny was bound to have some feelings on the matter. He might very well be waiting for her at the door, naked under the bunny bathrobe, and with a rose clenched between his teeth. And a bottle of champagne cooling on ice.

She put her foot down on the accelerator again.

By the time she reached home, she had popped the top two buttons on her blouse and sprayed the contents of a travel bottle of perfume down her front.

Lenny was not waiting at the front door.

'I'm home!' she said.

She found him in the kitchen.

'Hello,' he said. Very neutrally for one who had kissed her so passionately on the beach a matter of hours ago. And felt her bottom. Oh, yes, he needn't think she hadn't noticed that.

She searched his face for some sign that he was barely concealing his lust. But he looked more as if he was suffering a bout of reflux.

'So!' she said. 'Do you, um, want to talk about this afternoon?'

Or, better still, re-enact it.

'I'm not sure this is the right time, Judy.'

What, did they have to schedule it in? Judy felt herself growing a bit cold. Fed up of game-playing, she said, 'I thought you enjoyed it.'

'Well, yes, I did, it was lovely. Listen, Judy — '

'What's the problem?' she asked, her voice rising argumentatively. 'Are you cheesed off that

326

we couldn't have a ride there and then?'

'Judy.' He looked past her.

Judy whirled around to see Mrs Fox standing in the doorway of the living room.

'Mrs Fox . . . ' Her throat felt tight. Had she overheard? And what was she doing with a trowel in her hand? Judy took a step back, just in case she *had* overheard.

But Mrs Fox was the one who looked embarrassed. 'Sorry about, um, last week,' she said rather grudgingly.

'That's OK.' Seeing as nobody else was going to mention the trowel, she thought she would. 'Doing a bit of gardening?'

'Oh. I was just down at the cemetery,' she said, heavily. 'This kind of weather brings the grass up in no time at all. Poor Gerry was practically under a jungle down there.'

Judy was impressed. In the absence of sleeping pills or a handy diagnostician in the shape of Barry, she had obviously decided to do something a little constructive with her time.

'Still, it's a nice evening for it,' Judy told her.

Mrs Fox didn't know whether Judy was pulling her leg. 'If there's ever a nice evening to visit a cemetery,' she said, just in case. 'But, yes. I suppose it was quite peaceful down there.' Then she said, 'Barry rang me this evening.'

Judy's stomach did a little flip. Out of her peripheral vision, she saw Lenny shift.

'What did he want?'

'He just wanted to let me know he was all right. And to check that you got his phone message.'

'I see.'

'He wanted to be sure that you did, Judy.' Mrs Fox seemed at pains to let her know this. 'He asked me to come around just in case. He didn't want you worrying.'

'Our answering machine functions perfectly,' Judy assured her. As Barry well knew. His request seemed a little manufactured. If he was that concerned, why didn't he ring again?

Mrs Fox hesitated. 'He wanted to know how you were, Judy. If you were all right. Were you back to work, had the surgery been on to you, that kind of thing.'

His concern for her was coming a little late in the day. But there was something precise about the questions. There was none of the detachment of his previous phone message. But she was probably reading too much into it. He would ask his mother questions that he wouldn't ask her. And he wasn't a monster. Of course he would want to how she was, and how the surgery was doing.

'I hope you told him everything was fine.'

'Oh, yes. I said to him that you were coping. That you were being very strong.'

Mrs Fox had probably told him that she was as tough as nails. After all, Mrs Fox had accused her of as much during the tussle over the prescription pad.

Judy didn't care. It wasn't strictly necessary to be sure that Barry be given a truthful account of her coping skills. Or any account at all.

'If he rings you again to find out how I am, maybe you'd tell him it's none of his business,' she told Mrs Fox. She'd rather have said something much ruder, but was conscious of Mrs Fox's delicate constitution.

Mrs Fox looked at Lenny, then back to Judy. 'Yes,' she said. 'I understand how you might feel that way, Judy.'

'Good.'

'But he did sound very concerned. And rather ashamed of himself.'

It smacked of groundwork-laying.

'So he should,' Judy said.

Mrs Fox lingered a moment. There was clay under her fingernails and a grass stain on her trousers. 'Anyway. I just wanted to let you know.'

'Thanks, Mrs Fox.'

'I'll let you get back to whatever you were doing,' she said, looking at Judy, and then at Lenny again.

Judy flushed guiltily. But Mrs Fox just nodded pleasantly and set off for the door.

Outside, she went quickly down the steps, surprisingly agile for someone who last year had sworn she needed a hip replacement.

'Mrs Fox? Did he . . . give any indication of whether he might be coming back or not?'

She hoped it didn't sound desperate, or needy. She was very aware of Lenny behind her, hearing everything. But she just wanted to know.

'No. Sorry, Judy. He didn't.'

She stood on the steps outside for a moment after Mrs Fox had gone. She wanted a few moments to collect her thoughts, to digest this latest piece of news.

Barry had been making inquiries about her.

He had sent his mother around to intercede on his behalf. He wanted to be sure that she knew that he was thinking about her; that he was concerned that she was OK.

For the first time since this whole thing started, he sounded like the old Barry. Considerate and kind and caring, and horrified that he would knowingly hurt someone.

Which he had. She didn't want to forget that.

Then she turned and went back in, to Lenny.

He was still in the kitchen, his hands dug into his pockets. 'How was the house?' he asked, very neutrally.

'Pretty awful. But Dad's getting the builders in straightaway.'

'Good, good. And Rose?'

'She's upset, obviously, but otherwise all right.'

'At least nobody was hurt,' he said.

When the polite inquires and platitudes dried up, the atmosphere was like lead. It was hard to believe that they had been locked in each other's arms on the beach earlier that day.

'It's good to hear from Barry anyway,' he said eventually.

She didn't know how to take that. 'I suppose,' she said. 'Listen, maybe we should talk.'

'Talk?' he said. 'Oh, I don't think there's anything to talk about, do you?'

Then he picked up his sunglasses off the counter, and his wallet and he made for the door. 'I'm going out.'

Judy was very taken aback. The way he looked at her, so cool and detached, you would think she had done something terrible to him.

But then she felt strange, too. After Mrs Fox's little news bulletin, it was like Barry was back in the room with them.

'I'll probably be late back,' he said, 'so don't wait up.'

25

Angie and Nick had split up on safari.

'He kept complaining about the food and the heat and the smell, and in the end I just walked off and left him by a crocodile-ridden river. I haven't seen him since.'

'Oh, Angie.'

But Angie didn't want any sympathy. 'We weren't right for each other, Judy. I knew that the night we drove to the airport.'

The same night she'd had the showdown with Biffo.

'Anyway,' she said efficiently. 'These are for Biffo.'

She dumped a collection of plastic bags on the kitchen floor. Judy peered in, wondering whether Angie had brought him back some souvenirs from safari or something.

But the bags were full of clothes and shoes, and not miniature plastic elephants.

'It's just some stuff he left behind at my place last year. Judging from what you're saying, he might need them.'

Biffo's woes had worsened as he had sifted through the remains of the bonfire and Cheryl's thoroughness became increasingly evident. Along with every item of footwear and clothing (including what was in the laundry bin), she had incinerated his electric shaver, his supply of disposable contact lenses, his coffee mug with the word 'Geoffrey' printed on it, and his entire collection of WW2 model airplanes that he had spent several years of his youth collecting and building, and which he had packed away carefully in the attic to pass on to his son, if he ever managed to persuade a woman to have one with him.

She had also burned his passport. The Passport Office were very sceptical of his story of a vengeful girlfriend and a large bonfire, and he'd had to delay his flight back to Orlando by several days while they took their time about issuing a new one.

Angie nodded at the plastic bags. 'Most of the stuff in there is too big for him — he used to be a forty-four inch waist, do you remember? — but maybe he could use a belt or a bit of string or something.'

'Thanks, Angie. I'll tell him that.'

Angie made a great show of hunting in her bag for her cigarettes. 'Was he burned? In the fire?'

'No, no.' She didn't want to say that he hadn't been anywhere near the fire, but instead sleeping off a hangover in her spare bed. If he was going to win Angie back, then he needed all the brownie points he could get.

'What about smoke inhalation? That can be serious.'

'He's absolutely fine, Angie.'

Apart from the fact that he was wandering around in a pair of Mick's corduroy trousers, and as blind as a bat without his contact lenses. Specsavers wouldn't accept an American cheque.

Angie swiftly lowered her eyes, but Judy could

333

see she was relieved. 'Good, good,' she said, efficiently. 'Well, that's all really.'

And she stood up to go.

'Angie, wait.'

'What?'

'Is that it? There's no message for him or anything?'

'No.'

It looked like Biffo was going to have to work a little harder at winning Angie back than he'd thought.

'Now that Biffo's broken up with Cheryl and you've broken up with Nick, is there no chance you two could work things out?'

Angie gave a short laugh. 'Me and Biffo? Get back together? You must be joking.'

'But I thought you'd cleared the air last week.'

'What we did last week was establish the fact that Biffo couldn't handle my job. That he is a man who is fundamentally threatened by women who are cleverer than him, and that his way of dealing with it is to throw tantrums and sulks and make the woman feel that she's brought it all on herself by being so bloody successful.'

Judy deflated somewhat. 'Well, yes . . . '

'Men like Biffo Brady probably account for the single biggest reason why women don't do as well as men in the workplace, Judy. We're all so terrified of offending them that, unconsciously or otherwise, we downplay our own abilities to the point where we're constantly watching our step just to be sure that we haven't done too well for ourselves!'

'I can see your point — '

'He should be on some kind of Most Wanted list in the Women's Institute, as the kind of pathetic and malevolent man that any woman should run a mile from if she wants to achieve her true potential. He's nothing short of poison!'

The air was scorching by the time she was finished.

'No message then,' Judy concluded.

Angie let out her breath in a little rush. 'I feel better now. I've been wanting to get that off my chest since last week, and I would have except that I was on safari.'

'Why don't you get it off your chest right now?' Judy encouraged. 'Take those plastic bags around to the house and give him an earful.'

Despite Angie's understandable anger, Judy felt that all was not lost yet. That if they could get over the job stuff, the two of them had something very special that shouldn't be thrown away.

'Judy, I appreciate what you're trying to do here. But there isn't any solution. Except if I give up my job, which I most certainly am not going to do. He's obviously a man who just can't stand playing second fiddle.'

'You could at least talk to him,' Judy begged. She didn't want to reveal that Biffo had a plan. 'Maybe there's some way you could work things out.'

'Accommodate his ego, you mean. Because that's what it would be, Judy. It certainly wouldn't be him saying that he was happy for me to take the role of breadwinner, would it?'

Judy could find no answer to that, because

Angie was right. Biffo's plan involved no such humbleness, but rather him squaring up to Angie in the financial stakes.

'You know, I'm fed up of men with hidden resentments and masked jealousies, pretending that everything is fine when really they're seething every time you take out your purse. Next time I'm going to find a proper, grown-up man who's able to accept the fact that I earn more than him, and be proud of it.'

And she made purposefully for the door, with Judy flapping after her, making useless comments such as, 'At least *try* and work it out . . . ' and, 'People change, you know,' until in the end she realised she was talking to a brick wall. Or rather the door, which Angie was closing in her face.

'Tell him goodbye from me,' she called back.

Then, from behind Judy, 'Hold the door.'

It was Lenny, in another change of clothes, and reeking of aftershave. He stepped out smartly after Angie.

He said to Judy, 'I'm going down the town. Don't wait up.'

★   ★   ★

Ber's house had never looked so good, she said. Every surface sparkled, and you could actually see the picture on the TV screen. She now had her own pair of rubber gloves in the kitchen, yellow ones with pink daisies on them. Before moving in together, the only rubber present in the relationship had been those saucy PVC

336

knickers that Vinnie had once given her for her birthday.

'I'm just taking it one day at a time,' she told Judy gloomily. 'I'm not aiming for Housewife of the Year or anything like that.'

The bright side of all this new domesticity was that Vinnie cooked dinner Monday to Friday. He had surprised everyone by being a marvellous cook and she had put on half a stone on his fondues and curries and strudels. He didn't mind a bit, and would console her with a leisurely foot massage and loofah.

Ber looked off wistfully into the middle distance. 'Neither of us usually feels like sex after that.'

They were sitting in Judy's kitchen. Lenny was still in bed. He had come home at 4 a.m. Judy had been in bed since ten the night before, with earplugs in, the radio on low, and a pillow over her ears for good measure, and yet she had still heard the blasted front door opening. She had heard his footsteps pass by her bedroom door and go into his own room, rather unsteadily she thought. At least there had been no accompanying totter of high heels.

She was turning nasty, she decided. And she had been such a pleasant, inoffensive person too, before Lenny had come into her life. They were, she decided, very bad for each other, and the sooner he left her house the better.

'But Ber, I thought you wanted security. Don't forget all those years you spent as the mistress — the uncertainly of it, the misery of not knowing whether he would *ever* leave his wife.'

'Stop,' Ber cried, 'before I get too nostalgic.'

'Don't tell me you want that back?'

'Well, no, on balance I suppose not.' She crooked an eyebrow at Judy. 'But it's a bit like Christmas: the anticipation is often more exciting than the actual thing itself.'

'I suppose it's about finding the balance.'

'You mean compromise again,' Ber moaned.

'Well, yes. And I have to say, I think Vinnie's going about the whole thing very well.'

He had cheerfully got rid of his Status Quo collection and did his nail-clipping behind closed doors. For someone who had presented himself as completely unreliable and feckless, he had turned out to be a model partner and housemate.

'Now he wants to get a dog,' Ber told Judy fearfully.

'What's so wrong with a dog?'

'Oh, Judy, can't you see? We've moved in together, and now he wants us to have a baby — only not a real one, obviously. A cocker spaniel pup instead. We'll be having even less sex than ever, because one of us will have to get up and walk the flipping dog at the crack of dawn.'

'Oh, Ber, it's not as bad as all that.'

But Ber was very glum indeed. 'We're on a slide, Judy, and I just don't know where it's all going to end.'

Lenny came in, up from bed at last, and wearing the bunny bathrobe. Honestly, there wasn't a man on this earth who enjoyed flaunting himself in front of women more than him.

'Morning,' he said, breezily.

'Hi!' Ber perked up, predictably.

Judy didn't bother replying. Instead she gave a pointed look at the clock: two o'clock in the afternoon.

'Late night last night?' she said, sweetly. As though she hadn't known the exact moment he'd walked through the door.

'Very,' he said back, just as sweetly. 'Is there any coffee?'

'No,' said Judy ungraciously. 'You'll have to make some. Or is that too much like hard work?'

It was a dig. She had worked out that she was too troublesome for him to bother with, hence his flight to the pub that night at the first sign of an obstacle in his mission to get her into bed. He obviously preferred women with less baggage, and preferably no fiancés popping out of the woodwork to spoil his romantic endeavours with phone calls from France. When there were so many other, less vexing women out there, why bother with her?

He gave her a rather unpleasant look back. He poured a glass of juice instead and declared, 'I'm going back to bed.'

Off he went, in a strop.

'My God.' Ber had been watching the whole thing round-eyed, and with her chin nearly on her knees. 'You two are sleeping together.'

'*What?*' Judy jumped guiltily, even though she had absolutely nothing to be guilty about. Well, not much.

Ber wagged a finger. 'Don't try and protest! I know vibes when I feel them, and believe me, those were some vibes.'

'Ber, how on earth did you manage to work that one out? We just had a row.'

'Yes, but it was to cover up the fact that you're sleeping together. And that wasn't a row. That was foreplay.'

The very word was enough to set Judy's thighs twitching nervously. 'We are not sleeping together!' Best not to mention how they had tried to do just that but that it had backfired.

'Nobody could blame you, you know,' Ber assured her. 'In fact, personally, I think a good ride is exactly what you need.'

'I'm sure no psychiatrist would agree with you.'

Ber was undeterred. 'You need a bit of fun after the whole Barry thing. It's nothing to be ashamed of, you know. And Lenny is absolutely gorgeous.'

'Two weeks ago you thought he was the biggest gouger this side of the M50. That even when he was a teenager he was never happy unless he had two girlfriends on the go!'

'I was thinking about that afterwards, and actually I was wrong. He only ever used to go out with one at a time. But he did change them pretty regularly.' She gave Judy a serious look from under her brow. 'In fact, very regularly.'

Judy wanted to laugh. Ber was warning her.

'I'm sure he still does,' she said. 'And then they go the way of Charmaine.'

Ber's face cleared. 'Oh, I'm so glad you realise all this, Judy.'

'That Lenny would just be a rebound fling?'

'Exactly. But a damn good one, Judy. Many of us have had to make do with shop assistants and waiters. If I could choose one man on this earth to have a rebound fling with, it would be Lenny. In fact, some women would *break up* with their men just to have a rebound fling with him.'

'Ber, I hate to spoil your little fantasy, but Lenny and I are not sleeping together,' Judy said firmly. Nor were they likely to be.

'What's he still hanging around here for then?' Ber demanded.

'I have no idea. My mother put him up to it, but I think she's got too much on her plate now to put any more pressure on him.'

'No, I'd say he's definitely got a thing for you, Judy.'

'Ber, stop it.'

'Sorry. It's just that between you and Lenny, and Biffo and the Lawnmower Girl, I just don't feel I have any excitement in my own life.'

'Lenny and I are too different,' Judy announced. 'He's not the type who's good for women with broken hearts, Ber.'

Right now she believed it. And, upon reflection, she didn't think she was made of the stuff necessary for one-night stands either. Lenny was right: she wasn't casual enough, laid-back enough. She couldn't kiss somebody as if it mattered and then go off to the pub.

'I think Barry wants to come back.' She surprised herself as much as Ber; where had that come from?

'What?'

'Well, he hasn't said anything,' Judy conceded.

'But I think he might be considering it.'

'Oh, Judy. What would you do? If he did?'

Judy had no idea. Except that right now she had an overwhelming urge for her life to return to normal.

But there was no 'normal' any more. It was pointless to be wishing it back. Yet, sitting there in the kitchen she could almost feel Barry in the house again. For a moment she imagined he had been in the bedroom all this time, and he would shout out any minute, 'Judy, have you seen my blue shirt?' and none of this would have happened.

26

Cheryl had one final sting in her tail. Biffo only found out by sheer chance; he could have been all the way over in a Florida airport before he'd discovered her last act of retribution, as he said to anybody who would listen. But as it happened the Passport Office were very late sending back a new passport and his visa had run out, and he'd had to make a trip out to the American Embassy in Ballsbridge to get them to reissue it.

They wouldn't. They told him, very pleasantly, that there were problems with his application.

'What problems?' Biffo had demanded.

The problems appeared to be on a computer screen in front of them, but no matter how much he craned his neck he wasn't able to read what exactly was wrong with him. They didn't appear to be under any obligation to explain it to him either. If indeed there was any one specific thing — they gave him the distinct impression that it was pretty much everything about him that was undesirable.

'This is ridiculous!' he had thundered. 'I have a job out there! An apartment. I pay my taxes, and my refuse charges. I have Medicaid!'

But no amount of health insurance was going to get him back into the country. And by then he had worked out that Cheryl was behind it; or, rather, her father in Washington. He quickly deduced that he would be unlikely to get back into the country at any time in the coming year. Or the next. She'd probably have him barred for life.

'I'm going to sue her for this too! For denying me my rights as a legal alien in America!' he ranted to Judy when she called over that afternoon to see how progress on the rebuilding of the kitchen was coming along. Plastic sheeting cut off the kitchen and back garden from view, but there were fifteen jeeps and vans parked in the drive, and the noise of hammering was deafening.

'Surely there must be something you can do?' she shouted over the din, even though she had no idea in the wide earthly world what. How did you go about proving that your bitter ex had recruited her politician dad to subversively tinker in the immigration department to keep his daughter happy? It would sound just a tad implausible. But then so did the notion of Cheryl riding around the Bradys' back garden on a lawnmower, drunkenly singing 'We Shall Overcome.'

'She's probably got contacts in the FBI, too. And the CIA. Even if I did manage to get back in, she'd have me followed and arrested on some trumped-up charge, and sent to a high-security prison,' he finished up, somewhat hysterically.

The honeymoon period of him being the subject of a semi-obsessed woman was well and truly over.

Personally, Judy would have thought it quite an impressive coup de grâce on Cheryl's part had it not been played out on Biffo.

'I suppose no woman likes to be told that she was never even a contender,' she advised Biffo.

'So, what, I brought it all upon myself?'

'No, but maybe you need to do some serious revision on the way you break up with women, Biffo.'

'You make it sound like I'm a serial monogamist.' He looked very bitter. Then he said sombrely, 'By the way, you know that this is the end of the time-share I was going to give you in Orlando?'

'I can live with it,' Judy said bravely. 'So what are you going to do now? Stay in Ireland?'

'I don't see that I've any choice.'

'Maybe you could get your old job back.'

'Driving around in a shitty white van putting up signs? You must be joking. Anyway, I have a few weeks yet. Mum and Dad said I can stay on here until they demolish my bedroom.'

'They're demolishing your bedroom?' Judy was mystified.

'Have you not seen the plans yet? You're in for a treat.'

At that moment three burly builders squeezed down the stairs past Biffo, wearing hard hats and yellow reflective jackets over skimpy little vests.

'Don't turn on the shower unless you want to be electrocuted,' one of them advised Biffo kindly.

There was no danger of that. Biffo hadn't been anywhere near water in several days judging by the look of him.

One of the builders winked at Judy. She had been in a relationship for so long that she didn't

345

immediately know how to respond. In the end, she winked back. The builder looked a bit taken aback and hurried on out the front door.

'Well, if you need some cash or anything, or some company in the pub . . . ' Judy offered Biffo.

'Thanks, Judy.' His mouth twisted. 'You know what this means for me and Angie, don't you?'

She had been wondering when he was going to bring her up. She certainly wasn't, not after Angie's diatribe the other day.

'Well . . . '

'How can I ask her to take me back when I've no job now, or car, or even a decent pair of shoes?' He was wearing flip-flops under his corduroy trousers. 'Talk about irony! I'm worse off than I was a year ago. Even more pathetic compared to her. She'd laugh her head off.'

'I don't think Angie's finding much to laugh about right now.'

'I wouldn't give her the satisfaction,' Biffo said grimly.

'Oh, Biffo, stop all this one-upmanship. Why don't you just go over there and talk to her honestly. Tell her you still love her. The fact that you've no job doesn't matter a damn.'

But Biffo just shook his head stubbornly. 'I just need a few weeks to get on my feet, that's all. I'll draw out some money from my US bank accounts, and get some references, and set myself up here properly. With my foreign sales experience, I'll walk into a job here no problem. In fact, I'll drive around tomorrow in the car with my CV.' Slowly the realities of the situation began to sink in. 'If I had a car. Or a CV.' Then, with a whimper, 'Or even a reference.'

'She can't stop you getting a reference,' Judy said strongly.

'She'd be the one writing it.' His voice began to rise again, but he got a hold of himself. 'I'll work something out. Then, when I'm on the up again, when I'm Angie's equal, I'll go and see her.'

'Biffo, Angie doesn't care about you being her equal. Just that you accept her success.'

'Fine. I have no problem doing that.' He added, 'Just so long as I'm successful too, that's all.'

He set off up the stairs in his flip-flops. 'By the way, if you've left anything in my room I'd get it now if I were you.'

'What are they doing to your room anyway?' There hadn't even been any smoke damage.

'Did Mum not tell you? It's being turned into a bar.'

★　★　★

'Mind that pipe, for fuck's sake, it's only just been put in!' That was Mick, hollering at a builder who was traipsing across the lawn swinging a shovel haphazardly.

'If he keeps that up, they're going to kill him,' Rose murmured.

They were sitting on two deckchairs in the back garden drinking tea and watching the circus. Mick appeared to have taken on the role of foreman, which, along with completely pissing off the *real* foreman, gave him the excuse to impart his priceless advice to the hapless builders.

'To the left a bit,' he instructed nobody in particular, whilst hitching up his pants.

'Builder's bum,' Rose told Judy. 'At his age. Thank God the black dye has nearly washed out.'

Mick's hair was back to its normal grey. But if anything the dye had only aged him. Today as he strutted back and forth, Judy could scarcely credit that he was the same man as the pale, tired-looking version who had sat in his burnt-out house only last week.

When he had told Rose he would fix it, he had meant it. Whatever miracles it had taken, he had got an architect on site within twentyfour hours, and had then proceeded to poach a team of builders from Mr Brennan's extension up the road. Mr Brennan would never speak to him again, but that was of secondary importance to getting a roof over Rose's head.

'They're mostly from the country,' Rose informed Judy, eyeing the builders. 'They come up on the bus on a Monday morning and go home on a Friday evening. And none of them drink tea at all, even though I got in five hundred tea bags and a catering tin of fig rolls. But they won't touch anything, only bottles of mineral water.'

They all seemed very familiar with Rose, and nodded respectfully to her as they passed by carrying pipes and bags of cement and several square white filters.

'What are those for?' Judy inquired.

'The swimming pool,' Rose said.

Judy laughed. Then she realised that Rose was deadly serious.

'You're having a swimming pool?'

Rose shrugged. 'It was Mick's idea. He says it's a marvellous way of exercising. A couple of laps every morning and I'll never have to diet again. We're putting it over there, right about where Cheryl lit the bonfire.'

Judy couldn't believe it. People in Ireland didn't have swimming pools. Wasn't the whole country wet enough without bringing in more water? Not to mention the cold. And the wind, and rain, all of which lasted about eleven months of the year.

'What will you do in the winter?' she asked.

'Mick says we'll just cover it over and hit the bar.'

Judy had thought Biffo was winding her up about that. 'As in, a bar that serves drink?'

'That's right. Dallas-style, Mick says, with high stools and everything to sit up on.' She didn't sound particularly excited or grateful. 'All I wanted was a flat-pack kitchen from Furniture Direct.'

That wasn't true. She was always moaning about how pokey and old fashioned the house was. And Mick was always putting her off by telling her how hideously expensive it would be to renovate. And now not only was she getting a brand new swanky kitchen, but also a swimming pool and a bar on top of it all.

Her mouth was set in a thin line now. But the

dust had scarcely settled on the whole thing, of course.

'Has there been any news on suing Cheryl?' Judy asked.

'Oh, we decided to drop all that.'

'What?'

The last Judy had heard they were going to hire an American lawyer with Biffo and split the costs.

'We talked about it, and we decided that it would be a lot of hassle and mental stress, and that we probably wouldn't get anything out of her anyway.' She shrugged. 'So we're just going to get on with the rebuilding, and when we have a new kitchen we'll all be as happy as bloody Larry.'

She placed her cup back into her saucer with a sharp crack.

'Sorry,' she said. 'Oh look, we're fine, Judy. It was just one of those stupid things, wasn't it? She's gone now and that's the end of it.'

She turned to look out at the builders again rather joylessly.

Judy was trying to suppress a yawn. Lenny had been out on the town every night that week. Despite an extra pair of earplugs, and the radio on loud, Judy had heard him come home every single night. Sometimes it was two o'clock, sometimes four. She had bags under her eyes that you could camp out in, and had mislaid most of the crime section on the computer in work that afternoon.

'No word from Barry since?' Rose asked suddenly.

Judy jumped. 'No.'

'Perhaps it's best. There's no sense in taking off like that unless he's going to do some serious thinking. You might be surprised at the change in him.'

Judy hadn't really thought about that before, that Barry might have changed. But she supposed he must have, after such a dramatic flight in search of himself. Would all the torture he had gone through (presumably there had been a bit, along with strip clubs and expensive lunches out) show on his face? After his initial splurge on the credit card, was he now in the French countryside somewhere, deep in his own thoughts and subsisting on a simple diet of baguettes and cheese? Perhaps he would occasionally look up from his navel-gazing to ponder the sunset and think of her, and what a horrible mistake he had made. His voice might even have got deeper. More serious or something. 'Judy,' he would say, in gravelly tones, when he finally came home, '*Excusez moi.*'

But no, that was too lightweight for the enormity of his crimes. He had run off on a woman, after all, not merely burped. It would have to be, '*Pardonez moi.*' Said whilst on his knees, grovelling. That wouldn't do it either. It would take a great deal more than just saying sorry for her to take him back.

In fact, substantial change on his part would be completely necessary, she decided. He would have to have grown up a bit. Taken responsibility not just for his actions but also for the relationship. He had been content for too long to

351

sit back and let her run the show. In France he would have to fend for himself; no Judy there to find his shirts or organise a hotel room or generally take charge. It would be interesting to see how he coped, she thought.

It was the first time she'd consciously wanted to see him again since he'd disappeared.

She wondered what that meant.

Mick came over. He said to Rose, 'I got them to put lagging down on those pipes like you wanted.'

He waited anxiously for her reaction, wanting her to be pleased.

'Thank you,' she said, and duly managed a smile.

'And the window guys want to know do we want sliding or French doors for the patio.'

'You decide.'

It was all very polite.

'You're the one who's going to be opening them more than me,' he pointed out.

'It's a door, Mick. So long as it opens that's all I care.'

'Right,' he said, after a moment. 'I'll tell them that.'

27

When Judy got back to the house, she found Lenny packing. He had piles of things laid out on the bed and was efficiently placing them into a suitcase pile by pile.

She stood there for a minute, watching him. 'Are you going to visit relatives again?'

He didn't interrupt his packing for her. 'No. I'm going home to Australia.'

'Oh.' It felt like a kick in the teeth. Which was ridiculous. Of course he would be going home. He lived in Australia. What had she thought, that he would stay in her house for ever and ever, like some kind of lodger? Who might snog her every now and again?

'I tried earlier in the week to bring my flight forward but I couldn't,' he said.

Another kick in the teeth. He would have been gone already had the airlines facilitated it. He obviously couldn't wait to get out of her house.

'I see,' she said, giving him an inane smile. It seemed very important to be as efficient as him. 'Right, well, enjoy your trip!'

He threw her a look. 'I'm not going right now this second.'

'Oh.'

'I fly out tomorrow afternoon.'

'Lovely,' she said.

But that only seemed to annoy him because he

threw at her, 'Then I'll be out of your hair for good.'

Well, she wasn't going to take that. Not after putting up with his shenanigans all week. 'To be honest, I've hardly noticed you've been here.'

'I'm sure you haven't,' he agreed. 'I'm sure you've been too busy planning for Barry's imminent return.'

Judy's jaw dropped. 'What?'

'Oh, come on, Judy. I never saw anybody snap to attention so fast as the night Mrs Fox told you Barry was asking after you.' He gave a rather grim smile, as though the whole thing amused him.

Judy was so angry that she could barely speak. 'And I never saw somebody run to the pub so fast either!'

Lenny shrugged. 'I wasn't going to hang around while you drew up huge lists of things to do. Let me see — air the beds, put on a wash, stock up the freezer with his favourite meals.' His tone was condescending, insulting.

'You have no idea what you're talking about.'

'Haven't I? Face it, Judy. You'd take him back like a shot, for all your talk. And, indeed, your actions.'

Her face exploded with colour. 'What does it matter to you what I would do if Barry were to come back?'

'It doesn't.' He lifted a shoulder again. 'But it's a bit of a passion killer when the woman you're with would dump you like a hot brick if Mr Reliable came back on the scene.' He added

354

under his breath, 'Not that he's proven himself all that reliable.'

In between the swirls of angry mist in Judy's head, she realised he sounded rather jealous.

'You know, I always thought I was pretty worldly wise,' Lenny told her. 'But to think that I've let myself be insulted not once, but twice, by you . . . ' He shook his head very grimly. 'The international models have nothing on you, Judy.'

'I have never insulted you!' Judy protested strongly. 'At least, not intentionally.'

'Really?' he said. 'You just walk all over people's feelings by complete accident?'

He had never mentioned feelings before. Judy peered at him suspiciously, wondering had he been drinking. But he seemed sober, and rather hurt.

'What about *my* feelings?' she retaliated. 'You went out to the pub every night this week! Just because things didn't go according to your usual seduction plan. What's the matter with you, can you not accept a challenge?'

'A challenge!' He hooted derisively. 'You mean, would I fancy having my self-confidence dashed just a little more?'

Judy looked at him incredulously. 'I'm very sorry I can't completely block Barry from my mind the second you walk into the room.'

'It's not about that, Judy.'

'But it is. You just said it.'

'I'm not asking you to ditch Barry or anything like that, OK?'

'Good,' she said. 'Because you're going back to Australia tomorrow and you really don't have any right to ask me for anything.'

He threw a few more things into the suitcase. You would think she was some kind of she-devil he couldn't wait to get away from.

'Fine,' he told her. 'I'm delighted to be going, to tell you the truth. I'm sure you won't be long finding someone else to amuse you.'

Judy's jaw dropped altogether now. 'I was never amusing myself with you!'

'Oh, come on, Judy.'

'If anything, it was the other way around!'

'You, amusing me?' he said. 'Have you heard me laughing recently?'

He abandoned the packing altogether at this point. They faced each other across the big bed.

'Well, I'm sorry I've made you so miserable,' Judy said.

'Yes,' he agreed. 'In fact, I don't think I've ever come across a woman who's made me more miserable.'

The sex thing was starting to happen again, Judy just knew. The temperature in the room had gone up by ten degrees in any case. And it was ridiculous, because he was going the next day, and she would probably never see him again, and they should both walk away now.

Lenny wasn't going to. She knew by the look in his eye.

'Judy,' he said softly.

And she knew she wasn't going to either.

★   ★   ★

Judy had never had the kind of sexual experience that she regularly and jealously read about in books and magazines: lights flashing and her skin being on fire, and things exploding in her head and other places. She hadn't really believed in it, sure that it was fabricated to make ordinary folk feel very inadequate as they staggered through their weekly conjugal obligations. And if it wasn't made up, then the people having that kind of sex were weird — hormonally overloaded, and fans of strange books on heightened awareness, and usually had beards, even the women. Or else they were Sting.

But no! Happily such sex did exist. Not only did things explode for Judy that night, but she also figured she must have lost about two pounds' worth of calories in expended energy.

She didn't know whether this sexual bliss was to do with her being newly single and liberated (kind of), or whether it was down to Lenny, who had undoubtedly picked up a few handy tips along the way. Perhaps there was something erotic about making love in her own spare bedroom with a man who had his suitcase already packed at the foot of the bed. Or else it was the usual suspect, chemistry, of which they seemed to have more than their fair share.

Whatever it was, the minute Lenny touched her she was a lost cause. Everything just felt so wonderful and right and full of passion that she knew that this was the way making love should feel.

She had been slightly embarrassed at first by the amount of noise they were generating and she had kept saying, 'Sssh!'

'We're in your house, Judy. Who do you think is going to hear us?'

'I don't know,' she fretted. Mrs Fox, perhaps, even though she lived at the other side of town. But that was just her guilt making her feel that way. And anyway, she had absolutely nothing to feel guilty about. She owed nothing to anybody.

She couldn't have kept quiet anyway, even if she'd tried. Not great big manufactured screams or anything like that, but lots of contented little murmurings and sighs of bliss.

At first she had expected Lenny to be very gimmicky, and was worried that he would start suggesting all kinds of sophisticated things that she wouldn't even understand. Like, 'Let's try a 79.' Or, 'Could you tickle my perineum?' And she herself was so used to Barry that she was terrified she wouldn't know how to have sex with someone else. At any moment would she slip into her usual little routine, and kill every ounce of passion stone dead?

But it all worked perfectly. Better than perfectly. He was surprisingly gentle and thoughtful and slow, although he could whip up quite a bit of surf when he wanted to. There was a moment when Judy had been worried that the bed was listing dangerously to one side. And every time he kissed her it was as though he really meant it.

'Judy,' he said at one point.

'What?'

But then he thought better of it and just kissed her again.

Judy didn't want to think about her own feelings. That would just spoil everything. So she didn't. She just took Lenny's advice and let the moment take over again.

Afterwards she was prepared for some awkwardness. Surely what they had done was like sleeping with the boss at the Christmas party, and she would wake up at any moment with an appalling hangover and her toes curling in shame.

But she didn't. In fact, the whole thing still felt so right that she was happy to just lie there, gloriously naked and slightly damp.

Lenny seemed to be in similar contemplation. Surely if she were any old model he would have been up and dressed and gone by now. Although all his stuff was here, and he would have to finish packing first.

Eventually, he said, 'Judy?'

'Hmmm?'

'My arm's gone dead.'

'Oh! Right. Sorry.'

'No, no, I didn't mean . . . come back. There, that's better.'

They readjusted themselves and settled down again, and Lenny went back to stroking her hair.

But it wasn't the same as before. There was something missing. Judy hunted about for what it was, and then it hit her.

It was the post-sex endearments. The 'I love yous' and the 'your skin is like organic fuzzy peaches' and 'I've never felt like this before'.

Those things weren't going to be said because it wasn't that kind of sex. For Lenny anyway. For

Judy, the lines were a little more blurred. But if she came out with anything remotely intimate he would probably dive straight under the duvet, or run for the bathroom or something.

Besides, there was no point in laying herself open to hurt or, worse, amusement. He might give her a wry smile and say, 'Oh, Judy, I knew you wouldn't be able to just enjoy it for what it was.'

No, if anybody were to stray into emotional territory here, it had to be him. But he didn't.

And no matter how much Judy tried to tell herself to enjoy the moment (she found she was beginning to dislike that phrase), she was starting to feel that awkwardness that she'd been sure wouldn't come.

'Are you OK?' Lenny asked, when she stirred.

'Me? Oh, super duper. Never better!' What could possibly be wrong? She had just had a fantastic night with a great guy. It was nobody's fault that after tomorrow she would probably never lay eyes on him again. She might as well get used to it.

She sat up and reached for her robe.

'Don't do that,' Lenny complained.

'I should probably let you get on with packing,' she said. Miss Practical. Miss Efficient. Nobody could accuse her of getting all weepy and sentimental after sex.

'Wait, Judy.'

Oh, now he wanted to get all smoochy. He sat up too and took her into his arms, robe and all. He held her so tight that she was taken aback.

'I'm going to miss you, Judy,' he said softly.

360

There was a change in the air. Judy felt all light and free. She wasn't expecting him to immediately drop to one knee or anything like that, but she was very glad to know that it had meant something to him. She meant something to him. It wasn't just sex.

'I'm going to miss you too.'

And there was a gorgeous tender moment, and Lenny drew her back down into the bed. He curled himself around her and she felt so warm and happy that when her eyelids began to droop a few minutes later, she let herself drop off to sleep.

28

When she awoke the next morning she wasn't immediately sure of where she was. Then she realised she was in the spare bedroom of her own house, and that Lenny was snoring softly beside her.

It had been a great many years since Judy had woken up beside anybody apart from Barry, and she lay there for a moment wondering exactly what the protocol was.

But while she figured that out, she could at least have a good look at him without being observed. He was a pleasantly tidy sleeper, apart from the snoring. He wasn't dribbling, or splayed out across the bed, or with his face mashed unattractively into the pillow. He slept like people on the telly slept, all composed and sexily rumpled, and not like a rhino in pain.

She would quite like to have touched him, to guiltily fondle him while he was asleep. It wasn't as though there would be a chance again tonight. He was leaving for Australia that afternoon, and however good last night had been, she doubted it was enough to make him change his travel plans.

But she wasn't going to get bogged down in that. She had known what she was getting into; she had no illusions about last night, however much she wanted to.

She needed to go to the loo, but didn't want to wake him up by getting out of bed. Last night may have been all lust and passion, but it was a different story when daylight broke, and it came to walking across a room completely naked, displaying wobbly bits and other imperfections.

She looked at the bedroom door to try to gauge how many steps she would have to take. Maybe she could just bolt and run, and she would be out the door before he opened his eyes.

When she looked back Lenny was awake and looking at her.

'Hi,' he said.

'Oh. Um, hi.'

She had been fine up to now, quite blasé even about the previous night's activities, but suddenly her whole body felt suffused with colour.

Also, it just struck her that she may have failed to shave under her arms yesterday. It hadn't seemed important last night, but it certainly was now, and she rigidly snapped her arms in tight to her chest.

'Are you OK?' he asked.

'Me? Fine! Never better.' She gave him a brilliant smile. 'Starving actually.'

Maybe he would be gentlemanly and get up to pour her a big bowl of cornflakes, and she could get up and put some clothes on, and cover her mortification.

She hadn't, she realised, shaved her legs in a couple of days either. He had said nothing about nasty stubble last night, but he had probably been too kind. This morning they had the feeling of a wire brush. She scuttled away from him in the bed and brought her knees up just for good measure.

He hoisted himself up onto one elbow. 'Judy, what's wrong with you? Because *something* is.'

'All right, if you must know, I'm a bit embarrassed,' she said.

He looked astonished. 'Embarrassed?'

'Well, yes! Look, I know you obviously do this all the time, so it's kind of second nature to you, all this morning routine, but it's not to me and I'm a bit . . . embarrassed.'

'I think you just insulted me again there,' he mused, 'but I'm going to let it pass this time, in the circumstances.'

'Thank you,' she said, then wondered why she was thanking him.

They looked at each other for a moment from opposite sides of the bed. Lenny smiled, and she found herself smiling back.

'Judy,' he said, 'come over here and give me a hug.'

'I can't,' she said apologetically. That would mean unwrapping her arms from her chest, and letting her legs come in contact with his.

But then he hadn't shaved either, she thought. What about a bit of equality in all this?

'Maybe a small one,' she said. Then, in another strike for equality, she said, 'And you can come over here.'

He did, in a flash, and Judy forgot all about her unshaven bits as they wrapped their arms around each other under the warm, dark duvet.

He kissed her. She forgot all about breakfast too.

Then, because it was obviously niggling him, he said, 'Just for the record, I don't do this all the time.'

'You do it fairly often, though.'

'It's never as nice as this though.'

'I bet you say that to all the girls.'

'You think I'm just spinning you a line?'

'Look, relax, Lenny. I'm not looking for anything from you, OK?'

'And what if *I* wanted something from *you*?'

'What?'

'Or would it break the terms and conditions that we've already set?' He was half teasing, but there was something in his eyes that told Judy that he was being very serious indeed.

'I don't know,' she said. She didn't want to blow this one. It was too important. 'I suppose we could go into negotiations.'

'I'm all for negotiations,' Lenny said.

It became clear that they weren't getting up any time soon. After the 'negotiations' there might well be another energetic round of sex.

It all sounded absolutely marvellous, except that Judy still wanted to go to the loo.

'I'll be back in a minute,' she promised. 'Don't watch.'

He lay back on the pillow looking rather pleased with himself as she eased herself out of the bed, completely naked, and sprinted for the door.

'I said don't watch!'

'Why not? It's a great view.'

'Oh shut up.'

'Hurry back,' he said.

In the event, she didn't actually make it back at all. When she stepped out of the bedroom the phone began to ring.

Without thinking she picked it up and said, 'Hello?'

There was a lot of crackle the other end and not much else.

'Hello?' she said again, impatient to get back to Lenny.

Then: 'Judy? It's me.'

'Barry?' She froze. All the times she had expected him to ring, and he had never had. And now here he was, with the worst possible timing in the world.

'Judy, there's been a bit of a . . . ' The line broke up.

'Barry, I can't hear you. The signal is terrible.'

Lenny came out of the bedroom behind her. A few seconds later she heard the bathroom door shut quietly up the hall.

When Barry spoke again, he sounded a bit on edge. 'Judy, I'm in trouble.'

★ ★ ★

Barry was in a police station somewhere in Paris. It was difficult to get the full story, not least because the line went completely dead halfway through the conversation and Judy had no joy trying to persuade directory inquiries to put her through to all the police stations in Paris one by one.

She had thought at first that he must have been mugged, and that the police had kindly

366

taken him in. Possibly he needed some money to get home. And it turned out that he did need money — two thousand euro bail, to be precise. Bail? said Judy. Yes, Barry had mumbled. As soon as possible. And a decent solicitor. Preferably one who spoke English, because they were all talking at him in French, and he didn't understand any of it, but he knew it wasn't complimentary. And there was another detainee clicking his tongue at him right at that moment in a rather alarming way, and he needed to get out, now.

He had sounded bewildered and on the verge of hysteria. 'Please, Judy. I know it's a lot to ask.'

Judy had taken a breath and opened her mouth to let him know exactly how much it was to ask, but she only got out, 'Well!' before the line went dead. Either network coverage had collapsed completely, or the tongue clicker had ambushed Barry.

And she still had no idea what he was being detained in a police station for.

'Drugs,' said Ber, immediately. She liked to think that she knew about these things now from hanging around with Vinnie's teenage sons.

'Don't be ridiculous,' Angie said impatiently, although you could see she was worried. 'It's probably something very simple, Judy. It may even be a misunderstanding.'

Nobody really thought that. But then neither could anybody think of what Barry might do that would be bad enough to land him in a jail cell.

'Kerb crawling,' Ber said, definitively. Whether

she had got this from Vinnie's sons also was unclear.

'You're not really helping here, Ber,' Angie pointed out.

And help was what they had brought over that morning, in the shape of croissants and a smoothie from Ber, and good, solid organisational back-up from Angie. She'd already got Judy a flight, and was now on the telephone to someone else, a cigarette dangling from the side of her mouth.

Judy herself didn't know what to believe. Barry, in trouble with the law? For kerb crawling or drugs? (On reflection, she thought she would prefer the drugs.) Barry in prison, being cursed at in French, and propositioned by other law breakers?

'How much was the bail?' Angie inquired.

'Two thousand.'

'That's too little for a murder charge,' she reassured Judy.

'*Murder*?' said Judy, weak now.

'I wouldn't pay it if I were you, Judy. He got himself into this mess, let him get himself out,' Ber instructed protectively.

'At least you'll have company to the airport with Lenny,' Angie said consolingly.

'Yes,' Judy agreed, hoping to God her face didn't betray the fact that she'd had wild sex with him about fourteen hours ago. That she had scarcely stopped thinking about him since.

He had been so long in the bathroom after Barry's phone call earlier that Judy had begun to worry for his safety. She had paced up and down the living room in her bathrobe, cursing fate, and Barry, and the telephone company. Whatever might have been said between them before Lenny had left, whatever they had been tentatively working towards, all lay in tatters. Ruined by Barry's SOS call. Oh, how she wished she hadn't answered the damned thing.

But she had, and Barry was back in her life just like that. He might as well have plonked himself in the bed between her and Lenny.

When Lenny eventually came out he had said nothing. Not a word about negotiations or them or anything else. He'd had a face like thunder and had gone straight for the bedroom again.

He had only paused long enough at the door to say, 'I suppose you'll be going to France.'

It wasn't a question, it was a judgement.

It made her angry. He had made no commitment whatsoever to her, yet was acting as if he had.

'And I suppose you'll be going to Australia,' she said.

That wasn't a question either.

Angie hung up the telephone now. 'I booked you an optional night in a hotel over there just in case.'

Judy's head snapped up. 'In case what? Me and Barry are so overcome with passion that we can't wait until we get home?'

'In case it takes more than one night to spring him from jail, you eejit.'

'Oh. Sorry, Angie.'

'That's OK. I know you're a bit all over the place.'

369

To say the least. It was difficult to take in: that he was back in her life as suddenly as he had left. Unannounced. Throwing everything into disarray all over again.

A part of her was angry, furious. Since when did he think it was OK to go asking her to rescue him, after leaving her like that? Did he really believe that she wouldn't mind? Maybe he was so delusional that he thought she would be so relieved to have found him that she would be glad of the chance. Anybody with any sensibility at all would have phoned someone else.

But who could he phone? His mother, his aunts, his friends? He had walked out on them all. It would be difficult now to turn around and beg help, especially when it involved a trip to France and the not inconsiderable sum of two thousand euro.

He had known she would come. He knew that however much she might hate him right now, she would not leave him in the lurch, no more than she would abandon anybody she had known all her life. She was too earnest, too loyal. He was trading on their history together. It was cheap, she decided.

She shouldn't go, of course. It would probably be a service to him *not* to go. Let him sort the whole thing out his end. She was sure it would be very character-building, even though he might not appreciate it at the time. She wasn't his mother, even though she had done her fair share of mammying him up to now.

She decided she would do it one more time. Rescue him. Then he was on his own.

And she was doing it for her, too. He had been found, finally. Whatever happened now, at least that horrible surreal feeling of her life being suspended was over. Her going to France to get him would draw a line under this whole episode.

'I'll come with you,' Ber offered.

If someone was going to the supermarket these days, Ber offered to go. Just to spice up her life.

'No, I'm fine.'

'It's bound to be difficult, seeing him again,' Angie said.

'We'll all go,' Ber decided.

Before the whole thing turned into a party, Judy said, definitively, 'Thanks anyway, but I need to do this by myself.'

Angie shook her head. 'I feel a bit sorry for him. A big dramatic exit to France, and now to come home like this . . . '

'I know,' Ber agreed.

It was as though neither of them had really expected anything else; Barry, displaying his hapless streak again.

Judy didn't want to pity him. If she began to pity him, then all was truly lost.

Which it might be anyway.

She just didn't know yet.

⋆   ⋆   ⋆

They left for the airport an hour later.

Lenny had put on what Judy privately termed his International Outfit for the trip home: everything was black, mostly leather, all labels, naturally, and topped off by a gadgety mobile phone and the requisite pair of sunglasses that Judy couldn't see through. It was as if he had already left Ireland, and was mentally in some glossy bar in Amsterdam sipping a whisky and wondering who he might run into at his stopover in Singapore.

Judy, in travelling clothes of jeans and a T-shirt, couldn't believe she had slept with this man last night. This sex god! Was it possible that she had imagined the whole thing?

'You hardly need your sunglasses,' she said tartly. 'It's raining.'

He gave her a very haughty look from behind them. Or least she assumed it was haughty. 'I have a headache,' he ground out.

They loaded their luggage into Judy's boot. His was bound for Amsterdam. Hers, Paris.

'What time is your flight?' she said, in some attempt at communication.

'Four,' he said politely. 'And yours?'

'Two.'

After that there didn't seem to be a thing left to say.

Judy tried to distract herself by thinking of all the things she had forgotten to pack: her toothbrush, a money belt, chewing gum for the flight. It just went to show how useful lists really were, if only she hadn't sworn off them for life. But as the mental list grew longer and more worrying — had she packed underwear? — every inch of her was aware of Lenny in the seat beside her.

She could smell him. He was wearing some

kind of expensive after-shave. She herself had only used Sure, and probably not enough of it. Eventually she leaned over and put the air conditioner on full blast.

'Look, Judy,' he said. 'About last night.'

Her eyes flew to his. 'Yes?'

Perhaps now was when he was going to make some kind of revelation. Or even suggest a rematch in Australia. Just *something*.

'I obviously won't say anything to Barry.'

Judy stared straight ahead. Him bringing up Barry was the very last thing she had expected.

'I wasn't worried that you would,' she said carefully.

He shrugged. 'Fine. I just wanted you to know that I'll be discreet.'

She was furious now. He was making the whole thing out to be cheap and underhand.

'Oh, I'm sure you're very discreet,' she flung at him.

He took his sunglasses off, finally. He looked angry. 'What are you getting at me for, Judy? You enjoyed last night as much as I did.'

At least he was admitting he enjoyed it.

'Look, let's just leave it, Lenny, OK? You've made it perfectly clear where we both stand.'

'That's for sure. When Barry clicks his fingers, you really jump, don't you?'

Judy was open-mouthed now. 'What could I do? He rang from jail!'

'And so you'll swoop in and get him, and everything will be fine,' Lenny said. 'Still, you always made it perfectly clear where your priorities lay. Longevity, that was the word, wasn't it?'

She was furious at this attack. He was quite happy to ridicule her about taking Barry back, yet he himself hadn't said a single word that would made her feel that he felt anything for her.

She wouldn't explain that she had no intention of picking up with Barry where she had left off. Why should she? Lenny had done or said nothing that gave him any rights in her life.

She said, icily, 'I think it's best all around if, like you say, we don't mention this again.'

He was still for a moment. Then he shrugged. 'OK. It's all worked out fine for everybody then.'

It wasn't working out fine at all. Somewhere along the way it had all gone horribly wrong and now there was no way back. She drove along, blinking back tears, and unable to shake the feeling that she had lost something.

Which was ridiculous. With Lenny, there wasn't anything *to* lose.

At the airport, they said goodbye just inside the entrance.

'I hope you get on OK in France,' he said stiffly. 'I'm sure the two of you will manage to work things out.'

Judy kept her face blank. 'Yes, well, we'll see. Good luck with everything.'

'Thanks.'

There were no kisses, no hugs, just a quick handshake.

'Goodbye, Judy.'

'Goodbye.'

Then he turned and walked off, and was quickly lost in the crowd.

After a moment, Judy set off in the other direction, towards the check-in desk, and Barry.

29

Judy had learned French at school, but seemed to remember only the phrases, 'Can I buy two baguettes please!' and 'Is this the way to the public convenience?' neither of which would be much use in trying to spring Barry from a jail cell.

Although, in theory, he had already been sprung. While she had been on her way to the airport, Angie had been wiring through the bail money to Monsieur LeFevre, a French solicitor who had rather grudgingly agreed to come down and do the necessary paperwork to secure Barry's release.

Judy's mission, so to speak, was strictly collection.

She stopped for a cup of coffee at a sidewalk café within sight of the gendarmerie where he was at that moment waiting for her. She needed to clear her head, or collect her thoughts, one or the other. The plane journey over had been taken up with a dissection of her final run-in with Lenny — she had alternated between cursing and making low mourning sounds — and she felt she'd had little or no time to prepare for this momentous meeting with Barry.

Maybe it was best. That way there might be a chance to see how she really felt. Would she want to clobber him over the head with her handbag, or would the sheer familiarity of his face erode her anger and make her feel as if she was beating up a helpless puppy dog?

One thing was certain: this was not a glorious reunion. There would be no galloping into each other's arms amid cries of 'Marvellous to see you again!' and big passionate kisses. In fact, the way she felt right now, there was a distinct possibility that the gendarmes might have to step in to secure Barry's protection.

'Madame?' A waiter stood beside her, notebook held aloft.

'*Crêpe, s'il vous plait, avec le chevre,*' she said, rather pleased at how her French had come back. It only required a little practice, that was all.

He gave her an odd look before writing it down and walking off. A quick consultation of her copy of the *Language Survival Guide* confirmed that she had ordered her crêpe with a goat on the side, and not a fried egg on top at all. Oh, well. She probably wouldn't be able to eat it anyway.

She looked over at the gendarmerie, expecting all kinds of lowlifes and drunken hooligans to fall out of the double doors, kicked out by unsmiling gendarmes, saying, 'Beat it, you lout.' From Barry's phone call, the place had sounded like the pit of hell. But the only people coming out were dressed in suits, swinging briefcases and talking on mobile phones. If these were French criminals, then they had a lot more style than their Irish counterparts. There weren't even any iron bars on the window. Still, they probably kept the dangerous detainees out of sight, possibly in a high-security wing at the back, with barbed wire and electric fences and armed guards patrolling up and down. Barry was probably slammed up in some windowless cell with nothing but a hard bed for company.

She wondered what was going through his head right now. His humble tone on the phone said that he appreciated what he had done, on some level at least. He would not be expecting any instant forgiveness — which was just as well, because he wouldn't be getting it. Would he have excuses, explanations? Had he even worked out for himself why he had gone in the first place?

In a few more minutes she would have to walk in there and get him. And what then?

She had up to now refused to think ahead. What was the point? And if she had learned anything in this whole sorry affair, it was that you couldn't plan for everything, or sometimes anything at all.

But there were practical considerations to be taken into account. For instance, if he decided that he wanted to come back to Ireland with her, where would he now live? What would they tell people? Because they would have to tell them *something*. The engagement was obviously off, but was everything?

She didn't know. She didn't know how Barry felt either. But maybe it had already been decided by events; him disappearing to France, and her getting involved with Lenny.

Who was probably striking up a conversation with an attractive brunette in the airline seat next to him right at this moment. 'Can I borrow your in-flight magazine?' or something cheesy like that. He would throw the odd sardonic grin and rakish glance in her direction. By the time lunch arrived, they would probably have arranged to spend the stopover together, he knew a good hotel. Not giving Judy a single thought! Or if he did, it would be to admonish himself for straying outside his remit; for all her talk, Judy had read a little too much into a simple night of sex, and he would be better off sticking to his own kind from now on.

That might be a bit unfair. He could be downing whiskies to beat the band and sobbing quietly, 'I've been so stupid.'

But how likely was that? Not very, she concluded grimly. For him it had been a one-night stand, albeit with someone he knew a little better than usual. Sure, he liked her, maybe even a lot, but that was neither here nor there in the greater scheme of things.

And there she was, staring bleakly at her crêpe (which had actually arrived with a large red chilli on top) and wondering what genetic defect she possessed that rendered her incapable of sleeping with a man without imagining happy trips together to the post office to collect their pensions.

Because she suspected that last night was different because she had actually fallen in love with Lenny. A little bit anyway. Well, who wouldn't! He was gorgeous, and sexy, and unattainable and that just made her want him all the more.

She suddenly thought of the guys who used to

work on the waltzers and the other amusement rides down on the sea front when she was younger. They always had names like Al and Phil and Dec, dangerous kinds of names, and they wore tight jeans and white sleeveless T-shirts and an earring in one ear (gold hoops, no prissy studs or anything like that). They would zero in on groups of girls who got on the rides and would strut over to give them an extra push, and listen to their gratifying squeals.

A few of the girls, the really good-looking ones, got lucky with these guys, and would see them for a week of covert and desperately exciting late-night dates on the beach once the amusements had shut down for the night. She wouldn't have dared, of course — Ber probably would have, except that she was sure they were riddled with disease — yet she always envied the girls who did.

Of course, the amusements would move on a week later, and the girls were left heartbroken. And they would write to them for a while, long, anguished love letters on pink scented paper that they showed around in the toilets before posting them off, but they never got a reply. Of course, if you looked at any of these guys in the cold light of day, without the belting music and the flashing lights, they weren't all that special, and had they hung around, the girls would have gone off them pretty quickly. But it was magical and mysterious while it lasted, and these girlfriends sometimes still reminisced in the pub, 'Do you remember Phil? The waltzer guy? I was cracked about him!' And they would look all soft and far away, even though they had been married to Roger for ten years and had a clatter of kids.

Maybe Lenny was her waltzer guy, Judy mused. About twenty years too late, but she had always been a bit of a slow developer in that area. When she was older, maybe she too would have a far-off look in her eye, as she drove her protesting kids to tuba practice.

That was probably her reality, not having desperately exciting sex with guys like Lenny. She should recognise it for what it was, and walk away with that look in her eye, instead of bitterness and what-might-have-beens. He had been a great guy, at a time in her life when she'd needed a bit of passion.

Maybe it was as simple as that.

'Judy?'

Her head snapped up. Barry was standing on the pavement in front of her. She blinked a couple of times, wondering whether the August sun had made her light-headed and prone to visions.

But this was no vision. It was Barry, all right, looking exactly the same as when he'd left, except that he'd acquired a tan that Biffo would have been proud of. For some reason she had been expecting a tragic, tramp-like figure, with a grim prison haircut and possibly missing a shoe. She quickly checked out his forearms for a tattoo — maybe even the word *Judy* — but they were bare except for a rather nice watch.

Under her silent stare, he said carefully, 'I was hoping you'd at least say hello.'

'Sorry . . . it's just that, well, I thought you were in prison.'

'They let me out an hour ago,' he assured her. 'I've been sitting over there watching you.'

Oh God; as she had writhed and cursed under her breath and tried to order a goat. She felt as if she had been spied upon.

'I've been trying to pluck up the courage to come over,' he admitted sheepishly.

'And you did,' she said coolly. Well, she had every right to be cool. To give him the full Antarctic treatment if she chose.

He bowed his head in acknowledgement of this, and said, very humbly, 'Can I sit down?'

'I suppose.'

He sat. Then, 'Is that a chilli on your crêpe?'

'Yes. I happen to like them.' Now she was forced to pick up the damn thing and take a nonchalant bite off the top.

He was looking as her face so closely, so intensely, that she began to feel uncomfortable.

'It's so good to see you, Judy,' he burst out. 'I've missed you so much. It's been horrible without you. I've — ' Then he put up a hand, stopping himself abruptly. 'Sorry. Sorry,' he said. 'It's way too soon for all this.'

She nodded curtly. She refused to get drawn into any of that. Besides, her mouth was on fire.

'Why did they put you in prison, Barry?' she asked bluntly. She braced herself for the drug dealing and call girl revelations.

Barry shook his head in disgust. 'It was so stupid, Judy!'

'What was?'

382

'There I was in my car on the motorway, right? Minding my own business, keeping to the speed limit like I always do. In fact, I was driving even more carefully than usual because I'm in a foreign country and I respect their laws, right?'

Judy was wondering where all this was leading. Was he going to reveal that he'd had 5kg of hard drugs in the boot, which had been discovered when he'd suddenly got a flat tyre and been towed away?

'Next thing I know, this guy comes right up behind me, nearly runs me off the road! He must have been doing a hundred. Horn blaring and everything, like I was in the wrong.' He was quite het up now. Judy braced herself for the climax. 'Well, I wasn't going to put up with that kind of disrespect. So I drove after him. Put down my window, gave him a piece of my mind. Turned out he was the police. He did me for dangerous driving, obstruction of justice, and having no international driving licence.' He told her fervently, 'It was horrible, Judy. I didn't even have a toilet in my cell, I had to share with two others.'

Judy let out her breath slowly. 'You were in for a *traffic offence?*'

'Well, yes.' She must have looked very disappointed because he said, rather offended, 'You hardly thought I robbed a bank?'

Now that she really thought about it, it had never been a remote possibility. Or the drugs, or anything else.

'Thanks for coming to get me, Judy.'

'I probably shouldn't have.'

383

'I'm glad you're here.' He watched her in that long, careful way again. 'You look well.'

So did he. Maybe a little too well for someone who had been raking over the coals of his life for the past month. There weren't even any deep crevices down the sides of his mouth, brought on by hours of self-contemplation. But of course he would be keeping his emotions hidden at a time like this. She certainly hoped *she* was, and he wouldn't be able to tell from her face that she had happily bonked his best man last night. Just in case, she drew her mouth into a very sober line.

'Look, Barry,' she said. 'Let's cut the pleasantries. What exactly did you drag me all the way to France for? Because it wasn't for some piddly traffic offence.'

He looked a bit wounded that she was making light of his ordeal, but he wisely didn't pursue it. 'I was hoping we could talk. On neutral ground. Away from Cove, and everybody.'

'Shame you didn't suggest that a month ago. We could have saved ourselves all this hassle.'

He looked pained. 'Judy, I don't blame you for being angry. In fact, I wouldn't blame you if you want to slap me across the face.' He braced himself as if she might actually take him up on the invitation. 'I did a terrible thing to you, Judy. It was an appalling breach of trust. Unforgivable! I behaved like a total and utter creep.'

Judy could have come up with something more colourful than that, but perhaps expletives weren't all that useful right now. And he *was*

384

taking responsibility for the whole thing, she supposed.

Which he seemed to be at pains to point out. 'It was nothing to do with you, Judy. I just want you to know that. It was completely my fault. Stupidly, foolishly, I let my head be turned.' He looked at her. 'I think you know by whom.'

'Yes,' she said.

In a way, so had she. And now that he was gone, there was just her and Barry left. Two casualties of a holiday romance.

'Go on,' she said.

He took great encouragement from this. He dared to pull his chair in another inch.

'When you look at someone like Lenny, someone who's left the small town life behind and made a success of himself like that, well, you start to doubt yourself, Judy.' He gave a self-deprecating shrug. 'I began to think that I'd missed out by staying in Cove. I began to think, here I am, thirty-four and I've never done anything, never seen anywhere.'

'You became a doctor, Barry. You have a thriving practice, not to mention a huge following of devoted patients. You have nice friends, a decent social life, you travel a couple of times a year. You were going to get married at one point, maybe have kids. You have the life you chose for yourself, Barry.'

'Oh, I know all that *now*,' he cried, animated. 'But a month ago I thought that I had the most boring life on the planet. No, not even boring — downright dull! Plodding. No excitement anywhere in it!' He saw her face. 'Jesus. Not *you*,

Judy. No, you were the best thing in it.'

So good that he'd had to creep off under cover of darkness to get away from her. But anyhow.

'Why didn't you talk to me, Barry? Was I that wrapped up in the wedding plans?'

'Pretty wrapped up,' he said. But he rallied, and announced, 'But that's no excuse for my cowardice.'

'It certainly isn't.'

'I don't know why I was so afraid.' He said, rather ardently, 'It was ridiculous. I should have known that you'd have understood. You're such a compassionate person, Judy.'

'Let's not get carried away here, Barry.'

'I mean it.' He looked as though he wanted to take her hand, but restrained himself. 'I see everything so clearly now, Judy. It took me a month away to appreciate how good my life was in Cove. Everything I ever wanted was there: my work, my family, my friends.'

For a minute she thought he wasn't going to mention her at all. But no, he was obviously working up to a grand finale. 'And you, of course. I can't tell you how much I've missed you. I knew I'd made a terrible mistake within the first week.'

'Yes, yes,' she said. 'Listen, about your month away.'

'Yes?'

'I want to know all about it.'

He looked a bit taken aback at having to revisit the scene of his previous crimes. 'There's nothing really to tell.'

'There must be *something* to tell, Barry. You

left because you were looking for something. Did you find it?'

He didn't immediately understand what she saying. 'Yes. It's at home. It's you, Judy.'

'No, no, no. I mean, was France good? The fancy hotels, and the resorts and the strip clubs.'

He looked very wary now. 'Judy, I'm not sure what you're accusing me of here.'

'I'm not accusing you of anything. Honestly. I'm just interested to hear what you did. What you saw. That's all.'

He relaxed at that. She waited to hear the tall tales of his credit card spree and his romps up and down the Riviera.

'It wasn't worth it, Judy,' he assured her importantly. 'Oh, sure, the jet-set life is exciting for a while. The hotels were kind of nice, and eating out and all that. But in between it was mostly trying to make sense of the motorways. The next car we get, it's going to have air-conditioning,' he told her.

Judy tried again. 'Yes, but surely you must have done some really exciting things. You didn't go all the way to France to drive around the motorways?'

He thought for a bit and then his brow cleared. 'I went to one of the largest ten-pin bowling alleys in France.'

'What?'

'A place called La Piste Rouge.'

The alley bit became clear to Judy now. It wasn't semi-naked girls falling down in such places, but skittles.

'It was marvellous, Judy. You'd have loved it.

Maybe we would go there some day together.' Then he remembered himself and said, 'But obviously all that is something for the future.'

Judy said nothing.

'And I got a nice watch,' he finished up rather limply. 'My other fell down the toilet in the hotel. And a few new clothes in some hideously expensive boutique. I nearly collapsed when I saw the price of things.'

He must have taken her deepening silence for disapproval because he said, 'I'll clear the credit card debt, OK? Obviously you won't have to pay a thing.'

She just nodded.

'Judy, I know all this is a lot to take in. And I'm not going to rush you or anything. But I was thinking — well, hoping — that maybe we could try again.' This time he did reach over, and touched her hand lightly. 'I've been thinking about you every moment while I've been in France. Going through all the good times we've had. And we've had some really good times, Judy.'

She said, loudly, 'We didn't have sex, Barry.'

He looked around a bit nervously. Several other diners looked over.

'Yes, well, that's obviously something we'll have to . . . it was the wedding, Judy. We were too busy.'

'Balls,' said Judy.

Now Barry was distinctly nervous. He hissed, 'If it's just the sex thing that's bothering you, we'll work at it. I promise you.' He added (rather disapprovingly she thought), 'But there's a lot

388

more to life than sex, you know.'

'True,' said Judy. There was passion and energy and risk, and someone who looked at you like you were the only woman in the whole of Cove. Or even Wicklow. In fact, why not push the boat out: the whole of Ireland!

Barry seemed relieved that she had stopped cursing and wanting to have sex, and that the reconciliation was apparently back on track. 'So what do you say? Will we try again?'

She looked at him. He had come all the way to France to find some part of himself, leaving her behind. Yet she was the one who had moved on. He hadn't budged an inch.

'No,' she said. 'Thanks anyway.'

He flinched, but otherwise remained stoic. 'I understand. You obviously hate me right now.'

The thing was, she didn't. You couldn't really hate Barry, with his uncomplicated face. But he was the boy next door. And having had a twirl with the waltzer guy, Judy just couldn't go back.

'Maybe you'll change your mind in time.'

'No, Barry. I won't.'

'I won't give up, you know.'

'Do,' she urged him, 'for your own sake. *Garçon!*'

The waiter completely ignored her. In the end she just left some money on the table and stood.

'Goodbye, Barry. I'll see you at home.'

He wasn't defeated that easily. He stood and, uncaring of the other diners, called zealously, 'I love you, Judy Brady! Whatever it takes to change your mind, I'll do it! I'll make you marry me yet!'

you are invited to join

Rose and Michael Brady

For a Renewal of their Wedding Pledge
at the Church of the HolySaints, Cove,
at 3pm on Saturday the 23rd of December
and afterwards at a reception at the
family home.

RSVP by December 8th

30

'I suppose at least we can show off the new house, seeing as we've practically rebuilt it,' Rose confided in Judy.

She was on a very strict weight loss regime in anticipation of the occasion. By her calculations, she would only have to drop two pounds a week to get into the new burnt-orange suit she had already bought.

Unfortunately, she was already behind by three weeks, but she wasn't going to let it get her down. She had started a whole new diet only yesterday, and the fridge was chock full of chicken breasts, noodles, pork cutlets and bean sprouts, the principle being that it was not how much you ate but how you cooked it that counted. If she could only get the hang of the new wok, she'd be away. Plus, she was finding it hard to face into a stir-fry for breakfast. But she was persevering. It wasn't every day that your husband proposed all over again, and she wanted to look her best for him.

Although, if she were being perfectly honest, she could have done without it coming so soon after the renovations, and with Christmas only around the corner. And having to go on another blessed diet, and so soon after the last one. If she were given the choice, she'd have a preferred a week in Majorca, which would cost less and at least you'd be guaranteed the sun, but she wasn't going to say any of this, naturally. Or, at least, she only said it to Judy. Loudly. And several times.

'You should have seen him,' she told Judy now. 'Got down on one knee and everything. I thought he was after slipping another disc. Then he produces champagne and roses, the whole works, and he says he's having two eternity rings made to exchange at the ceremony. Nice rings, Judy, not his usual stingy affair.'

She looked out of the window at Mick who was pottering in the garden, and she shook her head slightly as if she couldn't quite credit the whole thing.

'We don't know anybody who's renewed their wedding vows. He must have read about it in a magazine or something.'

Her tone surprised Judy. Things had been so civil for ages now. Cheryl had seemed nothing more than a dim and murky memory, a blot on the landscape of their otherwise sedate marriage.

But perhaps not.

'He obviously wants to show you how much you mean to him, Mum.'

'He hasn't finished paying for the new kitchen,' Rose said bluntly. 'And now this?' Then she seemed to catch herself, and with an effort at a smile said, 'Still, it'll be a good party anyway. We're having sixty guests, and a DJ who's going to play the Beatles until midnight, and a bartender for the bar upstairs in Biffo's room. And, of course, we'll have the same caterers again.' The Indian food had gone down so well at the party for Barry's disappearance that they had decided to go ethnic again.

The whole thing was causing quite a stir on Sycamore Drive. The neighbours had only just recovered from the drama of Barry's disappearance and sudden return, not to mention three units of Dublin Fire Brigade fighting the blaze that day. Now not only had the Bradys rebuilt their house like something you'd see on the TV, they were also renewing their vows two days before Christmas like some Hollywood couple. You wouldn't see the like of it on *Coronation Street*.

Mick got an awful slagging down in the pub from the men. At his age, too — would he not be better off doing his Christmas shopping than getting all dolled up in a suit to get married to the same missus all over again? Had once not been enough for him? Mick wasn't a bit put out by any of it and remained tight-lipped about his motives. All this lent Rose a great air of mystery, and the men in the pub began to start doubting the worth of their own womenfolk, and they got fractious at home in the evenings, and judgemental, and rows started over the smallest thing at all. It would sicken you that Mick Brady, who did nothing only complain about his back and the price of things, should suddenly be lording it over the rest of them in the romantic stakes.

As more details of the lavish day began to leak out, the women of the road began to feel very unappreciated and hard done by in comparison. What had Rose Brady got that they didn't? Only a husband who lashed out money on a brand new house for her, including a waste disposal unit in the sink, that's what, before dropping down on one knee to ask her to marry him all over again! It was galling, especially when their own pathetic excuses for men spent their Christmas bonuses down in the pub talking nonsense and coming home expecting a hot meal on the table. And then criticising it. Loudly.

It was a wonder there weren't marriage breakdowns up and down the length of Sycamore Drive that winter.

'I feel a bit awkward asking you this, but will you be my bridesmaid, so to speak?' Rose asked.

'Of course I will, Mum.'

'Are you sure?' She watched Judy keenly. 'Because I can ask someone else if you don't feel up to it. You know, after everything.'

'It'll be an honour.'

'I didn't want to *not* ask you. In case you thought I felt sorry for you, or something. Because I know how much you'd hate that,' she fretted.

'Mum. Stop. It's fine.' She complained lightly, 'I can't believe my own mother is getting married again before I am.'

Rose looked relieved at the tone Judy was determined to take. 'Biffo said the same. He seems very embarrassed about the whole thing, and says he's not coming to it at all if there's going to be lots of kissing and mushy speeches and all that.' She gave a sigh. 'I'm worried about him. He's not himself these days.'

Well, it was only natural. In the space of a year he had gone from lowly estate agent to high-flying foreign sales executive and then back to an even lowlier estate agent. It was bound to take its toll.

'He says he's not bringing anybody to the wedding.'

'I suppose he's not.'

He hadn't been on a date since he and Cheryl had broken up. He didn't go out much at all, according to Rose. It didn't help that there was a fully stocked bar in his room, and he could drink himself stupid every night before falling into a sleeping bag in the corner.

'I don't suppose you are?' she said hopefully. 'Bringing somebody?'

'No,' Judy said bluntly. 'I'm afraid me and Biffo will both be going to your wedding on our own.'

'Oh God, I feel bad now,' Rose declared. 'I hope people don't think we're rubbing your noses in it.'

'Not at all. They already know that I drive men to different countries, and that Biffo has a preference for pyromaniacs.'

'Stop that now,' Rose scolded. 'You're both good, kind, decent children and it's neither of your faults that you ended up alone and unmarried in your thirties.'

'Thanks, Mum.'

'And anyway, didn't Barry come back? Isn't he over in his mother's house right now, counting the cost of his terrible mistake?' She cast a rather anxious look out the window. 'At least, we hope he is.'

A couple of weeks back she had gone out one

night to put the rubbish out and had found Barry in his car sitting in the dark. She had let out a scream, obviously frightening the life out of him because he had driven off at speed. Afterwards he had denied any knowledge of the episode. 'What on earth would I be sitting outside your mother's house for?' he had asked Judy, with an incredulous little laugh.

Judy had let it go. Possibly Rose had been mistaken. And it had been a difficult few months for Barry, facing back into the community he had turned his nose up at, and without his partner.

A week later she had found him outside her own house. He had dropped immediately to his knees and begun ripping up weeds. 'It's my house too, Judy,' he said, when she pointed out his presence. 'And if you don't mind me saying so, you've really let the garden go.'

She was getting a bit concerned about him. But she didn't want to be too hard on him, even after everything. He seemed very lost, and unable to find his feet again.

Mick came in now, ruddy-faced from the cold, and rubbing his hands together loudly.

'Did she tell you all about the wedding plans?' he said to Judy.

Rose cut any such talk short by commanding. 'Don't walk all over my floor in those bloody boots. Wait till I put down newspaper.'

The new tiles they'd had put down in the kitchen were absolutely gorgeous, except that you could see every damn speck of dirt and dust, and Rose was killed going around with a mop.

'I think she's excited, but she's trying to hide it,' Mick said hopefully, as Rose went off, cursing loudly.

'You've certainly taken her by surprise anyway.'

In fact, Mick looked no more excited about the whole thing than Rose. 'I was thinking and thinking what I could do to gizz things up again. You know, after everything. I thought, well, if I take her away for a week in the sun she'll only say that anybody can do that, it's nothing special. And then I heard about this wedding renewal thing, that lots of people our age were doing it — well, mostly famous people — and I thought, maybe that's it. Maybe that's what we need to, I don't know, patch things up properly.' He gave a little sigh. 'She says she wants to do it, but I don't know if she really does.'

'Maybe when it gets a bit closer she'll perk up a bit.'

They heard her coming back, and he covered by saying, loudly, 'So, Judy, are you bringing anybody with you?'

'I've already asked her,' Rose snapped, giving him a look as though he were completely tactless.

'I didn't know that, did I?'

Judy said reasonably, 'It's not even been six months, OK? I'm just not ready yet.'

'Well, of course you're not!' Rose cried. She said to Mick accusingly, 'Don't be rushing her. Her heart is still broken after Barry.'

The six months Judy was referring to was not the length of time since the break-up with Barry, but rather that hot night spent in the spare bedroom with Lenny, and naked as the day she was born. Having been loved until she hadn't an ounce of energy left in her whole body.

'Look at that little face!' Rose clucked. She turned on Mick. 'You've upset her now.'

Mick said, 'I'm going out,' and he turned on his heel and left.

Rose gave a big sigh. 'Listen to me,' she said. 'And we're supposed to be renewing our vows in a couple of weeks' time.'

'He's only trying to please you, Mum.'

'I know he is. For the last six months that man has tried to please me. And the more he tries, the more bloody annoyed I get!'

Judy's mobile phone rang, taking the heat off Mick. She looked at the caller display. She turned off the phone.

'Barry?' said Rose.

'Barry.'

* * *

Christmas was the scourge of single people.

Judy tramped down Grafton Street that evening, surrounded on all sides by couples holding hands, or with arms wrapped around each other, or else snogging in doorways. The couples that weren't embracing had a clatter of children traipsing behind them like a line of ducks. 'Keep up, little Jimmy!' they would call indulgently. Occasionally, Judy would spot another person on their own, but they all had huge, self-satisfied grins on their faces, and

400

would nearly knock Judy sideways with their massive shopping bags that she just knew contained a whole Clinique counter or a Playstation for their other half at home.

Even the Christmas window displays had it in for single people: elves were in twosomes, reindeer in threesomes, and in one window Santa's Little Helpers were having nothing short of an orgy.

Judy stopped for a takeaway coffee. 'Just the one,' she whispered miserably, and the girl gave her a sympathetic look.

Her shopping list was embarrassingly short. Without Barry to buy for this year, there was nothing on it, only the usual multi-pack of socks for Mick and a bottle of perfume for Rose. She could buy something for Angie and Ber, she supposed, but they didn't usually exchange Christmas presents and she would just make them uncomfortable. Would it be going over-board to get Annette and Marcia at the library a little gift? She could just wrap it up and put no tag on it, and they wouldn't even know it was from her.

Listen to her: she was pathetic. But she couldn't just give up and go home. She'd only been in town an hour. This was a trip she and Barry would normally make, spending hours debating the merits of the 'joint present', which in past years had been a DVD player or a home computer. 'Something sensible,' they would say, and the afternoon would pass pleasantly in discussions on hard disk space and various drives, and how to get the damned thing home.

There was such great comfort and security in being part of a couple. You always had someone else at your elbow to validate your choice in Christmas presents, and in life.

That was what she and Barry had become: reference points for each other, and security blankets. And it had worked out fine because they had liked each other. They had been friends, they had grown up together with the same life experiences and values and the same goals.

And had they got married, it would probably all have worked out fine until maybe ten years down the line when they would both have this hollow feeling that neither could quite explain, this sense that something was missing.

It was just her luck to have found her missing piece with a man for whom two dates in a row constituted a long-term relationship.

A shop door swished open as she passed, and Frank Sinatra blared out, extolling her to 'Have Yourself A Merry Little Christmas.'

I will fucking not, Judy wanted to shout back, but she knew that that kind of loutish behaviour would only spoil the warm, fuzzy Christmas atmosphere for everybody else; all those couples laughing merrily, no doubt going home soon to have mad sex. Even the pandas in China, who only mated once in a blue moon, and that was only if they could find another panda to mate with, stood a better chance than she did of having sex tonight. How sad was that?

She might as well face it: she *was* sad. In fact, she was miserable. She was worse than miserable. She was heartbroken and weary and lonely and riddled with regret, and fed up of trying to pretend that it was all because of Barry.

Because it wasn't.

'You'll get over him eventually,' people liked to say consolingly.

'Actually, I already am,' she wanted to say back cheerfully, but she knew that people would be shocked, and would think she had a very superficial and flighty attitude to a relationship that had been going on since they were three and half. Especially after all the weeping and wailing out of her over the summer, and the trips to the Garda station to try and get them to look for him, and the aborted poster campaign (somehow that had leaked out). The taking to the bed for three days (that had leaked out too) and the drinking of all that white wine. These were clearly the actions of a woman who had lost the love of her life — her soul mate! her rock! — and you could be forgiven for thinking that she would never be able to stand up straight again.

Everybody said that it must have been a very difficult and brave decision on her part not to take him back when he came crawling. When she could so easily have done so! Nobody would have thought any less of her, given her rampantly advancing age, and the fact that they had a house together, and a car, and a joint savings account — the whole set-up. In another six months his temporary aberration would have been forgotten and nobody would have lowered their opinion of her for having swallowed her pride and given it another go.

And it wasn't for the lack of trying on his part. Holy Mother of God, you never saw anything like it: the flowers, the letters, the daily trips to the library. A bunch of heart-shaped balloons once. The embarrassing intervention of Dr Hairy Stevens, who tried to set up some kind of reconciliation session at the surgery, with tea and fig rolls, except that only Barry showed up. They had nearly expected him to take out a full-page ad in *The Chronicle* begging her to take him back. But she had rejected every advance, spurned every overturn, and with great dignity too, everybody said, which was more than could be said for Barry these days.

Secretly, they'd have done the same. Well, how could you ever trust a man like that again? Every time you sent him out for a pint of milk there was a fair chance he wouldn't come back. Then there was that time he went up to Dublin for an overnight conference without telling anybody, and the whole town was saying the next morning, 'Did you hear? Barry Fox is gone again.' How could any woman be expected to put up with that?

Even his patients, the ones who had doted on him and even fancied him, had got a bit antsy. A good number of them who had been moved over to Dr Stevens and Dr Jacobs during Barry's time in France were very reluctant to be shifted back to him. Nobody was saying that he wasn't a good doctor — of course not. He was excellent, the very best. But did anyone really want to take their top off in front of a man who might step out of the room and never return?

Still, Judy must be heartbroken. You didn't get over a thing like that overnight. And nobody was expecting her to. No, it would be many months more, possibly years, before she could put the entire thing behind her.

What they didn't know was that Judy already had.

Pretty fully, she was sure. Things had fallen into place with great clarity at that café table in France. She knew absolutely that she did not want to spend her life with Barry. It was as simple as that. There was very little angst in it, and hardly any grief. In fact, she mostly felt a great sense of relief, and all the way home on the plane she had whispered to herself, 'Thank God, thank God,' until the woman in the seat beside her thought the plane was going to crash.

Judy felt she'd had a reprieve. Handed to her by Barry himself. Had he not believed there was something better out there for him, she would never have discovered that, in her case, there actually was.

Mind you, that something better was in Australia right now, probably bonking to beat the band.

But he had shown her what a real, proper, grown-up relationship could be about: challenge and laughter and passion, even the odd row or two, and with a bit of decent sex thrown in. Not two people ambling along in roles that they were both so comfortable in that neither ever stopped to say, wait a minute, what's going on here? What is this all about?

She wondered whether she had been so caught

405

up in the concept of longevity (the word made her want to giggle now, in a schoolgirl kind of way) that she had lost sight of what was really important: the person she was actually with. Or wanted to be with.

Which seemed to boil down to a waltzer-type guy with a vaguely sluttish smile who knew how to whip up a good argument before showing a girl a good time. He would be free-spirited, throw two fingers up at convention, be kind to his mother, and wear an apron well. He would also be devilishly handsome, and have maybe the merest hint of an Australian twang.

Oh, she wasn't fooling even herself. It was Lenny, pure and simple.

The tragedy of it was that it was completely pointless. Because he believed that any kind of long-term relationship obliterated passion, romance, interest in each other, then interest in food probably, and then extinguished life altogether. For him, commitment was like weed killer. Why else was he on the other side of the globe, and she here?

Just thinking about him gave her a pain. She stood in the men's department of Marks and Spencers trying to decide between pairs of diamond-patterned socks, and the pain grew so bad she had to clutch the rail.

Barry had never given her a pain like that, except in the neck maybe. Judy gloomily concluded that she was lovelorn, a word she had scarcely thought about in her life before, and certainly never uttered out loud. But all the signs and symptoms were there: the aching heart, the aforementioned pain in the nether regions, the violent waking during the night from semi-pornographic dreams set in the spare bedroom, the big long miserable face on her. 'Just looking at you makes me want to jump off a cliff,' Ber had said only yesterday. 'I hope to God you get over Barry soon.'

Even Angie and Ber thought she was still upset over Barry. She was glad in a way. It was easier. The alternative was explaining that she had actually fallen for Lenny after a one-night stand, and they would clasp their hands to their mouths in horror and say, 'Judy Brady! We thought you, of all people, would have known better!'

Well, she had. Lord knows he had made no attempt in the world to conceal the type of scurrilous person that he was. But it had made no difference in the world. Her emotions didn't seem to follow logic at all, damn them to the pit of hell. And now here she was, lovelorn to the back of her teeth, while the unsuitable and flightly subject of her affections was doubtlessly whooping it up in Australia, completely unaware of her feelings.

Thank God. She would die. Oh, she could just imagine his amusement. No, his *mirth*. When he had stopped laughing eventually, he would kindly point her in the direction of the local divorce courts just to get her feet back on the ground.

Well, he needn't bother. As if she harboured hopes of actually marrying him! She'd be lucky to see him on a flying visit a decade from now, when he came back for another wedding. She would be in her mid-forties by then, with everything starting to droop even more than it was already, and he probably wouldn't even recognise her, never mind remember that he had jumped on her one night and ravished her.

And broken her heart, the big bollox.

Although he didn't know it.

'Can I help you there at all?' A shop assistant was watching her curiously. Judy realised she was pressing a pair of socks to her mouth.

'Oh! Ah, no thanks.' She quickly dropped the socks into her basket. Mick wouldn't mind if they were a bit wet.

She was wondering what to do now — she couldn't string out the shopping any longer — and thought she might torture herself by sitting alone in a pub full of happy couples, when she turned round and crashed straight into Barry.

'Oh! Judy!' He looked astonished, 'Sorry.'

'No, it's my fault . . . ' She retrieved her basket while he fell over himself to pick up the socks.

'There you go.'

'Thanks.'

'I take it they're for your dad.' He gave her a muted grin.

'Um, yes.' There was a bit of an awkward silence. 'Barry, what are you doing here?'

He looked taken aback at this line of questioning. 'Same as you. Shopping.'

'Oh? I didn't realise you had anyone to buy socks for.'

Well, his father had been dead for a number of

years now. And he didn't have any uncles. And diamond-patterned socks were hardly something you'd buy a friend.

'I'm actually buying socks for myself,' he told her, very reasonably.

Judy blushed; she felt low and suspicious. Yet there weren't any socks in his basket. There wasn't anything at all.

'I've only just arrived,' he explained, catching her looking.

'I see,' she said, wondering how things had arrived at this place: her always questioning, him always defending. Both of them on edge.

They used to be so easy with each other. After all, they had spent most of their lives as friends.

'How are you, Judy?' he said. He was trying to be casual, but underneath it he was alert, nervous, watching her closely. He smelled of fresh aftershave and there was a little nick on his chin. He had never really taken to the whole shaving thing.

'I'm OK,' she said. 'And you?'

'Oh, fine,' he said, nodding vigorously.

'And work?'

'Couldn't be better,' he said confidently.

She knew that wasn't strictly true. Along with the patients who had refused to go back to him, there were rumours of lateness. Irritability with some of the older patients. Well, they could go on a bit, in fairness. He had been complaining for years about how some of them saved up their symptoms and then expected them all to be dealt with in a ten-minute consultation.

There was another awkward pause. 'What are

you doing for Christmas?' She didn't really want to ask. But the nick on his chin made him vulnerable. He seemed about eight. Maybe she felt sorry for him, which was a horrible thing to feel for anybody, but he seemed grateful for her inquiry.

'I'll be at Mum's. And my two aunts are coming over from Surrey.'

Once upon a time he would have delighted in it, three women hanging on his every word. But today he just looked a bit depressed at the prospect.

Of course, by rights he and Judy should have been settling down to their first Christmas dinner as a married couple.

The knowledge sat between them like a stone.

'I'd better go,' Judy said. 'Happy Christmas, Barry.'

She meant it. She hoped that he would be able to relax, think things over. Maybe move on a bit in the New Year.

'Judy, wait,' he said. She braced herself. 'Maybe we could go for a coffee or something. You know, if you're not busy.'

'Barry, I can't.'

He gave a little laugh. 'It's just a coffee, Judy. Come on, it's Christmas time.'

'No, thanks anyway.'

'Not even for old times' sake?' His smile suffered some slight slippage.

Judy took a breath. 'Barry, you have to stop doing this.'

He looked very surprised. 'Doing what? Inviting you for coffee? Correct me if I'm wrong,

410

but I think this is the first time I've done it since we broke up.'

'You know what I mean.'

'I'm afraid I don't, Judy.' He was going to be stubborn about it. She knew now that he had not turned up in Marks and Spencers by mistake. He had probably found out she was going Christmas shopping and had made an educated guess that at some point she would turn up in the men's department, as she had for the last twenty years.

'We're both going to have to accept that this is over.'

He looked offended. 'Judy, I assure you that I know full well it's over. You've made it perfectly clear that you don't want me back in any shape or form.'

'I never said that, Barry.' In fact, she felt she had been pretty mature about the whole thing, given the circumstances. Lots of other women would just have cut him dead. But she had entertained his numerous phone calls; had been understanding all those times he had called around to the library.

She saw now that perhaps this had been a mistake.

'Look,' said Barry, 'let's forget all this hostility, Judy. All right, so maybe we're not going to get back together — '

'We're definitely not, Barry.'

'But at least we can stay friends, can't we?' He looked at her eagerly.

'I have to go,' she said.

31

'Christmas is the scourge of single people,' Angie said viciously. 'I know that, I just said that,' Judy said with a sigh.

They were both a bit snappy with each other. They were supposed to be on the annual girls' Christmas night out, but didn't Ber pull out at the last moment because Vinnie was taking her late-night shopping to buy something mysterious but which he said was 'large, expensive and shiny'. Ber had come to the conclusion that it was a new washer dryer. She had broken the last one by trying to wash things like carpets and beanbags in it. There was some urgency on the issue because, for the first time in her adult life, Ber was hosting Christmas dinner in her house and needed to wash a tablecloth. It would be her, Vinnie and his two strapping sons. They had invited his ex-wife too, but she was spending Christmas at a luxury hotel in Malaga with her new, younger, boyfriend.

'Malaga,' Ber had spat. 'Meanwhile I'm stuck in the kitchen trying to cook a fucking bird for three men and a dog.'

The dog wasn't working out too well either. He refused to be house-trained for starters, and Ber spent most weekends following him around with a dustpan and brush and a bottle of Dettol. He got lonely a lot during the night too, which didn't improve her temper or her looks. And he didn't like Vinnie at all, only Ber, and would scratch at the bedroom door until she eventually let him in, and he would plant himself on her feet at the bottom of the bed and sleep, until, of course, it was time to get her up again to let him out for a pee.

She had come to the conclusion that she was being punished for having an affair in the first place. 'Someone up there has decided that I'm the bad one and should be taught a lesson, while his wife, the victim of the piece, gets rewarded by offloading her old man on me and trading up to a new, younger model.'

'Honestly, I don't know what she's complaining about,' Angie said now. 'At least she's not going to wake up on Christmas morning in the bed she had as a child. And Santa won't even have come.'

Angie was going down to the family home in the country for Christmas. All her brothers had girlfriends and wives, so she alone would be sitting at the Christmas table with her parents and a huge turkey, and at some point her mother would be bound to say that, with all her money, it was a pity that she hadn't found a nice man yet.

'And the worse thing is that she won't say it nastily. She'll be genuinely sorry for me that I wilfully turned my back on love and romance in favour of a glass office and loads of money. You just can't win, Judy. Or, at least, I don't seem to be able to win. You can either have a great career, or a great man, but it doesn't seem possible to have both.'

413

'You're just a bit down over the whole Gary thing,' Judy said.

'Yes, I bloody am down over it. Wouldn't you be?'

He had seemed so perfect too. Angie had met him during her lunch break on a park bench near the office. He was a voiceover artist, and indeed had a meltingly gorgeous voice.

He was also handsome, funny, intelligent and great in bed.

'I really think this could go somewhere,' Angie was confident enough to say after a week.

And everything appeared wonderful at first, and they went for cosy dinners in Temple Bar, and shopping on Saturdays, and to an exclusive spa hotel in the country only last weekend when Angie got her Christmas bonus (the first of three; they usually held off the largest until Christmas Eve, when they would hire a Santa to walk around the office handing them out in red envelopes with a 'Ho Ho Ho!' and a bottle of Krug).

It was only after a month together that Angie slowly realised that she was paying for everything. Not that she *minded*, she emphasised to Judy and Ber. The voiceover business was notoriously precarious, and Gary was often between jobs. But look at how he had splashed out on a bunch of flowers for her when he did that commercial for drain cleaner. Every time she heard the ad on her car radio, she would glow with pride. They had gone out to dinner to celebrate. Naturally, she had paid. But she hadn't minded in the least. It fact, it was a relief to be able to enjoy her money freely without worrying about embarrassing her boyfriend.

Gary certainly wasn't embarrassed. Quite the opposite. In fact, he would sometimes whinge if they didn't go out for dinner often enough. But most of the time he was such good fun to be with that Angie went on financing the relationship — after all, she had plenty of money compared to him, and hadn't she done enough moaning about men who made an issue out of her superior earning power? Refreshingly, Gary had no problem whatsoever about her trouncing him in the earnings stakes.

Which wasn't all that hard. The drain commercial didn't lead to any new job offers. But things looked up when he got an audition for a yoghurt commercial, and he and Angie had spent an evening rehearsing the line, 'Mmm, taste the difference.'

She had met him after work the following evening. 'Well? How did it go?'

He had pulled a little face. 'I didn't get it.'

Angie was outraged. After all that rehearsal too! 'They just don't recognise talent,' she said to cheer him up.

He didn't look that downhearted. 'Well, actually, I didn't bother going. There were twenty others up for it, and the money was crap.' He had given her one of his winning smiles. 'So, where are you taking me for dinner tonight?'

That was the end of that particular relationship.

'I became a sugar mummy without even realising it,' Angie complained now.

415

'You're not old enough to be a sugar mummy,' Judy said consolingly.

'The worst thing is, I saw him sitting on that park bench again today. It's obviously a trick of his — he hangs around the financial centre in the hopes of picking up career woman who'll look after him.'

'I'm sure he's not that manipulative.'

But Angie was still smarting. 'Are they really all such toads, Judy? Or is it just me? Have I let my life become defined by my career? Maybe I should just jack it all in and pack bags at the supermarket.'

'You'd never be happy doing that.'

'No, I wouldn't. But I'm sick of my job getting in the way, Judy.' Then she brightened. 'On the plus side, my first Christmas bonus would cover a really good shopping trip. Will we go to Brown Thomas?'

'No,' said Judy baldly. 'I couldn't bear all the couples and the Cliff Richard Christmas songs.'

'Let's go drinking then. I know a good sports bar.'

'They'll all be full of lechy rugger types who'll think we're only there to be picked up.'

'I'll take out my platinum American Express card, that should scare them off,' Angie said, gloomily. 'Come on, Judy, please.'

'No. I have to see my solicitor about something, I can't go in stinking of beer. And anyway, if it's drink and sports you want, the perfect candidate is sitting across town right now in a white van.'

Biffo had got his old job back. He was last

seen putting up a FOR SALE sign in Greystones, and then running away very fast with a large black dog on his heels.

Angie flushed. 'That's not funny, Judy.'

'You're right. It's not. You know, maybe this isn't about your job getting in the way at all, Angie. Maybe it's about you *letting* it get in the way.'

Angie waved a hand dismissively. 'That's just semantics. There's no future for me and Biffo Brady unless he swallows every last ounce of pride and comes crawling back on all fours.'

'That's a bit of a tall order.'

'There's no other way.'

'We all know that he was in the wrong over the break-up and all that. But he has to be allowed *some* pride, Angie.'

'I don't think he's ever been short on that,' Angie snorted.

'He is at the moment. After his great year away, here he is back in Ireland, right back where he started.'

'Well, yes,' Angie conceded. 'Did he find an apartment yet?'

'No.'

Biffo was still stuck at home with Rose and Mick, because what with the car rental company debt and the rebuilding of the kitchen, he hadn't a penny to his name. He was so broke that he hadn't been able to afford any new clothes yet and was still wearing Mick's diamond-patterned jumper around the house at weekends. He'd even had to borrow money off Judy to buy her a Christmas present.

'I suppose it's all a bit of a step down for him,' Angie said, who had never in her life had to worry about money.

'Yes,' Judy agreed. 'So if you were waiting for him to come crawling on his hands and knees, well, I think he's already on them.'

Angie was silent at that.

★ ★ ★

The following Saturday morning, Judy rang the surgery to make sure that Barry was there. Then she packed the last of his belongings up into boxes, which he had stubbornly refused to come and do himself, and drove around to his mother's house.

The smell of Vick's vapour hit her the minute the door opened. Mrs Fox's nose was red and streaming, and her eyes rheumy.

Her demeanour didn't improve upon the sight of Judy. 'I wouldn't come in if I were you,' she said, rather ungraciously. 'I have a filthy cold.'

'I'll risk it,' Judy assured her.

Mrs Fox watched silently as Judy made several trips in with the last of Barry's stuff.

'And here's his post. It's mostly Christmas cards. Some of them are still addressed to both of us — obviously word hasn't reached everybody yet.' She handed them over. 'Maybe you'd ask him to go down to the post office when he has a chance, and get them to redirect his post. It doesn't cost much, and it makes everything much easier.'

'For you, maybe,' said Mrs Fox.

418

Judy was prepared for hostility. 'For both of us, Mrs Fox. At some point we have to draw a line under this whole thing and try to move on.'

'It just trips off your tongue, doesn't it?' said Mrs Fox. 'This isn't some soap opera, Judy, where everybody gets over things in a weekend.'

'It's hardly a weekend. We broke up six months ago.'

'And don't I know it.' She blew her nose loudly before breaking into a violent coughing fit.

Judy felt sorry for her. For once, she was genuinely sick.

'Maybe you should be in bed.'

'Don't you start,' said Mrs Fox.

'What?' Normally Mrs Fox would have been delighted with any bit of sympathy at all.

But she looked at Judy balefully. 'Barry's after listening to my chest twice already today and no doubt he'll bring me home a selection of cough mixtures and antibiotics from the surgery. And all over a blessed cold.' She wiped her nose and burst out, 'Oh, for heaven's sake, he made a mistake, Judy! He learned from it. He's changed, all right? Is there not any way at all you could take him back, or are you just playing some kind of a game, making him suffer for as long as possible before you give in?'

Judy said evenly, 'Mrs Fox, you're obviously not feeling too well today, so I'm going to put that down to a high temperature, OK?'

'All I'm asking is that you be straight with him.'

Judy was getting angry now. 'Barry knows exactly how I feel.'

'Well, you're not making yourself clear then! Because he's still under some illusion that he'll win you back if only he waits long enough. I've tried telling him, you know. I've said to him, she doesn't care any more, get over it, find someone else, because you can be sure she will. If she hasn't already. But he won't. Instead he sits in my house night after night dreaming up ways of running into you by accident, and driving me mad.'

'I've just brought over the last of his things,' Judy pointed out stiffly. 'Everything else will be wound up next week.' There was a solicitor's letter in the bundle she had just handed over. 'If he doesn't know it's over by then, well, it's nothing to do with me.'

She turned to go.

Mrs Fox blurted, 'My sisters in Surrey want me to move back with them when they come over for Christmas. To retire.'

'That sounds great,' said Judy, not really sure why Mrs Fox was telling her this.

'We get on well, and I could rent a house near them, and we'd go walking, and there's a bridge club and tennis courts near them. I played some tennis while Barry was in France, did I tell you?' She looked a bit defensive, as though Judy was going to be shocked that she had enjoyed herself while her son was missing in France.

'Good for you,' she said.

'Yes,' she said. 'I think it's time. To start doing things again. You know, after Gerry.'

Judy said, 'That's really great, Mrs Fox.'

'But how can I possibly go!' she cried. 'With Barry moping around the house like a child again! I can't just leave him. Not after all he did for me since Gerry passed away.'

Including helping her turn into a hypochondriac, Judy wanted to say.

'Do you not think that sometimes people are best left to get on with things in their own way?'

Mrs Fox gave her a look. 'Possibly,' she said stiffly. 'And if I thought he was starting to put this behind him at all . . . ' She shook her head.

'He'll get there in his own time.'

'I knew you'd say something like that.'

The implication was that Judy was a cold, detached person who didn't care about what suffering others had to go through.

'What do you want me to do, take him back just because you want to move to England?'

Mrs Fox didn't appreciate this. 'Just make him know that this is over, Judy. Then he really might be able to move on with his life, and me with mine.'

Judy was fed up of the conversation now, and not about to take on the task of helping of Mrs Fox successfully relocate. 'Goodbye, Mrs Fox.'

'I mean it, Judy,' she called after her. 'Because it's not fair on anybody!'

Judy had no idea what she meant by that. She dismissed it, and Mrs Fox, from her mind and drove off.

32

The large, expensive, shiny object Vinnie had taken Ber shopping for was an engagement ring.

'He let me think we were on our way to Power City for the new washing machine, but at the very last minute he took a detour and next thing I know we're driving up O'Connell Street towards the Happy Ring House,' Ber said. She still looked stunned. 'They recognised him from the last time, and they broke open the champagne and the manager himself came over to serve us and everything.'

The ring sat on her fourth finger very ostentatiously. Ber would rather have had something a bit more discreet, but Vinnie insisted that she had gone long enough without any official recognition, and that she wouldn't be palmed off with any mean little diamond, and that he was going to spend the full month's wages on it as per tradition.

His full month's wages could buy quite a large diamond, unfortunately, which was why she had ended up with one that stood right up off her finger and was almost as large as her knuckle. But she hadn't the heart to spoil the moment, not when he was as proud as punch, and declaring to anybody who would listen that they had waited years for this day, and that it was best of his whole life.

'It got a bit embarrassing at one stage, when

he actually broke down crying, and the manager said that it was usually the woman who cried, and he had to go and get him a tissue.'

Judy thought it all sounded very sweet. 'And you had no idea at all?'

'None at all. Well, we're both so shattered with that bloody dog, and Christmas, and trying to fix up the spare bedrooms for his sons.' She looked at the ring again, rather distrustfully Judy thought, as though wondering how it got on her finger at all, or if indeed it belonged to someone else entirely. 'I wasn't expecting it,' she reiterated, a bit limply.

'So have you set a date or anything?'

'Jesus Christ, Judy, would you stop!'

'What?'

'I haven't even worked out how to get dressed yet without the thing snagging every jumper I have, and you expect me to have worked out a *date*?'

Well, yes. For many years now, Ber had had the dress chosen, and the menu for the meal, and the seating plan for the guests. Mind you, she would have to update that, as several of the guests had by now passed away from old age.

'Do you realise,' Ber thundered, 'that I have a twenty-two-pound bird to cook in exactly seven days, and have just worked out that I'll have to get up at six o'clock in the morning to put it in the oven? And you expect me to think about my *wedding*?'

Judy wondered if Ber had become unhinged

from all the cosy domesticity. Because she didn't seem like herself at all. But then she hadn't for a number of months.

'And anyway,' Ber went on in a rush, 'you know very well that Vinnie has to get divorced first, and that's going to take him at least five years under Irish law.'

She sounded oddly relieved. She must have become aware of this, because she frowned and grumbled malevolently, 'It's archaic! Disgraceful! Shouldn't be allowed.'

But it sounded a bit manufactured.

'I thought this was what you always wanted, Ber.'

'It is! Absolutely. I couldn't be happier.' Her ring snagged on her jumper again. 'Fuck.'

She eventually extricated herself, and laid out her hand carefully on the table as though it were something quite apart from herself. 'I suppose it's going to, you know, take a bit of time to get used to.'

This struck another odd note, seeing as Vinnie and Ber had been planning for their eventual union for the better part of a decade.

'But I suppose it's the next logical step, isn't it?' she said, with a brave smile. 'You move in together, then you get engaged, and then you get married.'

Judy knew the drill all too well.

'And then you have babies,' she said.

Ber paled. 'What? As well as a dog?'

'I was only joking,' Judy said.

Ber gave a little sigh. 'I thought the hardest thing would be the pressure to make it work. You

424

know, after him leaving his wife and everything. I remember thinking, God, it's going to be awful if, after everything, the whole thing goes belly up the minute he moves in.' She looked at the ring again, and then back at Judy. 'What I never reckoned on was how different everything would be. Having an affair, it's like a little dream world, Judy, full of romance and excitement and danger, and nobody ever stops to wax their back or worry about the credit card bill. Suddenly we went from seeing each other in a restaurant once a week to living together twenty-four hours a day. It's like he's a whole new person, and I am too, and there's hardly anything at all left of how we used to be.'

'Have you said any of this to him?'

'He doesn't seem to miss that part of our lives at all. In fact, he's delighted he doesn't have to lie or sneak around any more. And I suppose I am too, in a way. But some days I think I'm in an entirely different relationship to the one that I started out being in.'

'Maybe there's some way you can get some of it back.'

'Like how?' Ber scoffed. 'Dress up in something sexy and arrange to meet him in a room in the Holiday Inn, just like old times? Or ring his mobile phone and if he doesn't answer on the second ring, then hang up?'

'It sounds like you don't want to be back there anyway.'

'I suppose I don't,' Ber conceded. 'But God, Judy, where is it all going to end? The dog and the turkey are bad enough. And now this?'

And she waved her engagement ring dangerously.

Vinnie came in at that moment. He was the
most relaxed Judy had ever seen him.

'Hello,' he said, just the once. He hadn't
repeated himself in many months now, and
could look every single one of Ber's friends
squarely in the eye. Her mother, too, even more
importantly.

'Showing off your ring?' he said, indulgently.

'Um, yes,' Ber said.

'It took me a good many years, Judy, but I
finally managed to pin her down,' he joked.

And indeed Ber did look pinned down. But
she managed a smile for all concerned.

Then Vinnie seemed to think that he might be
being a tad insensitive to Judy, and so he said,
hurriedly, 'Not that marriage is all it's cracked
up to be. Not at all. No, love is the most
important thing. If you have that, then nothing
else matters.'

And he gave Ber a look of such shining
adoration that she went quite pink, and stopped
trying to hide the engagement ring.

'Thank you, Vinnie.'

'I'm only speaking the truth,' he said fondly,
and kissed her.

Judy stood.

'There's no need to go,' Ber assured her
hurriedly. 'We're not going to jump on each
other or anything.'

She had said it jokingly, but Vinnie weighed in
heavily with, 'Certainly not. We need to go and
buy a Christmas tree.' He fussed to Ber, 'We

426

don't want all the good ones to be gone.'

'I suppose not,' she said thinly.

Judy hastened her departure. 'I have an appointment at the solicitor's anyway.'

Ber's hand flew to her mouth. 'Here's me going on about myself when you have all this horribleness in front of you.'

'Hopefully it won't be horrible at all.'

'I'm coming with you,' Ber insisted.

'No, really, Ber. I'll be fine.'

'You need moral support at a time like this.'

'It's just a question of signing some papers, that's all,' Judy said. The truth was that Barry would not appreciate an audience that afternoon. And who could blame him? During the week he had threatened not to turn up at all. But perhaps the prospect of seeing her face to face had changed his mind, because he had suddenly announced yesterday that he would keep the appointment after all.

'Good luck, Judy.' Ber gave her a hug.

'Thanks.'

★ ★ ★

Their solicitor had all the papers neatly drawn up, ready to be signed. Barry had refused to appoint a separate solicitor for himself. 'Why should I be the one who has to get a new solicitor? Why don't *you* go get a new solicitor?' (This had been during the week, when he had still been very angry about the whole thing.)

He was late, probably on purpose.

427

'I'm presuming you've got the cheque ready?' the solicitor asked.

'Yes.' It was in a white envelope in her bag. From today, her mortgage repayments would more than double. She wouldn't be able to afford to go out again, ever. Not even to the cinema. Thank God she had already bought the socks for Mick and the perfume for Rose; they would be getting melted-down ends of old soap remoulded into shell shapes for their remarriage gift.

Annette had said that if there was any overtime going, she would put it Judy's way. But people didn't tend to flock to libraries at Christmas; in fact, it was one of the quietest times of the year, and she'd been sent home early yesterday.

But it was a small price to pay for her freedom, and a home that was hers alone. They should have tackled the issue of the house months ago, of course, but Barry had still been hopeful of a reunion, and Judy hadn't wanted to countenance the notion of selling up.

Thankfully that hadn't been necessary. The bank had, very reluctantly and after shining a torch into every financial corner of her life, decided to assist her in buying Barry out of his share of the house.

After today, there would be nothing left holding them together. And nobody would be able to accuse her of not making it perfectly clear to Barry that things were well and truly over.

That's if he ever showed up. She would have to go to work in a minute, and the solicitor's stomach was rumbling for his lunch.

Finally Barry appeared. Judy expected him to make some excuse about being held up at the surgery, but he walked in with no apology whatsoever and flung himself down in a chair.

'Hi,' she said, awkwardly.

He gave her a very cold look. Well, she hadn't expected a hug and a kiss on the cheek. This was the final nail in the coffin, so to speak. Naturally, things were going to be difficult.

'Let's just run through all the paperwork, will we?' the solicitor said, moving quickly to smooth things over.

Judy listened as he shuffled papers about, and explained that the value of the house had been arrived at by two separate auctioneers, and that Judy was prepared to pay Barry his share of the higher valuation. He had the deeds in front of him, and the assignment, and the declaration that the property was not a family home.

All the while Barry kept staring at Judy rather malevolently. She tried to ignore it, and concentrate on what the solicitor was saying, but the atmosphere seemed to be going from cold to freezing.

'So if you're both in agreement, then maybe we could start signing the documents,' the solicitor finished up.

'And what if we're not?' Barry said loudly.

'Sorry?'

'In agreement?'

The solicitor looked from Barry to Judy; she could tell he was watching his lunch break disappear.

'Judy's the one who started all this,' Barry said fractiously. 'What if I don't *want* to be bought out? She can't make me, can she?'

'Well, no. But she's making a very generous offer, and in the circumstances — '

'Oh, we're all aware of the circumstances,' Barry spat.

Judy tried to appeal to his reason. 'Barry, what's the point in maintaining a home together when we don't live there as a couple and never will again?'

'You still can't make me sell.'

It seemed that he hadn't come here to facilitate the orderly transfer of property at all today, but to cause a great big scene.

'You're right, Barry. In that case, we'll have to go to court, and they'll make us sell the property and divide up the assets, and we'll spend a fortune in legal fees, and we'll probably end up hating each other's guts.'

'Oh, and we're so friendly now,' he jeered.

'We have been, until today,' she said, carefully. She had gone out of her way to be nice to him, even after everything he had done to her.

He gave her another very nasty look, and she was taken aback by it. But she told herself there was nothing she could do about it: if he couldn't act in an adult fashion over the splitting of assets, then it was his own problem.

'It's your choice, Barry,' she snapped. 'You either sign here today, or I'll issue court proceedings and you'll have to sign then.'

He shook his head slowly, as though she were something particularly undesirable that he had just discovered on the sole of his shoe. 'And to think that I spent the last six months trying to get you back,' he said venomously.

'Are we going to get on with it or not?' she inquired tersely. She wasn't going to get drawn into a discussion about their relationship.

'How stupid of me,' Barry said. 'Ridiculous of me! Because you never had any intention in the world of taking me back, did you?'

The solicitor shifted uncomfortably. 'If we could . . . ?'

'If you looked at your own behaviour it's easy to see why,' Judy said. Best to throw it back at him. Make him defend himself.

'Well, of course!' Barry cried dramatically. 'It's obvious! I ran off. It couldn't have been anything else, could it?'

His eyes were a bit glittery, as if he'd consumed a couple of vodkas before coming in, and Judy had a sudden ominous feeling.

'There couldn't possibly be any other reason, Judy, could there? For you refusing to take me back?'

'No,' she said, mystified. 'There couldn't, and there isn't.'

'Like Lenny, for example?'

At the mention of his name something must have shown on her face — shock, or lust, or even her lovelorn state of mind — because Barry latched onto it in a flash.

'Bet you never thought I'd find out about that, did you!' he cried triumphantly. 'Well, I did! My mother told me.'

So it was all going to come out in the wash

after all. Thanks to Mrs Fox, who seemed determined to secure her retirement in Surrey at all costs. Well, they were welcome to her.

Barry was looking at her with a mixture of revulsion and hope. 'Are you even going to deny it?'

There was a split second where Judy almost allowed herself to be manipulated into making stuttered explanations and excuses for behaviour that she had no reason to feel guilty about, even though she'd felt so at the time. For a moment, she was so wrong-footed that she almost believed that she was the one who had betrayed him, instead of the other way around.

But only almost.

'No,' she said loudly.

Barry looked more shocked. 'So it's true then? That my mother walked in on the two of you about to have a passionate clinch, and you with your blouse practically unbuttoned to your waist?'

'Sorry about this,' said Judy efficiently to the solicitor.

He just kept looking from one to the other.

'Were you sleeping with him?' Barry demanded, his face hot looking.

'That's none of your business.'

'It most certainly is my business!'

'I was never unfaithful to you up to the day you walked out the door. I'm not accountable after that.'

Barry gave her a look as though she were the most brazen hussy that had ever crossed his path.

432

'You know, I didn't believe my mother at first. I said, there's no way Judy would do something like that. She's too decent, too loyal, to even think about having cheap sex the minute I was gone. And with Lenny, of all people! I said to her, there is no way Judy would let herself be taken in by someone like him. Let's face it, he'd do it with anybody. But she said that you were the one who was coming on to him that night, that he was the only one with any decorum!'

He gave her another disgusted look.

'But I obviously misjudged you badly, Judy. Even after all our years together, I'm starting to think that I never really knew you at all.'

'Are you going to sign or not?' She'd had enough of this.

'Oh, I'll sign,' he said grimly. 'I want nothing more to do with you. To think that all the time that I was missing in France, you were having it off with another man!'

That was the final straw. Judy was afraid that if she opened her mouth at all, she would spill out bile. She could scarcely believe him. He wasn't lovely, kind, harmless Barry at all. He was stupid, and selfish, and she was so very glad that after today she needn't even bother with the pretence of being nice to him.

'Yes,' she said, eventually, when she could speak again. 'Exactly, Barry. And just for the record, you weren't 'missing'. You ran off in the middle of the night like a coward. And, just for the record, that is why I ended the relationship. Not because of Lenny. If I'd never met Lenny, I still wouldn't be with you.'

433

He shot an angry, embarrassed look at the solicitor, before grabbing a pen. 'Tell me where I have to sign these damn things and let me go.'

It was all done as quickly as possible. Judy handed over the cheque and then Barry stood so brusquely that he nearly knocked his chair backwards.

'You needn't worry that I'll be bothering you again,' he told Judy, his lip curling.

Mrs Fox's ploy had worked, then. In a way, Judy was glad. After today, things were truly over.

Barry had one last parting shot. 'He didn't hang around then? Lenny.'

Judy felt sick. He knew how to get the boot in all right. 'There was never a question of him staying.'

She wanted it to sound like a joint decision, but it came out sounding weak and pathetic, as if she was making excuses.

He gave her a falsely sympathetic look. 'I could have told you that. He's a bit out of your league, Judy. Still, I hope you enjoyed it while it lasted.'

33

Biffo was refusing to go to his office Christmas party.

'It'll be the same as two years ago — a meal in the Happy Valley restaurant, with the boss at the top of the table and everybody else seated according to their sales figures for the year. The nearer the boss, the more houses you've sold. Which means I'll probably be put in the fucking kitchen.'

They were sitting in the pub like a couple of sad losers, trying to eke out their drinks because neither of them had any money to buy another.

'You're only back six months. You have to give it a chance,' Judy said to cheer him up, although she was a ball of misery herself.

'Six months! And I still haven't got my old desk back,' he said moodily. 'I have to share with Des, who stinks of garlic all the time.'

It had all been a very inauspicious end to his glorious career in America. Without references, his exotic experience in beachfront apartments was all but useless. He didn't even have a decent suit to go to interviews in, because he had great difficulty accessing his US bank accounts from Dublin. Cheryl, of course, was immediately suspected as the culprit even though she didn't know his pin numbers or anything like that, and it was unlikely she'd managed to get her father to interfere with bank clerks. But it didn't matter, she got the blame anyway. In fact she was a handy scapegoat for nearly everything that went wrong, even on this side of the Atlantic. Take dinner last week at Rose's, when the bulb had blown in the kitchen, and she had muttered, 'That fecking Cheryl,' before getting up to change it.

Anyway, with no references, Biffo was back at square one. He'd ended up begging for his old job back. But the firm was none too impressed at the way he'd dumped them for the glamour of America, and he'd had to start at the bottom all over again — arranging viewings, photocopying millions of brochures and, of course, putting up the FOR SALE signs. At least they'd given him his white van back.

'You know what the sad thing is?' he said. 'I was quite happy with my job before I ever went to America. I didn't know any better. But now that I've had it all, being back at the bottom really sucks.'

He knocked back his pint, then said, 'Damn. That was supposed to have lasted me another half hour.'

He was back on the cigarettes too; twenty a day, and thirty at weekends. And plenty of pizzas too, and chips, judging by his expanding waistline. His tan had completely disappeared, leaving behind acres of pale, pasty skin. If he still had any toned muscles, they were well hidden beneath his voluminous Liverpool shirt.

But it was nice to have him back. The new, improved Biffo had been a bit of a stranger. It was the one part of Judy's life that had settled down for the better.

'Are you bringing anybody to the wedding?' he inquired gloomily.

'No.'

'I suppose you're a bit off men right now,' he said sympathetically.

'Just a bit.'

He was quick to assure her, 'Nobody believes him, you know — Barry. And all those things he's been saying.'

All week long, Judy had endured a fresh round of scandalised looks from the library regulars. Several of them had congregated behind the Travel section yesterday to discuss this latest development in the saga. She had cornered one of them and demanded to know where the gossip had originated. It transpired that Barry had been telling patients in the surgery at the end of every visit. She had phoned up yesterday and told him that if he continued she would sue him. That had stopped it. But it was too late; the damage had already been done.

Biffo said authoritatively, 'It's a clear attempt to besmirch your name because you refused to get back with him. Everybody knows that, Judy. There's not a single person in the whole of Cove who really thinks that you were sleeping with Lenny.'

'Thanks,' said Judy, through a clenched jaw.

Biffo gave an amused little smile now. 'Barry must be on drugs or something. No offence, Judy, but I can't imagine you and Lenny.'

It was the first time somebody had said it out loud, but Judy guessed it had been said plenty of times during the week out of her earshot.

'Why not?' she asked loudly.

'What?'

'Because I'm not an international model? You think Lenny's that superficial that he only goes out with women who are six foot tall and with hair like a horse's tail? You think I have nothing whatsoever going for me that he might find remotely attractive? Even if it was just to sleep with me once?'

Biffo looked a bit taken aback by this diatribe. 'Well — '

'For all you know, I could be fantastic in bed! I might be the wittiest, sexiest, most exciting woman in the entire world! Only nobody ever knew it because I spent half my life joined at the hip to a plonker!'

Biffo said nothing for fear of inciting further wrath. When it became obvious that she was finished for the moment, he ventured, 'I'm sure you're, um, fantastic in bed, Judy. But when I said I couldn't imagine you and Lenny, I meant that you would never go for someone like him. Not the other way around.'

'Oh,' said Judy, deflating completely. Then, 'Why not?'

Biffo looked alarmed at having got her going all over again. 'Nothing — '

'You think I'm so straight-laced that I can't appreciate a big gorgeous hunk even if he's got the morals of an alley cat? If you must know, Lenny is one of the most charismatic, interesting, sexy, provocative men I've ever had the pleasure to meet!' Not to mention sleep with. It was just a shame that he had a slight biological fault when it came to hanging around.

Biffo was watching her very closely. 'Are you telling me that what Barry is going around saying is true?'

Judy was tempted to say yes. At least it would give her an air of mystery. Biffo might even look up to her for a while. But why add fuel to the fire? People had enough to talk about already without her chiming in with confirmation that she had, indeed, been sleeping with Lenny. Even if it was just the once.

'No,' she muttered.

'I knew it,' Biffo said, annoyingly. Then he mused, 'I wonder what he's doing now. Lenny.'

'Who knows,' Judy said shortly.

'He'll probably be spending Christmas on the beach,' Biffo went on enviously. 'That's what they do in Australia: pack up a few crates of beer, a couple of steaks, and have a big barbecue by the sea.'

Judy had a sudden and wrenching vision of Lenny in a tiny little pair of swim trunks. Followed by an even more wrenching vision of a seven-foot redhead standing beside him in just the bottom half of her bikini.

'Meanwhile, the two of us will be attending our parents' wedding with not a date in sight,' Biffo went on gloomily.

Judy wanted to kill him. 'It's not going to be as bad as all that.'

'It's going to be awful. I don't even know why they're doing it. Mum keeps looking at Dad as though she wants to murder him. And he keeps making her sweet tea and trying to buy her new things for the kitchen that she doesn't even want. I don't know what's up with the pair of them at all.'

Biffo had remained blissfully unaware of Mick's brief infatuation with his ex-girlfriend. Nobody had thought it constructive to enlighten him. Also, nobody wanted to bring up Cheryl's name unnecessarily in any civilised conversation.

'It'll be romantic,' Judy insisted, even though she wondered whether it would be at all. Maybe she just desperately wanted something nice to happen in her life. Something positive.

Barry's words in the solicitor's office that day were stuck in her brain, as he had no doubt intended. Men like Lenny *didn't* hang around for women like her. Mind you, he didn't hang around for any woman, it seemed, but that was scant consolation.

She wondered now whether she had harboured secret hopes that he would phone, or write her a big long letter saying that, on reflection, the night with her had been best of his entire career, and that he would like to come back for more if she were agreeable. He would say that he couldn't stop thinking about her, that she was on his mind constantly. He would admit that, after many sleepless nights, he had decided that casual sex wasn't all it was cracked up to be, and that he wanted to embrace commitment. With her, Judy. The whole monogamy lark. Give it a year, and he might even do the whole till-death-do-us-part bit, if she really, really wanted it. He was ready. He was hers.

But of course this was real life, and not only had there been no long, anguished letter, but there hadn't even been a Christmas card. Still, he mightn't have felt it was that appropriate to be sending one, seeing as he had boffed her six months previously. Viciously, she decided that he must have a very short Christmas card list if he had to leave off all the women he'd loved and left.

'How much of a Christmas bonus did she get then?' Biffo burst out.

Judy was startled, even though she shouldn't have been. After two pints, Biffo generally started talking about Angie.

'Ten grand?' he said disparagingly. 'Twenty? Fifty?' His Adam's apple bobbed nervously over that last amount. He could only dream of that as a yearly salary.

'I have no idea. Angie doesn't discuss her bonuses with me.'

'She didn't discuss them with me either. Looking back, it was a form of power,' he said regally.

'Oh, rubbish. You know very well that she didn't want to upset you by rubbing your face in it.'

Biffo brooded over that for a moment. 'There are worse things your face could be rubbed in.'

As only somebody on a very low salary could appreciate.

Judy looked at him quizzically. 'Oh?'

'On reflection, perhaps I didn't properly appreciate the holidays and the presents and the nice meals out that she used to pay for. I could

441

have enjoyed them but I didn't, because I was so busy being resentful.' He was quick to add, 'Not that it makes a whit of difference. Not that it changes anything now. But it's funny, Judy, all that time wasted, not being honest. We just started everything off wrong, both of us pretending madly that the money didn't matter.'

'And does it really?' Judy asked.

Biffo gave a sigh. 'Judy, it's too late.'

'I'm just asking if the money would matter now.'

He thought about it and then said, in a defeated kind of way, 'Maybe I'd still have some stupid male thing going on. And even if I didn't, people can be desperately thick, Judy. All those comments about being a kept man. Nobody lets you forget it.'

'You're right, Biffo. Those kinds of comments are hard to live with. It would take a very strong person to able to put up with that.'

Biffo gave her a rather testy look. 'Don't give me all that stuff, because I already know it, OK? How it takes a bigger man to accept that his partner earns more, and all that.'

'Well, it does.'

'I bloody know it does. Try parking a crappy little van next to her gas guzzler every evening. Don't talk to me about how secure a man needs to be in himself to live with that. Very fucking secure, that's what.'

'And are you not?'

'I always thought I was grand in the security stakes until I met her,' he mused. 'I never thought there was a thing wrong with me.'

'But there isn't, Biffo. Well, not a lot anyway.'

He shot her a look. 'I just don't know if I can handle it. On a long-term basis anyway. I mean, what if we did get back together, and we end up having kids? Am I going to turn into a stay-at-home dad? Can you imagine the lads in the pub at that one?'

'There are lots of stay-at-home dads nowadays. In fact, it's the very coolest thing to be.'

Biffo lifted an eyebrow at that. 'Are you trying to say I'd be 'special'?'

'I'm trying to tell you that there might be advantages as well, Biffo. But you need to talk things out. Acknowledge it. Find ways of making it work for everybody.'

She saw the first stirring of hope on Biffo's face. But he remained fearful. 'She's thinks I'm anathema to all career women. Oh, I heard what she's been saying around town, that I should be taken into classrooms and shown to young girls as an example of what to avoid if they want to make anything at all of themselves in the future. What makes you think she'll have me back?'

'Oh, I don't know, Biffo,' Judy burst out, fed up of both of them. 'The two of you obviously love each other, but that's not enough, it seems. You just keep on putting up these stumbling blocks all the time. If you want to throw it all away, then go right ahead.'

She got up and walked out.

443

34

Everybody who worked at the library agreed that there was a general misconception that librarians were, on the whole, a rather earnest, hard-working lot who would rather go home to bed early with a cup of drinking chocolate and a good book than do almost anything else.

That was why, each year, they held their annual Christmas party in the most outlandish place they could possibly find.

The rule was everybody brought their party clothes into work, and only when six o'clock came would they decide exactly where they were going.

'It's Christmas party time!' Annette would holler in a blood-curdling voice, and they would all doff their librarian clothes (in the toilets, of course) and start throwing out suggestions for the venue.

'And they say librarians aren't spontaneous?' Annette would say dangerously.

The best party so far had been in a supposedly haunted house in a remote part of the Wicklow Mountains. They had driven up in Annette's camper van loaded up with alcohol and music equipment, and had a blast. It had been chilly, and very dark, but after a couple of Annette's lethal cocktails nobody had minded a bit, and everybody had howled with laughter when Bill, the security guy, had pretended to bang on one of the walls in the house just to scare everybody (afterwards they discovered he had been out in the van at the time, and that the banging couldn't possibly have been him).

This year they were relying on Marcia's experience. Being young and happening, she would undoubtedly know some hot spots where a gang of librarians could shuck off their stereotypical image.

'I know where there's going to be a rave,' she said.

'A rave!' squealed Annette in delight. 'I didn't know they did those any more.' She was wearing a short red spangled dress and a pair of kinky heels.

'There might be drugs and things,' Marcia cautioned them.

'We'll take that on board,' Annette said stoically. 'What do you think, Judy?'

Judy was thinking that a rave was one of the very last places she wanted to be on the last Friday night before Christmas, but she didn't want to be a spoilsport and so she said, 'Great! I haven't been to a rave in ages.'

Ever, actually.

'Will we understand the music?' she inquired after a moment.

'I wouldn't think so,' Marcia said apologetically. 'Oh, look, maybe it's best if we go for a nice meal instead.'

Judy was just thinking what a good idea that was when Annette declared, 'Absolutely not. We have a reputation to uphold here. A tradition. No, lead the way, Marcia.'

Marcia checked her watch. 'It's probably not going to start until about two a.m.'

On reflex Judy started yawning.

Annette was undeterred. 'We'll go drinking first. Where's my camera? Oh, this is going to be great fun!'

In January, she always put up a selection of the more risqué photographs taken at these outings. 'What on earth is that?' the regulars would inquire, looking at them from every angle, trying to make sense of the debauchery. 'Just the staff do,' Annette would tell them cheerily.

Before they left, there was a minor altercation over whether people would be allowed to bring their partners.

'Why not? It's just a big party,' Marcia protested. She had been going out with someone for a month now and they were at that stage where they couldn't bear to be separated from each other, even for five minutes.

'Yes, but we don't do partners,' Annette said firmly.

Judy knew that this was for her benefit; Judy, who had no one, only a bitter ex who was going around town telling everybody that she was more or less a slut.

'Let people bring partners if they want to,' she said cheerfully, even though a rave was bad enough without having to watch Marcia crawling all over her boyfriend.

But Annette wasn't budging. 'It's staff only.'

'Probably just as well,' Bill chipped in. 'The missus wouldn't be too keen on a rave.'

She wouldn't be the only one.

'Right!' said Annette. 'Let's go!'

★ ★ ★

When Judy finally got home it was nearly five o'clock in the morning and her head didn't seem to belong to the rest of her body. Plus, she seemed to have lost her hearing.

'Thanks!' she screamed at the taxi driver who had driven her home. But it was OK, because it turned out she had lost her voice too, from trying to communicate with Annette and Marcia over the deafening din of the 'music'.

She wasn't drunk, though. There didn't seem to be any place to buy alcohol, although you could have as many drugs as you wanted. Annette may well have indulged, judging by the way she had danced the whole night long with a bunch of scruffy-looking twenty-somethings who had welcomed her wholeheartedly into their group.

Judy had hung at the back, trying to tap her foot to the music, before giving up and dreaming about her lovely soft bed.

The phone was ringing when she got into the house. Or maybe it was still the music in her head. One of the tracks at the end had sounded like a protracted fire engine.

But no, she was pretty certain it was the phone.

She checked her watch. Not a good time to be

getting phone calls. The last time she'd had a phone call at that hour, Aunty Noeleen had passed on.

She picked it up and croaked, 'Hello?'

She braced herself for the bad news.

There was a silence. 'It that you, Judy?'

Her heart did a flip. It was Lenny.

She went into immediate defence mode and pretended she didn't know who he was. 'Yes,' she said haughtily, even though she sounded like the monster from the deep. 'To whom am I speaking?'

'It's Lenny,' he said impatiently.

There was a big long tense silence. After its flip, her heart was now galloping like the favourite in the Grand National.

'Happy Christmas,' she said, just for something to say.

He obviously wasn't in a seasonal mood because he complained, 'I've been trying to ring you for the last ten hours.'

'I've been at a rave.'

'What?'

'A rave. You know, a music thing.'

'I know what a rave is.'

He sounded astonished.

'It was quite good, actually,' Judy said airily. That was one in the eye for him: predictable Judy, whooping it up at an all-night rave. He needn't know that her hearing was probably permanently impaired and that her feet were absolutely killing her.

Then it really hit her: Lenny was ringing her. At five o'clock in the morning. From Australia.

She hadn't heard from him in six months and now this.

'Has anybody died?' she inquired.

'Not that I'm aware of,' he said slowly.

He obviously was not au fait with late-night phone etiquette. 'You should have said that at the outset. Otherwise people automatically assume the worst.'

There was another little silence.

'I'll bear that in mind for the next time,' he assured her.

Now that nobody was dead, Judy got back to wondering what he wanted. Her hand was slippery on the phone receiver. She was lovelorn, after all, and the subject of her affections was at the other end of the line.

Saying very little, come to think of it. He wasn't blurting out that he hadn't been able to stop thinking of her for the past six months, or that he was ready to renege on his life of looseness and amorality.

'Did you ring for any particular reason?' she asked.

'Well, actually, yes,' he said.

She had missed his voice. That slow drawl, with the little sardonic twist, and the occasional Australian twang.

'Oh?' she said. She hoped she wasn't panting.

'I had a very strange phone call from Barry,' he told her efficiently.

Judy's heart went into freefall. It was about blasted Barry, and not them at all.

'Did you?' She tried to sound mildly interested, even though she would be very happy if she never had to think or talk about Barry again.

'He accused me of sleeping with you.'

'Yes, I imagine he did.'

'You told him?'

'No, I didn't tell him. His mother told him. She wants to move to Surrey.'

'What?'

'Oh, it doesn't matter.' She couldn't bear to lead him through the petty little chain of events.

'He said some pretty nasty things.'

'Yes, he's not been himself this past while,' Judy explained. 'Don't worry, he said some pretty nasty things to me too.'

'I'm not ringing up looking for sympathy, Judy.'

'Oh? What then? You're worried about Barry, is it? Like I said, he's a bit bitter at the moment, but I'm sure he'll come round eventually and be back to his sunny self in no time at all.'

'Judy,' he said, 'why are you speaking to me like this?'

Because you bloody well deserve it, she wanted to say. Because they'd spent the night together six months ago and he hadn't even inquired about her health.

'Because I'm tired, Lenny, and I want to go to bed.'

He was frosty now. 'Right, well, I won't keep you.'

'You haven't even told me what you're ringing about.'

He had said he had spent the last ten hours trying to get hold of her. Surely it must be important.

'He said you're not together any more,' he said, into the silence.

'Well, no, we're not. Otherwise I'd imagine his mother wouldn't have told him about us having some nookie while he was in France.'

'Judy, don't be flippant.'

'Why not? I thought you liked flippant. Lots of fun and games and nothing too heavy, isn't that right?'

'Judy, stop it.'

'No, you stop it. You ring me at five o'clock in the morning and you interrogate me, and you don't even ask me how I am! So, for your information, yes, Barry knows we slept together, no, we're not together any more, and now I'm going to bed. And I'm fine, thanks for your inquiry.'

She hung up and went to the bathroom to take off her make-up. And, actually, she needn't have bothered, because most of it seemed to have washed off her face in the heat of the rave.

She banged around the bathroom a bit, picking up pots of things and putting them back down again very roughly, and gargling her poor sore throat. And now she wouldn't even be able to sleep. She'd lie there tossing and turning over Lenny, who didn't even deserve it.

The phone rang again just as she was pulling the duvet up over her head. She took the receiver into the bed with her.

'Hello?'

'It's me again. I'm sorry. You were absolutely right.'

451

'About what bit in particular?'

'I didn't ask you how you were. I was going to work up to it.' There was a little pause. 'How are you, Judy?'

She was going to say fine, and pretend that everything was just super, but she was too tired to bother, and her heart was too sore, and so she just said, 'I'm actually not too good. I have a headache like you wouldn't believe, and Barry has been horrible, and I'm sick of Christmas.'

'So am I,' he told her. 'All those Christmas songs. And it's thirty-six degrees here, and everyone's in shorts, and it's not a bit Christmassy.'

Judy was suspicious at his chattiness. Normally he was too cool to let himself get involved in conversations about things like the weather, and shorts. She got the impression he was buying himself time.

'What are you doing for Christmas?' she inquired. Two could play at this game.

'Oh, it'll probably be the usual barbecue on the beach.'

Biffo was right. There would probably be brunettes there too, and blondes, and a smattering of redheads.

Although he hadn't mentioned them. But then again he wouldn't. He would realise it would be tactless to mention his current clatter of girlfriends to one of his exes. If you could even call her that. After only one night together she probably hadn't clocked up enough time to be conferred with that title.

'What about you?' he said.

'I'll probably go to Ber's', she said. She must mention it to Ber first. But Mick and Rose would be on honeymoon in Scotland so she could hardly go over to their house. The alternative would be to have Christmas dinner by herself, in her lonely little kitchen, before watching the family movie on the TV whilst getting through a large tin of Roses.

Her depression must have affected Lenny at the other end of the line because he had gone very quiet.

'Are you still there?' she asked.

'When did you and Barry break up?' he asked suddenly.

'Ages ago,' Judy said. She didn't want to tell him it had been less than twenty-four hours after they'd slept together. His head was already big enough. 'It just didn't work out after France.' She couldn't resist adding, 'Despite my insane urge to get married.'

She really wished she could see his face. You couldn't tell anything at all by silences.

'You're finally getting sense,' he said.

She was all set to be outraged, but found that she wasn't. Maybe it was because it was so nice to be talking to him on the phone. Or maybe they'd had this particular argument so many times now that it was hard to sustain any kind of outrage.

'I take it you mean that I've finally recognised marriage for the empty shell that it is?'

'Well, I wouldn't go that far,' he said.

She sat up a bit in the bed — it was difficult to sound authoritative on the flat of her back and she said, 'I'm sorry to disappoint you, but you're wrong. Despite everything, I still believe in commitment and even marriage. It was just that Barry and I weren't right for each other at the end of the day.'

'Still an incurable optimist.'

'Whereas you, I suppose, are still a pessimist. Which is just a fancy way of saying you get a bit nervous around the C word. That's commitment, by the way.'

'I know what the C word is. And as I've told you numerous times before, I have no problem whatsoever with commitment.'

'Just so long as it doesn't involve you.'

'Just so long as it doesn't involve any trips up the aisle dressed like a monkey and being watched by four hundred assorted friends and relations.' He sounded as if it was the worst possible thing that could ever befall him.

'I don't think there's any danger of that ever happening to you,' Judy assured him.

She had missed this: the sparring, the back and forth. Even though it involved momentous questions about him, and them. But right now she didn't care. She was just enjoying the conversation.

'Come over for Christmas,' he said.

'What?'

'To Australia.'

She was stunned. It was out of the blue. Or maybe not so out of the blue. He had rung because he knew she wasn't with Barry any more. He'd had it all planned.

'I don't know what to say, Lenny.'

'Say yes.'

'It's not as simple as that.'

'Why not, Judy? What's so complicated about it? Just hop on a plane. It's beautiful here right now, we'll go to the beach, we'll eat turkey in the sun. Come on, live in the moment.'

He was always extolling her to live in the moment. And it sounded very tempting. She should be over the moon. The man she was lovelorn for had just invited her to spend Christmas with him in an exotic place. As a couple. Why not go and enjoy it for as long as it lasted?

Because she had tried that already and it hadn't worked. Instead she had ended up miserable for the past six months.

'I'd love to, Lenny, I really would,' she said sincerely. 'But I can't.'

'Please, Judy. I've really missed you.'

'Lenny, don't start that.'

'What?'

'Don't start saying things that will just make it harder for me not to go.'

'I'm saying them because I mean them.'

'I'm sure you do, but it's not going to make any difference.'

There was a little pause. 'What *would* make a difference, Judy?'

'Look, Lenny, you were right all along. We're too different, you and I. I can't live by your rules and you can't live by mine. So maybe it's just best to leave it.'

She had dreamed the whole winter long of him ringing up begging to see her again. Now he

455

had, and she was saying no.

She huddled under the duvet, the phone pressed hard to her ear.

'So that's it?' He sounded disappointed and incredulous. 'You're not going to come over just because we happen to disagree on a few things?'

It wasn't as simple as that and he knew it.

'Do feelings not come into it at all?' he inquired.

Feelings had everything to do with it. She'd be gone like a flash if she didn't have so many of the damn things. They were already fragile enough without exposing them to further trauma.

'Lenny, there's no point in making this harder than it already is.'

'If that's what you want,' he said at last.

It wasn't what she wanted at all. It wasn't what he wanted either. But it was becoming increasingly obvious that he wasn't going to say or do anything that was going to change her mind.

And at this stage of the game she wasn't going to settle. Not again.

'I'd better let you get some sleep then,' he said.

'OK. Goodbye, Lenny.'

'Goodbye, Judy. Happy Christmas.'

'Happy Christmas to you too.'

35

'Judy, are you completely mad?' Ber demanded.

'Probably.'

'You just turned down a fantastic invitation to spend Christmas on a beach with one of the sexiest men this town has ever seen!' She was looking at Judy as though she had committed a very serious crime. But then again she had spent the morning making a plum pudding, which had all but unhinged her. Whatever way she had pressed it into the mould, it had come out in the shape of a bullet.

'Give me his phone number,' she said shortly. 'I'll go.'

Judy was starting to regret having told Ber. But she needed someone to confide in; the mirror at home in the bathroom wasn't giving her any answers. She wished she had a tape of the phone conversation so that she could listen to it all over again and try to make sense of it; to be sure that she hadn't indeed made a horrible mistake.

'Poor Barry,' Ber said. 'Nobody in Cove believed him when he said you and Lenny were sleeping together, and all the time it was true.'

'There's no need to go feeling sorry for Barry,' Judy said shortly.

'I know,' said Ber. Her nose wrinkled. 'But I kind of do, all the same.'

Actually, so did Judy. She wasn't even angry

457

with him any more. It was difficult to be angry with a person who refused to learn a single thing from their mistakes; a person who went about blaming everybody else for their misfortunes before shooting themselves roundly in the foot. Several times, in Barry's case.

'And, just for the record, Lenny are I weren't 'sleeping together'. You make it sound like we were at it the whole summer long. It was just the once.'

Ber gave her a wink. 'It obviously left quite an impression on Lenny.' Judy went red to the roots of her hair. 'This dilemma is not about sex,' she said primly.

'No, but you'd probably be guaranteed a fair bit if you *did* go to Australia,' Ber said practically. 'There's a lot to be said for good sex, Judy.'

'I know that.'

'And fun. And having a laugh. Being with somebody you really want to be with.'

'Yes — '

'It's completely obvious the two of you are mad about each other, even though you denied it to my face. And what can be more romantic than ringing somebody up and inviting them over for Christmas?'

When she laid it all out like that, Judy began to worry all over again that she was foolish not to go. Lenny had come seeking her out. In the intervening six months, he hadn't forgotten about her at all; he had thought she was with Barry. And the minute he knew she wasn't, he had come looking for her.

458

With a definite plan, too. A proper invitation, and not a case of, 'Oh, come over whenever you have a free week or two.' For someone like Lenny, who could barely see past next weekend, it was a pretty significant gesture on his part.

What had she expected, anyhow? That he would ring her up after six months apart and ask her to move in with him? After only one night together? Or announce that he was permanently relocating to Ireland just to be with her? It was naïve to expect something like that. And shortsighted. They barely knew each other, after all. It had taken her and Barry fours years before they'd even moved in together, never mind anything else (still, look how that had ended).

But they knew each other well enough for Judy to have lost half her heart to Lenny. Well, more than half. Three-quarters probably, if not four-fifths. A couple of weeks in Australia would take care of the rest of it, and then where would she be? Back in Ireland, probably, once the 'moment' was over, only worse off than before. She wouldn't be so much lovelorn as wandering around like the tin man, with no heart at all.

'Ber, I know what you're saying. But we had the good sex thing last summer, and the fun, and the laughs,' she said. 'We've done that bit already.'

'You're sure you couldn't do it again?' Ber looked hopeful.

'I can't go back there. And he doesn't want to move on.' That was pretty much it, and she didn't see any way out.

'You're assuming the worst here, Judy. Maybe

everything would go wonderfully in Australia. You might end up staying there permanently.'

Judy gave a bit of a laugh.

'What? You think he only wants a holiday romance? Maybe he doesn't. I bet he'll end up falling madly in love with you, which I suspect he already is, and he'll beg you to set up home in a nice little beach hut and you could run a mobile library or something.'

She was delighted with her projections. Judy hated to pour cold water on them.

'Lenny doesn't do the beach hut thing. He doesn't do the whole commitment thing, OK?'

'You're making him out to be some kind of sex monster, Judy, who goes around lapping on women before disappearing into the night. You think he's invited you over just to have sex with for a couple of weeks before loading you efficiently back onto the plane again?'

'Oh, I don't know any more! Except that things have gone too far, for me anyway, to go all the way over there without some kind of expectations, Ber. I'm not talking about dragging anybody up the aisle here, either — I'm a bit off that myself at the moment. But I can't love somebody if I'm thinking that the whole thing could well be over tomorrow. I'm thirty-three years of age, I've done the whole holiday romance thing, I'm not interested in that any more. What I *am* interested in is finding somebody to have some kind of a meaningful relationship with, somebody who's willing to be intimate for more than just a weekend, maybe even somebody to settle down with, and if Lenny thinks that sounds like too bloody much, well tough!'

She was out of breath when she had finished.

'I think you've made your point,' Ber said, rather fearfully.

'But do you think I'm wrong, Ber? Do you think I should be all modern, and progressive, and pretend that I'm happy to go with the flow, let's-see-how-things-work-out, and not put any pressure on men because it just shows what a hick I am?'

'Of course not.'

Judy threw her hands up. 'Oh, maybe I *am* a stick-in-the-mud. In which case it wouldn't work out anyway and I'm better off staying here. By the way, can I come over here for Christmas dinner?'

Ber looked alarmed. 'What?'

'I won't be any trouble. I could even bring something, like the stuffing.'

And maybe a plum pudding too. Ber's was listing dangerously to one side.

She tried to prop it up now, whilst consulting the recipe. 'I don't think you're supposed to take it out of the mould until you're about to eat it,' she muttered.

It was then that Judy noticed.

'Where's your engagement ring?' she asked.

'Oh. I gave it back.'

For a moment Judy thought she meant to the shop. She wouldn't blame her for exchanging it for something a little more tasteful.

But then Ber said, 'The engagement's off.'

'What?' Judy was completely confused. Vinnie

had walked out past her only half an hour ago to take the dog for a walk. Mind you, he'd had a face on him that would stop a clock. 'But Vinnie . . . '

'Oh, he still lives here. I mean, we haven't broken up or anything. It's just we're not getting married any more.'

'Ber, I'm so sorry.'

But Ber didn't want any sympathy at all. 'No, it's fine, it's not traumatic at all. In fact I'm delighted, and not just because of the awful ring. Vinnie's another story, naturally, but he'll see in the end that the benefits outweigh any temporary upset.'

'But why?'

'Because of what you said that day you were here.'

'What?' Judy was horrified. Not only had her own engagement failed, but now she also going around breaking up other couples' engagements. Once this latest got out around the town, people would be afraid to come within ten feet of her. In the olden days, she would have been put up against a tree and set on fire.

'You said that maybe there was some way I could get some of the old excitement back.'

'And you think you can achieve this by throwing Vinnie's proposal back in his face?'

'Exactly,' Ber said brightly. 'Oh, look, Judy, it would have been the final nail in the coffin. Can you imagine me as Mrs Vinnie Smyth? When once I used to be a mysterious, undomestic mistress? I'm already finding it hard enough to cope with the adjustments involved in being a live-in lover. I'm certainly not ready to be a wife.' In defiance, she pushed the plum pudding away. 'To hell with that. I'm going to buy one.'

That would probably be a welcome relief to all concerned.

'I felt better the minute I took that ring off. It was like I got a bit of myself back, Judy.'

And now that Judy looked at her properly, she did look more like herself. She had on a rather glamorous top and her hair looked freshly done, and she wore a good smattering of make-up for the first time in ages.

'Even better,' she said, 'I've hired somebody to come in and clean the blasted bathroom twice a week, and the kitchen. Maybe I'm unnatural or something, Judy, but I just don't get the whole cleaning thing.' She added, unnecessarily, 'Or the cooking thing.'

'And how is Vinnie taking it all?' Judy was beginning to enjoy Ber's rebellion.

'Oh, terrible,' Ber said cheerily. 'He said what was the point in him leaving his wife if I wasn't going to go the whole hog and get married? He accused me of letting down my side of the bargain. He said that we'd had years of being unsure of each other, and now we finally have the chance to settle down, except that I'm refusing to get married, and now he's unsure all over again.' She added, 'Still, he got dressed up for dinner last night. As in, he put on a pair of shoes and socks.'

Judy began to see the way Ber was working things.

'I thought you weren't going to get involved in

any game-playing, Ber.'

'This isn't a game, Judy. I'm not holding out to keep him on his toes or anything. I just don't think marriage is going to benefit Vinnie and me. In fact, I think it might be the death of us. And I don't want that to happen. I love Vinnie. I have for years and years.'

'Have you told him all this?'

'He's not really talking to me at the moment,' Ber confided. 'But when I explain to him properly that marriage would kill stone dead any remaining bit of excitement, I'm sure he'll see things my way.'

It was debatable how open Vinnie was to any kind of discussion, judging by the black look on his face when he came back in with the dog five minutes later.

He held up three of the little plastic bags that they used to clean up dog poo.

'I don't know what you're feeding that dog,' he said to Ber accusingly. 'And he tried to bite me too.'

The dog lent weight to this by going wild with excitement the minute he caught sight of Ber. He yipped and barked the house down, straining towards her on his lead with pure adoration.

'Oh, come here, baby,' Ber cooed. She had got fond of him recently, she told Judy.

Vinnie shot Judy a look. 'I suppose you know the engagement is off,' he said, his voice stiff with embarrassment and rejection.

'Ber told me, yes,' Judy said. She didn't know whether to commiserate with him or not, especially as Ber was chuckling delightedly beside him, and in the best form Judy had seen her in ages.

She ended up trying to make a little joke at her own expense. 'We've all been there.'

But Vinnie just looked alarmed. 'You're not going to run off on me or anything, are you?' he asked Ber.

'Oh, Vinnie. Of course not. Don't you know that I'm mad about you?'

Vinnie went a bit pink. 'You haven't said that in ages.'

'I know,' she agreed. 'I've been too busy trying to stick to the cleaning rota.'

'If I tear that up, will you agree to marry me?' he pleaded.

'No, Vinnie. But let's tear it up anyway.'

'What?'

'That way we'll have far more time to say nice things to each other.'

Vinnie was starting to see the light. 'I suppose,' he said.

Ber ran her newly painted fingernail down his arm. 'I thought we might go out for dinner tonight,' she murmured. 'Or else, if you want, I could cook.'

It took Vinnie only a split second to say, 'We'll go out.'

36

Two problems arose on the afternoon of Mick and Rose's renewal ceremony. The first was that Biffo, who had been appointed to drive them to the church, failed to turn up.

'I told him to be here at two o'clock sharp,' Mick thundered. 'I told him ten times if I told him once.'

'Did you try ringing him?' Judy inquired.

'Of course I've tried ringing him! I've been trying since yesterday. He didn't come home at all last night. If I wasn't so angry I'd be worried.'

Judy was far more sanguine about such things these days. There was almost always a reasonable, if not downright obvious, explanation. 'He'll turn up, Dad.'

'He'd better,' said Mick.

He seemed very nervous about the whole thing. He kept checking and rechecking the rings, and going over his after-dinner speech, and wondering to Judy if Rose would be offended if he mentioned her age in it. Then he decided that it was best if he didn't. He would stick to the stories about their first honeymoon. Then he worried that they were too smutty, and that Rose would be mad at him, even though there was usually nothing she liked better than a bit of smut.

He was not like a man who was renewing his vows to a woman he had lived with for nearly forty years. He was edgy, unhappy, anxiously pacing up and down looking for Biffo.

'If we're late getting to the church, she'll kill me.'

The second problem was that, despite all the stir-fries and pak choi, there was no way that Rose was going to get into the burnt-orange suit.

'It's Christmas time,' she ranted in the bedroom. 'Nobody should be expected to lose weight at this time of the year. There we were, in the neighbour's house last night, and himself tucking into mince pies like he hadn't care in the world. And me having to watch every sip and morsel, knowing I had to squeeze into this thing today!'

The point was that there was no hope at all of her squeezing into it.

'Did you not try it on during the week?' Judy asked, even whilst recognising the futility of the question.

'And where would I have got the time to do that?' Rose inquired dangerously. 'Between organising the caterers, and trying to get past the DJ's girlfriend on the phone, and ordering some half-decent flowers for the church? Do you know how difficult it is to get wedding flowers two days before Christmas, Judy? I'm lucky I'm not walking up the aisle holding a poinsettia.'

The little diatribe was all sounding horribly familiar. That had been Judy six months ago: the hassled, demented bride who, for two pins, would call the whole thing off, except, of course, that it was going to be the happiest day of her life.

Certainly, nobody could accuse Rose of being happy right now. She was hot and tense and belligerent, and it was obvious whose fault the whole thing was.

'He went and invited the neighbours last night as well. When we had already said family and friends only. He thought I would like it. He thought I would actually enjoy having the street come and watch us . . . *parading* up the aisle this afternoon like we were in the first flush or something!'

And she flopped down on the bed furiously. The burnt-orange suit fell on the floor in a heap.

'Mum, what's wrong?'

'Nothing,' she said. Then she shrugged and said, 'Oh, maybe this is just not me. That's all.'

'Tell Dad you don't want to do it then. He won't mind. He only wanted to do it in the first place because he wanted you to know how much you meant to him.'

'Oh, yes,' said Rose. 'The grand gesture. That'll make everything all right.' She ordered, 'Get me that yellow dress I wore to your cousin Susan's graduation last year, would you? I'll have to wear that, even though it makes me look like a big lemon.'

Judy went to the wardrobe. Right at the back of it, behind all the other clothes and wrapped in protective plastic, she saw something better.

'What about this?'

Rose looked. 'Judy, I have no sense of humour at all this morning.'

It was Rose's wedding dress, which she had married Mick in thirty-seven years ago.

468

'Why not, Mum? I bet it still fits.'

'I'm not sure whether to take that as a compliment or an insult.'

'And it's so old that it's back in fashion.'

'You pup,' said Rose. Then something about it seemed to tickle her because she said, 'Give it here then, I'll try it on for the laugh. But I'm not wearing it, I just want to see if it still fits.'

She got into it, and when Judy zipped it up at the back there were little folds of material left where it was loose around the hips.

'Imagine!' Rose hooted in delight. 'One of those diets must have worked after all.'

The dress was a simple affair with a flattering empire line, and in a gorgeous shade of cream that set off Rose's newly dyed hair just right.

'It's beautiful on you, Mum.'

'It's not bad, all right. Now, help me take it off.'

'Why don't you wear it?'

'No.'

'Why not?'

'Because everybody will think it's corny, and that we're trying to say something deeply significant about the day,' Rose snapped.

She burst into tears.

'Sorry,' she said. 'Sorry. You know me. Cry at the drop of a hat. Oh, sugar — now look at my make-up.'

But this wasn't crying at the drop of a hat. This was a deep and fierce upset. Judy let her be for a minute and went down the hall to get a box of tissues from the bathroom.

When she got back, Rose was a bit better. She

took a handful of tissues and mopped her eyes.

'You set out so happy, Judy. So optimistic. And here I am today all over again, but only because he let me down and now he's trying to make it up to me.'

It was unnerving to see Rose like this; she was so big and colourful and lively that you never really expected her to get very down.

'He knows it too. All this effort to win me back. The swimming pool. The bar. This charade this morning.'

'If you think it's a charade, then you shouldn't go through with it.'

'Maybe I won't.'

'Is there any way you could see it as a chance for you both to try again?'

Fresh tears rolled down Rose's face. 'If I'd known the first time around that I'd be sitting here nearly forty years later trying to resuscitate the whole thing, I wouldn't have bothered at all!'

'You would have. You know you would have.'

'I thought I was fine about it, Judy. That she was gone, and things were back to normal, and it was all over and done with. But it's not.' She scrubbed at her face with the tissue. 'You just keep thinking, at what point did it go wrong?'

'I know.'

Rose lifted her head. 'I suppose you do, better than most of us.'

They sat there in easy silence for a moment, except for Rose's hiccups. As they were being very honest with each other, Judy decided to come clean. 'I'm not upset about Barry any more, Mum. I haven't been for ages. There's been somebody else.'

'I see,' said Rose. If she was surprised she hid it well. She didn't ask who it was. But Judy supposed she had heard as well as anybody else what Barry had been saying around the town.

'And is there any hope . . . ?'

'No,' said Judy. 'I'm afraid not. I think we want different things at the end of the day.'

'It's funny,' said Rose, 'but I've found that we all want the same thing. Love. Companionship. Intimacy.' She cocked her head to look at Judy. 'You don't think he could give you all that?'

'Well, yes, maybe. I think so. But I'd never feel that I was secure. I'd feel it might all end at any moment.'

'Oh, Judy. It might all end at any moment anyway. There are no guarantees there.' She cast a rather bitter look down at her wedding dress. 'But if you have something special now, then is that not a good start?'

'It's too risky, Mum. I'd only end up getting hurt.'

'So what are you going to do? Be bridesmaid to every other woman in town? Including me?'

And she managed a smile.

Judy complained, 'You're my mother, you're supposed to be advising me against fast men. You should be telling me to run a mile and find a nice steady boy to settle down with.'

Rose raised an eyebrow. 'I think you've tried that one already.'

'So, what, it's on to plan B?'

'You were always a great one for the plans,' Rose said affectionately. 'Maybe it's time to tear

471

them all up once and for all, and listen to your heart, Judy.'

'That's a very flowery thing to say,' Judy told her, teasing. But really it was to divert attention from herself. She found her resolve starting to weaken again. Her mind had been all made up and now here was Rose, more or less extolling her to hop on that plane after all.

Still, it was too late now. It was 23 December. Her parents were getting married this afternoon — or maybe not. Either way, there was no way she'd get a flight to Australia. It was impossible.

She tried to find comfort in that, in the decision being taken from her, but she couldn't.

The bedroom door opened and Mick came in. 'There's still no sign of that pup,' he said.

When he saw Rose sitting on the bed in her wedding dress, he went still.

'This is not what you think,' she informed him evenly.

Mick registered her red eyes, and the wet tissues in her hand. 'What is it then?' he asked slowly.

'I don't know, Mick. I'm trying to figure it out. I'm trying to see when we stopped being nice to each other, I suppose.'

Judy moved towards the door fast. 'I'll go keep an eye out for Biffo.'

'No, Judy, stay,' Rose said. She turned to Mick again. 'I don't even know why we're getting married again today,' she said. 'Unless it's a last-ditch attempt to paper over the cracks.'

Mick answered at once. 'Not for me, it's not.' He looked at her levelly. 'I don't know about you. I don't think you've liked me for a couple of years now.'

Rose brushed that aside. 'Oh, that's because you've been moaning all the time. It would drive anybody mad.'

'If I don't moan, nobody will ever listen to me.'

'If you moaned less, I might listen more.'

'But you don't. You think everything is a big joke, and sometimes it's not.'

Rose was defensive. 'I never went outside our marriage looking for anything, Mick.'

'Maybe that's because you don't need as much, Rose. Some of us take a bit more propping up.'

'You could just have asked, you know.'

'Maybe I would have, if we were being nicer to each other.'

'Back to that again,' she said.

'Back to that again,' he agreed.

Judy made her way to the door. 'I'm just going to nip home and get my own car in case Biffo doesn't show up, OK?'

She left, closing the door quietly on them.

★ ★ ★

It was a freezing day, and her wedding attire of rather glamorous purple trouser suit and hat was no barrier at all against the cold. She should have bought that long purple winter coat to go over it, but had been afraid of looking like a giant aubergine.

She turned a bend in the road hurriedly, her

hands like blocks of ice. Her nose was undoubtedly giving Rudolph a run for his money too.

In the distance she thought she could see somebody sitting on the front steps of her house.

It was Lenny.

At least, she thought it was. He was wearing a T-shirt and shorts and sunglasses, and was huddled up into a ball on the steps, a hand jammed under each armpit for warmth and his feet impatiently tapping the ground.

When he looked up and saw her he went still. So did Judy.

She had spoken to him on the phone two days ago, they had agreed that whatever was between them was now over, and now he was here, in Cove, on her doorstep.

She stopped at the bottom of the steps. They were about on eye level.

'It's thirty-six degrees in Sydney right now,' he told her between chattering teeth. 'We could have been on the beach. In our swimsuits. Eating barbecued ribs. But you'd have to be crooked, wouldn't you?'

She didn't know what to say. She had no idea what was going on. 'You look cold,' she offered, rather timidly.

'That's because I am. When I left this country behind ten years ago, I gave all my duffel coats and woolly hats and thermal underwear to charity and have been living in a near-tropical climate ever since.'

Judy hoped that none of the neighbours were listening to this rather uncivil exchange.

'Would you like to come in?' she asked, eventually. He would catch his death sitting there in his shorts.

'I'm not sure yet,' he said, with great dignity. 'OK.'

Seeing as it looked as if they might be there for a while, Judy sat down on the steps beside him. She still hadn't a clue what he was doing here, but the fact was he was here, and she wanted to laugh, or smile, or do a little dance in the street.

Instead, she offered, 'If you get frostbite on those fingers, I know first aid.'

'I wouldn't have expected anything less. I'm sure you've also done a lifesaving course, and remember from Girl Guides how to generate fire from two stones. And if there was one woman in this world to have a heart attack around, you're the one.'

'I can't help it if I know some useful things,' she said.

'Don't be modest now. You pretty much know everything. The rest of us know very little in comparison.'

It really must be thirty-six degrees in Sydney because he was as brown as a nut. His hair was a bit longer too. His brown-flecked eyes were just the same, and they were fixed on her rather belligerently now.

She inquired, 'Did you come all the way over here just to insult me?'

'No,' he said. 'But seeing as you've forced my hand in all this, I think I'm entitled to be a little bit put out, don't you? At least for a while. I'm sure I'll thaw out in a few minutes.'

'What do you mean, forced your hand?'

'Well, you wouldn't come over to me, would you? So I had no choice but to come here to you.'

He lifted his chin a little, rather defensively, as if expecting rejection.

Judy just stared at him. It was a twenty-two-hour flight, with a stopover. He must have got on it about five minutes after he had put the phone down to her.

'Say something,' he encouraged her. 'Anything. Even just a 'nice to see you, Lenny'. Go wild.'

'Sorry,' Judy managed. 'It's just such a surprise, that's all. And it *is* nice to see you. Very nice.' It all came out sounding very uptight. But what was she supposed to do? Immediately straddle him on the steps? 'Lovely,' she said, hoping that sounded a bit warmer.

'I'll tell you, Judy,' he said grimly, 'You really make a guy work.'

'Sorry,' she said again.

They looked at each other for another long moment. After all, it had been a while.

Lenny said, 'What are you doing in all that purple gear?'

Judy was a bit offended; she had thought she looked gorgeous.

'I'm going to a wedding.'

Lenny laughed out loud. 'I should have guessed that. I should have known that we wouldn't last five minutes without marriage cropping up in some context.'

Judy decided she wouldn't even rise to that.

'It's my mother and father's renewal of vows ceremony,' she told him haughtily. At least, it might be if Mick said nothing to set Rose off all over again. Or she didn't slag him off about his hair or something and he stormed off. 'If you had phoned ahead I would have told you that.'

'But you know me, Judy. I don't phone ahead.'

'No, you just come by unannounced, despite what we agreed, and no doubt you'll expect me to drop everything just because you're here.'

'I thought that perhaps you might *want* to drop everything. I dropped everything for you. I got on a long-haul flight for you!'

'And you think that somehow makes everything OK?'

'No,' he said, 'but I think it shows that my feelings are stronger than yours because you wouldn't do the same for me.'

'That is not true!' Judy cried.

'Oh? Would you like to elaborate?'

'Well, I . . . I mean . . . ' She found herself struggling for words. They had only very fleetingly touched on the whole territory of feelings before. In fact, Lenny had given the impression so far that the very mention of feelings would send him into a dead faint. And now he wanted to give them all a good airing half an hour before she was due to be her mother's bridesmaid?

'My feelings,' she told him, 'are very strong indeed.'

'Don't bowl me over here, Judy.'

'Well, I'm sorry it's not very romantic,' she told him. 'But there are things we need to sort out, Lenny, even though it would be much easier to get swept away by the moment and go into the house and . . . just bonk!'

'I'm far too cold to bonk,' he assured her. 'So we have a bit of time before I have my wicked way with you, and jump immediately on a return flight to Australia and never contact you again.'

'Lenny — '

'Look at you, sitting there so suspicious of me! Like I have some kind of agenda. Jesus Christ, Judy, what more do you expect me to do?'

He looked thoroughly fed up now. And jet-lagged. And absolutely freezing.

Judy began to see his point of view. But there was no time to discuss it now unfortunately. 'Will you come to Mum and Dad's ceremony with me?'

He looked startled. 'What?'

'It's not an attempt to ram the whole marriage thing down your throat,' she assured him. 'But it's the only place we'll get a chance to talk, and if I don't go now I'll be late.'

Lenny rose, shaking his head. 'I haven't seen you for six months and the first place you take me is a church.'

'Cheer up,' she told him. 'You might even enjoy it.'

37

Biffo's white van was parked in the driveway when Judy and Lenny arrived at the house five minutes later.

He was in the kitchen, hastily putting on a tie. He looked completely wrecked, as if he hadn't slept since yesterday.

'What's going on?' he complained. He jerked a thumb towards the ceiling. 'I knocked on the door to tell them that we'd better get a move on, and they told me to go away.'

He looked past Judy. 'Lenny?'

'Hi, Biffo,' said Lenny easily. 'Listen, you wouldn't have a jacket or anything you could lend me? I came straight from Australia and I forgot it would be winter here.'

Biffo was boggle-eyed. He looked from Judy to Lenny and then back again, obviously trying to compute this information.

'Or even a jumper,' Lenny prompted. He looked down at his shorts and said to Judy, 'I suppose these aren't appropriate for your parents' wedding either?'

'Well . . . ' said Judy. He had lovely legs. It was a shame not to show them off, even in December.

'You came all the way from Australia for Mum and Dad's wedding?' Biffo was completely confused now. 'I didn't even know they had invited you.'

'They didn't,' Lenny told him. 'I'm going with Judy.'

It smacked of coupledom. Judy looked askance at Lenny. He seemed quite comfortable with the notion. And they hadn't even sorted a single thing out yet!

'It's not like that,' she told Biffo briskly.

But Biffo had put two and two together, or so he believed, and his eyes had grown as wide as saucers. 'So it was all true?' he chortled. 'What Barry was saying?'

'No!' said Judy. Then she was forced to admit, 'Well, yes, some of it.'

Biffo let out a low whistle and looked at Judy as though she was the world's darkest horse.

Squirming at her love life being laid bare like this — Lenny didn't seem to mind at all, but then his sex life had always been an open book — Judy said, 'Look, this is not what you think, Biffo. Lenny and I are not . . . we're just . . . '

Lenny said kindly, 'Why don't I go upstairs and borrow some of Biffo's clothes and let you explain things.'

He set off for the stairs.

'Don't mind all the stuff on the floor,' Biffo called after him. 'And there's a bar up there as well if you fancy a drink.'

When Lenny was gone, Biffo turned to Judy and said, 'Are you sure about this?'

'Biffo, stop! Look, he only arrived half an hour ago. I don't even know what's going on, OK? So don't give me any lectures.'

Biffo puffed out his chest a bit. 'I'm your brother, Judy. It's my job to warn you off the

480

kind of man that secretly I want to be, but who I wouldn't want my sister to go out with.'

'I thought you liked Lenny.'

'Judy, the guy is great. Handsome, funny, reasonably well-off, fantastic career, a bit short but then so are you, and who wears a pair of shorts very well.' He looked off up the stairs after Lenny rather longingly.

Then suddenly he turned very serious. 'But Steady Eddie? No way!'

'I don't want a Steady Eddie any more,' Judy said. She wondered how she had got embroiled in such a conversation at the foot of her parents' stairs.

'Judy, just because your engagement ended the way it did doesn't mean you should go to the other extreme,' Biffo said solemnly.

'If I was going to the other extreme, I wouldn't be here. I'd be in some bar somewhere.'

But Biffo was in no mood for lightness. He was obviously going to take his brotherly obligations very seriously.

'I could have a word with him. Man to man. Warn him not to mess you about.'

'If you do that, I will never speak to you or look at you again,' Judy informed him clearly.

Thankfully she was spared any further discussion on the matter by the downstairs toilet door opening behind Biffo. Angie stepped out.

She was all dressed up in a peach flowery wedding outfit, and a huge floppy hat. The effect was somewhat marred by the cigarette she was waving about, and her bloodshot eyes.

'I'm so hung-over I don't think I'll be able to

make it through the ceremony,' she complained to Biffo.

'That's all right, sweetie,' he said. 'I'll catch you if you collapse.'

'Thanks, honey,' she said gratefully.

Sweetie? Honey? After a whole year of pitched battle, recriminations, and vows never to give in?

'Hi, Judy,' Angie said chirpily.

'We managed to work things out,' Biffo told Judy unnecessarily.

They didn't even have the decency to look sheepish. In fact, they scarcely gave Judy a glance at all so busy were they pawing each other, and fixing each other's clothing, and popping mints, no doubt to cover the stench of stale drink.

'Stop it, you two,' Judy was eventually forced to say. 'Before you sicken me altogether.'

Biffo looked offended. 'I thought you'd be delighted that we've finally managed to see eye to eye.'

And a lot more besides, judging by the way Angie was rubbing his back. In fact the two of them looked so happy that they would surely overshadow Rose and Mick on their wedding day. If Rose ever showed up, that was. It was about two minutes to three o'clock, and the priest would probably be on the blower in a minute wondering why the happy couple were a no-show.

'Well, of course I'm delighted,' Judy said. 'I'm thrilled! Even if I haven't a clue how you managed it.'

Angie looked proud. 'He drove up outside the office at lunchtime yesterday in his white van with a big bunch of flowers for me.'

'I picked them myself from Mr Brennan's garden on the way,' Biffo admitted to Judy. 'I couldn't afford to buy any.' He looked at Angie rather shyly. 'Normally I would never admit that I couldn't afford something, but we've decided we're both going to have to live with a few things.'

'They were all my favourite flowers,' Angie said fervently. 'That's the important thing. Not how much they cost.'

Judy didn't want to point out that they hadn't cost anything, as they had been stolen. It would be a shame to spoil the moment.

'They wouldn't let him into the office in the beginning, because they thought he was there to clean the drains or something,' Angie said. 'They couldn't believe that he was there to see me.'

'But I didn't take offence,' Biffo said stoically. 'When you're going out with a high earner like Angie, you have to take a few things on the chin, Judy. So in future those kinds of remarks will just go right over me. Water off a duck's back!'

Angie squeezed his arm approvingly. 'So he went back to his van, took a FOR SALE sign out of it, and put it up in front of the building. And when they were all out looking at it, and ringing London and New York to find out what the hell was going on, he nipped up in the elevators to see me.'

'We got three very good offers on that building actually,' he told Angie now. 'I could have sold it no problem.'

'Well, of course you could have. Once you get

483

your desk back again.'

'I lost my desk again,' he admitted to Judy. 'They nearly fired me.'

Angie clucked, and said to Judy, 'I'd take him away for a weekend to Barcelona to cheer him up, only we've decided that there won't be any more of that. It makes him feel too uncomfortable.'

'Unless, of course, it's a weekend away to see a match,' Biffo quickly clarified.

'Absolutely. Then it's allowed.'

'Did we discuss your bonuses yet?' he suddenly wondered.

'I think we've discussed enough for one day,' she decided. 'I'll just keep stashing them away in the account in the Caymans until we get around to it.'

'Good idea.'

'They might come in handy for that house we were going to buy on the cliff road,' she ventured.

There was a tense moment when something ominous crossed Biffo's face; a resistance, a resentment, a slight choking down of pride. But it passed in an instant, and he said cheerfully, 'Maybe. Because God knows I can't continue to live with my parents.'

'You could always move back in with me,' Angie suggested. 'We don't have to wait until we buy a house together.'

Until Angie's bonuses bought them a house, she meant, but that didn't seem to matter any more. Or at least it didn't seem to matter as much as it used it. Which was probably as good as it was going to get.

'OK,' said Biffo slowly. 'I'd really like that.'

Angie glowed. So did Biffo. But only for a moment.

'We should never have gone on the tear last night,' Angie groaned.

'I know,' said Biffo, looking rather green. 'Here, give us a cigarette, that'll perk me up.'

There was a noise at the top of the stairs. Judy turned, expecting to see Lenny, and bracing herself for the inevitable explanations to Angie.

But it was Rose. She was wearing her wedding dress. Her eyes were a little red but otherwise she looked, well, normal.

Mick followed behind, not too near and not too far.

They walked in silence down the stairs with no fanfare, no dramatics.

Judy searched Rose's face for some indication that things were all right. She tried to take hope from the wedding dress, but that probably didn't mean anything, given that there was no possibility of her getting into the burnt orange.

'I hope you two weren't getting up to any funny business in that bedroom up there,' Biffo joked.

That landed like a stone.

'What?' he said, looking around.

'We just had some things to sort out,' Rose said neutrally.

Biffo was looking fussily at his watch. 'We'd want to get a move on.' He looked at Mick. 'I presume we're taking your car, unless you want to hop into the back of the van?'

485

His second attempt at levity landed like a stone too. He looked at Judy as if she might be able to tell him what was going on.

Rose turned to Judy and said, 'Did I just see Lenny in Biffo's room?'

'You did,' Judy admitted.

Angie's head swivelled around. 'You mean it was *true*? What Barry was saying?'

'Yes!' Judy shouted. 'The whole lot of it! We were bonking morning, noon and night!'

For the first time Rose smiled. 'Great!' she said. 'I'm delighted, Judy. Absolutely delighted.'

Mick looked at Rose and shook his head. 'How come any conversation in this house turns to sex sooner or later?'

But it was said gently.

'Oh, shut up,' Rose said to him.

But it was said affectionately.

'Are we going to the church at all?' Biffo said complainingly. 'Because I'm losing the will to live here. Call your boyfriend there, Judy, and we'll go.'

Lenny, of course, chose that moment to appear at the top of the stairs in a pair of Biffo's work trousers, which were two sizes too big for him and had a shiny backside.

He gave Judy a wicked little look. 'Here I am,' he said.

Judy's face burned.

Then, finally, when everybody was gathered and looking at each other expectantly, Mick turned to Rose and asked, 'Will we go?'

'We will,' she said.

The ceremony was lovely. The priest said some nice words about the sanctity and resilience of the marriage bond, and the rewards that were to be had from enduring one person for forty years, although the phrase he used was sharing one's life. Biffo played 'Love Me Tender' on the church CD player, although the priest frowned. Rose cried bucketloads of tears, and even Mick looked a bit moist around the eyes at one point.

'I hope you're not going to start crying too,' Lenny whispered in Judy's ear.

Actually, she *was* blinking back a tear or two. It had been a rough day on the emotional front for everybody, and it wasn't over yet.

'Only because I'm happy,' she said.

It was true. Her parents had made the peace and Lenny was beside her.

And the doors at the back were closed, so it was unlikely he would make a bolt for it, at least without causing a great disturbance.

Not that he seemed in any great rush to go anywhere. He was listening very closely to the ceremony, and was managing to keep up with all the genuflecting and kneeling that was required at various points, although he had to keep one arm clamped around his middle to stop Biffo's trousers falling down and giving the two ladies in the row behind him an awful fright. Or an unexpected treat, depending on how you looked at it.

'And now if we could have the eternity rings?' the priest prompted.

Biffo pretended that he couldn't find them. Then, when everybody had properly appreciated the joke, Mick and Rose exchanged the rings whilst saying some simple, and suspiciously secular, words of gratitude and promises to be nice to each other and not to complain too much or make excessive fun of the other person, sending the priest running to consult the order of the ceremony. But Mick and Rose didn't notice; they were very solemn and serious as they looked deep into each other's eyes.

'See?' Judy whispered to Lenny. 'It's not all doom and gloom and boredom, and sex dwindling off to nothing, and ending up not being able to stand the sight of each other.' Although Rose and Mick had come close.

'This is hardly the time or place for this conversation,' he whispered back.

'I don't see why not. I think it's the perfect time.'

'With your mother and father getting married all over again?'

'They are not getting married all over again. This is about love, and commitment.'

'I know, and it's very moving.'

She shot him a look, wondering whether he was making fun of her, and her parents and the whole set-up today.

'What?' he said. 'It's something I'd like for myself.'

Judy laughed. 'Then you must be getting old.'

'Age has nothing to do with it.'

'It is. You're reaching your late thirties and

you're fed up of one-night stands and you want to settle down.'

'That is so cynical,' he said, looking highly insulted.

'I know, it's usually something you'd say.'

'When I met you first you were so idealistic. And now look at you.'

'Tough as old boots,' Judy agreed.

'I was going to say that age has nothing to do with it, it's finding someone that you actually want to be with that matters.'

'What are you saying, that you've finally decided to throw in your swashbuckling lifestyle for the love of a good woman?'

'Yes,' he said.

That took the wind from her sails. 'Oh. Well, um . . . lovely!'

She didn't know what else to say. She was, literally, without words. It certainly hadn't been the kind of declaration she had expected.

'And what about you, Judy?' he said. 'What do you want out of all this?'

Judy looked at him for a very long moment — he had a lovely tan after a summer in Australia — and said, 'I want somebody who's not going to move on the minute the romance wears off. You know, like in the middle of a conversation about bathroom tiles, or what flavour soup to get in the supermarket.'

'You make it sound so attractive,' he mused.

Judy stood her ground. 'Great sex is all very well, Lenny, and excitement and passion, and I think we probably don't have any problems there.'

489

'Do you reckon?' he said, giving her a teasing look that reduced her knees to jelly.

'Yes,' she said, managing to remain standing. 'But at some point someone's going to have to get up out of the bed and make the bloody tea!'

The priest cleared his throat loudly and looked down at them. 'If we could bear in mind the significance of the occasion . . . ?'

Heads swivelled towards them. Judy lowered her head, trying to look very holy. Lenny looked back at them all, brazen as you like.

At the altar, Mick and Rose stood obediently as the priest mumbled some final, long-drawn-out prayer involving God, the Virgin Mary, and a good many of the saints, until Biffo began to cough a couple of times. This had an unfortunate chain effect on the congregation until, in minutes, the whole place was spluttering and coughing involuntarily, and the priest had to raise his voice to a shout to be heard.

Finally, with some relief, he brought the whole thing to a close by announcing to Mick, 'You may now kiss the bride. I mean the . . . ' He trailed off, confused as to what Rose actually was.

'The missus,' Biffo supplied, and everybody had a little titter at the confusion. But it didn't matter, because Rose looked a bit like a bride in the white dress, and Mick brushed aside the modest offer of her cheek and gave her a great big kiss.

Even Lenny seemed a bit affected. That was, until Judy jabbed him in the ribs and whispered, 'Come on.'

'What?'

She got quietly to her feet. 'They'll be busy taking photos now. They won't miss us for a moment.'

She left the church discreetly, Lenny following behind in his big baggy trousers.

It was very cold outside on the church steps, but they were used to it by now. Besides, Judy was glad for the crisp air. It cleared her thoughts. And she needed to have clear thoughts right now, unclouded by wedding sentiment or emotion or 'Love Me Tender' playing mushily in the background.

Lenny seemed more alert too.

They looked at each other for a long moment.

'What did we just decide in there?' Judy inquired.

'I'm not sure,' Lenny conceded cautiously. 'Except that I will discuss bathroom tiles. And cook.'

'I see,' she said slowly.

'And that both of us believe in love and commitment.'

'Right.'

He gave a half grin. 'If only we'd known it was going to be this easy all along.'

She didn't grin back. This was too serious. And they hadn't even discussed the Big Issue yet.

She didn't want to bring it up. Not on the day her parents were having a big, soppy ceremony. Not on the very day that Lenny had decided that she was worth sticking around for.

But she had to. 'And what about the whole marriage thing?'

'No,' said Lenny.

'OK,' she said. At least now she knew where they stood on that front. God knows she was ambivalent enough herself. But it was what they had spent most of their relationship arguing over.

She could live without marriage. The most important thing, as Lenny had said, was to be with the person she loved.

'Or at least nothing in a church,' he said.

There was a little silence. She looked at his face for signs of pain, and indeed there was a rather resigned stoicism about him.

He didn't want to do it. But he would do it if she really, really wanted to.

'We wouldn't do it in a church,' she said. 'If ever the day came when we felt like we might like to do it.'

'We wouldn't?'

'No. Maybe a beach in Tahiti, but not a church.'

He looked slightly relieved. 'But only if we felt like it, as you say. And it wouldn't be something we do to revive things, or copper fasten things, or liven up a boring year. And it wouldn't involve choirs or second aunts from Ballyhaunis.'

'They'd never go all the way to Tahiti.'

'That's true.'

Then Lenny gave a big sigh, as if he had been holding his breath in for about two weeks, and he said, 'Oh, Judy,' and he put his arms around her.

And for a moment Judy felt nervous; she hadn't been that close to him in six months. Supposing it all felt flat and wrong? Supposing the time and distance had eroded whatever they'd had that night, and they'd just expended all that time and energy hammering out a deal for nothing?

'You look terrified,' he commented.

'Do I?'

'Maybe I'm a bit nervous myself,' he confessed.

'What, because you haven't stood this close to a woman in six months?' she said, teasing him.

'I haven't,' he said simply.

At that the last of Judy's nerves disappeared. She relaxed in his arms, and raised her face to kiss him. Wow, she remembered thinking, before thought processes deserted her completely and she was lost in the feel of him. Every last ounce of uncertainty finally melted away, and they held each other as if it was forever.

And indeed they might have, had something not occurred to Judy. She tried to ignore it but it kept popping into her head, and in the end she reluctantly dragged herself slightly away from him. 'There's just one small problem.'

'What?' said Lenny. He was gratifyingly hot looking, despite the freezing temperatures.

'Well, right now you live in Australia.'

He thought about this. 'We'll have to commute for the moment.'

'Commute? To Australia and back? Are you mad?'

'Judy, stop trying to plan ahead,' he complained, pulling her close again.

'Somebody has to,' she whispered robustly.